Juno ... my, ... you on the ... ass heroes and ...mes fighting ... ...ves as well as their ...ly-ever-afters. As a veteran air force intelligence ...ficer, she uses her background supporting Special ...orces to craft realistic stories that make you sweat and ...woon. Juno currently lives in the DC area with her ...ient husband, two rambunctious kids and a spoiled ...scue dog. To receive a FREE book from Juno, sign up ... her newsletter at junorushdan.com/mailing-list. Also ... ...ure to follow Juno on BookBub for the latest on sales ... ...it.ly/BookBubJuno

Tyler Anne Snell genuinely loves all genres of the written ...ord. However, she's realised that she loves books filled ...th sexual tension and mysteries a little more than the ...st. Her stories have a good dose of both. Tyler lives in ...labama with her same-named husband and their mini ...ns.' When she isn't reading or writing, she's playing ...eo games and working on her blog, *Almost There*. To ...low her shenanigans, visit tylerannesnell.com

Discover more at millsandboon.co.uk

TRACING A KIDNAPPER

JUNO RUSHDAN

SURVIVING THE TRUTH

TYLER ANNE SNELL

MILLS & BOON

Published in Great Britain 2021
Mills & Boon, an imprint of HarperCollins Publishers Ltd
1 London Bridge Street, London, SE1 9GF

www.harpercollins.co.uk

HarperCollins*Publishers*
1st Floor, Watermarque Building,
Ringsend Road, Dublin 4, Ireland

Tracing a Kidnapper © 2021 Harlequin Books S.A.
Surviving the Truth © 2021 Tyler Anne Snell

Special thanks and acknowledgement are given to Juno Rushdan for her contribution to the *Behavioral Analysis Unit* series.

ISBN: 978-0-263-28348-8

0821

MIX
Paper from
responsible sources
FSC™ C007454

This book is produced from independently certified FSC™ paper to ensure responsible forest management.

For more information visit: www.harpercollins.co.uk/green

Printed and bound in Spain
by CPI, Barcelona

TRACING A KIDNAPPER

JUNO RUSHDAN

To my patient husband and understanding children,
thank you for your love and support that made
writing this book possible.

Prologue

Organized chaos. The only way to describe Corporate Family Day, Jackson thought.

"Daddy," Emma said, coming up to him and interrupting the chairman midsentence. "There's a puppy. I want to go see it."

"Just a second, sweetheart." Jackson patted his six-year-old on the shoulder.

"She is so adorable, dressed in that little pantsuit," the chairman said.

Emma beamed. "I wanted to be twinsies with Daddy." She looked at Jackson. "I have to hurry if I want to pet the puppy."

His assistant, Brittany Hall, had hired a magician and had mentioned an animal in the act, but he thought it was a bunny.

"Please, Daddy." Her blond curls framed her angelic face and her brown eyes sparkled with determination that'd one day serve her well. "It's right over there." She pointed to the atrium, but Jackson couldn't see anything through the crowd. The space was jam-packed with two hundred Emerald Technology Corp employees along with their kids and spouses.

"Patience. We'll see it together. Go grab a bite to eat."

This day was already testing his multitasking skills in new ways; he didn't need Emma having a hangry meltdown, too.

With a deflated look that pinched something in his chest, she trudged over to the catered food on the table.

The chairman cleared his throat, drawing Jackson's attention. "As I was saying, our current stock prices reflect the fact that the board made an excellent decision with you."

"It was an honor to be chosen as CEO." Jackson pulled on a smile. At the job, he gave one hundred percent, but when he was with Emma, she was his number-one priority. He hated making her wait.

"There's someone I'd like you to speak with." The chairman gestured for a woman to come over. "Her son wants to meet you. A teenager who is a big admirer."

"Certainly." Jackson turned to get Emma for introductions, but she was no longer at the table. He glanced around the room. "Emma?" Through a break in the crowd he caught a glimpse of the atrium. The magician was speaking with Brittany, but he didn't see Emma. "Excuse me a moment. My little girl has wandered off." He stepped away, searching the conference room, checked every chair, corner, even under the table.

Jackson cut through the crowd into the atrium and looked for a gaggle of kids who'd be drawn to a cute puppy, but everyone was milling about, chatting. Unease churned in his gut.

Brittany came up to him. "The band just arrived. Bouncy castle and face painters are outside in the courtyard. Plenty of arts and crafts Emma will love."

Jackson looked around past her. "Have you seen her? Is she in the courtyard?"

"I just came from there. We haven't opened it up to everyone yet. Maybe she's eating."

"She's not in the conference room. I think she took off to see a puppy. Does the magician have one?"

Brittany shook her head. "Only a bunny for the show. I haven't seen any other pets."

Cold dread swept through him, but he pushed it aside. He was surrounded by hardworking employees, good people who had their kids there. This was a safe place.

"Take a look in the restroom," he said, "and I'll check with security at the front."

"Okay." Brittany hurried down the hall.

Jackson ran to the security desk. "Has Emma passed by here?" All the guards knew his daughter. Each one had complimented her on her outfit, which had made her grin with delight.

"No, sir. She hasn't come this way and she certainly hasn't gone through the front door."

His mind raced as he hurried back into the atrium where the conference room was.

"She wasn't there," Brittany said, rushing to him. "No one inside has seen her."

A sinking, hollow sensation spread in the pit of his stomach.

Where are you, honey? Jackson clasped the back of his neck and rubbed the tension gathering there. "Everyone! I need your attention." The crowd quieted. All eyes turned to him. "I can't find my daughter, Emma. She's six, blonde, wearing a blue pantsuit. Look around you. If you see her, call out." She had to be here. He'd looked away from her for a minute. Thirty seconds. Less.

Heads turned on a swivel. A murmur rippled through the crowd. Jackson waited and waited, clenching his jaw against the suffocating pressure building in his chest. The mutter of voices withered and died. Parents clutched their

own young kids closer. Compassionate gazes found his as
every nerve ending burned with terrible certainty.

No one had found Emma because she was gone.

Jackson took out his cell phone and dialed 911.

Chapter One

"Stop whatever you're doing." Supervisory Special Agent Miguel Peters poked his head in Special Agent Madeline Striker's small office. His designer suit and dark stubble gave him a deceptively suave air, but he was tough and no-nonsense. "I need to brief everyone now."

Without further elaboration, he strode down the hall, rounding everyone else up. The team's communications liaison with the local police, Caitlyn Yang, was hot on his heels.

Madeline logged off her computer, anticipating that one or more of them would be headed out the door once the emergency meeting was done. Sometimes the ops tempo was fast and furious, and they had to be ready at a moment's notice. Grabbing a notepad and pen, she stood, facing fellow Special Agent Nicholas James, who'd stopped in her doorway.

"I wonder what type of bomb just dropped," Nick said.

There was no telling. At the Behavioral Analysis Unit—BAU—they handled the gamut from serial killers, explosives, cybercrimes, fraud, counterterrorism to kidnapping—Madeline's specialty.

"No doubt the ugly kind." The kind that kept her awake most nights and pushed her to work twelve-, sometimes sixteen-hour days, but there was no need to mention that.

Being a part of the BAU took a toll on all of them. Though they each had their personal reasons for doing the job.

Tall with an athletic build, Nick walked alongside her to the large conference room in the Bureau's Seattle headquarters.

Madeline entered the sleek boardroom, where Liam McDare, their tech guru, already had slides set up on the large digital screen for the briefing. Hands down, he was the best and quickest at research and compiling data.

Flicking a glance at the oversize FBI logo on the wall, Madeline pulled out a leather chair next to Caitlyn as Dashiell West—Dash, as everyone called him—hustled inside the room, followed by David Dyson, the office intern and Nick's protégé.

"This is time sensitive." Miguel spoke from the head of the table before everyone had a chance to sit. When Director Olivia Branson traveled, which was often, he filled in for her. "We have a child abduction case. An hour ago, the daughter of Jackson Rhodes, the new CEO for Emerald Technology Corp, was reported missing."

Madeline's stomach clenched like a fist. Almost half a million children went missing every year, but landing this type of case got to her each time.

Everyone's attention flickered to her, but she focused on Miguel's intense gaze. He tended to defer to the agent with the most relevant expertise for the investigation to take the lead once in the field.

This one would be hers. It was something she dreaded but was also eager to tackle. She wouldn't let him down. "What do we know so far?" she asked.

Miguel gestured for Liam to start the slideshow. An image of a handsome man holding a little girl came up on the screen. "This is Emma Rhodes with her father. The girl was kidnapped at ETC's annual Corporate Family Day event. She's only six years old."

Madeline ignored the quick chill that sprinted up her spine as she stiffened in her seat.

Six. The same age as her sister when she'd been kidnapped twenty-three years ago. Madeline had been eight. They'd gotten off the school bus and had stopped at the playground on their way home. One minute her sister had been there and the next she was gone.

After an exhaustive search, she was never found. No suspects had been arrested. No closure for their family.

Madeline looked up and met Nick's gaze, his green eyes assessing her. He turned away as if he'd been caught staring.

"Anything on the company's surveillance feed?" Dash, the team's cybercrimes specialist, asked.

"Nada." Miguel shook his head. "Every video camera that could've captured someone speaking with the girl or taking her was disabled."

"The timing of the abduction at the event," Madeline said, thinking aloud, "and disabling the cameras indicates this was premeditated. Someone planned and waited for the right moment when no one would notice."

"How many people were at the event?" Nick asked.

"It was loud, crowded and quite busy." Caitlyn tucked a lock of long black hair behind an ear as she scrolled through her phone for an answer. Her point of contact with the local police texted her with information as soon as they received it, updating her in almost real time. "A hundred and fifteen employees and catering staff, but that number doesn't include all the other kids or spouses." She looked up from her phone. "No one can even say for certain if every employee was present."

Madeline made a note. "Any demands?"

"None so far," Miguel said.

Not unusual in the early stages, but the first seventy-two hours were critical. As time went on there were fewer bread crumbs to follow. "What do we know about the parents?" Madeline asked.

Most kids were taken by a noncustodial parent, a family member or acquaintance. It was very rare for it to be a stranger. That only happened in less than one percent of missing children cases, but in those instances, it was even more crucial for them to work fast because the child could be in imminent danger.

Liam toggled to the next slide, bringing up a picture of Jackson in a polo shirt and shorts. Thick blond hair, blue eyes, tanned, the sculpted body of a Greek god with a face to match. Classically shaped features and a chiseled jaw. A haughty expression like he was prepared to conquer the world.

"Born and raised in Seattle," Miguel said, filling in the background information. "Business degree from Harvard. MBA from Wharton. He climbed the ranks quickly at Emerald Technology Corp and beat out stiff competition to be named CEO last month at thirty-four."

Madeline had gone to school at Yale and knew the type: an elitist golden boy born with a silver spoon in his mouth who never even had a bad hair day. WASP credentials came with lineage and the right connections. "Does he come from money? Have a trust fund?"

Whether a kidnapper's motive was money or notoriety, millionaires and high-profile executives proved to be tempting targets for abduction. Kidnapping insurance was a big deal for a reason.

"Nope." Liam advanced to an article on Jackson in *Cascadia Business* magazine. "According to this, he comes from a middle-income family. Received financial aid, student loans, and worked while in school to pay the rest of his tuition."

The same as Madeline. Ivy League institutions didn't offer academic or athletic scholarships. Getting a degree felt like a full-time job, but the hard work paid lifelong dividends for the top-notch education.

Taking a deep breath, she took another look at Jackson Rhodes. In the picture featured in the article he wore an impeccably tailored suit. His smile was bright and flawless, but this time she spotted the hint of sadness in his eyes. There was far more to him beneath the surface. "What about the mother? Do we know anything about their relationship? Hostile divorce? Nasty custody battle? Trouble of any sort? Or are they happily married?"

"Francesca Hyltin-Rhodes is deceased," Miguel said as Liam advanced to the next slide. "She was a principal ballerina in the Pacific Northwest Ballet company until she got sick. She died of cancer when Emma was two. Jackson has raised his daughter on his own for the past four years. The magazine article described him as a doting father."

How awful for a child to lose a parent so young. It must've been hard for Jackson to raise her alone. Despite the rough patches, Madeline's parents were still together, and she couldn't imagine her father trying to cope on his own when she had been little.

Madeline stared at a photo of Francesca and Jackson, him standing behind her, with his arms wrapped around her, his hands resting on her pregnant belly. *Beautiful.* A picture-perfect couple. Emma favored her father, but she had her mother's eyes. "Other family members?"

Liam shook his head. "There are no living relatives on either side."

"Abductions by strangers are the rarest type of cases of missing children, and even then," Madeline said, "the kids are usually taken as the child is going to or from school. In this situation with a new executive who's received a lot of recent media attention, I think the girl is alive and that the father will get ransom demands. Soon. The kidnapper targeted Emma Rhodes specifically for a reason."

Caitlyn's cell phone buzzed. She picked it up, swiped through on her screen and looked at a message. "Madeline, you must be psychic. My point of contact with the police on-site said the father just received ransom demands. He must step down as CEO within twenty-four hours if he ever wants to see his daughter again."

Dash let out a low whistle that underscored the surprise etched on everyone's face. "Maybe an ETC employee who isn't too happy about Jackson's promotion took the girl."

Miguel nodded as if thinking the same. "Or a rival at another company."

"Did the police say anything about the caller's voice?" Madeline leaned back in her seat, drumming her fingers on the arm of the chair. "Male, female, the tone used?"

"There wasn't a call." Caitlyn set her phone down. "The father received the demands via text."

Madeline froze. "Text?" Now, *that* was unusual.

Jackson Rhodes wouldn't have a cell number that was easy to obtain. Not that it would stop a determined person, but something about the kidnapper sending a text rather than making a call bothered her.

"All right," Miguel said. "Madeline, you're the lead on this. I want everyone to head over to the scene and pitch in any way you can."

Everyone rose and gathered their things.

"It's good we didn't have a Family Day here to bring your kids," David said.

"None of us *have* kids." Miguel opened the conference

room door. "We're all married to this job. I'm not so sure if that's a good thing or just plain sad."

Nick hustled around the table, filing out behind Madeline. "Hey, are you going to be all right on this one?" he asked in a low voice, coming up beside her. "I know it hits close to home."

She'd been with BAU for five years and Nick for four. They'd worked together on several close-call cases. Nick was privy to a little more about her past and what drove her than some of the others on the team.

He used to know better than to ask her such a question.

Ever since he started dating Aubrey Flood, an ER doctor he reconnected with two months ago while trying to stop a copycat killer, he caught a severe case of feelings and started lowering his walls around everyone.

It was equal parts inviting and invasive.

Straightening her posture as she quickened her pace, Madeline pulled on a tight smile. "When have you ever known me not to be all right?" No matter how challenging, scary or gruesome things got, she didn't simply muster through. She stayed at the top of her game, always, and never let anything, personal or otherwise, stand in the way of her doing her job.

He ran a hand through his dirty blond hair. "What we do is tough. It takes everything we have until there isn't much left at times, but we rise to meet the demands. That doesn't mean we aren't human. It's natural if a case gets to us sometimes."

Madeline appreciated the well-meaning concern, no matter how unnecessary. "I should be asking how you're doing now that you're finally in a serious relationship."

"Better than I've been in a long time since falling for Aubrey." A ghost of a smile touched his lips, but whenever he mentioned her name his eyes lit up in an unmistakable way. "I highly recommend monogamy. You should give it a try."

She shrugged as she entered her office.

Who had time for love, much less an opportunity to find it? Nick's situation was an outlier. Then there was Liam and Lorelai Parker, the administrative assistant to Director Branson. A slow-burn office romance that was about to be sealed with marital vows didn't count either.

She slipped on her navy blue windbreaker that had FBI printed across the back.

Nick grabbed his jacket from across the hall. "But I'm guessing your earlier deflection means I struck a nerve."

More like an old wound that healed a little bit each time she rescued a child, but she didn't confirm or deny his astute assessment.

"And for the record," Nick continued, "you never answered my question."

"I'm fine." She'd joined the FBI with the goal of becoming a kidnapping expert. Sure, whenever they got a case like this, it burned Madeline's gut that another innocent child had been snatched, but this was what she lived for: a chance to save a young life and spare a family an agonizing loss.

She was going to do absolutely everything in her power to bring Emma Rhodes home alive and well. No matter the personal cost.

Chapter Two

"I've already answered this question." Jackson Rhodes bit back impatience as he paced in front of the first-floor conference room. Seattle Police Department officers swarmed around the atrium, buzzing like bees in a hive, collecting statements from employees and vendors for the past hour. Still, they had nothing to go on. "Shouldn't you be trying to find my daughter instead of making me repeat myself?"

"It's important for us to go over every detail of your statement." Detective Dowd's flat, indifferent voice only ramped up Jackson's anxiety. "Make sure there are no inconsistencies."

Inconsistencies? Jackson stopped cold and glared at the detective. "What are you implying? That I might be lying about what happened?"

The detective sighed. "This is standard procedure, sir." His gaze shifted to something over Jackson's shoulder. "Finally," he muttered.

Turning, Jackson spotted the FBI team crossing the atrium. Four of them, maybe more. After exchanging a few hurried words, they each took off in a different direction. One made a beeline his way, badge hooked on her waistband on the opposite hip from where her gun was holstered.

Dowd tipped his head at the statuesque woman. "You have no idea how good it is to see you." He looked back at

Jackson with relief stamped on his face. "Mr. Rhodes, this is Special Agent Madeline Striker, one of the FBI's best kidnapping experts."

Agent Striker proffered her hand. She was attractive with golden brown skin, long dark hair swept up in a low, loose chignon and a steely demeanor.

Jackson stepped forward, accepting her hand. Warm fingers wrapped around his and squeezed with surprising strength, sending an electric prickle down his spine. He quickly dropped his hand, ignoring the sensation that pulled him from his thoughts for a nanosecond.

"Mr. Rhodes, we're going to do everything in our power to get your daughter back as quickly as possible." Her confident bearing and the utter lack of pity on her face loosened the tightness in his chest.

It gave him the glimmer of hope that this nightmare might not end badly. "Thank you. Please call me Jackson."

Another woman in her midtwenties approached them. She was younger than Agent Striker by a handful of years. Tall and slender, she greeted him with the type of worrisome expression that he was beginning to dread.

"This is my colleague, Caitlyn Yang," Agent Striker said. "She's our communications liaison."

Jackson acknowledged her with a nod.

The younger woman flashed a forced smile in return and then glanced at the detective. "Thanks for the timely updates."

"Only doing my job," Dowd said. He looked at his notepad. "I was just about to go over Mr. Rhodes's statement."

"For the second time," Jackson snapped, renewed frustration mounting inside him.

"I can't imagine how difficult this must be for you," Ms. Yang said. The compassion in her voice rubbed Jackson raw and it was almost more than he could bear. "Why don't you have a seat?" she suggested, taking his elbow and gesturing to a chair.

Jackson jerked his arm away. "I don't need to be handled." He was an expert at managing people. Reading them during a negotiation and knowing precisely how to respond. The reversal of being on the receiving end was a pointed reminder that for the first time in his life he was completely powerless.

"I was only trying to help," Yang said.

"The police have been here over an hour and they don't have a single lead. Not one. More than a hundred people are out there and you mean to tell me that no one saw a damn thing? If you think trying to coddle me is helpful, you're mistaken."

Yang lowered her shock-filled gaze while Dowd released a heavy sigh and pursed his lips.

Jackson's heart hammered like a brutal fist against his rib cage. "I don't need to repeat my statement. You should be taking action. Questioning the vendors again. Scouring through the surveillance footage. Combing the streets to find my daughter!"

Instead of squandering precious time.

Time that should be spent searching for Emma.

He'd read that the first forty-eight hours were the most critical. The longer she was missing, the odds of finding her alive dwindled exponentially. The thought that his little girl might never come home again made his knees shake.

Jackson was hanging on by a thread, but he managed to push the weakness aside.

It wouldn't do Emma any good if he broke down. He paced in the conference room, needing space to breathe, but the suffocating sensation didn't ease.

Agent Striker gave Jackson a probing stare. Her sharp

brown eyes simmered with a beguiling energy. Her un-readable expression didn't change. She didn't even blink.

He gritted his teeth at not having any inkling as to what she was thinking.

"Detective," Agent Striker said, "why don't you share his statement with Caitlyn while I take over the family support role with Mr. Rhodes."

Dowd raised a conciliatory hand. "No arguments here." The gray-haired man flicked his pad closed. He turned along with Yang and the two left the conference room.

"Mr. Rhodes, I assure you that neither I, nor any law enforcement officer here, have any intention of wasting your time since we have none to spare," Agent Striker said matter-of-factly, as if reading his thoughts. "I understand the inquiry process can feel tedious, frustrating even, but it's necessary." Grim resolve settled across her face. "Our only goal is to find your daughter, and I give you my word, I'll do everything possible."

The statement broke through the haze of his panic, steadying him. This was what he needed. A solid professional unencumbered by sentimentality running the case.

"All right." He took a deep breath. "I'm sorry for raising my voice and trying to tell everyone how to do their job." That was so unlike him. Not the part about issuing orders or giving constructive criticism, but losing his temper. He could be brusque at times. Never rude. "To be honest, I'm angry at myself. Emma wanted to go somewhere to see a puppy. She even asked permission the way I'd taught her." Like a good girl following the rules. "I was distracted, told her to wait. Then the next thing I knew she was gone." Vanished without a trace. "Turns out there wasn't any puppy on the premises."

"Kidnappers often entice and lure children away with

the prospect of something that's hard to resist, like going somewhere fun. Getting candy. Petting a puppy."

"The nanny had offered to come. Had said it wouldn't be any trouble. If only I hadn't given Liane the day off."

"Her last name?"

"Strothe. With an e at the end."

Madeline withdrew a smartphone from her pocket and began typing. "How long has she been with you?"

"A little less than two years. Why? You don't think Liane had anything to do with this, do you?"

"Why didn't you want her to come?"

"Emma was going to be with me the entire day." He had promised her no work under any circumstances. "I had arranged to leave early because I wanted to take her to the Space Needle, for a ride on the monorail and treat her to ice cream." They had spent a week planning what they were going to do together. "I relish the time I have with her. Liane never takes personal days, and I didn't see any reason to waste her free time." All true, but there was a deeper, underlying truth he couldn't admit out loud. On Family Day, everyone brought their kids and spouse. Not their nanny. People at ETC already thought him an elitist snob. He hadn't wanted to perpetuate the distorted perception. "Worst-case scenario, I knew I could rely on my assistant, Brittany, to help me out, but I was foolish not to bring Liane. This might never have happened if I had."

Damn trying to repair his image.

"This isn't your fault, Mr. Rhodes."

Maybe not, but it didn't lighten the crushing weight of guilt bearing down on him. Or the simple fact that if he had paid closer attention to Emma, she'd be in his arms right now. Not missing. "It's Jackson. Please."

This federal agent was his best chance at getting back the

most important person in the world to him. Fostering some familiarity couldn't hurt. It might even prove beneficial.

"Call me Madeline."

"Is Liane a suspect? I got her through a highly respected agency I've used for a long time. They do background checks, drug testing, the works."

"We'll need to question everyone who has had close contact with your daughter before we can rule them out. The nanny. Your assistant. Do you have a housekeeper? Personal chef? A driver?"

"Time is my most valuable resource, but I don't have that kind of household staff." He never fit in with the jet-setting, country-clubbing one percent who did. But he wanted to make sure his daughter felt at ease around anyone, whether it was in a soup kitchen or on a yacht. "I have Liane to help, I use a cleaning service and I have groceries delivered. I do the cooking for Emma and myself unless we eat out. As much as possible, I prefer to be hands-on."

Madeline raised an eyebrow. "Considering you're a single parent with a high-pressure position at ETC and the means to hire a personal staff, that's commendable."

To him, it was the least his daughter deserved. "How will you figure out who took Emma?"

"We'll look at the evidence, compile a list of suspects and run everything to the ground," she said. "Do you have any enemies?"

"No."

Madeline's eyes narrowed as though the response had been delivered too fast. Or she suspected it had been a lie. Her cell phone pinged, and she read her text message. "You were recently named CEO, a position that comes with a lot of power, money and prestige. I'm sure you didn't achieve that without ruffling a few feathers."

"You're right. I didn't get this job by trying to win a

popularity contest, but you're asking if I ruffled feathers to the point someone would want to kidnap my daughter."

Her gaze settled hard on him. "Yes."

Success had required making tough choices. He had bruised egos and hurt feelings during his climb up the ladder. All for the sake of business. Nothing personal, and he had always treated everyone fairly. It wasn't as if he was a monster. "No. There's no one."

Doubt rocked through him. *Someone* had taken Emma. For every action, there was a reaction. Basic physics.

The chasm of guilt inside him deepened.

"Have you had a bad breakup recently, say within the last six months? Ended a relationship when the other person wasn't ready to say goodbye?" Madeline asked.

Jackson scoffed. "No relationships. No dalliances. No breakups. Not even a one-night stand." His love life had been one big black hole for four years, much less the past six months.

"Who stands the most to gain from your resignation?"

The most obvious implication hadn't occurred to him. "The vice president. Andrew Phillips. He's next in line. Always wanted the job."

Madeline typed on her smartphone, again.

"Excuse me, but may I ask what's so important on your phone?"

"I'm checking red alerts from the team, any potential suspects they come up with, and inputting what I learn in a shared document. The process is efficient and timely, but I'm still focused on everything you say." She looked up at him. "Please continue."

"Andrew would be the one to fill in for me. At least temporarily, until the board officially designates my replacement." Andrew had been there at the start of Family Day. When was the last time anyone had seen him?

Jackson spun toward the atrium and scanned the crowd, looking for him.

Madeline glanced in the same direction, then caught his eye. "The kidnapper contacted you via text?"

"Yes." Jackson nodded, recalling how terrifying it had been to receive the demand, the acknowledgment that Emma had been taken, but it had also been a relief. He had something to act on. A reason to hope there was a chance to get his daughter back. "Don't kidnappers usually issue ransom demands through a phone call?"

"Most times, but not always. We'll need your cell phone to trace the text."

"My IT person, Rivka Molnar, is cracking away at that as we speak. She's one of the best there is in the business." As soon as Rivka had given her statement to the police and dropped her own daughter off at school, she'd gotten to work on it.

"No doubt. Nevertheless, we'll need to have our people take a look."

"Of course." Surely the FBI had their own protocol and needed to verify everything.

Another ping on Madeline's phone drew her attention to the screen. "Where can we find Ms. Molnar?"

"This floor. In a restricted area, beyond security. You need a badge to access it."

With a nod, she began typing. "Apparently, our techie, Liam McDare, is in security now, reviewing the surveillance footage. He'll take care of it."

"I suppose I should contact the media, set up a press conference so I can resign publicly per the demands." The sooner he did so, the sooner he might get his daughter back.

"I'd advise against that." Madeline lowered her phone. "I don't think it's a good idea."

His heart twisted into a knot. "Why? It was the one thing

the kidnapper demanded." The only thing. Not money. Not power. "My resignation in exchange for Emma's safe return."

She opened her mouth to respond, but Rivka darted past two police officers into the conference room.

"Jackson!" Rivka rushed to him with his cell phone in her hand.

"Agent Striker—Madeline—this is Rivka Molnar. The head of the IT department I was telling you about."

"I traced the number," Rivka said, cheeks flushed, stray red curls that had escaped her ponytail hanging around her face. She handed him the phone. "It was easier than I expected considering the circumstances. Almost too easy, now that I think about it."

"I won't look a gift horse in the mouth." Riding a fresh surge of adrenaline, Jackson stepped closer. "What's the location where the text was sent from?"

"Believe it or not, one of our remote work sites. Off I-99 across from the Duwamish Waterway."

"What?" Jackson shook his head. "That doesn't make any sense."

"I agree, it is strange. I cloned your phone for the FBI. They have all the metadata and can monitor any further communication in real time. Liam McDare is going to have an Agent West verify the trace."

"If Ms. Molnar missed anything," Madeline said, "I have every confidence that between West and McDare they'll find it. What's the exact address of the work site?"

Questions whirled in Jackson's mind and there was only one way to get answers. "I'm heading over there." He started toward the atrium. "It's less than ten minutes away. You can follow me or ride along. But don't think of suggesting that I stay behind. Not when the text originated from ETC property and it looks as if it might've been an employee who has taken Emma." The thought of such a betrayal burned his gut. "I have to go. That's nonnegotiable."

Madeline hurried ahead of him, bringing him to a quick stop with a raised palm. "No one can force you to stay here, but riding *with us* would be faster," she said in a firm, impassive voice that he found oddly soothing. "You'll have to stay in the vehicle while we check the facility and question employees. That's also nonnegotiable. Can you do that, Jackson?"

He would do whatever was necessary to get his little girl back. Emma was his true north, his whole world. Without question, he would make any sacrifice to protect her. Lay down his own life in a heartbeat. Truth be told, if it came down to it, he would take a life, too. "I can."

Madeline led the way through the atrium toward two FBI agents who were questioning the chairman and Jackson's assistant, Brittany, separately. A succession of pings had all three agents glancing at their phones.

Both agents broke off their interviews and approached Madeline.

"Jackson Rhodes, this is Supervisory Special Agent Miguel Peters," Madeline said, gesturing to a man with dark hair, "and Special Agent Nick James." She indicated the other somber-looking agent as perfunctory handshakes were exchanged. "Jackson would prefer us to dispense with the formality of titles and surnames."

"We just got the update on the location of the trace from Liam," Miguel said to Madeline. "I'll stay with Dash and handle things here, finish collecting statements and reviewing the surveillance footage." He handed her car keys.

Nick's gaze shifted to Madeline. "I'll go with you."

Miguel nodded. "Take Caitlyn as well and a few of the police officers standing around."

"Jackson is also going to come," Madeline said. "It might be useful to have him on-site."

Miguel glanced at Jackson and looked him over a moment, then he turned back to Madeline. "If you think it's best for him to go along, I won't question it."

Jackson and Madeline made their way outside the front of the building while Nick rounded up the others. Madeline climbed in behind the wheel of one of the two black SUVs that were parked near squad cars. He slid into the front passenger seat beside her.

She cranked the engine and entered the address he rattled off into the GPS.

The second Nick and Caitlyn hopped in the back of the vehicle, Madeline peeled out of the spot.

With blue-and-red lights flashing on the dash and the sirens blaring on the police cruisers that followed them, Madeline wove through traffic at a speed that had Jackson clutching the armrest.

In this situation, there was no such thing as too fast. He was relieved Madeline acted as such.

"Why do you have a remote site?" Madeline asked.

"It's not uncommon. We have several for different reasons. Sometimes the issue is space. Out at the Duwamish site, it's for secrecy. Top-of-the-line security. The facility has metal detectors, and no one can even bring a cell phone inside. Everyone who works there has been through the most stringent of background checks."

Madeline's gaze flickered to him. "What is ETC working on?"

Years of secrecy caused Jackson to hesitate. Under normal circumstances, a civilian would have to sign a nondisclosure agreement before he answered the question. Nothing about today was normal. "Cloaking technology.

The team is finishing a prototype. We're hoping to get a government contract."

"With DARPA?" Caitlyn asked, referring to the Defense Advanced Research Projects Agency.

"Yes. They deal with all the breakthrough technology for national security. We're talking the potential for billions in profit." Jackson had fought to expand the company, take ETC in a bold, innovative direction. Against all odds, he had scraped together the money to save the company from the brink of bankruptcy while funding the venture. "It's my pet project. Sort of my..." He swallowed hard, nearly choking on the words sticking in his throat.

Caitlyn and Nick stared at Jackson in the rearview mirror.

"Your what?" Madeline asked.

"Everyone at the office jokes that it's...my baby. My second child." A cold finger ran across his heart.

Jackson clenched his hand and leaned back against the seat. He didn't know exactly what it meant that the text had been traced to that specific location, but there was no doubt in his mind that it held horrible significance.

"Are visitors allowed inside the remote site?" Nick asked. "For deliveries? Repairs? Standard maintenance?"

Jackson looked back over the seat. "No, we have strict protocols in place. Only cleared personnel. Anyone who steps foot inside the facility has been thoroughly vetted."

"We need to know all the employees who have access to the Duwamish site," Madeline said. "See if any had a grievance or might be vulnerable to blackmail."

"I'll call Dash," Caitlyn said, taking out her phone. She dialed and relayed the message, then listened. "Okay. Thanks." She disconnected. "They verified the trace. The text did originate from that location. Dash said there was no attempt to mask the trail. Also, the surveillance footage inside ETC headquarters was on a loop. That's why there's no coverage of who took Emma."

Something about this was wrong. The details didn't add up. "The kidnapper was savvy enough to put our surveillance feed on a loop, but not cover their tracks of the text message?" Jackson asked.

No one said a word. They didn't have to. The cagey looks from the others told Jackson all he needed to know. They were thinking the same thing.

Almost too easy. Rivka's words came back in a rush, filling him with foreboding.

Madeline exited I-99 and took Alaskan Way to East Marginal. Once they made a right toward the work site, the gated facility was visible.

Alarm crept over him.

Employees were gathered outside the building in the parking lot. Twenty of them, which accounted for the entire team plus security, stood about a hundred feet from the building near the fence line.

"What in the hell?" Nick muttered.

Madeline and Jackson traded wary glances as she stopped at the entrance and rolled down the window.

Jackson leaned over and waved to the security guard. "What's going on?"

"Mr. Rhodes." The guard's eyebrows rose in surprise. "The carbon monoxide alarms went off in the building. Everyone had to evacuate. I called the fire department and gas company. The SFD should be here any minute."

Almost too easy. Now a carbon monoxide leak?

Jackson stiffened. "What if Emma is inside?" The stray thought struck him as irrational. The odds of his little girl being in there, without anyone noticing, were as slim as someone who worked at the site being the culprit. But the events of the day had already taught him anything was possible.

"Is this the only way in and out?" Madeline asked Jackson.

"Yes. Single point of entry for added security."

Her gaze swung back to the guard. "Has anyone entered or left the premises in the past hour?"

"No, ma'am," the guard said.

The news kept Jackson from doing something rash, like leaping from the vehicle and racing inside the building against Madeline's instructions, though it wasn't nearly enough to bring him a shred of relief.

"The funny thing is," the guard added, "there's a strange smell in the building."

"But carbon monoxide is odorless," Madeline said.

"That's what makes it so weird."

"Think this is some kind of a diversion?" Nick asked. "A slew of uncleared people are about to circumvent protocol and get access in there."

"It's possible," Madeline said. "We shouldn't rule anything out." She looked back at the guard. "Make sure no one leaves the premises unless they've been cleared by the FBI or the police."

"You've got it." The armed guard buzzed them in. A second later, the heavy gate rolled open.

They drove past the gaggle of employees, closer to the one-story building, and parked. The state-of-the-art facility was small. The east side of it was comprised of a meditation room, break room with a kitchen, gym and locker room since the team spent long days hard at work. The other half of the building—which faced the Duwamish Waterway, giving the team a western view and natural light through the privacy-tinted wall of windows—was entirely for research and development.

"Sit tight and let us handle this," Madeline said.

Jackson nodded in reluctant agreement.

The others jumped out of the vehicle and huddled up by the open trunk.

Madeline and Nick took off their jackets and strapped on bulletproof vests while she doled out orders. "Caitlyn, have the officers help you collect statements from everyone. We'll do a sweep inside to make sure there's no one left."

The communications liaison and the uniformed officers headed to the cluster of ETC employees.

Nick and Madeline both drew their weapons. As they advanced toward the building, Jackson hopped out of the SUV.

Pulse hammering, he edged forward, desperate for definitive proof as to who had taken his daughter. But he stopped, fighting against the overwhelming urge. Better to leave this part to law enforcement. Though nothing, other than finding Emma unharmed, would make this better.

Tension coiled through him, what-ifs stacking up in his mind. What if whoever had sent the text was no longer here? Or what if the trace was a dead end?

Madeline and Nick were side by side, their guns raised.

Watching the Feds draw closer, Jackson scrubbed a hand over his jaw. His heartbeat pounded in his ears. He ached to do something, other than wait, but at the same time, he couldn't shake the sense that something about this was wrong—really, really wrong.

The two agents got within ten paces of the front door. And then...

The west side of the building exploded.

Chapter Three

Madeline and Nick staggered to a halt as a blaze consumed the interior of the building's west side. Heat surged from the broken windows, exploding the remaining panes, but her blood chilled.

If the timing had been different—two minutes, maybe less—they would've both been inside. She risked her life on a regular basis—that came with the territory. But this had been a close call.

Too close.

Fire licked the air through the shattered opening. Gray smoke billowed out across the water.

Madeline looked over her shoulder.

Jackson stood aghast, gaping at the building. At the ruins of his pet project. His baby.

Madeline holstered her weapon and went to him.

His eyes were glassy with horror. His skin, his coloring was too pale. The same paralyzing fear she'd seen on countless other parents rolled off him in waves.

She put a hand on his shoulder. "The fire department will be here shortly. They'll search the building and confirm if it was empty."

For a long moment, she wondered if he'd heard her. Even Nick gave her a concerned glance that had her regretting the fact that she'd allowed Jackson to come along.

"Thank you," Jackson said in a low voice, still staring at the fire.

She let out a small breath of relief that he'd spoken. "For what?"

Finally, his gaze met hers. "Not asking me if I'm all right."

It was obvious he wasn't. In a few short hours, everything that mattered most to him had been taken away. This man was suffering from a pain beyond what the physical could inflict and it was etched all over his face.

"You said that you don't have any enemies, but…" Madeline took a second, needing to find the right words. "This was well-timed. Meticulously executed. I need you to think hard about who might want to target you in this way."

He stepped back, shrugging off her hand. "If I knew something that could be useful, anything that might help me get my daughter back, don't you think I'd tell you in a heartbeat? I have no idea who did this." He threw a hand up at the building. "No idea why."

The kidnapper hadn't asked for ransom money. Only his resignation. Which meant that Jackson did know who was responsible. He just couldn't see it yet.

"What about Andrew Phillips?" Nick asked. "Your assistant told me that in the event you step down, he'd be the one to fill in for you. Or how about Charles Albrecht, the CEO of AlbrechTech? I overheard the chairman mention that you two have a combative rivalry."

"That's true. There's been infighting between me and Andrew since day one. And as for Chuck, *combative* is putting it mildly." Jackson's cheeks turned a mottled shade of red. "But to think that either of them would go to such lengths…" He glanced at the fiery ruins of his project. "It's unimaginable."

Nick rocked back on his heels and peered up at the sky. "Well, what do we have here?"

Madeline followed the direction he pointed in, spotting the whirring device at once. A small quadcopter drone fitted with a camera hovered above the parking lot.

How long had it been there?

She couldn't hear the rotor blades due to the roar of the fire, but if the drone had been overhead when they stepped out of the vehicle, she would've noticed the noise.

"We're being watched." Nick hiked his chin up.

"By the person who kidnapped Emma?" Jackson asked.

"Safe assumption," Madeline said. Her gut told her any other explanation would be too much of a coincidence, and she didn't believe in those.

"Why use a drone?" Jackson asked. "Did the sick bastard want to watch the explosion?" He glared up at the quadcopter, fists at his sides. "I'll give you whatever you want! Just release my little girl! Please. Let Emma go."

"They're usually only equipped with video, no audio," Nick said.

Dropping his head, Jackson slapped the hood of the SUV and muttered a curse.

Madeline got the sense he was a man used to being in total and complete control, of himself, of everything in his orbit. Even now, looking on the verge of falling apart, he was working hard to hold it together.

She turned to Nick. "See if you can shoot the drone down." It was within range and Nick was a good shot. "We might get lucky. Pull a set of prints." Everyone made mistakes sooner or later. Maybe the kidnapper got sloppy, hadn't considered this possibility. If so, they could use it to their advantage.

"Sure."

While Nick quickly took aim, Madeline opened the

front passenger door and ushered Jackson inside the vehicle. Fortunately, he sat without a fight. Giving whoever was watching the video more footage of Jackson unraveling wouldn't help the situation. If anything, it'd only feed the perpetrator's ego.

Madeline stayed between the door and the frame.

A pair of gunshots rang out, making Jackson flinch. She was used to the sharp sound, but the loud report always came as a surprise to most civilians.

Nick had managed to drop the quadcopter to the ground on the second shot. He grabbed an evidence bag from the trunk and tugged on gloves before retrieving it.

"I know commercial drones aren't equipped with audio." Jackson loosened his tie and pulled it off over his head. His tailored suit did nothing to hide the bulk of his muscles or the unbearable weight he was carrying. "If it were, at two hundred feet high, it'd capture very little audio from the ground. Factor in prop noise and it'd be useless." His shoulders slumped forward, his brow creasing as a hand jerked the top button on his collar open. "No point in screaming at it the way I did. Like an idiot. I think I'm in shock from it all."

There was something in his voice, a deep, dark underlying sadness that caught her breath. That made her soften in a way she hadn't for a long time.

The desire to comfort him was startling in its intensity. She clenched her hand to keep from touching him. The rest of the BAU team thought the impact on the parents was never her concern, but they couldn't have been more wrong. The reason she kept her distance from the victims' loved ones, normally letting Caitlyn handle the support role instead, was that she understood their suffering all too well. The closer she got to the family, the easier it was to get caught in the emotional undertow. Then how would she be able to save the victim?

She swallowed to clear her throat. "What you're feeling is only natural. To be expected."

Sirens wailed in the distance. It was convenient the fire department had already been called and was on the way. They might be able to get the blaze under control quickly.

"Did he hit the drone?" Jackson asked.

"Yes." She gave an encouraging nod. Any glimmer of hope she could offer she would gladly give. Not only for Jackson's sake, but for her own as well. Far too many kidnapping cases, like the one involving her sister, didn't have a happy ending. The families were left devastated. Broken. Sometimes beyond repair. She shook herself, refusing to let ugly memories distract her. "It's pretty much intact. We'll have it dusted."

She glanced back at Nick, who was sealing the evidence bag.

Movement in the sky snatched her gaze. Another drone was following, and a second. *Oh, no.* Whoever planned this had indeed taken into consideration the prospect of losing one. Slim odds they'd find any prints. There went a possible lead.

Her heart sank.

"What is it now?" Jackson asked.

Madeline chided herself for reacting and wiped the expression from her face which had given away that something else was wrong. "More drones."

The sirens grew louder from the approaching fire trucks.

Jackson's phone chimed. He fished his cell from his inner jacket pocket.

"Another text, from an unknown number." He swiped the screen and read the message out loud.

"Behold the demonstration of my resolve. Appreciate the mercy shown to your employees. Understand the FBI can't help you. Resign on camera when the press arrives. Fail and your daughter pays the ultimate price."

Unease twisted Madeline's stomach into a knot. The carbon monoxide alarm had been deliberately triggered. This was all a ploy to evacuate the building and spare the workers' lives. "Let me see it." After reading it once, she'd have the text committed to memory.

Jackson handed it over. "I bet this time it won't be traceable."

She was inclined to agree, but she knew better than to voice the concern. "Our team will still try everything possible."

"What won't be traceable?" Nick set the bagged drone down in the trunk.

"Second text message," Madeline said. "Further demands."

Nick closed the door and came around the side of the vehicle. She passed him the cell phone.

Two fire trucks pulled through the gate as Nick read the message. "Another doozy. Let's see if the number will receive a text." He thumbed a few quick words. A second later, he shook his head. "Message delivery failed. One-way communication."

Jackson buttoned his collar, put his tie on and adjusted it.

"What are you doing?" Madeline asked.

"Preparing to go on camera." He combed back his blond hair with his fingers, not leaving a strand out of place. Within seconds, he appeared polished and poised. "Resign like the kidnapper wants. The press will be here any minute."

There was no doubt in Madeline's mind that every local

news station had received an anonymous tip about the explosion, ensuring full press coverage would be imminent.

As if on cue, a KIRO 7 *Eyewitness News* chopper zipped through the sky, taking a position over the water with a prime vantage point of the blazing inferno.

The kidnapper was smart and miles ahead of them, tightening their control of the situation at a brutal pace. Madeline had to change the dynamic, shift the balance of power somehow and buy them time, even just a little. "You can't resign. It's the only card you have to play."

"Can't?" Jackson's eyes narrowed, growing cold. He got out of the SUV, towering over her and sucking up the air with his fury.

Madeline stood her ground. Jackson was a distraught parent. Terrified. Angry. Frantic. Although the whirlwind of emotion raging inside him was directed at her, it wasn't because of her. "You *shouldn't* resign. It's not the right play."

"I don't have a choice." He pushed past her and Nick.

"Please listen to me." She kept her voice calm and firm despite the panic welling in her gut. "I do think you should go on camera."

Jackson stopped and turned. "And say what?"

"Demand proof of life. A video of Emma telling you something only she would know. Maybe the name of her favorite toy. Footage could reveal clues to help us find her, and the kidnapper won't expect it." There were no guarantees, but she was fairly certain Jackson issuing a demand would throw the unsub—unknown subject—off-kilter. Emma's captor wanted to avoid direct confrontation and expected everyone to play by their rules. Perhaps that's why the demands were sent via text. A phone call invited discussion, negotiation. A one-way text left no opportunity for debate.

"Which also means not doing as I was told might antagonize him," Jackson said. "Provoke the psycho to lash out. Retaliate."

A point she couldn't deny. "I'm well aware of the risks. But this is worth taking the chance. Her abductor, whoever it is, has thought this out. He's prepared. Even worse, he's changed the terms as he sees fit, according to his timetable. First you had twenty-four hours to resign and now you've got, what? Twenty minutes before there are camera crews out front. We need time to catch up. I'm right about this." She was sure of it.

"I don't know." Jackson shook his head. "Sounds too risky."

"You should listen to her," Nick said. "She's the best kidnapping expert I've ever seen. She knows how to handle an unsub. If anyone can get Emma back with the least possible risk, it's Madeline. You need to trust her judgment."

Jackson's steely gaze bounced between them before settling on her a beat. He stroked a hand over his mouth, the troubled expression on his face not fading. He was assessing her, deliberating. His silence signified he didn't trust her. Not that she would let that rattle her.

Faith in self was essential in this business. She needed the unshakable kind that would get Emma home safely.

Given the chance, her plan would work and prove to Jackson that he could rely on her expertise. But if it backfired, she could have an emotional parent going rogue to contend with.

She had to convince him. "The kidnapper made sure to evacuate the building and detonate the bomb before we went inside," Madeline said, closing the gap between them. "This person doesn't want the situation to escalate to murder. When you're on camera, talk about Emma, use her name a lot. You have to humanize her to her abductor."

"I'll need my phone back," Jackson said. "To show the press a few pictures."

"Good idea." Madeline gestured to Nick and he gave the phone to Jackson. "Remember, winning a negotiation requires patience and keeping our heads. But whatever you do, don't resign. Not yet. As grim as it might sound, we need to know that Emma is alive. Then and only then should you comply with the demand."

GUILT THRUMMED THROUGH Jackson faster and hotter than the blood in his veins as he stood in front of a gaggle of reporters. Cameras and mics were pointed at him. Everyone waited for him to make a statement after the communications liaison, Caitlyn, had explained the circumstances regarding the kidnapping and the explosion.

Everything was on the line. Emma's life. His own life because he wouldn't survive losing his only child.

It was his fault she had been taken in the first place. He'd let down his guard, looked away for a moment too long, brushed aside his daughter's eagerness to see a puppy.

No more mistakes.

"I appreciate the assistance from local law enforcement and the FBI." Jackson swallowed in an attempt to clear the emotion thickening his throat. "I'd like to address the person holding my daughter captive. Whoever you are, I beg you not to hurt Emma." He held up a picture of her on his cell phone, giving the cameramen an opportunity to zoom in on the photo of her taken this morning, posing in her pantsuit, before he swiped to the next one of her. "She gets cold easily and is allergic to strawberries. She's a sweet, loving child. Creative. Spirited. Kind. She has the biggest heart."

A favorite image of Emma—curly blond halo of hair and her face lighting up when he had surprised her with her first horseback riding lesson, the way she threw her arms around his neck and squeezed—rose in his mind like an apparition.

Pure joy bled into stark fear.

Proof of life.

Madeline was right. He needed to know his daughter was still alive, but at what cost?

The kidnapper had been startlingly persuasive with that fiery demonstration. Someone who was willing to kidnap an innocent child and blow up a building was capable of anything.

More images flooded him, holidays, birthdays, breakfasts, bedtime. He struggled to stem the tide.

Fail and your daughter pays the ultimate price.

His mind spun, but tremors erupted in his heart. They spread down his arms, tingling in his fingers. The phone shook in his hand.

No matter what happened to him, he only wanted Emma to be safe. To grow up and live a long, happy life. No sacrifice on his part was too great.

"Per your demands, I hereby resign as CEO from ETC effective immediately. But I need to know that my daughter is okay. That you haven't hurt her. I need to see her, do you understand? Send me a video of Emma showing that she hasn't been harmed and in it have her tell you what she wished for on her last birthday. Once you do, ETC will release a press statement confirming that my resignation is officially binding and permanent."

Jackson turned his back on the press and stalked away from the flurry of questions the press hurled at him and made his way back through the Duwamish gate.

The fire was being contained. Gray smoke filled the sky above the building. Nick was busy coordinating with the fire department while Madeline was on an intercept course with Jackson.

He kept walking toward the SUV.

Though he could no longer see her behind him, he was aware that she was hot on his heels.

"What was that?" Madeline asked once they were out of earshot of the press and employees.

He stopped and faced her. "I'm sure you're good at your job. Hell, you might even be the best, but I haven't vetted you. I don't know your track record, if there are any red flags, what's your success-to-failure ratio, the number of hostages who haven't been rescued. The only thing I know for certain is that every instinct I have is screaming that compliance was the right call. And I always trust my gut."

"I can understand that. Respect it even. I always trust mine as well. But vetted or not, I am an expert for a reason. I've been through this many times. What you did was in direct opposition of the play I advised."

"With all due respect, this isn't a game. You may be a kidnapping expert, but the one thing I specialize in is risk assessment. This is my daughter we're talking about here, and it was too risky to antagonize the person who has her. I will not take unnecessary chances when it comes to Emma."

"Kidnapping situations can go wrong. There have been casualties in my previous cases, but none of them a victim. I have never lost someone."

"Not yet." No one had a perfect record forever.

She drew herself up, standing taller, and stared him dead in the eye. "I don't intend to let Emma be my first."

"Do you have children, Madeline?"

A flicker of emotion slashed across her face before she tensed and staggered back a step as though the question had been a physical blow. Then she went completely still.

"No." All the strength that had been in her voice a moment ago was gone. "I don't."

"Then you can't possibly understand my position. For all your effort and good intentions, you and the rest of the FBI will walk away from this case once it's done and move on to the next. But this is my life. And this was my choice to make. One only I have to live with." Strip away the credentials, the experience, sense of duty, and this boiled down to something far more organic. A parent's love. "I will not, under any circumstances, gamble with my daughter's life."

Chapter Four

"I can't believe he went rogue, on television, to the press," Madeline said, standing in the smaller, more personal conference room at BAU headquarters. She clenched the back of a chair, letting her fingers dig into the leather. "I thought we had an understanding."

She had hoped she'd convinced Jackson Rhodes to trust her professional expertise. To work with her and follow her instructions.

It was a good thing Caitlyn had taken over with him to oversee the setup of the tap on his home landline and personal computer while the rest of the team regrouped. If she was standing in front of him right now, what she had to say to him might not reflect the most diplomatic choice of words.

Miguel swallowed a bite of his sandwich from Emerald City Roasters and wiped his mouth. "The situation could've been worse. At least he asked for proof of life," he said, and she agreed, but the situation could have been better, leaving them in a stronger position. "Don't beat yourself up over this. It happens to the best of us."

"Not to me. Not on my watch." An emotional parent going rogue could jeopardize this case just as much as her getting the profile of an unsub wrong. That's why she always took her time, analyzed every angle and relied on her training to help her connect the dots. Sometimes in the field a split-second decision had to be made, but only rookies made a rash call.

"First time for everything." Dash leaned back in his chair with a smug look and folded his arms.

How could Jackson be so...

She wasn't sure what he was. Reckless. Infuriating. Good-looking to the point of distraction. A wild card.

A parent acting out of conviction. And love. Madeline's heart softened a little more as her temperature cooled.

There was no denying that giving in to the demands against her advice took a great deal of courage, even if it had made her job harder.

With a shake of her head, she suppressed her reluctant admiration, yanked out a chair and sat. "Where do we stand on statements from those who were there?"

"I prioritized the catering crew of three, the magician and the band," Dash said. "Every year, ETC uses the same catering company, but their staff has a high turnover rate. A lot of college kids who need part-time employment. No one working on the crew that day knew each other. I ran checks on them but turned up nothing. They were all clean. Same with the magician and band. Everyone was so busy doing their job, they didn't notice anything."

"We still have hundreds of statements left to review." David munched on fries from his to-go container. "The cops didn't flag anything as suspicious. No one saw a young girl being led away. It'll take me a couple of days to go through them all, compare for discrepancies. Honestly, it's going to be a nightmare of busywork. I know that's what us interns are here for, but the kidnapper picked the worst possible day."

"Actually, the kidnapper picked the perfect day." Madeline sipped her coffee, still wound too tight to stomach any food, despite the tempting aromas in the air. "We're going to be stretched thin with a mountain of statements to comb through. I bet most of them will be meaningless. Tracking down anything useful will be like trying to find a needle in a haystack."

David sighed. "Great. I'm looking forward to it."

"You won't be alone." Nick clasped his shoulder. "I'll be digging in the weeds right along with you." He turned to everyone else. "Forensics is dusting the drone I shot down for prints, but I wouldn't hold my breath that they'll find anything. I jotted down the model number and looked it up. It's commercial. A popular brand called ABC Icarus. According to the specs, the drone's max speed is fifty miles per hour, and it can fly for up to thirty minutes. Whoever was operating it was within a twenty-five-mile radius."

Madeline perked in her seat at the small nugget of useful information. "That means Emma wasn't far when the building exploded. The kidnapper wouldn't have a chance to drive her out of state and return in time to maintain a visual of the Duwamish site once the ransom demand was sent. The child might've even been in the metropolitan area. Definitely within a thirty-to-forty-five-minute drive. Hopefully, she's still close by."

"What were the fire department's preliminary findings about the bomb?" Miguel asked.

"Another drone was used to deliver what appears to be a homemade explosive device along with an accelerant," Nick said. "The drone entered through the ventilation shaft on the roof. They also found soiled cat litter in the air vent, which they believe triggered the carbon monoxide alarm."

"That would explain the strange smell the employees mentioned," Madeline added. "Since the kidnapper used drones to trigger the alarms, deliver the bomb and monitor the situation, how did the text message originate from the building?"

"The text was traced to the vicinity of the Duwamish site," Dash said. "Not necessarily the building. The cell phone was detected within a small radius of three different cell towers. The area where each tower overlapped is where it was pinpointed. The person could've sent the text half a block away from the building without ever needing to go inside." His brows drew together as if he was thinking of something. "Traffic cam footage around ETC didn't turn up anything viable, but we might have better luck around the Duwamish site." Dash made himself a note.

"We have statements from the employees there," Madeline said. Each one of them seemed heartbroken over the loss of their project. All their hard work on a prototype down the drain. "I don't think any of them were involved."

"I have to agree," Nick said. "They were pretty shaken up. Even more rattled when they each learned that Rhodes's daughter had been kidnapped."

"Any clarity on the profile of our unsub?" Miguel asked her.

"After the bombing, I got the feeling that this goes deeper than business." The unsub's motives were becoming clearer. This was all about Jackson. "It's definitely a personal grudge. Someone who not only wants to hurt Jackson but also manipulate him." But to what ultimate end? She wasn't so sure this was only about him resigning anymore. "There's still something about the text messages as the form of communication that bugs me. It's one-way and doesn't give Jackson a chance to barter. This person wants Jackson to suffer, yet they haven't exploited the opportunity to hear him beg over the phone."

"Whoever it is saw him plead on TV," David said.

Nick nodded. "And he screamed at the camera on the

drone. I'm sure that made for lovely footage someone could watch and revel in over and over again."

"The televised speech was tempered," Madeline said. "The drone didn't provide audio. Neither showcased his suffering. More importantly, the kidnapper hasn't bragged."

"'Behold the demonstration of my resolve,'" Dash said, reading the first line of the transcript from the last text sent by the kidnapper.

"*Resolve*. Not power. That's not boasting." Sitting forward, Madeline rested her forearms on the table. "That was persuasion. Someone doing their best to convince Jackson what kind of devastation they're capable of inflicting, but without actually hurting anyone by having the building evacuated and using three drones to ensure no one went back inside. Three. Quite clever." She drummed her fingers on the table. "The passive form of communication, the great care with the specific wording in the texts, using the promise of a puppy as the lure, not boasting—instead seeking validation. My gut tells me it's a woman. Not a man. Caucasian. Educated. Midtwenties to midthirties. I wish I could say I was a hundred percent on that, but not yet."

"Why not?" Miguel's gaze narrowed, and she stiffened under the tangible weight of his scrutiny. "What's holding you back?"

"Two things. First, I don't know why the kidnapper wanted Jackson to resign. Second, who are our top suspects?"

"Andrew Phillips and Charles Albrecht," Dash said.

Madeline nodded. "Exactly. Both men." Regardless, she couldn't shake that gut feeling, which had never led her astray. Then again, maybe Dash was right and there was a first time for everything. This could be the first time her instincts were wrong. Too many elements about this case were throwing her off. The texts. The unusual ransom demand. The wild card father with those piercing blue eyes. But when all else failed, the one thing she could rely on was her training. "We need to check the nanny and Jackson's assistant." Rivka Molnar also fit the profile. "The IT supervisor, too."

"I spoke to Ms. Molnar in depth," Dash said. "She was with her own nine-year-old when Emma was taken. She didn't leave the premises until after the police arrived and it was to take her kid to school. Then she came straight back. We also have a brief statement from Brittany Hall, the assistant. Sounds like she was either doing something with the catering staff, the magician or the band at the time. But I went ahead and ran preliminary background checks on both as well as the nanny. No red flags."

Doubt churned through Madeline. What if she was wrong? Or she was off track with the kidnapper's profile?

Whittling down the list of suspects was a good thing, not bad, she reminded herself.

"We're looking at too many people right now for me to run a more extensive background check on everyone," Dash said.

"I did call the nanny like you wanted." David closed his food container. "Liane Strothe is coming in tomorrow."

"Thanks," Madeline said.

"Also, I noticed there wasn't a statement from Phillips. Should I schedule interviews for him and Albrecht?" David asked.

"There were numerous reports of no one seeing Phillips around the time Emma was taken," Miguel said. "He wasn't at ETC headquarters when we arrived. According to his administrative assistant, Natascha Campbell, she was with him all day up until the time he departed for Spokane for a meeting to acquire a smaller company."

"His assistant is his alibi?" Nick asked. "Do you buy her story?"

Miguel shrugged. "I'm not sure. She was a little too cagey. A gatekeeper of the first order. Fiercely loyal to Phillips, very protective. But the chairman confirmed the meeting in Spokane has been on the books for weeks. Phillips will be back tomorrow and available for an interview. With his lawyer. I'm going to speak to him first thing in the morning at nine."

Any attorney worth his salt wouldn't allow his client to say anything incriminating. Good thing Miguel was going to question Phillips. He was one of the best at reading people and had the strongest interrogation tactics on the team. Even with a lawyer, Miguel would be able tell if Phillips had anything to hide.

"Don't bother calling Albrecht," Madeline said. "Too easy for him to take the precaution of lawyering up, too. I'd prefer to surprise him, catch him off guard. Make him feel as though he's doing a great service by answering a few questions."

"Sounds like a smart way to handle it," Miguel said. "In the meantime, I want them under surveillance ASAP. Reach out to the field office in Spokane. I want eyes on Phillips."

Nick nodded. "I'll take care of it."

"Have we considered the prospect of an angry ex-girl-friend behind this?" Dash asked.

Of course she had. "I asked Jackson if he had any romantic entanglements lately. He claims there hasn't been anyone. Not even a one-night stand."

Dash gave a low chuckle. "I guess his whole world revolves around his kid."

"And his job," Miguel pointed out.

The unsub had just taken away both in one day. A devastating blow.

"An unrequited crush could also be a possibility," Nick suggested.

That was a tougher angle to explore. Jackson might be oblivious. Men sometimes were.

Miguel smirked. "'Hell hath no fury like a woman scorned.'"

Madeline rolled her eyes. "Have I ever mentioned how much I despise that saying?"

"Yes," the guys said in unison.

Shaking her head, Madeline smiled, refusing to give any of them the satisfaction of seeing her annoyance.

"The unsub could contact Rhodes again at any time," Miguel said. "We'll be monitoring his communications, but I think one of us should be on hand, spend the night at his house just in case. Since he went rogue once, he's capable of doing it again."

Miguel didn't ask for volunteers because he didn't have to. Someone on the team was always able, willing and ready. This was her case. Her responsibility.

"It makes sense for me to do it," she said. "I'll eat, sleep and breathe nothing but this case until we bring Emma home." Though she doubted she would do much eating or sleeping.

"I'll have Caitlyn tell him to expect you and smooth things over if he has a problem with the Bureau maintaining a presence in his home."

Raised voices from the hall penetrated through the glass door of the small conference room, drawing everyone's attention.

Madeline leaned to the side of her chair, giving her a partial view of the hall.

"I'm only asking for two minutes." Worry was plastered all over Lorelai's face as she chased after her fiancé down the hall.

Liam huffed a breath, stopped walking toward the conference room and faced her. "Two minutes turns into five and then ten. The next thing I know I've wasted twenty minutes on wedding nonsense."

"Nonsense?" Lorelai rocked back on her heels, clearly offended.

Trouble in paradise again. Ever since those two lovebirds got engaged, it had been one fight after another. Lorelai had shared with Madeline and Caitlyn every wedding detail and inevitable problem that came along with it. Maybe the arguments were due to jitters, stress from planning the event of the year.

Or maybe it was proof that romance and happily-ever-after only worked in fairy tales.

Liam hung his head. "I didn't mean it like that. I'm sorry. It's just that there are more important things for me to focus on right now. This case is—"

"There's always a case." Lorelai crossed her arms. "But our wedding is once in a lifetime."

"Tell that to my parents, each headed for a third divorce."

"You and I are not them. I just wanted to know if you got fitted for your tux. They need time to make any alterations. The wedding is in two months."

"I know when it is and no, I haven't had a chance to get fitted. I'll get around to it."

"This is important, too, you know. I want everything to be perfect, for it to be the most spectacular day of both our lives when you seem like you could care less."

"I don't care whether there are roses or tulips in the place settings, notched lapel or peaked lapel on my tux, the style of the invitation or the endless list of things you want me to weigh in on. That's the kind of stuff you could ask my mom about to include her more. Listen, I looked at a gazillion venues, tasted food until I was stuffed and sampled more cake than I've ever eaten in my life. Why can't that be good enough?"

"Good enough?" The hurt resonating in Lorelai's voice had Madeline tensing in her seat. "I didn't realize you were doing me such a huge favor by helping to plan *our* wedding. Do you have any idea how many decisions I've made without bothering you about any of them?"

"No. Thank God for that small mercy."

David snickered.

Madeline was about to shoot him a warning glare when Nick prodded him in the side with an elbow.

"Can I get back to work now?" Liam asked.

Lorelai spun on her heel and stalked down the hall.

Not a good sign. Lorelai was never at a loss for words when it came to Liam.

True love was probably rubbish people clung to for hope, but Madeline wished those two, who seemed like a perfect match, every happiness together.

Liam strode into the conference without making eye contact with anyone. Holding a folder under his arm, he closed the door behind him and took a seat on the other side of David. His cheeks were a bright red from emotion. A normally vibrant thirty-year-old, he looked completely sapped of energy. "The last text couldn't be traced. I think the unsub was bouncing the signal around between cell towers. But I dug deeper into Mr. Rhodes to see if there was anyone who might target him for any reason, and I found this." He opened the folder and passed the contents around. "A couple of years ago, the Red Right Hand set their sights on him."

"I've heard of them," Madeline said. "Domestic extremists who take their name from Milton's poem *Paradise Lost*. View themselves as the embodiment of divine wrath."

"A pleasant bunch, spreading joy and cheer wherever they go," Liam said. "They've protested against ETC business practices outside of their headquarters while holding up signs that called Mr. Rhodes 'the Butcher of the American Dream' and even threw acid on the hood of his parked car after he was named CEO, but no one was inside the vehicle, so no injuries."

Madeline scanned the sheets of information. That seemed to be the worst of it, but there was a list of harassing incidents a page long, from sneaking into a cocktail party at a hotel and throwing a drink in Jackson's face to posting flyers around his daughter's school of him depicted as the Grinch, complete with photoshopped green-tinted skin.

"Apparently getting children involved isn't off-limits," she said.

"They don't officially claim to have a leader," Liam said, "but in fact, they do, and I found out who it is. Samantha Dickson."

Madeline turned to the last page. She stared at a picture of Dickson standing on a hill, waving her fist in the air, holding a bullhorn and firing up a crowd. The woman's eyes were filled with pure rage.

Ethnicity: White
Age: 26
Education: Bachelor's Degree from the University of Southern California
Parents: Sylvie and Donald Dickson, owners of Dickson Chemical Company

"She's *that* Dickson?" Madeline asked. "Heiress to billions?"

"Yep." Liam nodded. "Not that I'm sure if Mommy and

Daddy are still leaving her their fortune considering she turned whistleblower on them. She reported the petrochemical company for dumping toxic waste that polluted a town's water source. The town filed a nasty lawsuit and Dickson Chemical lost millions in a hefty settlement."

"Bingo," Dash said. "Rich kid turned radical with a pattern of escalating aggression toward Rhodes. Her group made their unhappiness over him being named CEO unmistakably clear when they threw acid on his car."

The question was why. What on earth could Jackson have done to draw their ire? More importantly, why hadn't he mentioned it to her?

Miguel put the information sheet down. "She does fit the profile and has a motive to want the Butcher of the American Dream to resign."

"We need to bring her in for questioning," Madeline said. "Now."

Liam closed the folder. "That's where we run into a bit of a problem. We have to find her first. There's no known address for her. No utility bills in her name."

"What about the rest of her merry little band?" Madeline asked.

Liam shrugged. "I haven't had time to look into them yet, but I will."

This case was going to need everyone to work flat out.

"The group is still active?" Nick asked, stealing the next question from her lips. "Targeting others and fighting the good fight?"

"Yeah." Liam nodded. "In the past ten days, they've protested a restaurant for not paying their undocumented workers a reasonable wage and a cosmetics company for testing on animals. At the latter, they fired red paintballs at the CEO as he left the building."

Even if her entire crew lived off the grid, which was a

highly doubtful *if*, there was a way to track them down or flush them out. "Then we can find the Red Right Hand," Madeline said, "and Samantha Dickson."

Chapter Five

Caitlyn Yang inwardly cringed as Miguel rattled off her marching orders over the phone.

"It's imperative we stay close and keep an eye on him. His emotions are running high and justifiably so. The kidnapper will make contact again. When that happens, we need to be there. Hopefully he won't have an issue with Madeline staying the night," Miguel said in her ear.

Wishful thinking.

Rhodes had had a problem with everything else thus far. From how long it took the tech team to set up to the endless round of questions he hammered her with, demanding answers about the case that either she didn't have or wasn't her place to provide.

His frustration was normal. His anger understandable.

His entire world was hanging in the balance.

He was a guarded man who valued his privacy and was used to being in charge. Sitting around doing nothing while surrounded by strangers was probably the hardest part for him.

Now she had to be the one to drop the bombshell that he wouldn't even have his home to himself tonight.

"I'll take care of it," Caitlyn said, standing in the foyer, where she'd excused herself to take the call.

"As always," Miguel said. "I know I can count on you.

Madeline should be there within the hour. She needed to grab some things from home first."

What did Caitlyn have to complain about? Madeline was the one who would be stuck here, dealing with Rhodes all night. No break to decompress and hit the ground running fresh tomorrow.

Caitlyn's heart went out to her. Madeline avoided taking on the role of family support during kidnapping cases. Not that she wasn't capable. Staying laser focused on finding an abducted child alive—always the burning goal—took precedence over the impact to the parents. Her job exacted a heavy emotional toll. Required a cool detachment to see things objectively and stay in control. Mix in handling the relatives and friends of victims, an already tough task which often pushed Caitlyn to her limits, and anyone could get overwhelmed.

It was a lot to manage. A lot for someone to be.

At times, Caitlyn suspected there might be a deeper reason, one more personal, that kept Madeline at a distance from the families. Perhaps she was haunted by ghosts from her past. Had lost someone close to her.

In the five years they had worked together at BAU, they'd become friends, though not close enough for Madeline to share her history or reveal what had motivated her to join the FBI.

Whatever tormented Madeline also drove her to find and rescue victims, even at the expense of having a personal life of her own. As though her job was her reason for living.

"Okay," Caitlyn said to Miguel. "I'll hang here until Madeline arrives." She disconnected the call.

Her specialty was smoothing over ruffled feathers, whether civilian, media or local law enforcement, and Rhodes was testing her skills today.

Taking on the role of family support was usually effortless for her. Comforting the victims' loved ones gave her a sense of professional satisfaction that no other aspect of her job provided. The trick was figuring out what kind of support a person needed.

Everyone was different. No one-size-fits-all technique worked.

Her initial approach with the doting father had been way off base. The more she offered to do for him, the more anxious and snappish he became. She had to go against her natural instincts, dial down her efforts to console him while minimizing the sense of intrusion when the tech team had been in the house.

Once they had cleared out, it had been touch and go with Rhodes.

The one thing that she had found worked no matter age, gender or personality was distraction.

She stuffed her phone in her pocket and followed the music.

Sad and familiar, the melody being played from the piano rose and fell gently, reaching deeper inside her until her heart ached. She slipped into the living room, not wanting to disturb him as his fingers glided over the keys of the baby grand in the corner.

Dear God. She never would've guessed that he had such talent inside him.

The way he played was entrancing.

He struck the last chord. The melancholic melody hung in the air, resonating in her soul, and goose bumps broke out on her arms. She wanted to weep.

Staying seated, he rested his hand on the top of the piano.

This was as good a time as any. "That was Supervisory Special Agent Peters on the phone. He would like to have an agent stay the night." She geared up for the rest of her speech. "The volatility of the situation—"

"Which agent?" he asked, his voice flat and low, keeping his back to her.

"Madeline Striker."

"Madeline," he said with a strange emphasis. A statement, not a question. For a beat longer, he didn't move. Then he swiveled around on the bench and looked at her, his face impassive.

Was he going to complain? Fight this?

One of the most important parts of her job was to reduce the stress for the agents whenever and however she could in her dealings with the police, the press and public.

Caitlyn raced through a list of potential objections he might make and chose the best proactive counterargument. "Once the kidnapper makes contact again, we want to ensure you're not compelled to take action you might regret. Especially if the form of communication changes from text to a phone call. With Special Agent Striker present we can manage an appropriate response, as well as act on any new information quickly. She's on her way here now."

"It's fine."

Wait, what? "Really?"

"Yes. I'll do whatever is necessary to get Emma back."

Caitlyn wiped the shock from her face. "I'll stay until she arrives."

"To watch me and keep me under thumb." He rose. "Can I get you a cup of coffee or tea while you wait?"

"Tea, please."

THE NIGHT HAD grown chilly. Fat splats of rain pounded the car, accompanied by a long growl of thunder. Madeline drove her Volvo to Madison Park, a far more affluent area than where she lived. Her Wedgwood neighborhood was safe, affordable, allowed her to get away from the busy city center while the commute to work was still quick via I-5.

But it was a far cry from the chic enclave of legacy properties lying on the shore of Lake Washington that many business executives sought to live in.

Out of all the high-powered, wealthy CEOs in Seattle, and they were in abundance in this city, why had Jackson Rhodes been targeted?

Better still, why work out the grievance through his child?

Jackson was driven, smart, self-assured without being arrogant. Capable of rising to the top. Whoever did this must view his love for his daughter as his weakness.

Children made you vulnerable. Opened you to the possibility of unimaginable pain. The very reason she never wanted to bring a life into this world. She'd watched her parents suffer for years, bore witness to how their grief ate away at their family like a cancer.

For all the guts she had every day on the job, she was still too much of a coward to be a mother.

The GPS chimed, indicating she had reached her destination. She parked the car in front of the house and killed the engine. Lightning flashed through the sky.

Storm clouds made the evening an unusually dark one. Everything beyond the wet windshield seemed to be dissolving, as though the whole world might drain away through some cosmic hole. She tightened her grip on the steering wheel, not wanting any part of herself to get sucked into the void, set adrift in the darkness, alone. It had been so long since she had needed to hold on to anything, but this case was dredging up the agonizing memories of that life-changing day when her sister, Kimberly, had been kidnapped.

For so many years, one question plagued Madeline.

Why Kimberly and not her?

Guilt tightened around her like a noose.

She'd worked so hard to move past it, to convince herself that she was stronger than the loss, than the pain that had nearly crushed her family.

Burying her face in her hands, she gave in for a fleeting moment to the dread and pain churning inside her. The memories made her want to curl within herself. Disappear.

Pull yourself together. You don't do pity parties.

That innocent little girl needs you.

So many in her field entered this profession as a way to do good. For Madeline, it was a way to drive out the darkness.

Dropping her hands, she hauled in a steadying breath and realigned her focus to one thing. Finding Emma Rhodes. Nothing else mattered.

She had to come to an understanding with Jackson that working together was in his daughter's best interest. Then she had questions for him, and his answers had better be damn good.

The rain slowed. The last rumble of thunder sounded farther away. The storm was passing. One good thing at least.

She leaned over to the passenger seat, grabbing her umbrella and overnight bag. After leaving the office, she'd made a pit stop at her condo and packed a few changes of clothes and some essentials. She would be holed up with Jackson for as long as it took to find his daughter and prayed that wouldn't be more than a day or two.

Madeline hopped out into the drizzle, hoisting the open umbrella over her head.

The rain crackled against the pavement as if it were oil in a deep fryer. She looked up and down the quiet street, taking in the surroundings. Only a handful of cars were parked along the curb. She noted makes and models. The rest of the vehicles were in driveways or she assumed the garage by this late hour.

Shivering against the chill, she walked up the stone path to a charming cottage set on a large lot. According to the GPS, the house was only steps from the lake.

The nip in the air had her hurrying up the wooden stairs and under the covered porch. She closed her umbrella, giving it a good shake.

The glass panes of the front door provided a view of the lit foyer and short hall that led deeper into the house.

Before ringing the bell, she sucked in the rainy night air, seeking a little more emotional distance. Then another deep, cleansing breath.

Still, she hesitated.

Compartmentalization allowed her to operate at the top of her game. She'd learned techniques to detach and deal with the emotion later—while out on a run, unwinding in the bath, during her kickboxing class, any time or place she wasn't on the clock and didn't have to be a consummate professional. That was the only way to do her job.

Yet all of her tried and tested tactics were failing her.

Something, or rather so many things, about Jackson and this case made it hard not to feel when the last thing she could afford was any sort of attachment to a victim's father.

Professional investment was necessary. An emotional one would only cause distraction.

She rang the bell.

Less than a minute later, Jackson and Caitlyn rounded the corner into the foyer, engaged in easy conversation. No one appeared on offense or defense.

Jackson opened the door. "Madeline." He gave her a smile, broken and weak, fragile as a wounded bird.

There went that catch in her chest, which came each time she saw his sorrow.

"Come in." He stepped aside, beckoning her to enter.

"Thank you." The space was bathed in soft golden light.

"I know it's an inconvenience to have someone in your home, but I'll do my best to make sure my presence doesn't feel like an intrusion. With any luck, you won't notice I'm here."

"That will be an impossible task." His gaze locked onto hers. "This is a small house, but it would be difficult not to notice you even if it were a sprawling estate."

Was that good or bad? Considering how they'd left things when they'd last spoken, she wasn't quite sure.

Jackson had changed clothes, ditching the suit. He wore jeans and a cobalt blue long-sleeved T-shirt that matched the color of his eyes. The clingy material hugged his broad shoulders and biceps, stretching across a muscled expanse that tapered to slim hips.

All the oxygen emptied from Madeline's lungs. She swallowed, tightening her grip on her bag. Never had she reacted to a man in quite this manner.

It wasn't as if she could click it on or off. A part of her feared blocking the sensation of feeling so routinely that she might construct a wall too thick and tall to be able to get through one day.

"The surveillance on his landline and laptop are good to go," Caitlyn said. "The team will be able to monitor everything. I should head out." She walked to the door. "Try not to worry, Mr. Rhodes."

"It's Jackson." His tone toward her had warmed considerably.

Caitlyn flashed a gentle smile, but Madeline noted it was more reserved than usual.

The evening must have been tense. Jackson coming home for the first time without Emma, surrounded by strangers. For Caitlyn, she probably had to navigate an emotional minefield, but if anyone could handle it with finesse and compassion, it was her.

Madeline turned to Caitlyn before she slipped through the door. "You might want to give Lorelai a call. I think she'll need to vent."

Caitlyn gave her a knowing nod. They were used to being the proverbial shoulder for Lorelai to lean on since the engagement. Both of them adored Lorelai and were happy to listen whenever she needed.

With a curt wave, Caitlyn was gone.

He locked the door and put the chain on. "Let me show you to the guest room."

"That won't be necessary. I can catch a few winks on the sofa."

"I won't hear of it."

He headed down the short hall, leading her past a formal living room with a piano. The dining room sat across from the kitchen. Beyond that was the family room, lit from the glow from the fireplace. Large windows overlooked the dark front yard. Next, they passed what appeared to be his office. At about two thousand square feet, the one-story multimillion-dollar home was cozy, welcoming. Tastefully furnished in a neutral palette, it was the kind of place where you wanted to sit down, have a glass of wine and snuggle in.

Finally, he opened the door to a room with a queen-size bed ready for guests. "There's no en suite, but the bathroom is next door. Emma's bedroom is right across the hall." Sorrow drifted across his expression. The muscles in his throat worked as if he'd swallowed gravel. "Mine is at the end of the hall."

Staying in the corridor, Madeline dropped her overnight bag on the floor inside the room, setting her purse on top, and kept her cell handy. He leaned against the doorjamb and their eyes met, his deep and unfathomable.

For one quiet moment, they stared at each other. She

fought not to squirm in her skin or shift her gaze under the unexpected jolt of power that came with that stare.

Why couldn't he get less attractive the closer she got? Instead, he was one of those men you couldn't help but look at. An aesthetic face that was all male, a slash of cheekbones and sculpted mouth. Blue eyes with such intensity of color she could lose herself in them. Hair that was thick and full. He was almost ridiculously gorgeous with a devastating presence that filled a room.

Before she melted into a puddle at his feet, she asked, "Can we sit down somewhere and talk?"

They needed to hash things out. Right now.

Jackson gestured for Madeline to follow him.

Lecturing him, extolling her success rate, trying to use her position to get him to fall in line wouldn't work on him. Only one thing would get him to trust her and treat her like a teammate in this because he sure as heck wasn't going to sit on the sidelines.

She straightened, steeling herself for what she had to do.

Chapter Six

Walking down the hall, Jackson led the way back through the house, sensing what Madeline was about to bring up.

She wanted to talk about the way he'd handled the press conference. Read him the riot act. Lay down the law. Make sure he understood who was in charge and how things would go from here on out. It was evident in her bearing, the way her tone had changed.

If they needed to clear the air and reach an understanding, so be it.

First, he damn sure needed a drink. Anger and adrenaline had drained from him, leaving him cold with a bone-deep fear.

Minutes had blurred together until hours had crept by since he had resigned on television. Still, there was no proof of life. No new text.

Only silence while he was forced to wait in purgatory.

Had he made a mistake? Had he ruined his one chance to find out whether his daughter was alive?

No, no, he mustn't think like that. Following his gut wasn't wrong.

He shuttered the doubt. Nothing was final. Not yet. He'd created a loophole rather than backing himself into a corner he couldn't escape.

The monster who'd taken his daughter wanted Jackson's

resignation to be final. The only way that would happen was to have evidence Emma was all right.

Inside the family room, he made a beeline to the discreet bar at the far wall. "Do you drink Scotch or brandy?"

"Brandy, but not while I'm on duty."

He pulled the cork from a bottle and poured amber liquid into two snifters. Crossing the room, he handed her one. "Calvados. Lecompte. You can't remain on duty 24/7. I got the impression from Caitlyn that you're here to make sure I don't do anything stupid. One drink won't prevent you from doing that."

Madeline considered him. "One." She accepted the glass, smelled the brandy and took a sip. "I haven't tasted Calvados this good since my last vacation, in Paris."

"How long ago was that?"

Madeline sat on the sofa that faced the burning gas fireplace. "I'm ashamed to say, but it's been too long since I've taken any time off."

She was a workaholic, the same as him.

Emma was the only thing to drag him out of the office. With one parent gone, he did his best to shower her with the love and attention that two would give. Sometimes that meant spoiling her a bit. At other times, he worried that he pushed her too hard to excel.

He turned from Madeline toward the fire. Closed his eyes, pictured Emma safe and warm and tucked into bed, waiting for him to read a story. Tears pressed against his eyelids. He recalled the sound of her giggle, the feel of her hair slipping through his fingers, the fruity scent of her shampoo mingled with her skin still damp from her bath.

Fathomless despair yawned inside him like an abyss.

Opening his eyes, the world blurred. He blinked back tears and took a healthy swallow of brandy, forcing himself to stop before he drained the snifter.

The doorbell rang.

Madeline shifted on the sofa, glancing toward the hall. "Are you expecting anyone?"

"I'm not. I'll be right back." He set his glass down on the coffee table and went to the door.

From the foyer, he spotted Brittany.

Jackson opened the door and let her in.

She stepped into the foyer, carrying a large brown paper bag.

"What are you doing here?" he asked.

Brittany tucked her straight black hair behind her ear. "Today has been a whirlwind. I haven't had a chance to say how sorry I am about what happened to Emma." She clasped his arm with her free hand. "I wanted to stop by and see how you were holding up. Thought maybe you could use some company."

"That's very considerate of you, but unnecessary." No one needed to make a fuss over him. Everyone's concern and energy should be directed toward Emma.

"I can't imagine what you must be going through. Not knowing where she is, who has her. It must be torture." Brittany's gaze shifted behind him.

Jackson looked over his shoulder. Madeline stood on the periphery of the foyer.

"I'm sorry." Brittany dropped her hand and shuffled backward. "I didn't realize you weren't alone." Her gaze bounced between them, a flush blooming on her cheeks.

"This is Special Agent Madeline Striker," he said.

"Oh, you're one of the FBI agents investigating the case," Brittany said. "There were so many police officers and agents at ETC earlier. I didn't think you guys would still be here this late."

Madeline strolled deeper into the foyer. "I'm staying

the night. The Bureau wants to ensure we have an around-the-clock presence."

"Really? I would've expected a police officer parked out front for that sort of thing," Brittany said. "Not an agent in the house overnight."

"Are you well versed in law enforcement protocol?" Madeline asked.

"I just assumed, you know," Brittany said. "From movies, TV shows, that sort of thing." She glanced down at the bag in her hand. "Takeout from Spinasse. I figured you wouldn't think about eating until you were famished."

How astute of her. He hadn't eaten since the Family Day event, but he wasn't hungry. The thought of food turned his stomach.

Brittany handed him the bag. "A few of your favorite dishes. You need to keep up your strength. For Emma's sake."

Jackson smiled at her. She was the world's best assistant. Always looking out for him. "Thank you, but I wish you hadn't gone to the trouble."

Brittany shrugged, throwing a glance at Madeline. "No trouble at all. Besides, I also picked up a late dinner for me and Aaron. Saves me the hassle of cooking."

"Who's Aaron?" Madeline asked.

"My boyfriend."

Another step forward and Madeline's expression softened. "Is it serious?"

"I should hope so. We live together and I think we're ready to take the next step." Brittany flashed an unfiltered smile, then her gaze darted to Jackson and the light in her eyes went out. "I saw your press conference on the news. Since you resigned, I didn't know if I should go into the office tomorrow. Did you want me to take care of anything for you?"

Jackson hadn't considered that far ahead. His mind snagged on the thought of getting proof of life, unable to go beyond the dark hypotheticals if one never came. He ran his hand over the cell phone in his pocket. "Stay home, for now. Enjoy your time off." She was only twenty-seven, worked fifty to sixty hours a week and needed to spend more time with her boyfriend. A break would do her good. "I'll contact the chairman and make sure they find you a new position."

"Are you really not going to come back to ETC?" Brittany asked.

So long as he got his daughter back, it didn't matter to him which company he worked for. Emma was the most important thing in the world. "That's not up to me."

"This is so unfair." Tears sprang to Brittany's green eyes. "I'll keep you and Emma in my thoughts and prayers. If there's anything you need, anything at all, day or night, call me."

He nodded, though he wouldn't call. But her dedication was appreciated. "I'll make sure the chairman gives you paid leave until you're reassigned."

"That's so generous of you. Thinking about me at a time like this when you're being put through the wringer." Brittany whisked away tears with the back of her hand. "Try to get some rest. You need to take care of yourself." She opened the door and stepped out into the night.

Jackson locked the door and switched off the light in the foyer. "Are you hungry?" He held up the bag.

"I'm good. But your assistant is right. If you haven't had dinner, you should eat something to keep up your strength."

"I can't right now." Not when he didn't know if Emma was safe. Had she been fed dinner, or was her little stomach rumbling with hunger pangs? He suppressed the anger and sheer worry rising inside him like a tsunami. "I'll put it away."

Jackson set the entire bag on the top shelf of his fridge and returned to the family room.

Picking up his glass, he sat near Madeline on the sofa. She pressed against the side of the couch as if he'd invaded her space. They were an arm's length apart.

"If I've made you uncomfortable, I can sit somewhere else." He motioned to one of the slipper chairs a few feet away.

"No," she said in a rush, shaking her head to emphasize the word. "It's not that. It's just…nothing. We need to talk."

He downed the rest of the brandy, letting the heat slide down his throat to his belly. Got up and poured another. Sat back down, this time an inch or two closer to her.

For some reason, the proximity unsettled this unflappable woman. As he saw it, that took away her advantage and gave him a fighting chance at staying involved in his own child's case. It hadn't occurred to him how much information the FBI might withhold from him until Jackson had shot off one rapid-fire question after another to Caitlyn, asking about the bomb, the statements that had been taken, the list of top suspects, the next steps in the process—and she had told him virtually nothing.

"Let's talk," Jackson said.

Madeline cleared her throat. "There was a misunderstanding between us earlier. This job isn't a game to me. I'm sorry if I made you feel otherwise." She shifted toward him, wrapping both hands around her glass. "This is my life's purpose. It's the reason I'm here."

He got the impression she didn't mean *here* as in his house, but more of an existential reason for being.

"I would never gamble with human life, especially a child's," she continued. "Neither will anyone else I work with. Not while I'm in charge of a case. I may not be a parent, but I understand what you're going through."

He looked up at her. There was an openness in her eyes, a vulnerability that hadn't been there before. As if she had lowered a wall. Now he saw what she hid so well.

Something haunted her. She understood pain. Loss.

"When I was eight, my sister was kidnapped," she said in a soft voice. "Taken from a playground while we were together. She was two years younger than me."

Shock surged like an electric current through his limbs. "The same age as Emma."

Madeline nodded grimly. "My sister was never found, but that was a different time, much different circumstances. Technology has come a long way in facilitating investigations since then."

The hell she had gone through as such a young child, and to come out on the other side without acting the victim or martyr. He had no idea. Then again why would he?

She swallowed and then went on. "I'm sharing this with you so you know that what I've been through, what my parents had to endure..." A stricken expression fell across her face, but just as fast melted away, leaving warmth and determination.

Jackson inched closer to her. He didn't touch her, but the urge to reach out and take her hand hit him hard. When their gazes met this time, it was more powerful than any physical connection. Never before had he experienced an instant common bond with someone.

Even one borne from tragedy.

"It's the reason I've dedicated my life to this," she said. "To spare as many families as I can that unbearable grief."

The perseverance and true grit it must have taken to become an FBI agent, choosing to face the same gut-wrenching scenario on a regular basis, all to save others. It couldn't be easy.

Madeline Striker was steelier and stronger than he'd first assumed, being one of few women in a male-dominated profession. While he understood her motivation and admired her dedication, her self-sacrifice to do this simply blew him away.

"On each case," she said, "getting it right means everything to me. I am fully invested. The entire team is committed to bringing your daughter home safely."

The way she said it, the promise in her voice, the sincerity behind the words, rocked him to his core, spreading calm within him.

"Thank you for telling me." Knowing that she did understand what he was going through in a way most others wouldn't changed everything. He wasn't alone. "I'm sorry about your sister."

Unable to resist the impulse, Jackson squeezed her shoulder, for a moment, but with tenderness as well as strength.

Madeline was fierce yet also a little wounded. Maybe a lot wounded.

Taking a deep breath, she nodded, allowing his sympathy without bristling, and he admired her more for it.

"I've often wondered why Kimberly was taken," she said. "Instead of me. Why I got to…" Her voice trailed off, but he filled in the blank.

Live. Love. Laugh.

For more than twenty years she'd battled survivor's guilt. He couldn't begin to comprehend what that must be like. He'd been without Emma for less than twenty-four hours and he was on the verge of losing himself. Right on the edge of the abyss.

Having Madeline there, with her calming energy,

grounded him. Kept him from spiraling. Much in the same way playing the piano did. But no one could play forever.

"I owe you an apology for what I said to you earlier." Asking her in the heat of the moment if she was a parent, like some litmus test, had been unfair. The emotion that had flashed across her face he now recognized as hurt. He regretted saying it.

"There's nothing to apologize for. I can relate to what you're going through. It's the flip side of a coin, but it isn't exactly the same."

He lowered his hand, grateful that they could move forward.

"We have to work together as a team, Jackson. That means listening to my professional advice, and if your gut leads you in a different direction, talk to me before you act. Okay?"

He couldn't pull his eyes from hers. The depth of pain, of affinity staring back at him, wouldn't let him go.

"Fair enough," he said. "I can, I will do that. I hope that means you'll keep me in the loop." Being kept in the dark would drive him stir-crazy.

"Sharing information is critical. It'll ease your mind a little and help us find your daughter. But you have to stop withholding information."

He flinched at the accusation. "I haven't withheld anything." He'd never dare compromise the safe return of his daughter.

"Then why didn't you tell us about the Red Right Hand and how they've harassed you when I asked you about enemies?"

What did they have to do with this? "They've gone after half the CEOs in this city for one reason or another." Others had faced far worse treatment from them. "They're just a bunch of tree-hugging hippies." A royal pain for certain. Occasionally, a PR nightmare, but nothing more.

Madeline shook her head. "They are violent domestic extremists whose beliefs lead them to commit crimes. Thus far they haven't sought to kill or injure anyone, but they're guilty of vandalism, cyberattacks, property damage and arson. We're trying to locate their leader, Samantha Dickson."

"She's a real piece of work." Unfortunately, he was well acquainted with her tactics. If he never set eyes on her again, it'd be too soon. "At every protest, she's rather vocal. Along with a young guy, Kane Tidwell. He was the one who threw acid on my car."

Madeline sent a text with the name. "Their pattern of aggression toward you makes the group a suspect, though we're focused on Dickson. What motivated them to target you in the first place?"

Jackson gritted his teeth, hesitant to get into the ugly details. "Andrew Phillips and the smear campaign he launched against me."

"This smear campaign, what was it about?"

"It started small and then snowballed. Andrew spread rumors amongst the employees that I was a coldhearted cutthroat who only cares about the company bottom line after I had some of our operations moved overseas and had all charitable donations stopped."

Madeline raised the expected eyebrow at his admission, but it sounded worse than it was in reality.

"Andrew also made sure I received a lot of bad press for it. Not that I can prove it, but I know it was him. Ever since, I've been on the radar of the Red Right Hand."

"Sounds like you gave a lot of people legitimate reasons to view you in a negative light. Is there more to this story in which painting you as the Grinch was unwarranted?"

He liked a woman who didn't hold her tongue and who cut to the point. "The company was on the brink of bankruptcy. Either we found a way to remain solvent or we were going to go under. Andrew was the first to propose having machines replace workers for some of our operations, quite ironically. Over time, five years to a decade, that would've saved us money. But we couldn't wait that long to stop hemorrhaging. I recommended halting our charitable donations, only temporarily, and sucking up the PR hit. Instead of machines, I suggested we move a limited number of operations overseas. The impact was bigger and faster. I also cut one of Andrew's departments. Video games."

Madeline tilted her head to the side. "Was the video games department his pet project? Something he was passionate about? A reason for him to blow up the Duwamish site?"

"I started that department. It meant more to me than it ever did to him. During a reorganization, he vied for it and won. He lorded it over me, rubbing my face in it every chance he got."

"Did you eventually cut the department to get back at him?"

Petty vengeance wasn't his style. "Of course not. I sold off the games to other companies for a quick, heavy injection of funds. Everyone in that department walked away with a very generous severance package. Half of them ended up making millions in the deal. I made sure to take care of them. It was a major win-win for everyone." Even provided the funds to expand ETC's reach in the industry.

"That doesn't change the fact you moved key operations overseas, which resulted in the loss of jobs. I'm guessing quite a few, and that earned you the moniker the Butcher of the American Dream."

The epithet still burned his gut. But that's what the Red

Right Hand did. They called you cruel names and protested. Though the acid splashed on his car had been disturbing, not to mention expensive, to fix.

"Also, you did stop the company from giving to charity."

"Everyone at ETC would've lost their jobs if not for those changes. I saved the company and hundreds more jobs. I'm no Grinch." Explaining to Emma why some people thought that he was hadn't been simple after those horrid posters depicting him as such had been put up around her school. For weeks, other kids had teased her. That had been worse than the acid. "After the most recent incident with the Red Right Hand ruining my car, I issued a press statement announcing that not only were we able to resume our charitable donations by Christmas, but that we'd double the amount from previous years. I thought that would pacify them, as well as doing something good."

"Dickson is one of our top suspects. Along with Charles Albrecht and Andrew Phillips. Are we missing anyone who might have a grudge against you? Are you sure there's no jilted girlfriend? Maybe think back further than six months."

Jackson snorted. "That's outside the realm of possibility. There hasn't been anyone since my wife, Francesca."

"No one, in four years?" she asked skeptically.

Hearing the status of his love life phrased that way even sounded sad to him. "No one."

"You must've loved Emma's mother very much."

Devotion to the memory of his deceased wife had kept him single? A lovely notion. Too bad the reality wasn't so picture-book. He'd never been honest with anyone about his marriage. Carried the truth for years like a dirty secret.

He was tired of pretending.

"I did care for her a great deal." Much more at the end when she had been sick and suffering than at the beginning. "She was a prima ballerina. We met at a fundraiser for membership donors such as me. It was only meant to be a fling for both of us. A fun distraction. She got pregnant. So we got married. Quickly, we realized we were polar opposites. Not even friends. She was miserable throughout the pregnancy once she had to stop dancing. Resented me because I didn't have to give up anything, even temporarily, to bring our daughter into the world. Then she got sick." And cancer redefined how he loved. "I took a six-month sabbatical to take care of her. She was gone so fast, Emma doesn't remember her." He wasn't sure why he'd told Madeline quite so much. He only knew that once the words had started, there was no holding them back.

Unburdening *was* good for the soul. Lightened the load he had been carrying.

"You sacrificed for Francesca at the end." There was unwavering sympathy in her eyes. "You've continued to sacrifice for your daughter."

He'd been single a long time. So long, he'd grown numb to the loneliness. Earlier this evening, when his house had been teeming with people, while Emma was missing, it was like a scab had been ripped off, leaving him raw. Forcing him to face the emptiness that had metastasized over the years. Sitting here with Madeline, talking, made him feel less alone.

Tonight, he needed that more than he had realized.

"I suppose I haven't been with anyone because I've been focused on Emma and work. Not much time for anything else." Dating required energy and effort he didn't have to give when Emma was a toddler. Once she started elementary school, he had no clue how to juggle everything. "I don't think there are many women who would accept that I already have two top priorities. Who would be willing to settle for third place?"

"Someone who has her own priorities wouldn't see it as settling, but as compromise. Give and take. But I get it." She nursed the brandy, indulging in another tiny sip. "There aren't many men who can handle my grueling schedule with odd hours and not sleeping at home when the job demands."

Only an idiot wouldn't understand. She was intelligent, full of drive, beautiful. The kind of beautiful that struck you at first sight but deepened the longer you looked at her. And she was out there in the thick of it saving lives. Literally.

"All you need is one," he said. "The right one."

Their thighs brushed. Their gazes connected in the firelight of the room.

Hyperawareness tingled through him, calling him to draw closer, like recognizing like.

Under different circumstances, when everything he cared about wasn't slipping through his fingers faster than grains of sand in the wind, he would've acted on it.

He got up and strode to the other side of the room near the window.

Leaning against the mantel, he drew comfort from the heat of the fire.

"At least we can rule out the possibility of a hostile ex," Madeline said, crossing her legs. "Tell me about your combative rivalry with Albrecht."

"Our relationship has always been contentious, but purely about business. We've gone in similar directions with the manufacture of products once or twice. Right now, he's vying for a military contract."

"The same as you. Could it also be for stealth technology?"

He shrugged. "I don't know, but if that is his latest breakthrough that would give him a reason to target the Duwamish site. Having me step down as CEO might just be for good measure, a smoke screen for going after a rival product that could win a government bid over his."

"That's what I was thinking. I wish there was a way to verify what he's working on. Confirmation of stealth technology would be enough for us to get a warrant to search every piece of property he owns and dig into his financials to see if he's made any large payments. Perhaps hired someone to kidnap Emma."

Thanks to Chuck's need to be in the limelight, there was a way. "He's having a black-tie cocktail party tomorrow at AlbrechTech to make a big announcement. The cocky bastard even had the gall to send me an invitation. He's the biggest narcissist."

"Literally? As in inflated sense of his own importance, a deep need for excessive attention and admiration, and a lack of empathy for others?"

"That about sums him up. His dad started AlbrechTech in his garage thirty years ago, building it into the *Fortune* 500 that it is today. Last quarter, Chuck talked the board into replacing his own father with himself. He's a cold-blooded snake."

Madeline frowned.

Whatever she was thinking, he wasn't going to like hearing it, but he had to know. "Please say it."

"People with narcissistic personality disorder are more likely to become child abductors. But that's usually in cases where the kidnapper is the parent. I'm sure whatever the announcement is will make the news the morning after the event. We'll have to wait and see."

To hell with that. This was a golden opportunity to get inside AlbrechTech, check things out and see firsthand for himself. "I'm not waiting. I can't." He raised a palm. "Please don't ask me to."

"You never hear the word *no*, do you?"

"It's been spoken in my vicinity on occasion, but somehow never directed toward me." He was persuasive and shrewd, had to be in his business, and he wasn't going to apologize for it.

Scooting to the edge of the sofa, she leaned forward. "We should expect the press to be there. The optics of you at a party wouldn't be good. You'd receive unwanted attention that could complicate matters for the case. For you personally."

"I wouldn't be there to have fun. Only to find out what Chuck is up to."

"They wouldn't know that. Freedom of the press could easily flip to freedom to be merciless. They'd have a field day telling the story of the father with a missing child who was kicking up his heels at a party. Misinformation, of course, but it'd sell a lot of newspapers."

He didn't care about getting roasted by the press, but assuming Chuck wasn't the kidnapper and pictures of him attending a party surfaced, then whoever had Emma might think he wasn't taking this seriously and seek to punish him further.

A hiccup he hadn't thought of, but for every problem there was a solution.

Madeline's gaze snapped up to something over his shoulder, her eyes widening as she jumped to her feet and rushed forward. "Oh, my God. What is that?"

Spinning a one-eighty, Jackson faced the window. He went slack-jawed at the sight in his yard.

Flaming lines that burned three feet long blazed on his front lawn.

In the darkness, four letters spelled out a single word in fire.

Chapter Seven

Madeline stood at Jackson's side and stared out the window. She opened her mouth to ask what the fiery word meant, but a flash of movement registered in the shadows off the left corner of the yard.

Someone dressed in all black, wearing a plain white mask with a hood pulled up over their head, turned and took off like a shot.

The unsub. It had to be.

Madeline withdrew her service weapon from the holster on her hip and bolted for the front door.

Heavy footfalls pounded after her.

She flipped a switch beside the door, bringing on the porch light, and had the chain off and was out the door before Jackson caught up.

With her Glock at the ready, Madeline charged down the wooden steps. She cleared the front yard, gun swinging in a careful arc as she made her way to the sidewalk.

She scanned the north side of the street. The left. No one was visible. No pedestrians out walking their dog. Nothing suspicious.

Jackson ran to her. A baseball bat was clenched in his hands. "Where did he go?"

His house was situated in the middle of a long lane. The

unsub wouldn't have had time to disappear around the corner on foot. Not even if they were an Olympic sprinter.

They were hiding. In a neighbor's yard. Or a car.

"Stay here," Madeline ordered Jackson.

She darted into the middle of the street illuminated by streetlamps and looked in both directions. She'd taken the time to scope out the block earlier. Knew which vehicles had been there.

Did anything stand out? Was something different?

There! A black van. Parked barely twenty yards away with the quiet engine running, headlights off.

She locked onto the white full-face mask behind the wheel. The unsub was watching.

The engine roared, tires squealing on the wet pavement, and the vehicle raced toward her.

Her arm moved on its own, raising the gun—pure instinct kicking in. She thumbed the safety off. Years of habit had her sighting down the barrel, her left hand coming over to steady the Glock in her palm, finger sliding inside the trigger guard as the car bore down.

Aim. Squeeze. You'll hit the bastard.

Emma. The thought of the child made her freeze. If she killed this person, the BAU team might never be able to find Emma.

Madeline shifted her aim away from the driver's head. She could wound the unsub and end this. She locked eyes with the person behind the wheel and squeezed the trigger.

Once. Twice. Three times. The darkness lit up with the flash of bullets. Holes blasted into the windshield.

The van swerved back and forth, still hurtling toward her.

Her breath shuddered in her chest, her pulse hammering in her ears. She braced for the inevitable pain if she missed one last time.

Steadying her aim, she squeezed the trigger.

But she was tackled from the side. Jackson had launched himself at her, hauling her out of the way.

A split second later, the van was breathing hot as it blew past.

The impact of Jackson's body knocked her off her feet. Tumbling with her, he held her tight to his chest. Momentum propelled them both down fast to the asphalt behind a parked sedan. He'd twisted, taking the brunt of the fall.

Madeline landed on top of him, the wind forced from her lungs. Her shoulder scraped against something hard. Jackson's head slammed on the concrete curb. A groan tore from his lips. He rolled again, deftly placing her beneath him as if to shield her.

His considerable weight pressed her to the cold, wet ground. Instinctively, she had clung to him with one hand as they were falling, but she had managed to hold on to the gun with the other.

Her fingers dug into chiseled muscle. Their legs tangled. His face lifted, putting his lips inches from hers, his breath fanning her cheek.

For a heartbeat, everything blended into one. Fear. Adrenaline. The feel of the damp pavement. The warmth of his searing heat. His strong arms wrapped around her. The scent of his aftershave and burning rubber.

She got her bearings. Regained her breath.

Brakes screeched. The transmission ground, making an ugly noise.

Madeline slid to the side, out from under Jackson, shoving herself upright to peer around the sedan's bumper. Her vision speckled and then cleared.

The driver threw the van in Reverse, gunning the engine, and headed back for them.

She squeezed one shot off, hitting the rear door.

The vehicle kept coming.

Jackson grabbed her by the elbow, yanking her to her feet. A wave of light-headedness swept through her.

They both stumbled up onto the sidewalk and back out of the way in the nick of time.

The van slammed alongside the sedan, metal scraping against metal, and then angled backward, mowing over the spot where they had just been.

She fired again. This time she aimed for the tires. Bullets pinged, striking steel.

The driver righted the car, threw it in Drive and punched the accelerator, burning rubber down the street. A hard left and the van careened around the corner out of sight.

Madeline's heart beat wildly in her throat. Relief coursed through her, but it was fleeting.

Emma's kidnapper had gotten away.

Madeline put her hand to Jackson's chest, thankful they hadn't been crushed by the van. "Are you okay?"

Tension rolled off him in waves. He inhaled, his muscular chest expanding beneath her palm. "Fine."

But he wasn't fine. Blood trickled down his temple from a cut over his brow.

"You okay?" he asked.

Her shoulder ached and the skin where she'd scraped it burned. "I'll live."

Lights started popping on in the windows of his neighbors. The cops would be there soon. Surely someone had called them by now.

They crossed the street, making their way back to the house. She moved stiffly at first. One pant leg was ripped and strands of her hair had slipped loose of her twist, falling around her face.

He picked up the baseball bat that he had dropped earlier, and she holstered her weapon.

In the yard, they walked up to the flames burning on his lawn. They drew close enough to feel the heat.

Sticks had been positioned to create four letters and then set on fire. "'Pony,'" she said, reading the flaming word. "What does it mean?"

"It's what Emma wished for on her last birthday. A pony. I got her horseback riding lessons instead. This is proof of life."

Madeline took out her phone. Thankfully, the screen hadn't been damaged when they hit the ground. She snapped several pictures of the letters before the fire died out and messaged the photos to the team along with a quick breakdown of what had happened.

"What about the video I asked for?" Jackson looked at her with haunted eyes. "Do you think he'll send it? Or is this it?" His gaze drifted back to the burning letters. "The only proof of life I'll get."

Honestly, she didn't know for certain. "Every action Emma's kidnapper has taken has been calculated and planned with one consistent goal. Hurting you. Torturing you. Manipulating you." First, Emma was taken right in front of him. That one act alone was enough to riddle any parent with overwhelming guilt. Then his pet project was destroyed. He was pressured to resign ahead of the deadline. Now this. A violation of his home, stripping him of any small peace of mind. All of it designed to mess with his head. "Not sending you a video would leave you to wonder. The imagination is powerful. Can conjure up all sorts of ugly possibilities. But you demanded to see Emma before your resignation is made official and you haven't. I think you'll be made to wait a little while longer. Then the kidnapper will make contact again."

Whoever it was wanted to stretch this out, make Jackson suffer, and Madeline feared they weren't finished with him. Not by a mile.

"But he just tried to kill me," Jackson said.

"Actually, the van was coming for me and you merely got in the way." The kidnapper had taken things to the next level. Attempted murder. Apparently, they were willing to kill under the right circumstances. That made them far more dangerous. "For the record, don't ever do that again."

"What? Save your life?" The hint of a smile tugged at the edges of his mouth.

"Put yourself in harm's way. Not for me." Part of her job was to keep him safe. Even protect him from himself if necessary.

Jackson closed the gap between them, stepping so close she had to tilt her head back to maintain eye contact. His wide shoulders and broad chest were like a wall in front of her. The rich scent of his aftershave, cedar and musk, had her softening again.

"In case you haven't figured it out yet," he said with the gleam of challenge in his eyes, "I'm not good at following orders."

"Oh, I've noticed."

"By the way, you're welcome."

The phone in her hand vibrated. A call from Miguel. Stepping away from Jackson and that scent which teased her senseless, she answered. "Hope I didn't wake you with the update." Doubtful since it was only eleven. The BAU team was accustomed to operating on little sleep.

"Are you and Jackson all right?" Concern flooded Miguel's voice.

She'd forgotten to highlight that they were okay in the message. "Yeah. We both are." Thanks to Jackson getting her out of the way of the van. She did indeed owe him her life. "Only some scratches."

"I'm going to have Dash check traffic camera footage and try to locate the van." A hotshot hacker, if anyone could cut through the red tape, or circumvent it to find an answer fast, it was Dash. "Did you catch a license plate number?"

"No. Everything happened too fast. But it wasn't a passenger van. It was one of those smaller service vans." She closed her eyes, tried to recall additional details. "A Ford Transit, I think."

"Okay. That'll give him more to go on."

"What about a description of the perp?"

"I couldn't make out much. The person was standing far away in the shadows. The white mask is what caught my eye. I only saw them for a second. Average height. Medium build. Nothing distinctive. Sorry."

"We'll track the van. Put out an APB." The all-points bulletin would have local law enforcement on the lookout for the vehicle.

As soon as two squad cars with flashing lights pulled up, an elderly neighbor across the street, whose sedan had been damaged, came outside.

This was going to be fun. "I've got to go," she said, wishing Caitlyn were there to handle this. "The police are here." She turned, glancing at the fire again.

"Go. We'll let you know if we find anything."

No news would mean bad news. A dead end.

Another thought occurred to her. "Hang on. One more thing. The burning letters. There's something odd about the fire. It still hasn't gone out. The branches are lying on top of wet grass. Never should have lit to begin with."

"I'll have Forensics come out ASAP and take a look."

"I'm happy to pay for the damages to your sister's car," Jackson said to his neighbor, Lawrence Travers.

Owner of the Wilderness Emporium chain stores, Larry

was a laid-back fellow in his prime at just under sixty who loved hunting, golf and his wife, not necessarily in that order.

Larry waved his hand, dismissing the suggestion. "Don't trouble yourself. Sounds like you have an unenviable amount on your plate already. Looks it too from the gash on your head." He tightened the belt of his robe covering his pajamas. "Insurance will take care of the car."

Once Madeline had explained the circumstances, Larry had graciously agreed that they could work out the specifics regarding the damage themselves. The police had made a report and left.

Standing on the sidewalk in front of Jackson's house, Larry shoved his hands in the pockets of his robe. "Is there anything I can do to help you out with this nasty business?" He nodded at Jackson's lawn.

The burning letters taunted Jackson. Made the hair on the back of his neck stand on end.

"Do you have a firearm in the house?" Larry asked. "I can outfit you with a piece perfect for home defense if you don't."

"A generous offer, but the idea of having a gun in the same house as Emma without a safe to store it properly doesn't sit well with me. Besides, Special Agent Striker has all the firepower I need." Jackson glanced at Madeline, and she gave him a supportive smile.

"That's the spirit," Larry said. "Emma's going to be back home before you know it. Although in the future, you never know when you might need a gun. I'll have a Rapid safe sent over along with a 9 mm and ammo. The safe uses Radio Frequency Identification for quick access. You'll get a RFID key. Best level of child-resistant security. Do you know how to shoot, or do I need to set you up with lessons at the Emporium's range?"

"I don't need lessons." A marine veteran, his father had made it a point to teach Jackson three things at an early age: how to shoot, fight, turn every obstacle into an opportunity to chart his own path. While his mother had taught him to play the piano, giving him balance he'd never taken for granted.

A silver sedan rolled down the street and parked in front of the house.

"That must be someone from Forensics," Madeline said. "They should be able to tell us how the perp got the fire started on wet grass and why it hasn't burned out yet."

"You don't need Forensics. I can tell you that." Larry rocked back on his slipper-covered heels and puffed out his chest. "Smelled it from across the street."

"Smelled what?" Madeline asked.

"Tree resin," Larry said as if the answer was obvious. "Pine, spruce or cedar would be my guess. Fire equals life in a wilderness survival scenario. Resin is your secret weapon to starting and keeping a fire going in wet conditions. Highly flammable stuff. One of the best natural accelerants since it contains volatile oils. Easy to get and use. Great for all sorts of things and it's a renewable source. Melt the resin, soak some rags or strips of bandanna, wrap it around thick branches and it'll extend the burn time for a while."

Thirty minutes later, Forensics had confirmed Larry's assessment.

The fire died out and the man from Forensics collected the remnants to compare with the accelerant used in the bomb at the Duwamish facility.

After Jackson and Madeline trudged inside, he locked up behind them.

He stared at the nine panes of glass in the upper half of his front door. A damn window.

It was so easy to break in through a window in the door. Not that it hadn't occurred to him when he had purchased the house seven years ago. At the time as a new resident of picturesque Madison Park, he had thought the glass-paned door was quaint. A reflection of the carefree, safe neighborhood. Like the large bay windows in the family room that had never been adorned with curtains.

There was no telling how long the kidnapper had been spying on him before lighting the fire.

The vulnerability of every aspect of his life now stood out with stark lucidity.

He stowed the solid-wood Louisville Slugger back in the hall closet, where he kept it for emergencies. Though this had been the first time he had ever been inclined to use it.

In the family room, Madeline shrugged off her jacket with a groan.

"Are you hurt?" He wasn't sure if the sound had been caused by pain or fatigue.

"I banged up my shoulder. Nothing serious." She brushed long strands of hair from her face and turned away from him, draping her jacket across a chair.

Blood stained the back of her white silk blouse. "You're bleeding."

She twisted her chin over her shoulder, trying to inspect the injury, but she'd need a mirror to see it. Her gaze flickered up, meeting his, then higher to his head. "So are you. Aren't we a pair?" Madeline smiled weakly, a brief upturning of her mouth, her posture relaxing, her face open.

The sight of her like this warmed him, banishing the heart-stopping image of that van hurtling toward her.

Not for a single second had she shown a hint of fear.

Right now, she still looked tough as iron, but also shockingly vulnerable. An appealing contradiction.

For all her beauty, brains, nerves of steel, not to mention her incredible magnetism, it was astonishing to think she didn't have someone special in her life.

Such a pity.

Madeline cleared her throat and looked away. "It's late. I'm going to get cleaned up." She grabbed her jacket and headed down the hall to the bathroom.

There were plenty of fresh towels in the washroom since it was the one Emma used, but no medical supplies. He went to the kitchen and retrieved the deluxe family first aid kit. Then he made an ice pack and took it to the hall bathroom.

Jackson knocked.

Madeline eased the door open. She had removed her silk blouse and was standing in slacks and a black sports bra—the kind that didn't look like underwear or flaunt a ridiculous amount of cleavage. The women at his gym paraded around in far less.

"Thought you could use some Neosporin and a bandage," he said.

"You have blood dripping down your face, and you're worried about me?" She opened the door wide. "Get in here and sit down."

Jackson stepped inside, passing behind her to the other side of the sink. With the two of them inside, the bathroom seemed to have gotten smaller, growing far too cramped. He cast a glance at the black semiautomatic in the holster on the vanity. It looked out of place beside Emma's Disney-themed toothbrush and her hand towel with a picture of a unicorn.

Madeline bent over, lifting the cuff of her torn pant leg. He shouldn't have been surprised at the sight of a second weapon strapped to her ankle. The special agent came across as a woman who was always prepared. She tugged at the Velcro fasteners. The gun was more compact than her Glock. The polished nickel gleamed when she set it on the counter.

He closed the lid to the toilet and sat. Holding the medical supplies, he was now eye level with her chest. His gaze slid over the swell of her breasts, her sculpted arms, taut abs and wicked curves that showed the discipline of someone who rarely missed a workout.

Clenching his hands, he curbed the urge to touch her, but he was so physically aware of her that it was like walking barefoot in the grass under a power line that sent a tingling rush under your skin.

He didn't mean to let his mind go there, but there wasn't a damn thing he could do to stop it.

"A good host takes care of his guest first," he said, breaking the silence and meeting her gaze.

Her eyes softened, and something sparked between them. Something warm. Something deep. Something strong.

"I'm not a guest." She sorted through the bag, taking the antiseptic and gauze. "I'm working."

Jackson fought for air as she stepped closer, leaning in until her breath brushed his face. He studied her features, trying to figure out what about them he found so captivating. Was it her high cheekbones, the flawless golden brown complexion, her well-defined lips or those riveting eyes, which seemed to see straight into his soul? Maybe everything—the whole was definitely greater than the sum of its parts.

He had never been attracted to weak women, no matter how pretty or charming.

There was nothing weak about Madeline. She was a force to be reckoned with.

She dabbed at the bloody gash on his forehead with a cotton swab, patting the skin gently. The tantalizing fragrance of her, vanilla and roses, stole into his lungs with each breath. He always loved the way women smelled, but her scent was so enticing that every muscle in his body tightened.

He closed his eyes, trying to shut out the sensations he knew he shouldn't have, but the absence of sight made it more difficult for him to think of anything else.

"You won't need stitches," she said, and he opened his eyes. She tore into a packet of butterfly bandages, closed the cut by holding its edges together and applied them. "You should put ice on it. Keep the swelling down." Turning, she chucked the gauze away in the trash.

The abrasion on her back was red and raw. Road rash from the pavement.

"Let me clean the scratch on your shoulder for you. It looks pretty bad."

"I can handle it."

Sure, if she was a contortionist.

"You're not used to accepting help from others, are you?" he asked. When she didn't respond, he said, "Quid pro quo. Only fair."

She studied him, her face a blank mask. Tension stretched between them, making the space in the bathroom feel even tighter before she nodded and faced the sink. "All right."

As he wiped at the blood, working toward the abrasion, she watched him in the mirror.

The second he touched the cotton swab to the ragged flesh, her spine stiffened, and she sucked in a sharp breath.

"Sorry."

She grabbed onto the counter. "Don't worry about it," she whispered.

Brushing the antiseptic over the scraped area, he worked

quickly. Her shoulders remained tense and a muscle flexed along her jaw.

He added a dab of Neosporin to the tender scrape, grabbed a piece of gauze and ripped off several sections of medical tape.

"Almost done." Taping the gauze over the injury, his fingers grazed her warm skin. Silky soft.

In the mirror, her mesmerizing gaze found his and didn't waver. Electric awareness shot down his spine, lighting up nerve endings along the way. Time suspended, and the primal attraction between them was undeniable.

He let his fingers stretch until his palms glided over her skin above the shoulder blades. Her muscles relaxed, her body softening, leaning into him. Something he didn't want to acknowledge and was helpless to suppress coiled through him. A dangerous combination of darkness and desire.

"Jack—"

His phone chimed, and the sound had them jerking apart. *A new message!*

He snatched the phone from his pocket, his pulse in overdrive.

Madeline spun around and looked at the screen alongside him.

No video. I'm in charge. Not you. Not the FBI. This is all you get. Make your resignation official.

With another chime came a grainy picture of Emma. She was in a room, sitting on a bed with a gray wool blanket. Newspaper covered the wall behind her. Emma's brown eyes were wide with fear. Tears stained her cheeks.

"She's alive," he muttered. *Thank God.* Then a horrible thought struck him like a bolt of lightning through his chest. "Do you think he hurt her? She's been crying."

"Tears are natural. She misses you, home, everything familiar." Madeline put a hand on his forearm, and the sudden tightness in his chest eased. "She's scared, not hurt."

He wanted to believe that. Needed to. "Are you sure?"

"Yes."

He needed to contact the ETC PR team and have them draft a statement. "Once I make my resignation official, you don't think he would…" The words stuck in his throat. He couldn't bring himself to say the worst thing imaginable.

"Emma's going to be okay. Look on the floor. There's a Happy Meal container. On the bed—a doll, coloring book, crayons. She's in fresh clothes."

A pink sweat suit.

Why hadn't he noticed any of those things until Madeline had pointed them out?

"If her kidnapper wanted to hurt her, they wouldn't go to the trouble of feeding her, giving her things to play with. Changing her clothes." She tightened her fingers on his arm and squeezed a little. "Emma's going to be okay," she said again, as if the statement needed reinforcing, and perhaps it did.

Madeline took out her phone, made a call and put it on speaker.

The phone rang twice. "What's happened?" Miguel said.

Madeline relayed the message and details about the picture.

"We'll have a copy of everything at the office from the tap," Miguel said. "I can get Liam on it. Just to let you know, Dash hacked into the CCTV. There are no traffic cameras in Madison Park or the surrounding area, but the police found the van abandoned under an overpass near I-5. It had been torched."

Would they be able to lift fingerprints off a burnt vehicle?

"Damn it. Another dead end." She pressed a palm to

her forehead. "The picture needs to be analyzed. I want to know everything. Which newspaper is on the walls, clothing brand, any shadows, reflections, absolutely everything," she said with a desperation that echoed Jackson's own.

"You're not saying anything that I don't already know," Miguel said. "We'll analyze every single inch of it. No stone left unturned."

Madeline nodded. "We have to find a solid lead. And soon."

Chapter Eight

The elevator doors whispered open on the top floor of ETC headquarters. The hallway was carpeted in pale beige. The walls were light green. Miguel Peters stepped off promptly at nine and proceeded to the vice president's office. The outer wall and its door were glass.

Natascha Campbell rose before he'd gotten through the door.

The rest of the room was paneled in wood. The door to Phillips's office was wooden, blocking the interior from sight. As though ugly secrets were hidden inside.

"Good morning." Natascha walked out from behind her desk with a smug smile.

Miguel took in the young woman. Once again, she wore a gray suit: the jacket and pencil skirt fit snug across her slender figure. But this time, her auburn hair was pulled back into a sleek ponytail that sharpened her features, making her look even younger today. Perhaps twenty-six. She was centerfold pretty, something he hadn't noticed in the previous day's chaos.

Natascha picked up the phone and pressed a button. "Agent Peters is here."

Miguel strained to hear the response but couldn't pick up so much as a murmur. The office door and walls were thick.

Interesting.

On the center of her desk was a copy of the press release ETC had issued earlier, regarding Jackson's resignation.

Natascha hung up the phone. "He's ready for you." Smile widening, she led him across the room and opened the door.

Miguel stepped into an enormous room that was lavishly equipped with furniture. His gaze swept across the table near the window, potted plants, a sofa, Andrew Phillips and his lawyers.

Plural.

¡Mierda!

One lawyer would be a pain. A team of lawyers would be a problem.

"Can I get you a coffee, Agent Peters?" Natascha asked.

Before Miguel could open his mouth to respond, Phillips said, "He won't be staying long enough for coffee."

We'll see about that.

Natascha left, shutting the door behind her.

Miguel sat in the chair facing the desk, beside a gentleman in an expensive suit. The man was gray haired and thin and colorless as though the years had leached the life from him.

"George Grohs." The older man extended his hand but not to shake. A business card was proffered in between his fingers. "Mr. Phillips's attorney."

Miguel took the card. Across the middle The Grohs Law Group was printed. "You're not ETC corporate counsel?"

"No, we're Mr. Phillips's personal attorneys."

Big companies such as ETC often had a legal team deeply involved in various aspects of operations from exploring groundbreaking new products, supporting growth, to managing legal risks. Providing counsel for a vice president wasn't unusual.

But Phillips's going outside company channels to bring in his own team was highly suspect.

The other two, a man in a navy suit and a woman in red, who Grohs neglected to introduce, stood flanking Phillips on either side of him behind the desk.

This was more than a precautionary measure. Phillips was scared for some reason. Enough to hire outside representation that had cost him a pretty penny.

Dressed in a pin-striped tailored suit, tanned to an unhealthy degree, dark hair slicked back with too much mousse, Andrew Phillips shifted in his seat, not appearing nearly as confident as his assistant. A green smoothie in a clear plastic container sat untouched on his desk. The top half of the paper wrapper still covered the straw. "Agent Peters. None of us at ETC know what to think, what to say. We're all still reeling from what's happened."

Funny. He didn't appear distraught in the least.

"Mr. Phillips," Miguel said, sliding the business card into his pocket, "I'm going to record this interview and give you your rights."

The VP squirmed in his chair, smoothing a hand back over his hair.

Miguel set a recorder in plain view on the desk and recited the Miranda rights. Then he asked, "Where were you yesterday afternoon when Emma Rhodes went missing?"

The woman tapped Phillips's shoulder, a light press of her hand.

"I can't say exactly." Phillips looked down and away. "Because I don't know when she was taken."

"Let me clarify. Where were you between twelve thirty and one thirty yesterday afternoon?" Miguel asked.

Phillips shrugged. "Working. Somewhere in the building."

"Somewhere?" Miguel repeated. "You don't know where you were?"

"I'm a busy man. There was a lot going on yesterday. So many moving pieces."

Miguel took brief notes on his phone as well in case he needed to follow up on anything during the interview. "What were you working on?"

Another whisper in the VP's ear, this time from the blue suit.

"I was preparing for my trip to Spokane," Phillips said.

Taking a deep breath, Miguel tried to tamp down his growing frustration at Phillips getting coached by lawyers. What was he hiding? "Why weren't you downstairs at the Family Day event?"

"I was for several hours at the beginning, but I'm single and not all of us had the luxury of taking the entire day off."

"Many employees have characterized your relationship with Jackson Rhodes as contentious." Miguel studied him. "Would you say that's accurate?"

The prune-faced attorney sitting in the chair crossed his legs. "My client can't speak to the opinion of others. Move on."

Miguel cut his eyes from the shark of a lawyer back to the executive. "Do you like Jackson?"

"We're not friends, if that's what you mean," Phillips said.

"Are you enemies?"

The woman in red leaned in and spoke low in the VP's ear.

"We're on the same team with a common goal." Phillips flashed a shaky grin, his beady eyes gleaming. "The success of ETC."

"Did it make you angry to see someone fifteen years your junior promoted over you?"

Phillips made a small sound, a little breath of distress. "It didn't put a smile on my face."

"You're the only person with something to gain by Jackson resigning," Miguel said with straining patience.

"I didn't hear a question for my client," Grohs said.

Miguel gritted his teeth. "Do you find it suspicious that the kidnapper's one demand was for Jackson to step aside, effectively giving you the promotion you were passed over for?"

Both attorneys flanking Phillips leaned in at the same time, but he raised a palm silencing them. "I'm suspicious of lots of things. All-you-can-eat buffets, hotels with low ratings, that some prizefights are fixed. I can go on endlessly about my suspicions."

Irritation snapped through Miguel, but he didn't let it show on his face or in his voice. "Do you find it suspicious that you're the only one to benefit?" he asked again.

"Have the FBI considered that maybe the kidnapper's ulterior motive is to make my client look bad?" Grohs asked.

"No," Miguel said, deadpan, keeping the intensity of his focus lasered on Phillips. "We have not." With the lawyers buffering every response, this was futile. Miguel began to consider a different approach, a change in tactics. "Andrew, have you considered there's a six-year-old child missing? She's alone and scared and wants to go home."

The vice president's chair creaked under his weight as he shifted back. "Look, I feel bad for Jackson—honestly I do. I wouldn't wish what he's going through on my worst enemy. I assure you I had nothing to do with the disappearance of his daughter."

"That's enough," Grohs said. "My client has shown considerable courtesy in giving you this much of his time. I think this interview is over."

If this was courtesy, Miguel hated to see contempt.

Relief poured over Phillips's face, and he picked up his smoothie for the first time, removing the wrapper from the straw and taking a sip.

The more Miguel thought about it the less likely it

seemed that Andrew Phillips cast the spotlight of suspicion on himself by kidnapping the kid and then taking Jackson's job.

But an irrefutable fact remained. Phillips was hiding something that required legal representation, and Miguel wanted to know what it was. "Actually, we're just getting started. And since I've been so courteous as to come to Mr. Phillips's office rather than giving him no choice but to answer questions in mine, I'll have that coffee now."

NICK JAMES ENTERED the observation room adjacent to the interview room and handed Jackson a steaming hot cup of coffee. The poor guy accepted it with a weary nod of thanks.

Jackson looked to be holding up well considering the holy hell he had been through over the past twenty-four hours. Though bags under his eyes, the five-o'clock shadow before noon on his jaw and the cut on his head showed the heavy strain he was under.

The press release from ETC announcing Jackson's official and permanent resignation had been released two hours earlier. But there had been silence from the kidnapper. Examination of the torched van had produced zero prints, and the culprit had been smart enough to remove the VIN number.

Nick stopped beside him and stared through the two-way viewing glass partition into the interview room.

"How long have you worked for Jackson?" Madeline asked the nanny.

Liane Strothe, a blond, curly-haired twentysomething, sat across the table with her hands folded in her lap. She wore funky catlike glasses and a long, flowered dress with Converse sneakers. "Almost two years."

"I spoke to the agency that placed you and they said you have excellent references."

Giving a shy smile, Liane pushed her glasses up her nose. "That's good."

"Have you been happy working for Jackson?"

"Oh, yeah. No complaints. The pay is great, the work is steady. It's so much better working for a family than at preschool. And I love Emma." Her eyes brightened as she perked up in her seat. The affection was genuine. "She's sweet and funny. Really smart for her age. Is she going to be okay? How is Jackson? I wanted to call him, but I also didn't want to intrude."

"Do you know of any reason why someone would take Emma to hurt Jackson?"

Liane's gaze roamed as she thought a moment. "No. I can't think of anything."

"How would you describe Jackson?"

The young woman's brows drew together. "I don't understand."

"Pretend I'm a girlfriend and you're describing your boss. Would you say he's hot?"

Jackson flinched as though the question had made him uncomfortable.

Liane gave a one-shouldered shrug. "I guess, if you're into that Norse-god kind of look. Thor isn't my type. I'm more of a Spider-Man gal."

Madeline had taken a shot in the dark and hadn't hit a target. Nick drew in a deep breath. "No issue of an unrequited crush with your nanny."

"Thank goodness for that," Jackson said, sounding relieved.

A lot of guys might enjoy it if their young, attractive nanny had stars in her eyes for them, but he clearly wasn't one of them.

"Where were you yesterday afternoon between twelve thirty and one thirty?" Madeline asked.

"At the movies. I went to see the new Marvel film at the Pacific Cinema since Jackson gave me the day off."

"Was there anyone with you who can confirm your whereabouts?"

Liane shook her head. "I was alone." She picked up her slim backpack that doubled as a purse, opened it and fished around inside for something. After a long sigh, she said, "I thought I still had my ticket stub, but I can't find it."

"When did you arrive at the theater and what time did the movie let out?"

Her mouth twitched. "I got there early. Maybe noon. I hate to miss the previews. It was done around three thirty, I think."

"That's a long time." Madeline's gaze slid over the woman, doubtful.

It sounded about right to Nick. The film Liane was talking about had a running time of 180 minutes. Three hours. Throw in previews and it added up. Still, it was easy enough to verify whether or not she had been there. "I'll be back in a minute."

Jackson nodded and sipped his coffee.

Nick left the observation room and headed down the hall. He rapped on the open door with a knuckle.

"Yep," Dash said, eyeing his state-of-the-art monitors with a frown.

"Hey, how long will it take you to hack into the Pacific Cinema and pull up security footage from yesterday?"

Dash's fingers flew over the keyboard. "Five minutes."

"I'm timing you." Nick waltzed in and strolled around behind Dash's chair to watch.

On one monitor the cybercrimes specialist brought up a black screen. Lines of code zipped across.

Between their tech guru, Liam, and Dash's stunning ability to crack computer systems and write code, the BAU almost always found what they needed if it was in the digital ether. Provided there was something to find.

"Was the new number that texted Jackson last night untraceable again?" Nick wondered as he watched his colleague work.

Dash blew out a heavy breath. "It was, unfortunately, but before you came in, I was doing a deep dive of the metadata to see if there was anything the kidnapper might have left behind." The camera feeds of the Pacific Cinema popped up, showing the ticket counter, concession stand and outside each numbered theater. "Child's play."

Impressive. "Less than three minutes."

"What are we looking for?"

"Not what, who. Liane Strothe. She claims she was there between noon and three thirty."

"Marvel movie?" Dash asked.

Nick nodded.

"Yeah, that's a long one."

"But a great one." Nick hunched over, getting a better look when time-stamped footage from yesterday appeared.

"You'll get no argument from me."

Nick zeroed in on the ticket counter. Liane Strothe sauntered into the lobby, wearing a purple long-sleeved top, jeans, Converse sneakers and had a backpack slung over her shoulder.

Dash typed something into the keyboard, and the screen shifted from the lobby to the concession stand, where she waited in line and bought a small popcorn and drink. Then they watched her enter theater number four. A few clicks on the keyboard, and Dash fast-forwarded. At three thirty, Liane left the theater, throwing her empty popcorn container and drink in the trash bin. "Her story checks out."

Nick thumbed a quick message to Madeline on his phone to let her know. "Thanks."

"No problem." Dash went back to plugging away.

Leaving the office, Nick stepped into the hall and bumped into Liam.

"Excuse me," Liam said with a grimace. Weariness added an edge to his expression and voice.

"Hey, there. You okay?"

"Yeah." Liam's frown deepened. "No. The wedding's off. I should feel relieved, thought I would, but I don't. This whole thing with Lorelai is messing with my head."

Oh, boy. "I'm sorry to hear that," Nick said sincerely. Before the engagement—correction—before the wedding planning, those two were so happy together. "Is this because of the fight you had in the hall yesterday?"

His cheeks reddened. "You all heard that?"

Reluctantly, Nick admitted, "We did."

Liam groaned. His mortification was obvious.

"Listen, we all understand couples go through stuff," Nick said. "I'm sure you and Lorelai will work things out."

"I don't know. I can't really think about that right now. I need to get back to analyzing the photo the kidnapper sent. I'm almost ready to give an update."

Nick patted Liam on the back, and they headed in separate directions.

At the observation room, Nick opened the door and slipped inside.

"Madeline is wrapping up with Liane." Jackson sipped his coffee.

Both women stood. Madeline was giving her the regular spiel about not leaving town in case they had more questions.

"We verified Liane's story," Nick said, closing the door. "She was at the movies."

Jackson's phone buzzed. Looking down at his pocket, he pulled it out and swiped the screen. Blood drained from his face and he swayed as though the world fell out from under him. "Oh, God. No." The paper cup dropped from his hand, splattering coffee on the floor.

Dread tightened in Nick's stomach. "What is it?"

"The kidnapper..." Jackson stared at his phone in horror, shaking his head. "He's not giving Emma back."

Nick took the phone from him and read the message.

You haven't paid nearly enough. I think I'll keep your daughter a little longer.

What the hell?

"I did what he wanted," Jackson said, tension and panic sharpening his words. "Why? Why is he messing with me like this?"

Madeline and Liane moved into the hall.

A second later, Madeline came into the observation room. Her expression fell as her gaze traveled between them. "What happened?"

Nick handed her the phone.

She read the message, her eyes widening, her lips tightening to a grim line.

The unsub was determined to make Jackson suffer as payment for something he'd done wrong. But what?

Madeline clutched Jackson's shoulder. "This isn't unusual. The kidnapper has already demonstrated that they like to change the rules as they see fit. I should've expected this. Don't worry. This is a setback, nothing more."

The door flew open. Dash hurried inside. "I found something."

"What is it?" Madeline asked.

"A match on the cell phone that sent the picture last

night. I couldn't trace the location, but I dug deep into the metadata. The same as I've done before. But this time the kidnapper got sloppy. I found a name. Natascha Campbell."

Jackson's face twisted in fury. "Andrew's assistant?"

"Miguel is at ETC now." Nick took out his phone. "He'll bring her in."

Chapter Nine

Madeline stood in the observation room next to Jackson. Behind them were Nick, Dash and David. From the updates rolling in, Liam was hard at work analyzing the photo. Madeline wanted him to stay on task until they either had a confession or Emma.

Miguel ushered Natascha Campbell into the interview room and sat her down in a chair.

It had taken less than twenty minutes for Miguel to read Natascha her Miranda rights and haul her in, but things felt a little off to Madeline. She preferred to watch this interrogation rather than conduct it. Sometimes distance provided clarity.

"I can't believe Natascha is behind this," Jackson said, shaking his head in shock.

Maybe she wasn't. She did fit the profile. Her boss had everything to gain. A promotion for him meant a promotion for her. Still, Madeline couldn't put her finger on what was throwing her.

"Am I under arrest?" Natascha asked. "Am I being charged with a crime?"

"Not at the moment. This is standard procedure. I need to ask you some questions about the kidnapping of Emma Rhodes and how you're connected."

"Connected?" Natascha reeled back in the chair. "I didn't kidnap Emma. Why would I take Jackson's daughter?"

"That's what we're going to find out," Miguel said.

"What makes you think that I'm connected?" Natascha demanded.

"You disappeared from the Family Day event yesterday around the same time Emma was taken. No one saw you for at least two hours. Where were you?"

"Working." She lowered her head and wrung her hands. "With Andrew."

"The two of you are hiding something. If you didn't help him take Emma, maybe kidnap her for him," Miguel said, and Natascha's jaw unhinged, "then what aren't you telling me?"

"Andrew said he'd send a lawyer. Maybe I should wait."

The lawyer had already arrived at the FBI office as representation for Natascha. A woman in a killer red suit. Caitlyn and Lorelai were running interference. Stalling. Miguel didn't need long. Maybe ten minutes to get to the truth.

"If you're innocent, you have no reason not to cooperate and answer a few simple questions. A little girl's life is on the line. Time is of the essence. I would think you'd want to help unless you're responsible somehow."

A classic technique. Most people who have nothing to hide felt compelled to talk. That it was their civic duty. All Miguel had to do was play on the emotion, apply pressure.

"I didn't do anything," Natascha said. "I swear."

Miguel nodded. "Then you need to explain something to me." He kept his eyes level, his tone cool. "Your name was found in the metadata of a text that was sent by the kidnapper. How is that possible if you didn't send the message?"

The metadata, the kidnapper making the convenient mistake of leaving it behind—that was what bothered Madeline about this whole thing.

"What?" Natascha's eyes grew so wide they looked as if they might bulge out of her head. "That's not possible."

"It is, if you were the one who kidnapped Emma and sent Jackson that text," Miguel said, pushing.

"No, no, no. I don't understand." Natascha's glassy eyes filled with tears. "Wait." Her brows drew together and her gaze roamed as if she had remembered something. "I lost my phone."

"Lost it?"

"Yes. But that was like two months ago."

A chill ran down Madeline's spine. If Natascha had lost the phone used by the kidnapper, two months was a long time for someone to plan.

"Where did you lose your phone?" Miguel asked.

"At the athletic club. Northgate."

"How can you be sure you lost it there?"

"I swim there three times a week. As soon as I got back into my car, I realized it was gone because I went to check my messages and couldn't find it. I reported it to the front desk, hoping someone might return it, but no one ever found my phone."

Miguel looked at the one-way mirror. "Get me verification."

"On it." David hustled out of the room.

"Why did Andrew have three lawyers during his interview?" Miguel asked.

Tears spilled from Natascha's eyes and rolled down her cheeks.

"He was afraid of saying the wrong thing," Miguel said. "Of incriminating himself. I bet you know of what."

"Please." Natascha lowered her head and wept. "It has nothing to do with Emma."

"Then you have nothing to worry about."

"Landing the position as CEO means so much to him. He doesn't want to risk losing it."

"What are the two of you hiding?" Miguel asked.

"Andrew and I snuck out of the Family Day event be-cause…because we went back up to his office…to have sex." Her gaze slid up at Miguel. "You can't tell anyone at ETC. They have a very strict policy about fraternization. Especially between a supervisor and subordinate. If it's not reported to HR, it's a fireable offense. And the fact that we had sex in the office is considered gross misconduct."

"It's true," Jackson said.

"Sounds like grounds to have him booted from the po-sition," Nick said.

Jackson rubbed the back of his neck. "I don't care who has the job. I just want my daughter back unharmed."

Natascha sniffled. "Andrew didn't want to go public with our relationship. So no one could know. He was wor-ried that you'd find out during the interview and that he'd lose his chance to finally be CEO. It's all he's wanted since he started at ETC."

"A chance that he only got because someone kidnapped Jackson's daughter," Miguel said.

Natascha shook her head. "Andrew would never do that. I would never. I swear, we went back upstairs."

Dash moved to the door, stopping with his hand on the knob. "There are cameras in the elevators and halls. Only those on the first floor were on a loop. I have a copy of the security footage for the whole building from Rivka Mol-nar. I'll check it."

Madeline nodded.

As Dash hurried out of the room, Miguel continued to hammer away at Natascha.

"She's telling the truth," Madeline said low.

"If she's putting on an act, she deserves to win an Oscar," Nick agreed.

Madeline fought the urge to drum her fingers as her thoughts churned. "There's no way an unsub who's been so clever suddenly gets careless on this one thing."

"What are you saying?" Jackson looked at her. "Don't criminals make mistakes?"

"Sure, but this kidnapper has been meticulous." Flawless, thus far. "They wouldn't get this sloppy, leaving the metadata behind."

"The perp wanted us to find it," Nick said.

"But why?" Jackson asked.

More dots connected in her head. "Misdirection. They want us spinning our wheels and running in circles. If we're chasing after the wrong leads, then we're not chasing after them."

David and Dash returned at the same time, one following the other through the door.

"The athletic club has a record of Natascha reporting her cell phone missing," David said.

"What about the club's security footage?" Nick asked.

David shook his head. "Their security system only keeps the footage for thirty days and then it's automatically deleted."

Damn it. "What about the footage at ETC?" Madeline asked Dash.

"At noon, Andrew and Natascha got on the elevator, alone. He snuck a few squeezes of her bottom on the ride up to the top floor. The camera in the hall shows her kissing him, removing his tie, stroking his groin before they disappeared inside his office, where they stayed for a little over an hour."

Madeline bit the inside of her lip and turned toward the

glass partition. They were right back where they started. Not a single step closer to finding Emma.

Her cell pinged along with most of the others. She glanced at her phone. Liam was ready to give an update.

She sent a message updating Miguel that they had verified Natascha's story and the young woman could be released.

The team and Jackson made their way down to the boardroom and took seats, but they waited on Miguel.

Liam looked awful. Hair disheveled. Unshaven. He paced back and forth as though he'd had too much coffee.

Madeline turned to Nick, who was sitting on her left. "Did Liam pull an all-nighter?"

"The wedding is off as of right now," he whispered. "I don't have details about the straw that broke the camel's proverbial back, but he's torn up over it."

Poor Lorelai and Liam. In spite of Madeline's reservations about relationships, she hoped those two would get their act together.

"Madeline," David said, "I don't know if you had a chance to see the update I submitted earlier since it's been such a hectic morning."

"No, I haven't seen it yet." All alerts she prioritized. The rest she would read as soon as she had a chance.

"I was going over the rest of the interviews, trying to find any discrepancies, and found one thing. Ten employees mentioned seeing four people as part of the catering staff."

"But there was only a crew of three," Dash said.

David nodded. "I know."

"Out of the employees, did anyone specify how many were men and how many were women?" she asked. They might be able to narrow down the gender. Reinforce her profile of the kidnapper or lead them in a different direction.

"There was no mention of gender," David said. "Only that there were four people on the catering crew."

Madeline drummed her fingers on the arm of the chair. "That's how the kidnapper went unnoticed."

"Led Emma away right in front of me," Jackson said from his chair to the other side of her with his head down.

It was a key thread of information David had found. If they pulled on the loose end, there was no telling what else they might unravel. "Check with the catering company to see what type of vehicle they used for the event."

"Do you think it's the same kind as the one from last night?" Jackson asked.

The kidnapper using a service van to transport Emma made sense. Reduced the likelihood of anyone seeing her and wouldn't have raised suspicion on ETC premises. "It's possible."

David pushed out of his chair and was moving toward the door. "I'll go call them right now."

Jackson scrubbed a palm over his jaw. His brow was furrowed with worry.

"I know the last message feels devastating, but this isn't over," Madeline said to him, keeping her voice low so that only he could hear her. "They're not going to keep her. The kidnapper is toying with you." Wanted to drag this out and wear him down. Break his spirit a little more with each message.

"Because he wants to make me as miserable as possible?" Jackson whispered.

"Yes." And she was sorry for it, ached for what he was going through. For someone to use an innocent child as tool for revenge. This case was eating at her, digging at her from the inside out. They had to find Emma soon.

"Then I'm sure he's imagined what kind of person could hurt a child," Jackson ground out through clenched teeth. "What the psychological baggage would do to me. I'd never offload it, not for as long as I lived if something happened to her."

"You can't think like that." She patted his hand under the table, and he covered hers with the palm of his other, his fingers squeezing hers. "No one is going to hurt Emma."

"The kidnapper almost ran us down last night. That proves they're capable of anything."

"They have no reason to cross that line." Not yet. "We will find her." Madeline was willing to go to the ends of the earth to get his daughter back.

In his eyes, she saw that he believed her. She would do everything in her power to make good on her promise.

Miguel joined them, and Liam got started with his update by bringing the picture of Emma up on the screen.

"The photo the kidnapper sent was grainy, and it took some time to improve the resolution," Liam said. "The sweat suit Emma is wearing is from the private label brand for a big-box retailer that has stores everywhere. The store also carries the doll and coloring book. So nothing to go on there."

Jackson muttered a curse under his breath.

"After taking a closer look at the room that she's in," Liam continued, "I realized that there are no windows. I think the use of the newspaper on the walls was to hide that fact. Also, the floor is concrete."

"Like she's being kept in a garage?" Jackson asked.

"That's a strong possibility," Liam said.

Madeline stared at the picture. "Did you figure out which newspaper was used?"

"So far two. The *Emerald City Times* and the *Seattle Chronicle*."

"Are those recent newspapers?" Miguel asked.

"I couldn't make out the dates. So I started cross-referencing the ads and images that are visible. Found one dated last week. Here's an article that wasn't on the wall but was in the *Chronicle* for that day."

Jackson straightened as the article came up.

The headline read:

New Emerald Tech Corp CEO Vows Cutting-edge Breakthrough This Year. Can He Deliver?

Whoever took Emma had a clear personal vendetta against Jackson, but one that was business related.

It took more than discipline and intelligence for Jackson to rise to CEO so young. It had required ambition. In her experience, ambition was a volatile fuel capable of great damage.

Maybe taking a closer look at AlbrechTech wasn't such a bad idea after all. Questioning Charles Albrecht was one thing. Getting proof of a motive was better.

Madeline glanced at Jackson. Stubborn resolve was stamped on his face.

David opened the door and popped his head in the room. "I spoke to the owner of the catering company. Their staff only uses one type of vehicle for events."

"Black Ford Transit?" Madeline asked.

"Yep, that's the one."

JACKSON SAT IN the passenger seat of the government SUV, more determined than ever to attend the event at AlbrechTech and see if Chuck was behind his daughter's kidnapping. Chuck had sold out his own father to get ahead. Would he sell his soul, too?

Madeline turned onto his block, headed back to his house. "I don't have anything to wear. After I drop you off, I'll swing by my condo in Wedgwood to change."

"Not necessary," Jackson said.

"It's black-tie. It is necessary. Unless you think this is appropriate." Madeline swept a hand over her shirt and slacks.

A change of clothing was essential and that was precisely what Jackson was relying on.

She pulled into his driveway. "Who is that?" Madeline asked, staring at the woman standing on the porch.

The slip of a girl had two stuffed garment bags draped over her arm.

"A stylist," Jackson said. "I didn't think you had an evening gown stashed in your overnight bag, and we don't have time for you to run home to get ready. I don't want to miss Chuck's big announcement."

"When did you call her?"

"I rang Petra while you were in Miguel's office talking to him about the party at AlbrechTech." He'd made *two* calls from the landline in Madeline's office since the FBI were monitoring his cell phone. "I've used her in the past for Francesca. She sent an assistant over with a couple of dresses for you to choose from."

Madeline arched a perfectly groomed eyebrow at him. "It's that simple. One call and the store comes to you."

"That simple. You're a six, right?" He opened the door and hopped out.

Madeline killed the engine and walked around the front of the car. "A what?"

"Dress size. A six." Being married had made him a good guesser in that department, but he'd asked Petra to send over options that ranged from a four to eight since cut varied by designers. All jewel-toned or pastel colors that would best flatter Madeline.

"I *am* a six," she said, sounding a bit shocked.

He knew it. "She also brought some undergarments to go along. I didn't know if a sports bra would work with the selections."

"Did you guess my bra size as well?"

He had. Guessed a 34C. Clearing his throat, he thought it wiser not to respond.

On the porch, he made a quick introduction.

"Petra told me to give you this." The assistant handed him a glossy black bag.

"Thank you." He took the bag as Madeline eyed him. "A disguise to throw off the press," he said to her and when she appeared satisfied with the response, he unlocked the door, letting them in.

Across the street, he spotted Larry leaving his house and making a beeline their way.

"Take your time, Madeline. I want you to be comfortable. If the selections don't work for you—"

"I'm sure it'll be fine," she said, staring at him. Her striking face was a blank slate giving away nothing, her tone crisp and cool.

Once again, he had no clue what she was thinking.

Madeline headed down the hall and the assistant followed as the two disappeared around the corner.

Jackson went out onto the porch to greet his neighbor. "Hi, Larry."

"Glad I caught you." In the late daylight, his thinning blond hair and golfer's V-neck burn were pronounced. He sported khakis with a crease sharp enough to draw blood, a blue blazer with a yellow-and-green lining, a matching pocket hankie that protruded like a clown's water-squirting flower, and loafers with no socks. "This is for you, my friend." Larry handed him a ten-by-eight black metal case with keypad access, along with a RFID wristband and key fob and a box of ammo. "If I had to recommend one handgun for the home, it'd be the Glock 19. Great for the range, your nightstand and on your person for concealed carry. There's a Gen 5 inside." With a bright white grin, he tapped

the top of the metal case. "I always store my ammo separately, but some folks like to keep theirs loaded."

"I appreciate it, Larry. What do I owe you for this?"

His neighbor waved a dismissive hand. "We never did
get you a welcome gift when you moved in. Consider this
it, a few years late." He shoved his hands in his pockets and
rocked back on his heels. "I see the FBI agent is back. Do
you keep the same one or do they rotate them?"

"If I'm lucky, there won't be any rotation." He hoped
that was the case. Madeline had looked more annoyed than
pleased. He might have overstepped by contacting the stylist, but that had been a risk he'd been willing to take. This
was the only way to cover what he had done in making
the second phone call, and he wouldn't make Madeline
complicit.

"I'll say. I wouldn't mind having her around 24/7." Larry
waggled his eyebrows, and his ruddy complexion deepened.
"She's a looker, that one."

"Excellent at her job," Jackson said. "I couldn't ask for
a smarter, more dedicated kidnapping expert committed
to helping me get my daughter back."

The small grin on Larry's lips fell. "I'll leave you to it.
If you need anything, let us know." With a wave, he hurried down the porch steps.

Jackson put the chain on, making a mental note to have
his front door replaced with a steel one without a window.

Passing the guest room, he overheard Madeline talking
to the assistant. From what he could make out, it sounded
as though it was going well.

In his bedroom at the end of the hall, he closed the door
and set everything on his dresser. Pressing the RFID key
fob to the reader, he opened the case, revealing the Glock.
He picked up the cold matte black pistol. Lightweight with

a low recoil, it was a solid choice for home defense. But he didn't have a need for the gun tonight.

Closing the case, he turned his attention to the glossy bag.

Madeline had made exceptional points about why he shouldn't attend the AlbrechTech event. All of them he had taken to heart. Inside the bag was a little something from Petra, the solution to the problem. A wig and fake mustache. Being noticed by the press wasn't on his agenda.

Also in the bag was an envelope—the contents of which were a product of his second phone call that he didn't want the FBI privy to. His contact had dropped the envelope off at Petra's studio as directed and collected a twenty-five-thousand-dollar fee in return.

No record of money changing hands between Jackson and the contact would exist. But Jackson would receive a hefty bill from Petra.

He checked the envelope. It contained exactly what he had expected. His plan wasn't aboveboard, nor was it definitive he'd have to go through with it. Always be prepared to seize an opportunity. That was what his father had taught him. A lesson that had served Jackson well for more than thirty years.

Jackson bathed and got dressed, putting on a tux. Applying the silicone-based adhesive to his face, he went slowly, working carefully to ensure the mustache wouldn't come loose at an inopportune moment later. He slipped on the brown wig that was streaked with gray and looked in the mirror. A different man stared back at him.

He drifted down the hall. The shower ran in the guest bathroom and the assistant was gone.

Jackson sat at the piano and ran his fingers across the keys like it was an old friend. In many ways, it was. A best friend that had never failed him.

He struck a few chords, waiting for the piece of music to choose him. Then he played.

Opening himself, he let his focus become so singular it was as if the music reached out and took possession of him. Let every emotion pour out over the keys. He thought of his mother, as always. But he also thought of Emma. Of her smile. Her laughter. Her tears. Of the little things that made her special. Of all the great things he hoped she'd one day achieve. She was his hopes and dreams wrapped up in pure, unconditional love.

When he finished, emptied of the pressure, he was breathing hard and fast. And this was why he played. So that he could breathe.

"Tristesse," Madeline said behind him, referring to the name of the piece, which meant *sadness* in French. "Also known as Chopin's Etude Number Three in E Major, Opus Ten."

It didn't surprise him that she knew it, but it did warm something in his chest.

"I've never heard it played so beautifully in person," she said. "Where did you learn?"

He lowered his head. "My mother. She went to Juilliard. Instead of realizing her full potential, she married my father and had me. She gifted me with her love of playing."

"And her talent."

Spinning around on the bench, he looked up at her and the breath stalled in his lungs.

A fuchsia sheath dress clung to her svelte figure. The vivid color contrasted beautifully with her radiant skin. A slit along the right side that ran from knee to midthigh was the one aspect of the sophisticated dress that wasn't subtle in its sex appeal. With her long dark hair flowing loose and wavy around her shoulders, there was only one word to describe Madeline.

Breathtaking.

"You look stunning." He stood and crossed the room. Her eyes were glassy with tears. "What's wrong?" he asked. "You don't like the dress or is my disguise that bad?"

"I love the dress, though I would've preferred something black to help me blend in rather than stand out, and low heels would've been nice. Your disguise works. Quite effective." She dabbed at the corner of an eye. "You moved me. Your playing touched my soul. If I could play like that I'd never stop. Why don't you do this professionally?"

He frowned and the mustache tickled his face. "Could you picture me in a lounge playing for my supper?"

She squinted at him. "No, I guess I can't."

"My father hammered into me the practicality of pursuing business over music. But Emma is free to follow her passion, wherever that leads. She has been playing since she was three. She's quite good. You should hear her play." His chest ached with the desire to make that a reality.

Madeline moved to him and cupped his cheek. Almost as soon as she had, she dropped her hand and stepped back. "Should we go?"

"I arranged for a car. It should be here any minute."

"Why did you go to the trouble?"

"Force of habit for this sort of thing. Besides, my car isn't exactly subtle." His blue metallic Tesla was too recognizable to take to the event. "And I didn't want you to have to bother driving yours. You're going above and beyond already." He gestured for her to proceed. "After you."

Madeline smiled at him, warm and genuine, and headed for the door.

Jackson grabbed the invitation from the coffee table and slid a hand over his breast pocket, feeling the outline of the contents from the envelope. Under the best set of circumstances, he wouldn't have any need to use it. If push came to shove and he had to move forward, then and only then would he let Madeline in on the details. It wasn't the most ethical plan after all.

The last thing he wanted was to jeopardize her career and burn the personal bridge they'd been building. The possibility of it made him sick, tore him right down the middle. He'd try to avoid that outcome.

But he was willing to do absolutely anything to get Emma back. Anything.

Nothing was more important.

Chapter Ten

In the confines of the back seat of the luxury sedan, Madeline was highly aware of how delicious Jackson smelled. She breathed him in, telling herself to relax and focus on the job.

The car passed a throng of protesters gathered outside of AlbrechTech and pulled into a line to drop them off at the entrance of the building.

Madeline scanned the crowd, looking for one of their prime suspects.

"She's here," Jackson said. "Samantha Dickson. Kane Tidwell, too."

Someone set a wooden crate down and Dickson climbed up on top of it. She lifted a bullhorn to her mouth. "We will continue to target these CEOs and make them pay. We're going to turn up the pressure. Make them suffer. Hit them where it hurts the most until they've learned their lesson. They want to pretend like we're not here, as if they can't see us. Well, let's make sure they hear us." Her light brown hair was loose and free, flying wild around her face as she raised her right palm, which was painted red, then clenched it into a fist and chanted, "Hell, no, we won't go! Hell, no, we won't go!"

The mob circling her repeated the furious words.

This was perfect. Nothing better than a glamorous event

with the press to lure the Red Right Hand like moths to a flame. Simply couldn't help themselves.

Madeline opened the clutch that matched her Tarik Ediz dress, shifted her FBI credentials to the side and grabbed her cell phone. She dialed Miguel. "Three guesses who is outside AlbrechTech right now protesting."

"Samantha Dickson," he said, excitement ringing in his voice. "I'll pull the guys surveilling Charles Albrecht and have them follow Dickson. This way we'll know where she's staying."

"Make sure they keep eyes on her in case she changes locations."

"Of course," Miguel said. "I was just about to call you."

"Did Liam or Dash turn up anything new?"

"It's not about the Rhodes case. I got a lead on the terrorist suspect responsible for those two bombings last year."

Finally. Madeline knew precisely how much this meant to Miguel. The terrorist on their watch list had claimed over a hundred lives and evaded capture. Like every member of the BAU team, Miguel would risk his own life to find justice for the dead and try to prevent any more people from dying.

"I need to follow this lead before the trail grows cold," Miguel said.

She'd expect nothing less from him. "I understand. Be sure to keep us in the loop."

"Will do."

She disconnected and stowed her phone back in her purse. The chanting cut through the silence in the car.

"What reason do they have to be angry with Albrecht?" Madeline asked.

"Take your pick. From new facial recognition software that he sold to law enforcement, which they claim is racially biased, to drone technology for US Immigration and Customs Enforcement that's used to separate families."

"Drones," she said, and understanding of where she was going lit up in his eyes. "What brand does he produce?"

"Two. For the government it's ABC Daedalus, and commercially it's—"

"ABC Icarus." The *AB* stood for Albrecht. The *C* for Charles. With them being stretched to the limit on this case, they had missed a small yet important detail.

His blue eyes narrowed, taking on an iciness. "Were Chuck's drones at Duwamish?"

"The commercial brand, but that doesn't prove anything. They're very popular and widely available."

The driver pulled up to the entrance, stopping the car. Jackson got out, came around to her side and opened the door.

He extended his hand. She put her palm on his and he helped her out. The simple contact, a slip of skin on skin, sparked a tingle she couldn't ignore.

A flurry of cameras clicked, flashes bursting like fireworks in front of them.

Taken aback by the onslaught of paparazzi, she lowered her gaze.

"Sorry," Jackson said. "I should've warned you what to expect."

They hurried through the press gauntlet, neither of them smiling, both eager to avoid the cameras. There was a small white tent set up.

The moment they entered, an armed security guard greeted them. "Good evening."

Jackson presented his special VIP invitation.

When the man swept over the custom holographic foil print with a handheld scanner, a bar code that hadn't been visible before illuminated.

"What time is the big announcement?" Jackson asked.

"You're just in time," the guard said in an accent that sounded Russian. "Should be any minute since the entire board of directors have arrived."

Jackson nodded his thanks.

Another security guard took her handbag and searched it. Spotting her credentials, he flipped open her badge. He met her gaze, stuffed her identification back inside and gave her the clutch. A third guard, holding a metal detector wand, motioned for her to step forward.

If he did a thorough search, her BUG—backup gun— that was strapped to her thigh would set off the alarm.

Madeline extended her arms while the guard waved the wand across her upper body, moving lower.

As he came to her midsection, she dropped her purse. The guard bent to pick it up, a natural reflex he probably wasn't aware of. She lowered along with him, moving too fast and close on purpose, and their heads collided.

"Sorry about that," she said.

"No problem, ma'am." He also spoke with an accent. The guard grabbed the clutch, handed it to her and gestured for Jackson to assume the position.

A quick swipe over his body, and they were cleared.

"Are the guards always armed here at AlbrechTech?" she asked.

"Since Chuck took over. He's paranoid to the nth degree." Putting his hand on her lower back, Jackson guided her into the building. The large, long lobby served as a reception hall. He pressed his mouth to her ear. "I'm fairly certain each invitation had a unique bar code. Chuck will soon know that I'm here. If he doesn't already."

That could present an unanticipated set of challenges or opportunities, depending on how the night went.

The decor inside was more lavish than she expected.

The lighting was low and there were huge arrangements of flowers everywhere. Servers passed, carrying trays with flutes of champagne and hors d'oeuvres. Ambient music flowed and glitzy guests mingled.

"Now what?" she asked.

"We wait." Jackson took her hand and led her to the designated dance floor in front of a makeshift stage that had been erected.

The first strands of a waltz began. He whisked her into his arms, bringing her close.

Ignoring the tightening in her stomach that had nothing to do with the stress of the case and everything to do with their proximity, she looked up at him. She was a tall woman, at five-eight, but even with three-inch heels, Jackson towered over her by several inches. Despite the wig and mustache, his tailored tux did nothing to hide the bulk of his muscles. With his formidable stature he looked both debonair and dangerous. A tantalizing mix.

They moved easily, fluidly together. He was a skilled dancer, confident in his lead. Was there anything this man didn't do well?

Relaxing in his hold, she struggled not to think about the feel of his wide, muscular body against hers. But it was impossible. He had a bold, dominant style that was inherently sexual. Not something he tried at. Simply the way he was.

There were hidden depths beneath that handsome face and chiseled body. It was almost unfair to the women of the world that he had brains, brawn, masculine beauty and talent.

He rubbed a hand up and down her back, making patterns against her skin. She wondered if it was deliberate or if he wasn't even aware of what he was doing.

His gaze traveled around the room. Not as though he

was worried about bumping into Albrecht, but like he was casing the place.

"Is there something you're not telling me?" she asked, banishing her unprofessional distraction.

He lowered his head and his blue eyes connected with hers. His face was impassive, the picture of calm, yet he vibrated with energy. It was his hesitation that made her certain he was holding something back.

Madeline's stomach knotted and rolled. "Does our agreement about information sharing stand?"

His hand glided up her spine, his fingers playing over her vertebrae as he pressed his body to hers in all the right places. Lifting his hand to cup her cheek, he caressed her skin with his thumb, and her heart fluttered.

"It does," he said.

She wanted to believe him, truly. But she didn't.

The lights came up in the lobby, going from intimate to bright, and the music stopped.

"Ladies and gentlemen," a man said into a microphone, standing on the stage, "please gather around and join me as we welcome to the stage AlbrechTech CEO and firebrand, Chuck Albrecht."

Applause resounded and everyone assembled around the platform.

Albrecht jogged out onto the stage, clapping for himself, wearing jeans, sneakers and a blazer over a T-shirt at his own event. He was about the same age as Jackson, but lanky, average height, forgettable face. Someone who wouldn't stand out in a crowd. Unless he was wearing the exact opposite as everyone else. She could tell he was the kind of guy that people loved to hate.

He took the microphone. "Thank you, thank you. I know this is the moment you have all been waiting for with bated breath, for me to arrive." The crowd clapped and laughed.

"Seriously, we're going to get to the reason you're all here in a second. But first, can I point out that we are about to have another rocking quarter?" Cheers and applause erupted. "Our earnings are through the roof! We are trouncing the competition like Emerald Tech Corp into the dust." The ovation grew louder. "No one can touch this." He pointed to himself, and the crowd egged him on with more laughter. "I would like to take a serious moment to acknowledge the horrific events a colleague is currently suffering. Jackson Rhodes, over at ETC, I'm sure you've heard. His daughter was kidnapped and one of his R&D facilities was bombed."

Murmurs rolled through the audience.

Jackson stiffened. His gaze was locked on Albrecht.

"I know, it's terrible," Albrecht said, shaking his head. "A tough set of circumstances. The guy was going to have a hard enough time already facing our next earnings report and his own limitations trying to cut the mustard as my competition. So, I've decided to offer a reward from my trust fund—not from the company—for any information that leads to the safe and speedy return of his daughter, in the amount of one million dollars."

A flurry of gasps turned into applause.

"What is he doing?" Madeline said to Jackson. This would only invite thousands of false tips to flood the hotline, pushing their resources, already stretched too thin, to the breaking point.

"Chuck is being Chuck. Showboating," Jackson said through gritted teeth. "I want to snap his scrawny neck."

"What can I say—I'm just that magnanimous." Albrecht put his hand over his heart and took a small bow. "And to Jackson, wherever you might be tonight," he said, letting his gaze travel slowly over the audience, "you're welcome, buddy!"

Madeline's lip curled in disgust. How could anyone be so pompous and callous at the same time?

Chuck Albrecht was many of the things she'd assumed Jackson might be before they had met—entitled, arrogant, a jerk. She couldn't have been more wrong about Jackson. Compared to Chuck, they were night and day.

Once the crowd settled, Albrecht said, "Without further ado, let's get to the nitty-gritty of why you're here tonight. To celebrate. I have achieved something no one else has and every shareholder is going to make a lot of money because of it. Our fully self-driving cars have reached Level 5 autonomy with ten million miles and zero crashes." Thunderous applause erupted.

Madeline leaned in toward Jackson. "Aren't there already self-driving cars?"

"Not at Level 5 autonomy, where the car can drive day or night, no matter the type of road or weather conditions. Without any need for human intervention. This is major. An endgame for self-driving technology."

"Next week," Albrecht continued, "I'll have another announcement related to the DOD, but mum's the word until the ink is dry on the contract. In the meantime, raise your glasses to toast me and you." Everyone holding a glass lifted it. "Let's celebrate!"

Upbeat dance music pumped from the speakers and the crowd resumed enjoyment of the festivities.

"This is big," Madeline said, "but it's not in the same league as what you were working on."

"We don't know what else he has in development, but I need to find out. He has a military contract in the pipeline, and it isn't for his self-driving cars. There's more in R&D. Something that's close to completion. Or since he's talked about the contract as though it were a done deal, my guess is that it's already been finished and tested."

"I suppose we'll have to wait until he makes an announcement." She put a supportive hand on Jackson's forearm, knowing it wasn't what he wanted to hear.

"Like I told you at the house, I'm not waiting."

Before she had a chance to reply, Jackson turned and stalked away. Madeline hurried after him. Where was he going?

She stayed alert to their surroundings: the location of the security guards, who Albrecht was socializing with and the positions of the security cameras.

A guard at the end of the lobby tapped his ear as though listening through his Bluetooth, and then circled around toward the crowd away from a door that led outside. Jackson homed in on the movement and headed for the exit that was far from the crowd.

A red roll 'n' pole sign warned of restricted access.

Ignoring the posted sign, he pushed through the door and she followed close behind him.

Fresh air hit them. The serenity and distance from the crowd was welcomed.

"What are we doing?" she asked.

Jackson pointed to a patch of trees at the rear of Albrecht-Tech headquarters. A lit path ran through the center of the woods, leading somewhere.

He started moving down the walkway adjacent to the building, headed in the direction of the unknown.

"What's out there?" she asked.

"On the other side of the thicket is the R&D facility." He kept walking. "The equivalent of my Duwamish site."

"How do you know?" she whispered. "Have you seen it?"

"Only aerial shots of the building, but inside information from a contact confirmed it. Whatever military-related project Chuck is working on is out there," he said, his voice low.

As they approached the corner of the building, the sound of footfalls drew near.

There must have been guards on patrol. One was headed their way.

Madeline grabbed Jackson by the lapels, yanking him to her as she rose on the balls of her feet and kissed him, long and slow. Without hesitation, he took her lead, wrapping his arms around her like they were a couple.

A guard came around the corner and shuffled to a stop. He cleared his throat quite forcibly. "No one is allowed out here."

Jackson pulled his lips from hers and lifted his head. "Give me a couple of minutes to take advantage of this opportunity, if you know what I'm saying."

The armed guard flattened his mouth. The bulge of the gun in his shoulder holster was obvious under his jacket. "The party is inside."

"And so is her husband," Jackson said. "I'm an important shareholder. All I need is five minutes and I'll be sure to let Chuck know how outstanding his security team is. Or I can make recommendations for changes. Your choice."

The armed guard looked around, his mouth twitching. "Two minutes. Not five. When I pass by again, you better not be here."

Jackson gave a suave smile. "I guarantee we won't." He brought his mouth down to her collarbone and nibbled up her neck to her ear, sending a frisson of desire skittering through her. "We better make it believable." The gravelly whisper was like a hot finger drawn down her spine.

He pulled her in a tight embrace as the guard began to walk away.

With one hand at the small of her back, he lowered his lips to hers. She welcomed the hot slide of his tongue against hers, wanting to taste him again as she drove her fingers into his hair. His mouth was warm and firm, more possessive than persuasive, making her pulse quicken and pound through her body down to her core.

The clunk of the guard's shoes disappeared around the corner.

But Jackson didn't stop, and neither did she.

The kiss grew rough and urgent. His hands clenched, pulling her ever closer.

She pressed against him, not knowing if this one chance might be her only and last. He pushed her back against the wall. The glass behind her was smooth and cold, causing her to shiver, but Jackson's clever hands molding to her ignited something inside her. She wanted more than a kiss. So much more.

Another minute of this and the guard would be the least of their problems.

"Jackson," she gasped, breaking the kiss. With the breath shuddering in her lungs, she looked up at him. His gaze was scorching. "The guard is gone."

Everything shifted in his eyes, turning sober and wary. Now full of something that sent a chill through her. Determination. "I have to go," he said.

"*We*, you mean."

"It's too risky for you to go with me. Head back inside. I'll check out what's in the R&D facility and come straight back."

Was this a joke? "You're not going anywhere without me."

"It's not safe for you. You shouldn't be involved in what I'm about to do next. Trust me." He cupped her chin and kissed her forehead. "We don't have time to argue. Please do as I say. Go inside."

Turning from her, Jackson ran to the corner of the building. He looked around and then he darted down a hill, avoiding the lit path, and disappeared into the darkness.

Unbelievable. Did he really think she'd be a *good girl* and do as she was told?

Madeline slipped off her shoes to keep her heels from making a racket against the paved path and chased after him. She passed a sign that read:

Stop. Authorized Personnel Only Beyond This Point. Trespassers Will Be Shot.

Once her bare feet hit the cool grass, she sprinted as fast as she could until she hit the tree line. Wood cracked and a warm line of blood scored her arm.

Stopping beside a tree, she put her shoes back on and searched the darkness.

Jackson was nowhere to be seen.

Damn it. Where was he? And how big was this property? She guessed an acre, maybe two, at least.

A palm slid over her mouth, and she reflexively threw an elbow toward the person's gut.

Jackson snared her arm, blocking the blow as he came up behind her. He'd managed to get the drop on her. The man was stealthy, too. She would have to add that to the growing list of his annoying traits.

"I knew you'd follow me," he growled.

She swatted his hand from her face. "*You're* upset with *me*?" she whispered.

"You didn't listen." He moved downhill at a quick pace through the thicket, trekking parallel to the illuminated path.

Madeline hurried to catch up with him, doing her best to balance on the killer heels. "You simply took off with no explanation."

"I considered telling you my plan, per our information-sharing agreement. Then I realized it wasn't fair to put you in that position."

"You mean the position I'm in now? But instead of having all the facts, I'm going in blind." She tripped over a tree root and stumbled.

Jackson caught her by the elbow, saving her from a nasty face-plant, and steadied her. "You weren't supposed to be going in at all. I was keeping you in the dark for your own good. I decided the less you knew, the better in the long run," he said. "That way you would have plausible deniability."

What damnable action was he planning to commit? "Did you make that decision for my own good before or after you kissed me?"

A smile curved Jackson's mouth, but Madeline caught the tightening of suppressed anger in it as he sliced a look at her. "Does it matter?"

To her, it did.

They cleared the woods and came out to a glade. There was a building, not unlike the one at Duwamish, sitting amid the tall trees.

"There'll be a sophisticated security system," she said. "We won't be able to simply waltz in and look around."

"I'm aware and have prepared accordingly." He took her hand, and they ran to the double doors.

As he reached into his left breast pocket and drew something out, she looked around for security cameras. Two were trained on the entrance, where they stood. Red blinking lights on several trees around the perimeter indicated there were more.

They wouldn't have long.

Jackson produced an entry card and swiped it through the reader.

"How did you come by that?" she asked.

The red light on the sensor flashed to green. The door unlocked with a click.

He opened the door and ushered her inside. "The less you know, the better." He slipped the keycard back into his jacket.

"Right. Plausible deniability," she said. "Which will mean nothing if we don't hurry up and get out of here before security guards show up."

A low whooshing noise captured her attention. A second later, the ten degree drop in temperature from outside registered. The sound was the cooling system recirculating the air.

They stepped forward, triggering motion sensors, and overhead lights popped on, bathing the space in bright white light.

"I'd say we have about two minutes before we have company," she said.

He nodded. "Come on."

They headed down the corridor. Labs lined either side of the hall that led to a large open bay. Beyond the glass walls of the workrooms, there were prototypes of new drones, biometric devices, semiconductors for a video gaming platform and equipment connected to a replica of a sink with water lines for what she guessed was the development of smart water tech.

"Do you see anything at all that could be stealth technology?" Madeline asked.

Getting closer to one of the rooms, he said, "No."

At the end of the corridor, they entered the large bay and stared at the centerpiece.

A military tank.

"How did I not guess?" Jackson said. "Chuck's contract

with the DOD is for self-driving tanks." Slamming his eyes shut, he hung his head.

"Are you sure? Maybe it's stealth technology for tanks."

A look of defeat shrouded his face as he shook his head. "Chuck achieved Level 5 autonomy for self-driving vehicles. This is the next logical step. The most efficient one for the greatest profit in the least amount of time. Of course the military would jump at the chance to get their hands on this." Clenching his hands, he swore. "I had this all wrong."

Chuck didn't have a motive to torch Jackson's facility, and after the speech he'd given, Madeline didn't see the rival CEO as someone who would stoop to kidnapping to be top dog. The self-aggrandizing blowhard Chuck Albrecht didn't think he had to resort to such drastic measures because he already viewed himself as the best.

"He didn't kidnap Emma," Jackson said in a harsh whisper, voicing her thoughts.

"No, I don't think he did." Another dead end. She could only imagine how crushed he must be. The investigation process wasn't easy, but it worked. At least Albrecht had been eliminated as a suspect.

"Then who has my daughter?"

Madeline wished she had the answer. Looking around, she noted the cameras in the bay. "We have to leave. Now."

Their time was up. She took his arm and tugged him back to the corridor.

They hustled down the hallway.

At the door, Jackson used the keycard to unlock it. The night was quiet. The air still. But Madeline knew it wouldn't last.

They dashed to the woods, steering clear of the path. As they reached the tree line, shouts and noise-suppressed gunfire erupted.

Madeline shoved Jackson behind a tree, taking cover with him.

They were too late. Security was onto them.

From the sound of it, at least three guards, using weapons with silencers, were in pursuit. The suppressors flattened the noise of the gunshots but didn't eliminate it entirely.

Madeline screamed, "Federal agent! Federal agent! Don't shoot!" She removed her badge from her purse in preparation to show her credentials. "Stay here, out of the line of fire," she said to Jackson. "I don't want you getting shot by these trigger-happy Neanderthals."

With hands raised, she stepped out from behind the tree.

Three men snaked through the woods, headed straight for them and opened fire.

Bullets split the air and peppered into a nearby tree.

Madeline dived back behind the tree with Jackson. Her skull prickled. Had they not heard her? "FBI! Don't shoot!" she said at the top of her lungs.

More bullets smacked into a tree less than a foot above her.

Her knees weakened a little at the realization that the guards had heard her identify herself. But they didn't care. Because they didn't have to.

She was the one in the wrong. Trespassing on private property. Searching a building without a warrant. In the aftermath, they could spin the story however they wanted, and a good lawyer would get them off scot-free.

Bastards!

Madeline grabbed her BUG. The Beretta Nano was sleek, thin and compact, but only offered seven rounds. Each shot needed to count.

If that was the game they wanted to play...

She ducked low, peeking around the base of the tree. Took aim. Fired.

The single shot hit a guard through the right upper arm. His weapon dropped to the ground, and he grabbed hold of his perforated biceps as he shouted in agony.

…then she'd play.

Chapter Eleven

I should've brought the gun after all.

Adrenaline ramped up Jackson's heartbeat, had the tight muscle hammering in his chest. The new rush of raw energy catapulted him into fight-or-flight mode. That was the thing about fear: the right amount could help you. Made you think clearer, faster, got you ready to tackle anything that might come your way. But too much fear could cause you to make a mistake. At a time like now, that could be fatal.

"Don't move," Madeline ordered. Then she took off, darting to a new position.

Glancing around the tree to assess the situation, Jackson did his damnedest not to expose too much of his head and invite a bullet.

One of the guards noticed Madeline and aimed at her. She fired first, and the guard dropped to the grass, clutching his knee. Seconds later, she vanished behind a cluster of trees.

The unsuppressed report of her weapon was shockingly loud compared to the shots discharged from the guns with silencers. It would capture the attention of everyone at the party.

Four additional guards were already rushing down the lit path. They cut into the woods, charging toward the action.

He and Madeline were outnumbered. Outgunned. Outmaneuvered. Still, Jackson had to do something to help her. Even if it meant taking a bullet to keep her from getting hurt. He'd created this mess and had to make sure she got out of it unscathed.

Calculating his chances, he seized an opening and worked his way from tree to tree. Bullets snapped and pinged. One whizzed so close to his head, he was forced to duck back behind a large oak. But he refused to stop moving until he caught sight of Madeline.

She had put down a third guard, once more without killing him.

Jackson was in genuine awe of her skill and restraint.

A burly guard, tall and thick, circled around behind Madeline, trying to sneak up on her. Perhaps to shoot her in the back. Like a coward.

The hulking man was six-five and a solid 250 pounds of pure muscle.

Jackson couldn't dodge a bullet. Nobody could. But one on one, in a tussle, Jackson could take him. Training, practice, size, all of it was a determining factor, but the key to a good fighter was natural ability. Quick reflexes and hand-eye coordination were two things Jackson had been born with. That didn't even take into account the years of training his father had given him.

The huge guard maneuvered past two more trees, drawing closer. He lifted his weapon, sights trained on Madeline.

Jackson bolted forward and slid feetfirst into the shooter, his heels connecting with knee joints that bent sidewise in an unnatural way. Bullets rocketed up to the sky, and the guy fell on top of him. Jackson flipped them both over, putting the bruiser's back to the ground. Without slowing for a second, Jackson slammed his forearm across the big man's face, breaking his nose.

Scrambling to his feet, Jackson kicked the man's weapon away.

Madeline had wounded a fourth man. Shot him in the shoulder. After disarming him, she grabbed him by the back of the collar and positioned him in front of herself, like a human shield. Her movements were quick and precise, but as smooth and practiced as a dance.

The remaining guards—Jackson counted three—closed in, focusing their aim on him.

"If you shoot him," Madeline said, gesturing to Jackson, "I'll make sure all of you are hospitalized." Her eyes remained flat and cool. "Not merely stopped with a flesh wound. But hospitalized. As in requiring serious pain meds and physical therapy for a very long time."

The guards exchanged glances and decided on taking defensive positions rather than pulling their triggers.

"Get your boss down here immediately," Madeline said, flashing her badge. "Tell him Special Agent Madeline Striker would like to have a chat about his security protocol."

One of the guards spoke into his mic, relaying the message.

Tension stretched between them during the nerve-racking standoff. Three guns against one. But it didn't take long for Chuck to show his face. A couple of minutes tops, and he was strolling downhill with an entourage of security guards.

"I'm here, Agent Striker," Chuck called from the illuminated path. "Would you and your cohort come out into the light for our little détente?"

"Move." Madeline nudged the guard she still held in front of her forward.

The other guards backed up slowly, stopping once they reached the walkway.

"Boys, lower your weapons," Chuck said, and they did as instructed.

Strolling closer, Chuck lifted his wrist to his mouth and whispered something. The lights along the path went from an amber glow to football-stadium wattage.

Madeline released the guard, stowed her gun in her purse and flashed her credentials in Chuck's face.

With a glib smile, Chuck proffered his hand. "Special Agent Striker. Chuck Albrecht. It's a pleasure to meet you."

Madeline glared at his outstretched hand with barely contained fury. "I wish I could say likewise."

Chuck's gaze slid to Jackson and the weasel's eyes narrowed. "Jackson Rhodes? Is that a wig and fake mustache you're wearing?" He gestured to a guard, who promptly snatched the headpiece off Jackson. "Well, well, wonders never cease to amaze me. Did you put on this getup because you wanted to come tonight and see what my announcement was about, but were afraid to face me?"

This jerk was full of perpetual hot air. "My daughter is missing, you son of a bitch, and I needed to see if you were behind it. But I didn't want the press to know that I was here. I don't want to make the situation worse for Emma."

Chuck held up the wig. Staring at it, he shivered as if disgusted. "This explains why I couldn't find you after your invitation was scanned. Despite a thorough search."

"What amazes me," Madeline said, "is that your security personnel continued to fire their weapons at us after I identified myself clearly as a federal agent."

A smug smile tugged at one corner of Chuck's mouth. "How were my men supposed to know you were a legitimate FBI agent? Why would they believe you, considering the two of you were trespassing out here? I have every confidence that once they saw bona fide credentials they would have stopped shooting," he said, holding that evil grin. "Do you have a warrant, Special Agent Striker? Probable cause? Because if you don't, then your presence and search of this part of the premises is illegal. There's a little thing called the Fourth Amendment." He folded his arms. "My men are Russian mercenaries and have a strict 'shoot first and ask questions later' policy regarding trespassers. I don't mess around when it comes to my intellectual property, and no one dares mess with what's mine because of them. They had every right to open fire on intruders who broke into a restricted facility where I have tech worth billions. And I have every right to contact your supervisor and demand your badge. This stunt you two pulled is highly irregular, not to mention against the law."

Everything Chuck had said was true. Madeline didn't have a legal leg to stand on and what made it worse, Jackson had been the one to put her in that position.

"I believe your grievance is with me, Chuck," Jackson said, wanting to draw the slick bastard's line of fire away from Madeline. "I needed to know what you were working on."

"Curiosity killed the cat," Chuck said.

Clenching his jaw, Jackson gritted his teeth. "I had to see if what was inside that building was similar to my tech that was destroyed at my Duwamish site."

"Oh!" Chuck threw his head back and barked a laugh. "As if I might have been the one who blew up your facility and kidnapped your daughter. You thought *me* that desperate." He rolled his eyes. "Hopefully after tonight you've come to your senses and realized that I don't have to snatch your kid, destroy your tech and strong-arm you into resigning to beat you. Because I'm smarter and better than you and have two things you never will."

Jackson didn't ask the obvious question. He waited for the answer instead.

"Prodigious talent and ruthless ambition," Chuck said. "I was willing to put my own father out to pasture to get ahead since the old man was holding me back."

As if that was something to be proud of.

"And I have two things you don't," Jackson said. "A light touch and a tight grip. Step a little closer—I'll show you."

Chuck quirked an eyebrow and backed up. "I'm signing a ten-billion-dollar contract with the DOD on Monday for my self-driving tanks. The only thing you have on me is about ten inches in height and those pretty-boy features. But I don't need that with my genius, money and talent. I truly do hope you find your daughter and take your job back at ETC. Do you want to know why?" A nasty grin spread across his face. "So I can have the satisfying pleasure of outperforming you. Every. Single. Quarter." Chuck had the nerve to wink at him. "Look, to show I'm sincere about hoping your daughter is returned safely to you, I'm going to have my guards show you the back way out, so you don't have to face the paparazzi without your disguise. I will not be held responsible for making things worse for Emma."

"Is this professional courtesy, one CEO to another?" Jackson asked.

More hearty laughter from Chuck grated on Jackson's nerves. "You're no longer a CEO. Remember? You resigned. Consider this a favor. Now you owe me, and the thought of you being in my debt puts a smile on my face."

The guards escorted them to the eastside exit, which was clear of snooping photographers, where Jackson's car met them.

On the drive back to his house, Madeline didn't look at him. Didn't say a single word. He could feel her justified anger, simmering below her calm exterior, but he decided it was best to wait to talk behind closed doors in the privacy of his home instead of giving the driver free entertainment.

Not that he was sure what to say.

The air in the car seethed with tension.

He was furious with himself. For not getting any closer to finding Emma's kidnapper and bringing her home. For his unethical plan backfiring. For endangering Madeline.

For not being able to erase from his mind that kiss he'd shared with her.

Suddenly, he could think of nothing else but the press of her lips against his mouth, her arms wrapped around him, her body molded to his, the wild heat flashing between them as natural and dangerous as lightning in a storm.

Shifting in the seat, he wished he could wipe out those images, forget the vivid sensations that had taken hold of him. But every time he glanced at her mouth, let his gaze trail down her bare arm, took in her scent with each inhale, they came flooding back.

The driver turned into the driveway and stopped the car. He and Madeline got out. Slammed the doors. Marched inside the house.

"Good old Chuck had it right, you know," she said before they'd made it out of the foyer. "What I did with you tonight was illegal. Do you have any idea what that could have meant to my career?"

He pressed on down the hall. "I know how much your job means to you. How important it is." He stalked into his bedroom, ripped off the fake mustache and shed his jacket. "I didn't want to make you complicit—that's why I asked you to wait for me at the main building. To protect you."

"It's my job to protect *you*. Not the other way around. Danger is a part of my career description, not recklessness. How could I wait for you at the main building while you ran off into the night to do only God knows what? You should have trusted me with the details of your plan. Given me a chance to think it through. But instead of working with me, like you promised, you went rogue. Again. And compromised me in the process."

"If had told you, you would've tried to stop me."

Her beautiful brown eyes blazed. "From trespassing? From breaking the law? Hell, yes."

Jackson stormed into the bathroom. Madeline followed.

Turning on the faucet, he gathered his thoughts and tried to squelch the emotion raging inside him.

"There are rules for a reason," she said. "Limits and constraints serve a purpose. If we had found any evidence in that building, it would have been inadmissible."

"But any evidence, inadmissible or not, might have led me to my daughter." He splashed water on his face and scrubbed the adhesive off his skin. "Sometimes you have to do the wrong thing for the right reason. If we hadn't, then we'd still be wasting time looking into Chuck. Spinning our wheels. Right?" He dragged a towel over his face and tossed it on the counter. Removing his tie, he brushed past her going back into his bedroom. "I had to get in there to see for myself. To be one hundred percent certain. Now we know he wasn't involved."

She was right on his heels. "If Albrecht decides to report me to the Bureau, I could be suspended."

He faced her, regretting that he'd put her at risk in any manner, professionally or physically. That had never been his intention.

"Fear is a powerful thing," he said. "Most people try to move away from fear, do what they can to alleviate it. Me? I lean into it, harness it so that I can make it work for me instead of against me. That's how I thrived in my father's house, with his expectations and high standards and efforts to tear me down so that he could rebuild me stronger. To this day, I still live my life leaning into the fear, heeding it, listening to it. Not running away from it."

Madeline stepped closer. "How does that have anything to do with what happened tonight?"

"The day Emma was kidnapped, I didn't listen to it. This is one of my worst nightmares come to life. Losing Emma in plain sight. It's the reason I don't take her to amusement parks, malls, parades. I should've listened and brought Liane instead of worrying about my image. Since Emma has been gone, there's this knot in the pit of my stomach." A cold fist squeezing his gut sometimes to the point where he couldn't breathe. "Tonight, fear of missing an opportunity to discover the truth, to find Emma, drove me to do what I did. You're living proof that not all children who are taken are rescued. I couldn't choose not to take action when I had the power to do something. I'm sorry I dragged you into it."

"You made me look unprofessional out there," she said, soft and low, the furious wall she'd thrown up cracking and crumbling. "Worse, you made me *feel* like a fool. I trusted you, Jack."

The hurt he'd caused her was unmistakable, making him even more furious with himself, but it wasn't lost on him that the vulnerability she had dared show him was a precious gift.

He brushed his knuckles across her cheek, and she pulled her face away.

"Say that again," he whispered.

Confusion clouded her expression. "What?"

"My name. Say my name like that again." He touched her cheek once more, sliding his hand around, cupping the back of her neck.

This time, she didn't pull away.

As his grip on her tightened, she softened against him. She lifted a hand between them and put her palm to his chest. Whether to shove him back or bring him closer, he wasn't sure. He closed his fingers over her wrist, and she only stood there, staring at him, trembling.

"Jack," she said softly.

He lowered his mouth close to hers until an inch separated them and he held her gaze. "You're not a fool, Madeline, anything but."

The dark promise of a kiss hovered there, had the breath backing up in his lungs and his pulse throbbing hard and heavy.

There were times when he negotiated to get something. And there were times when he simply took. This was entirely different.

If they started, there would be no stopping. So in this, she had the power, and he was at her mercy. Despite how much he ached to abandon control and release the stress of the past few days, and just ravage.

"I'm bound by rules," she said, "and can't indulge myself in every reckless whim."

Were they still talking about AlbrechTech? "To hell with the rules, so long as you make it count when you break them."

Her mouth captured his then, her arms going around his neck, her fingers sliding into his hair. His kiss was ruthless, his mouth never leaving hers, but she was equally wild and hungry.

With nothing more than a kiss, she held him captive. This craving he had for her went far beyond chemistry. Beyond lust. Beyond his control.

Raw desire unlike anything he'd ever experienced surged through him. Blood pounded in his loins. He backed her to the wall beside the bed. She ripped his shirt open, sending popped buttons to the floor, and held him tighter.

This amazing woman had so much passion buried deep inside her and he wanted to unearth all of it.

She ran her hands over his chest, her fingers caressing, exploring. The brutal ache that had started deep inside him now swelled. He swallowed the groan that rose in his throat, but when Madeline whimpered, rubbing herself against him, the dam broke.

He wrenched the front of her dress down with one forceful tug and took in her beauty, her skin gleaming in the moonlight. "You're gorgeous. So gorgeous you take my breath away."

Cupping her breast, he reveled in the heavenly weight in his palm. Suckled a pert nipple. Slipped a hand through the convenient slit of her dress and found that hot button of nerves just beneath lace. Moaning, she arched against him. He tore off her panties and placed his palm firmly on the smooth mound between her thighs.

Her breath hissed out. "Yes. I want you."

He slid his fingers into her, his groan melding with hers at the feel of her—wet, hot, tight. Desire coiled deeper inside him, snaking through him, gathering with the force of a storm. He wanted far more. Needed to be inside her like he needed air to breathe.

As if reading his mind, feeling the same hot desperation, she unbuckled his pants and lowered his zipper. Her warm hand closed around him, stroking the length of him. He yanked the hem of her dress up. She spread her thighs, giving him access that he capitalized on without a second of delay. He thrust his hips deeper, and she guided him home.

Everything melted away in the exquisite point of connection.

Their eyes locked on each other as the pleasure spread from the place where they were joined. It was then it struck him that they were still clothed except for the most intimate parts of their bodies.

He lifted her and in one fluid motion, turned and brought them down onto the bed.

Wild for her, he pressed his mouth to hers as he rocked into her, all his finesse evaporating. Her hands raced over him as she pumped her hips, driving him faster.

The need for release was fierce. All-consuming. Somewhere along the way, he lost his mind. Primitive instinct had taken over. His body was completely in charge. Nothing existed but Madeline, her sweet scent, the uncontrollable urge to plunge deeper, the ferocious need to satisfy the clawing hunger.

Madeline dug her nails into his back and clenched around him, coming undone beneath him.

With a guttural sound tearing from his lips, he quickly followed and the tension burst, setting him free.

BREATHLESS, MADELINE TRIED to recover as her skin rippled with the aftershocks of pleasure. Everything was a blur of heat and passion.

"Madeline." He rolled, bringing them onto their sides, and crushed her to him, pressing his damp face into the curve of her neck.

They stayed that way, chests heaving, clinging to each other until the haze cleared and reality dawned.

What on earth had she done?

Panic set in as she stilled.

All effort to maintain emotional distance had failed. Miserably. One minute they had been arguing. The next, he had touched her. Then they'd kissed, and desire had spread like a wildfire through tinder-dry brush.

That had been more than sex. A tangling of emotion with the physical. An assault of the senses that had stripped her bare. A release.

She hadn't thought, not for an instant. If she had, she

would have heard that little voice inside her head telling her that she was breaking all the rules. She had crossed a personal Rubicon and there was no going back.

With every second that passed, she sensed him withdrawing, the connection between them slipping further away as his arms fell from her body and he lay on his back.

All the warmth receded into a marked chill.

"I'm sorry," she choked out, her voice so small she wasn't sure if he'd heard her.

But she glanced at him. Saw the soul-deep sadness etched on his face.

Her throat tightened. "That was a mistake," she muttered, needing to be the first one to say it. She tugged her dress up over her breasts and rearranged the rest of the fabric down over her hips, covering her legs. "I shouldn't have—"

"It takes two. This was more my fault than yours."

Fault. Corroboration this had been a mistake. Her heart pinched. "I'm sorry," she said again. "This was wrong."

"I don't regret it, but…"

She waited on pins and needles for him to finish. He didn't.

There really wasn't anything to say. She had taken an inappropriate step, lost control without thinking about any of the repercussions.

Goodness, they hadn't even used a condom.

"You don't have to say anything," she said, her face growing hot from a different sort of heat. "I understand."

Jackson reached up, slipped his hand around the nape of her neck, bringing her closer, and kissed her softly. The stroke of his tongue into her mouth soothed the sting of his silence but didn't lessen her embarrassment.

"I do need to say it because you don't understand, Madeline. I barely understand it. You're everything I could want in a partner. Beautiful. Brilliant. Sexy. Independent. Full of guts."

But…that word and everything else he'd neglected to say echoed in her head. Loud and clear. He didn't need to explain his feelings or justify his actions. He was hurting, a parent stuck in one of the worst situations imaginable. While she was supposed to be the professional, his anchor getting him through this.

He looked into her eyes. "What happened between us wasn't wrong, but the timing *was*. I don't have the bandwidth to think about exploring a relationship. Not while Emma is missing. I feel guilty enough that I enjoyed myself with you just now."

Oh, God. That's what he thought. Jackson was fantastic when he wasn't infuriating her by going rogue. He was the kind of guy worth diving into a relationship with and taking a chance on to see if the fairy tale was possible, but she didn't want him to think that she was foolish enough to have any hope for something more between them.

The idea that he did set every internal rhythm haywire, had her heart and lungs battling for room inside her chest. "You needed comfort." Perhaps they both had. "That's all this was," she said, the words leaving her mouth in a rush. "A lovely distraction with no strings attached. No expectations. I promise."

He lifted up on his forearm and stared down at her. "So you took pity on me."

It would have been easier if the answer had been yes. "No. Adrenaline collided head-on with attraction." Electrifying attraction that neither of them could resist. "We slipped up. Gave in to a moment of weakness." One stupid, reckless moment. Nothing more.

"You're right. I couldn't stop myself from touching you." He brushed the back of his hand across her cheek and swallowed so hard it was audible. "Didn't want to because I needed you. I've never wanted anyone like that. I'm ashamed to admit that I still want you."

That made two of them. The ache deep inside her for him hadn't subsided either.

Madeline sat up. "I can call Nick or Dash and see if one of them is available to stay at the house with you tonight."

"I'd prefer if you didn't." The expression on his face turned heartbreaking. "But I'd hate for things between us to become awkward."

He was worried this would further cloud her judgment, that she might hold some grudge against him.

"It won't become awkward," she said, her voice confident despite the truth of how she felt. "We can be adults about this."

He took her hand in his. "Stay. In here tonight. I don't want you to leave. I know that must sound selfish."

Madeline drew in a deep, heavy breath filled with the scent of him that made her throb with a yearning for more than she ever would admit.

"It sounds honest." Honesty she respected, even when it hurt, but if she stayed, they'd have sex again, this time without their clothes on. Having this conversation all over again in the bitter light of day would be ten times worse. She needed to scrape together whatever dignity she had left and get out of his bed. "I'll stay. In the guest room. Things need to go back exactly as they were. Good night." She pulled her hand away and scrambled down the hall as quickly as possible.

She shut the door of the guest room, leaned against it and squeezed her eyes closed. She could smell him on her, that intoxicating fragrance printed on her skin.

Her heart was still fluttering in her chest, aching though it shouldn't. She cursed her reaction to him. Her stupidity for getting too close.

A nice hot shower—or rather a cold one—and a good night's sleep would clear her head. In the morning, she'd tackle the day fully focused and get back on track.

No more distractions.

Chapter Twelve

To set the right tone, Jackson made breakfast while Madeline was in the bathroom getting ready. If they could share a meal, then everything would be all right.

He wasn't delusional in thinking that things between them would return to *normal*. What did that even mean? None of this was normal for him.

But he had a connection with Madeline, something deep, electric. An undeniable attraction. Last night, they had both acknowledged it and had acted upon it. If things were different, his life *normal*, then he could open himself to the possibility of a relationship. A prospect that appealed to him more than he had first grasped. He'd had a sleepless night thinking about her, smelling her on his sheets. Wanting the warmth of her next to him. The sound of her voice to keep him from spiraling down the rabbit hole.

And hours to hate himself for that desire while Emma was missing.

His chest ached at the realization that without this tragic chaos, he never would have even met Madeline.

Stealthy as a cat, Madeline walked into the kitchen, her face an unreadable mask.

His throat closed at the sight of her. Beautiful. Sophisticated. Intelligent eyes.

"Good morning," he said, setting down two plates of scrambled eggs, bacon and toast on the eat-in island.

"I'm heading out. I have a location on Samantha Dickson."

Now he had two reasons to get her to break bread with him. "Really, where?"

She watched him with very cool, very suspicious eyes. "An abandoned warehouse."

No address mentioned. Right.

He picked up the coffeepot. "As I recall, you need a hot cup of joe in the morning." He poured some of the steaming brew in a mug. "The time it would take you to go through a drive-through, you could spend drinking the coffee that is readily available this second." A vital point for any caffeine junkie to factor into consideration. "And have a quick bite to eat since I cooked."

"Jackson—"

"Please, Madeline."

Drawing a deep breath, she crossed the room and sat. "Thank you." She sipped her coffee.

The politeness felt a little too formal and stiff, but he'd take it. "You're welcome." He sat beside her and began eating. "Dickson."

Before he could finish, she said, "No, you can't come."

"She's not on private property, is she? I believe you stated the warehouse is abandoned."

"It is."

"No danger of trespassing, then. What's the problem?"

"She may not talk if you're around."

"If I'm around, I guarantee she'll talk. The hothead won't be able to help herself. Samantha Dickson would never miss a chance to take a proverbial swing at me. In fact, get us in a room together without her seeing you. If she has Emma or is responsible in any way, she'll rub it in my face because she knows it'd burn deeper than the acid they threw on my car."

Setting down her fork, Madeline looked at him, her eyes narrowing. "That might actually work."

"I'm full of good ideas." He hadn't made it to CEO for no reason, and then he remembered his resignation and a vicious sting followed.

She quirked her brow. "We only do this on one condition."

Anything she wanted, he'd do so as not to be excluded and stay at the tip of the spear with the investigation. "Name it."

"You wear a wire."

THE FBI VAN sat down the road from the warehouse that Dickson was holed up in, hidden behind another deserted building off Pier 30. Madeline parked the government SUV beside it. She and Jackson got out and walked to the van in tense silence, the same way they had driven around all morning.

Madeline had gone to the office earlier with Jackson and discussed the plan with Nick and Dash. Her ability to remain objective where Jackson was concerned was questionable at best. Luckily, her teammates had both agreed the idea was worth a shot.

Opening the van door, she gestured for Jackson to enter. They climbed in.

Nick and Dash were seated in front of the surveillance equipment ready to go.

"Get him set up." Dash handed her a kit containing the wire and slipped on headphones.

"Where's the pen?" Madeline asked. "The one with the listening device hidden inside. I thought we were using that."

"My fault," Nick said. "I grabbed the van, thinking there was one inside. The regular wire will work fine. It's not as if he's about to walk into a mobster's den where he's going to get a pat down." He stared at her, his brows drawing together. "Is there a problem I'm missing?"

Yes. "Nope. No problem." She opened the kit. "Jackson, can you lift your shirt for me?"

He took off his leather jacket and raised the hem of his cashmere pullover, exposing the broad expanse of his bare chest, the contours so defined in the bright light of day, or rather the glow of the equipment, that his sun-kissed skin gleamed as if polished.

Her heart flipped over at the sight. Biting the inside of her lip, she pulled out the first electrode, peeled off the plastic backing and stuck it to his torso. His muscles tensed, his gaze shooting to hers while a deep stab sank into her chest.

They had sworn this wouldn't be awkward, but it was because the attraction was there, simmering beneath the surface, burning in the shared glances, smoldering when they touched. It was torture.

Hurrying with the second electrode, she pressed it to his skin, struggling not to linger. She turned on the listening device and handed it to him. "Clip it on the inside of your waistband." Once he did, she said, "Try it out."

"Testing, one, two, three. Testing," Jackson said low.

Dash gave a thumbs-up.

"You're good to go," she said. "If you run into trouble of any sort, or need us to come in, give us a sign."

Jackson put on his jacket. "What kind?"

"Say you need a cigarette. Wish you had a smoke. Something along those lines."

"Since I don't smoke, there won't be any confusion, is that it?" he asked.

Madeline nodded. "Exactly."

"Okay," he said.

The tone of his voice, the look in his eye, made her wonder. Was this another mistake? Samantha Dickson was their last solid suspect, and Jackson was desperate for progress with the case. He would push for answers, take things right to the edge. Maybe even over the line. Provided he saw the line to begin with.

"This isn't a challenge—you don't need to prove you can handle it on your own," she said. "You will let us know if you need help, won't you?"

Those blue eyes shimmered with steely resolve. "Of course."

Why didn't she believe him?

Jackson put a hand on her shoulder and gave her a look that screamed, *I've got this*. "We'll know if they have Emma." He climbed out of the van and headed for the warehouse.

"You didn't sound too sure about this a second ago," Nick said. "Can he handle this?"

"We're sending him in to push buttons and get them talking. I have no doubt he'll achieve the objective." And that's what concerned her.

JACKSON STRODE THROUGH the front door of the warehouse, determined not to leave until he knew for certain whether the Red Right Hand were behind Emma's kidnapping.

Their suspects were evaporating one by one, and he didn't know how much more of this he could take. The waiting. The worrying. Twisting in the wind, not knowing who had taken his daughter or why. Someone wanted to punish him, and they were doing a good job.

A door opened on his far left. A group of five, maybe six twentysomethings, was gathered inside, sitting on mattresses, talking. One man with a scraggly beard Jackson recognized as a member of the Red Right Hand walked out and spotted him. "What are you doing in here?" The guy strolled up to him and took a closer look, his eyes narrowing. "Hey, I know you."

"I'm Jackson Rhodes and I'm here to see Samantha Dickson."

The guy snickered. "It's your funeral." He passed some old pallets and started up a steel staircase. "This way."

The abandoned warehouse was ten thousand square feet of decrepit space spread over two floors. The main level looked as though it had once been used for storage. Dust and mold filled the air. Sunlight streamed in through broken windows. Why anyone with choices for better options would want to stay there was lost on him.

Once they reached the catwalk, the guy said, "Hang here." He knocked on the door of a former office, waited a second, then entered.

Before he closed it behind him, Jackson glimpsed the brown-haired Samantha canoodling with the red-haired Kane on a mattress in the center of the room.

When the door opened again, Samantha Dickson and Kane Tidwell strode out.

Samantha sported her perpetual wind-tousled look, face flushed, eyes narrowing, gearing up for a fight. "Well, if it isn't the Butcher of the American Dream in the flesh." She put her fists on her hips.

Kane stood beside her with his arms crossed over a wide, thick chest. He had a fleshy face and very small eyes. "You've got a pair of spuds on you. I'll give you that."

"Why do you stay here, living like squatters?" Jackson asked.

Samantha gave him a hateful smile. "As opposed to living in the biggest house, driving the most expensive car, burning electricity, wasting water, squandering resources and abusing Mother Earth until the future of the next generation is blacker than the oil extracted from her dying body?"

"It's not surprising that someone like you doesn't understand," Kane said. "Someone who doesn't care about his carbon footprint, global warming, fairness and equality, supporting Americans by keeping jobs in America or basic decency like giving a little bit of those profits to charitable institutions."

"I sent those jobs overseas and *temporarily* stopped charitable donations to save ETC. A lot more people would've lost their jobs if not for my actions."

"As if that absolves you," Kane said. "Who the hell do you think you are?"

"He's someone who still hasn't learned his lesson," she said. Anger suited her. Samantha's face glowed as she stalked closer.

"You think the Red Right Hand is capable of teaching it to me?" Jackson asked.

Samantha's smile spread. "No job. No fancy project. No kid. But I think you still have plenty left to lose. And once you hurt enough, your eyes will open. We're the perfect group to give you an awakening."

"Get the others," Kane said to his pal. "Trash his car. Make sure he has to walk home."

Mr. Scraggly Beard hustled past them across the catwalk and hurried down the steps.

"That's if we let him leave," Samantha said.

"You want to make me disappear like you did with my daughter?" Jackson asked, his temperature rising.

Confusion clouded Samantha's eyes.

But Kane didn't so much as blink.

The rest of their gang ran outside carrying pipes and pieces of wood.

They were in for a surprise.

"Our mission in life," Kane said, "is to make sure that people like you get exactly what you deserve. Balance the scales of justice."

"You call snatching my child justice?" Jackson demanded. "I call it reprehensible. Evil."

Kane stepped closer, putting them within arm's reach. "You don't deserve to have a child." He poked Jackson's chest. "Raising a mini you to help destroy the world and pick its bones clean."

"You shouldn't have put your hands on me," Jackson said, making it clear to those listening in the van that what happened next wasn't his fault.

He snatched the man's wrist and twisted his arm hard. Pressing his free hand into Kane's back, Jackson pushed the man's torso until it was parallel to the ground while wrenching his captured arm up. The pressure on the twerked shoulder was enough to elicit a shriek from Kane.

The others ran back into the warehouse at the same time. "There's no car out front." They gasped and made a beeline for the stairs.

"Get off him!" Samantha said. "Let him go." She pounded her fists on Jackson's back.

"Where's my daughter?" Jackson shoved down harder on Kane, making him scream in pain. "Let her go and I let him go."

"We don't have your stupid kid!" Samantha said. "We're not like you. We don't take advantage of the innocent."

"What do you say?" Jackson asked Kane. "Huh? Did you have anything to do with her kidnapping?"

Scraggly Beard and the others stormed down the catwalk toward them, holding up their pipes and hunks of wood.

"No!" Kane said.

"Sure?" Jackson pressed down.

"I swear!" Kane said. "We don't kidnap children. Not even the spawn of monsters."

Jackson believed them. He would've let Kane go, would've yelled for a cigarette, but it was too late, and everything unraveled too fast.

Scraggly Beard swung the pipe. So Jackson swung Kane, lowering the seized wrist and forcing Kane's body up to take the blow.

Metal connected with bone. Blood sprayed through the air from Kane's mouth.

Horror widened Scraggly Beard's eyes at his mistake. Samantha gave a spine-chilling scream.

The others stormed forward, brandishing their weapons.

Since letting go would be to his own detriment, Jackson held on to Kane, making sure he took more hits than Jackson received.

"FBI!" Nick said, racing in through the door.

"Stop!" Madeline's voice came next. "Put your hands in the air!"

Once again, too late.

A pipe slammed into Jackson's ribs and pain exploded through his side. The force of the blow knocked him back against the railing. Momentum carried him over the side of the catwalk. And still he held on to Kane, taking the man with him.

Chapter Thirteen

Two ambulances and four squad cars were on the scene. The entire Red Right Hand was already wanted for crimes committed last night: vandalism, for spray-painting graffiti on the AlbrechTech building, and destruction of property, for smashing the windows of Chuck's car. Now a couple of them would also face assault charges.

Kane Tidwell was loaded in an ambulance.

"Please let me go to the hospital with him," Samantha begged as she was handcuffed and put into the back of a police cruiser.

Madeline stepped into the back of the other ambulance, where Jackson lay on a gurney. She was grateful he was conscious and had the strength to argue with the EMT.

"I'm fine," Jackson said. "Kane broke my fall. Going to the hospital isn't necessary."

"Definitely a couple of broken ribs and a possible concussion," the EMT said.

Sheer panic had flooded her when Jackson fell from the catwalk. It had happened in slow motion. She hadn't been able to breathe, move; it had been as if her heart had stopped.

The funny thing was, when he opened his eyes and spoke, she had one overwhelming thought. *Thank God I didn't lose him.*

She'd had to remind herself that he wasn't hers. Once this case was over, they'd go their separate ways.

Still, Madeline found herself taking his hand before she realized she'd broken her rule and was touching him, and by then she didn't want to let go of him. "You're going to the hospital."

"I need to be out there, looking for Emma. I have to find her." His face filled with so much despair that Madeline's heart broke. "If the Red Right Hand didn't take her, then who did?"

Since she had no answer to give him, she frowned down at their joined hands. The need to find out who was behind this and save Emma was like a fire burning in her gut, spurring her on. Not to give up. Never.

She'd exhaust every possibility, chase down each lead. But she'd never stop trying.

Her phone rang. She pulled her hand from his and answered. "Yeah, Striker."

"It's Liam. I was going to update the file, but thought it was better to tell you."

"One sec." She glanced at the EMT. "Could you give us a minute, before you take him to the hospital?" After the woman nodded and hopped out, Madeline waved Dash and Nick over and put the call on speaker. "Go ahead, Liam. I have the others here along with Jackson."

"Some of the newspapers go back three years," Liam said.

"Three?" Madeline asked. "Are you sure?"

"Positive. I was only able to find two articles that were related to ETC and one also mentioned Jackson."

"What were they about?" Dash asked.

"One was about the video game department and the other was an obituary for a former ETC employee. The article talked about Jackson cutting the division and a big sale of the games."

"Did you have a bunch of angry engineers and designers?" Nick asked.

Jackson shook his head. "The one department at ETC that shouldn't have a grievance with me was Games. I made all of them rich. Except for one guy. Lou Jenkins. He received the smallest severance package, but it was still generous. I heard he rebounded and is thriving at a new company. This has to be a coincidence."

"Maybe," Madeline said. "But you do this job long enough and you stop believing in coincidences. You weren't really involved with the day to day of the video games department, were you?" she asked, thinking there might have been things going on in the office that he hadn't been aware of.

"I wasn't in the trenches with my people," Jackson said, "but I tried to keep my finger on the pulse of things. I have, had, an open-door policy."

"Who was the head of the video games department?" Madeline asked.

"Dennis Garcia," Jackson said. "A good guy. Retired now. I've had him to the house for dinner once or twice."

"What about the obit, Liam?" Madeline asked. "Who was it for?"

"Theon Lasiter, but it doesn't say what department he worked in."

Jackson sat up and winced. "You're right. It's not coincidence. Theon worked for me, in Games. But I don't understand how it could be related to Emma's kidnapping."

"How did Theon Lasiter die?" Dash asked.

Jackson shrugged. "I didn't even know he was dead. He walked away from ETC with the biggest check of all."

"There's a correlation with the games department," Madeline said. "We just have to find it. I should sit down with Garcia and talk with him. See what we're missing."

"I'll track down Lou Jenkins," Nick said.

Dash tilted his head, like he was thinking. "I'll go back to the office and see what I can find on Lasiter's death. Liam, keep plugging away at the articles."

"Where does Garcia live?" Madeline asked Jackson, wondering how long the drive would be.

"I can get you the address from HR." He reached into his pocket to take out his phone and groaned in pain. "I believe his house is in Olympic Manor."

Probably a thirty-minute drive, depending on traffic. "I'll pay him a visit. Talk to him in person," Madeline said. "No stone left unturned. And you are going to the hospital."

Madeline's estimation had been correct. After Jackson got her the address, it took her twenty-eight minutes before she parked in front of the Tudor-style house in Olympic Manor and made her way up the front steps. She knocked and waited.

The door opened. A man stood slightly taller than her on the other side of the threshold. With a round face and kind eyes, he smiled. "Hello."

She held up her badge. "I'm Special Agent Madeline Striker. Are you Dennis Garcia, the former chief of the gaming department at Emerald Technology Corp?"

"Yes, I am. What can I do for you?"

"I'd like to ask you some questions that might help us with the kidnapping of Emma Rhodes, the six-year-old daughter of Jackson Rhodes."

He rocked back. "I heard about that, but I don't understand how I can be of any help."

"Do you mind if I come in?" Madeline asked.

"Certainly." He opened the door wide, letting her in. "Would you care for something to drink?"

"A glass of water, please," she said, her throat parched.

"We can speak in the kitchen, if that's all right."

They walked through the tidy home, passing the living room, dining room, and Madeline sat at the small bistro-style table by the window.

Garcia handed her a bottle of water from the fridge and grabbed a can of soda for himself.

She opened the bottle and chugged some of the cool water. "I'm going to record this conversation, if you don't mind."

"Not at all. Go ahead."

She took the recorder from her pocket and set it on the table. "How would you describe the layoff of the games department at ETC?"

"In a word, profitable."

"Did you agree with Jackson Rhodes's decision to sell off the games and dismantle your department?"

Garcia opened his Coke. "Didn't matter if I agreed. I understood why it had to happen. Made complete sense. Allowed me to pay for this house in cash and have a comfortable retirement."

"But it wasn't profitable for everyone, was it? What about Lou Jenkins? Was he angry when he didn't receive a big fat check?"

Garcia chuckled. "Lou was grateful he walked away with as much as he did. He was at the bottom of the pack and knew it. Got a new position at another company. As an animator. I see him from time to time. He's much happier. Doing really well for himself."

"Do you recall another employee who worked under you—Theon Lasiter?"

His eyebrows shot up. "How could I ever forget?"

"Can you tell me about him?"

"Theon was special. Gifted, I mean. Singular in his vision. It took him a while to find his niche when he first started working at ETC. None of the games he developed had really taken off. But he had an interesting background that I thought he could use as inspiration for a game."

"Interesting in what way?"

"He grew up in a survivalist community. Real hard-core. Almost cultlike if you ask me."

"You mean like preppers?" Madeline asked.

Garcia chuckled. "I once foolishly thought they were the same thing, too, until Theon schooled me. There are some significant differences. Preppers and survivalists both plan and prepare for that doomsday scenario. A megadisaster. But how they prepare is where they diverge. One group is focused on stockpiling and the other on developing a finely honed skill set."

"So I take it, the preppers are the ones loading up their shelves with canned goods, water, powdered milk, that sort of thing."

Nodding, Garcia opened his soda. "That's about right."

"What type of skill set does the survivalist cultivate?"

"Instead of stockpiling massive amounts like preppers, survivalists become experts at fishing, snaring, foraging, hunting. They're the ones with the guns, make no mistake about that."

She couldn't help but think about the fire on Jackson's lawn. How tree resin was the secret weapon for surviving in the wilderness. "Survivalists are focused on building up an arsenal?"

"No, no. They like to stay light on their feet." Garcia sipped his soda. "They'll have a couple of guns in a bug-out bag and will train to be crack shots, but they'll have knives, too. Think of it like this, you and I have GEICO—they have body armor. Instead of building a garden, they're creating booby traps, making homemade bombs, that sort of thing. Defense and offense are key to survivalists. Not stockpiling."

A homemade bomb had been used to blow up the Duwamish site. Forensics confirmed tree resin had been the accelerant. The same compound used in the fire on Jackson's front lawn.

"Where was the survivalist group based that Theon grew up in?"

"Loon Lake. On the east side of the state. Four or five hours from here."

Madeline logged the place, updating the shared document, though it seemed too far away for the kidnapper. Seemed more likely that Emma's abductor was within an easy drive of Jackson.

"Tell me about the game he created," she said.

"It's called Survivalist Zone. Apocalypse scenario. Players build a zone, establish a home, and then they have to protect it. Sometimes a player will need to attack another player's position to claim vital resources. The game was an instant hit. But it still had a lot of untapped potential. Theon wanted to make the next version more elaborate and complicated. Jackson was still overseeing the department at the time and supported Theon when the kid wanted to create a real-life mock-up, complete with booby traps and everything. ETC had some land that they weren't using and gave him the green light. His older sister even came out to help him make it as realistic as possible. She never even asked for any name recognition or credit."

"Sister?" A shiver raced down her spine. "What was her name?"

"Chloe. Chloe Lasiter."

Madeline sent a red alert to the team with the name. She wanted Dash digging into the sister as soon as possible.

"She was devoted to Theon," Garcia said. "When the

video game was sold and our department was cut, I think she was as devastated as her brother."

"If the game was successful, why was it sold?"

"That's the *reason* it was sold. Because it was successful."

"I'm not tracking the logic," Madeline said. "Why sell a game that's making a solid profit?"

"Theon's game was computer based. Had a strong cult following. Wildly popular. It's an open world and users contribute content, making the game grow. Generated revenue and profits. Brought in millions. Double digits. But Jackson sold it to a company who already had a foothold with video game consoles. The other company could expand the game to their consoles and their dedicated app store. And make an even bigger profit."

"How much did the intellectual property sell for?"

"Two. Point. Five. Billion."

Madeline reeled back. "Goodness."

"Brilliant move on Jackson's part." Garcia nodded with a look of awe twinkling in his eyes. "He did the same with the other moneymaking video games in the department. It was simply more profitable for ETC to sell. But Survivalist Zone was by far the biggest. Theon and the others walked away millionaires. Like me."

"Then what was the problem?" Madeline asked. It sounded as if the entire department should've been kicking up their heels and moving on to greener pastures. "Why wasn't Theon happy about the sale even if it meant the loss of his own department?"

"The problem was Theon didn't care about the money. He wanted to remain affiliated with the game and future developments. But the buyer said no. They wanted to take the game in their own direction. Theon was crushed. He had poured his heart and soul into that game. Had spent so much time and energy working on it that his wife divorced him when it was in the beta stage. All he had left was that game. It was his baby. His brainchild," he said, putting pieces of the puzzle together for Madeline. "And when what he cared about most was taken from him, he lost it. Cracked. Spiraled into a dark depression. Then I heard he killed himself. So sad. He left Chloe all his money. Fifteen million."

She let out a low sound of surprise.

"Sounds like a lot. To most people it is, more than they'd see in a lifetime. But when you think about it, fifteen mil was only one percent of the profit Jackson and ETC made from the sale. Not that the cash mattered to survivalists like Theon and Chloe. I saw her at the funeral. She was heartbroken. She blamed ETC for his death. Blamed Jackson."

Chloe Lasiter was behind this. Madeline knew it deep in her heart. "Can you describe what Chloe looks like?" Madeline asked, urgency propelling her.

Garcia shrugged. "She's about thirty, maybe thirty-two by now. Fair skinned. Long chestnut brown hair. Hazel eyes like Theon. On the slim side but not petite. She was athletic and on the taller side."

The description didn't match any of their suspects. But it fit the profile for the unsub and gave a strong personal motive to target Jackson that was tied directly to ETC business.

"Those two put so much into the development of that game," Garcia said again, his eyes looking haunted. "You know ETC still has the site where they built their real-world mock-up. The company never tore it down. Probably forgot about it."

"Where is it? I'd like to check it out for myself." Walking around the site and seeing what Theon had created with his sister might be the best way for Madeline to get inside

Chloe's head. Understand what she was truly capable of and how far she might be willing to go for revenge.

Garcia wrote down the location for her since it was more a set of directions than an actual address.

"Going out there will shed light on what inspired the game. Reflects the darkness that was in their heads, much more than the video game would. Though that Survivalist Zone can get pretty dark with people stealing resources and killing each other. It's a bit of a drive, about an hour outside of the city up in the mountains. But once you see the site, it'll have you praying that you never come up against a survivalist."

AN ELECTRIC HUM from Dash's computer system purred in the air just beneath the clatter of his frantic typing on the keyboard. Since he'd gotten Madeline's alert, Dash had been parked behind his desk at BAU headquarters, feverishly trying to dig up whatever he could on Chloe Lasiter, including a picture.

It was like she was a ghost. No social media presence. No property records. No utility bills.

Maybe her brother had been more active and had left a digital footprint.

Dash redirected his search to Theon Lasiter. Once again, no Facebook, no Instagram, no Snapchat. No old property records either.

But all serious gamers were on Twitch—a livestreaming platform tailored for that crowd—and Discord, which was a means for people to easily communicate while playing PC games together.

Already his fingers were darting across the keys. The screens shuddered and flickered as he typed faster.

Sure enough, Theon and Chloe had profiles on both sites. No pictures. Only avatars.

Dash glanced at his second monitor, which showed the results of the search on Theon. There was a magazine article featuring Theon as the Game Awards winner for Content Creator of the Year three years ago. Clicking on the link, he scrolled through the article that touted Theon as someone to watch over the next decade. Theon had been quoted stating he was thrilled his sister had finally moved to Seattle and they were about to close on a house they'd bought together.

That meant there was a property in one or both their names. Maybe under an LLC—limited liability company—for privacy since he had been gaining a bit of fame in the industry.

Scrolling a little further, Dash came to a picture of Theon holding the Game Award up in one hand, his arm slung over the shoulder of a young woman, with their temples pressed together. The caption listed the smiling brunette as Chloe Lasiter.

She looked so familiar, but he couldn't place her. Was it the hair?

Dash zoomed in, two clicks, and his heart slammed against his rib cage as he stared at the picture.

"Holy hell."

He knew exactly who that was. Without a doubt. He'd done a background check on her personally, and hadn't found any red flags under the alias she'd used. How was that possible?

Reaching for the phone to call Madeline, he reconsidered. Before Dash called her, he needed to get Liam to help him do a deep dive and cull as much useful information on this woman as they could to find the Rhodes kid fast. Madeline was going to have a ton of questions for him, and he had better be prepared with answers.

Dialing Liam to save himself the time of running down the hall, he glanced back at the woman's face on his screen.

At the kidnapper.

Liane Strothe.

Chapter Fourteen

Jackson answered his phone, relieved it was a call from Madeline and not another text message designed to torture him.

"Are you okay?" Madeline asked.

Shifting in the seat in the back of his Uber, he stifled a groan. "Yeah. I'm fine. No concussion. Only a couple of broken ribs."

"Only? You're lucky a lung wasn't punctured in the fight."

"Tidwell looks worse." That was the truth.

"Are they holding you the night for observation?"

"They checked me out and an Uber is dropping me off at home as we speak." His Uber parked in front of his house instead of in the driveway.

"The doctor checked you out," Madeline said, "or did you take it upon yourself to simply leave?"

"Same difference." Jackson tipped the driver from the app on his phone and got out beside his mailbox. It had been a few days since he had last checked it. The thought hadn't even occurred to him with everything else going on. He opened the mailbox and grabbed the bundle of envelopes inside. "Did you turn up anything with Dennis?"

Walking up the drive, he sifted through the junk mail.

"Actually, I think I did," Madeline said. "I believe this might all be centered around Theon Lasiter and his suicide."

Jackson staggered to a halt. "Theon killed himself?" He was a bright kid, talented. A real wunderkind who had loads of potential. It was such a shame. "You know his re-vamped version of Survivalist Zone was an overnight success. Thanks to him, we made a large enough profit from the sale of his game that I was able to…" His stomach turned to ice. He hadn't seen it before, but the link solidified clearly for him.

"What were you going say?"

"I was able to fund my pet project at Duwamish. Moving forward on the stealth technology wouldn't have been possible without that sale." The ice spread up into his chest.

"My gut was right. This is about Theon."

This still didn't add up. Something else was missing. "But Theon is dead. So who took Emma?"

"I believe it was his sister, Chloe. Did you ever meet her?"

Jackson stepped onto his porch. "No. I almost did once. She attended the Game Awards with him. I was supposed to go to show my support, but Emma had a fever that night. I stayed home with her."

"Theon's sister worked with him on Survivalist Zone," Madeline said. "She helped him create the real-world mock-up to make the video game more intense and realistic. I'm headed out there now to take a look. I think seeing the place might give me better insight into who Chloe is and how her mind works since she helped her brother design it."

"Why don't you swing by here and we can go together?" Jackson suggested. He knew the lay of the land, more or less, and could show her around while making sure she didn't get hurt.

"You should rest. Besides, I've already passed Madison Park. I'm about to get off the 520 and hit the 405."

No one should go out there alone. Jackson had been to the site when construction had first started and once it had been completed. Theon had let his imagination run wild with the concept, and the end result was somewhat terrifying. Apparently, his sister had helped.

Two dark minds were better than one.

"Be careful," Jackson said. "You could get a flat tire on the road alone leading into the site. Pretty rocky terrain from what I recall and the place itself is quite dangerous. We put a fence up around the three-acre property to keep hikers from wandering in, getting injured and filing a lawsuit. You'll need a code to access it. Come and pick me up and I'll give it to you."

"There's no sense wasting time doubling back. What's the code?" The firm tone in Madeline's voice made clear that she would brook no argument.

He sighed with resignation. "If Andrew never changed it, and I doubt that he'd take enough interest to bother, then it should be 75688."

Madeline's line beeped. "Jackson, I've got another call. From Dash. Might be an update with information on Chloe. Listen, try to get some rest. Once I know something concrete, I'll call or come by."

"Stay safe." He hung up.

Closing the door behind him, he dropped the mail onto the foyer table. A flyer slipped to the floor. At the top of the pile on the table was an envelope with his name spelled out in letters meticulously cut from newspapers and magazines.

Jackson ripped open the envelope and pulled out a note. The message, created with the same type of letters from periodicals, was another sucker punch to his soul.

Get rid of the FBI. No police.

Then I will tell you where to meet. Alone. Midnight.

Do it if you ever want to see your daughter again.

MADELINE DISCONNECTED THE call with Jackson and clicked over to the other line on Bluetooth. "Please tell me you found something."

"I hit pay dirt," Dash said. "Chloe Lasiter is Liane Strothe."

Madeline's heart stuttered. *Oh, my God.* "The nanny?" They'd had her and let her go.

"Yep. I'm sending you a picture now of Theon and Chloe together."

Her phone buzzed. She tapped the message, bringing up the photo and zoomed in. Sure enough. Chloe had long, dark hair just as Dennis Garcia had described and didn't wear glasses, but the eyes, the nose, everything else was the same. *Liane.*

Madeline shook her head, but the shock didn't dampen. How had she not connected the dots and realized? Chloe… Liane had been right in front of her.

"She's been with Jackson and Emma for almost two years," Madeline said. Two years of scheming and planning, getting to know Jackson and what made him tick, to figure out the nastiest way possible to hurt him.

Jackson had told Madeline that his worst nightmare had been to lose Emma in plain sight. In front of him. Rather than easily snatching the girl at any time, Liane had strategized how to make that nightmare a reality that had left Jackson swamped with guilt.

"A long time, I know," Dash said. "Turns out that Chloe Lasiter bought the nanny agency that Jackson used. I spoke with the placement coordinator. She claims she's never met Lasiter in person, but that Chloe was the one who hired

Liane. Guess when? One week before Jackson's previous nanny had a car accident that forced her to quit."

She hired her own alter ego, then took out the caregiver in order to replace her. That was creepy.

The degree of deception Liane had gotten away with was staggering. It unnerved Madeline, chilling her to the marrow. The commitment. The patience. The high level of manipulation and organization. Liane was a psychopath. Calculating and carefully plotting each move, using focused aggression in a planned-out manner to get what she wanted.

No wonder Liane had been a mile ahead of them. She'd had two years to devise every step.

"But she had an alibi." Madeline thought about all the ways she'd been diverted from looking deeper into the woman as a suspect. "You saw it yourself. She was at the movie theater for three and half hours."

"We watched the footage again. During the playback we saw how she did it. After she hit the concession stand and entered the theater, she changed her top. Actually she put on a black hoodie and removed her wig and glasses. It must've been hidden in the backpack. We caught it this time because of her shoes. The same Converse sneakers. When we zoomed in, it was her. Not only that, but there's also more. Once I confirmed it was her, I checked the cinema's parking lot footage. She drove the black Ford Transit to the movies. That means—"

"Emma had been in the back of the van at the time."

"Liane parked at the far end of the lot away from any other cars," Dash said. "If the kid had been in there, tied up and gagged, no one would've heard her."

Madeline's stomach churned into a knot. "The last text Jackson received from her came through while she was sitting across from me in the interview room. How did she pull that off?"

"She must have used a timed app to send the message. Deliberately synced it to happen while she was at the office to throw us again," he said. "And you're not going to believe this. The name Liane Strothe is an anagram for Theon Lasiter. It's almost as if she wanted Jackson to figure it out. She's been right in front of us the whole time. We just didn't have all the pieces to see it."

Questions cascaded through Madeline's head in a deluge. "What about the background check you ran on her?"

"Looks like she must've paid a pretty penny for the extensive identity she had created. It was professional. Done by the best of the best. Detailed to look and feel real. The data trail went all the way to childhood medical records."

An identity invented and two years invested to get back at Jackson. The knot in her stomach tightened. This whole time they had been playing the wrong game. They didn't even know who the hell Chloe Lasiter was.

But Madeline was going to find out.

"We got an address for Lasiter. Purchased under an LLC Theon had formed with her for privacy," Dash said. "She owns a house on the north side of town. Near Sand Point." He rattled off the address. "Isolated area located far from any other homes. It's likely she's holding the girl in her garage or basement. Nick and I are headed there now with the police to search the place."

That would be easier said than done.

"If you're still in Olympic Manor, you've got time to meet us for the raid."

"I'm not." She was on the opposite side of Lake Washington. "Listen, Chloe Lasiter has been the epitome of careful, organized. You guys need to take extra precautions. The woman is an expert at bomb making and booby traps. She won't just let you waltz in and take Emma. She'll defend the house."

"Lasiter never thought we'd figure out her real identity. That's what she considers to be her safe house. Still, we're playing it by the book. Nick coordinated with the bomb unit and SWAT. We're all en route together. Every precaution that can be taken is. Seriously, don't…worry…the kid…be there," he said, breaking up. "…got this…covered."

If he was right and they took Liane by surprise, things could still go wrong. Getting caught wasn't part of her plan and she certainly wasn't finished with Jackson. No telling what else she had in store for him, and there weren't going to be any exceptions regarding the target of her vengeance. Liane had gotten a taste of power, enjoyed the sweetness of her revenge and wasn't ready to give that up. Being forced to deviate from her plan would make her panic.

Panic was a potent thing. Highly volatile like tree resin. It had the power to change a person. Robbed them of rational thought. Thus far, Liane hadn't killed anyone, but Madeline knew all too well that panic could turn a person into a murderer. All that was needed was the equivalent of a lit match.

Madeline clenched the steering wheel, her palms growing sweaty. "How far out are you?" she asked.

"We'll be…in fifteen minutes."

Madeline factored the time it would take her to turn around and drive clear across town to meet them. Forty minutes at best. "I'm almost at the Survivalist Zone site," she said, slowing down on the rocky road. "Be there in ten minutes." That was her best guess off the time estimate Dennis had given her since there was no address to load in the GPS. "I still want to check it out." No point in wasting the drive. "Call me as soon as you search the place and let me know what you find, one way or the other."

"Hello? Hello? Madeline, I…can't—"

The signal cut out.

Great. She checked her phone. No bars. She looked around beyond the trees to the hills and mountains of the valley she was in. The terrain must be interfering with the cell phone signal.

She passed an ETC sign warning against trespassers and to only enter the area at your own risk.

A QUARTER OF a mile from the Lasiter house, Nick stopped the vehicle, and everyone else pulled over behind him. It took two minutes to huddle up. The best route of approach was through the woods where the suspect wouldn't see them coming. She lived off the beaten path with the closest neighbor half a mile down the road.

"The suspect should be considered armed and dangerous," Nick said to the team of law enforcement assembled. "She's proficient in homemade explosives and setting booby traps. SWAT will check the rear entrance, which is the target ingress point, for any explosive devices. If they find something, the bomb squad will take care of it. Once inside, we need to move quickly but cautiously. Sharp eyes as you clear rooms because we don't know if there might be any nasty surprises waiting for us. Remember, the suspect is holding a six-year-old girl captive in a room with no windows, a garage or a basement. Our number-one goal is to get the hostage out unharmed."

They needed to bring this case to a close. The right way. No shots fired and no casualties was preferred.

Everyone acknowledged the directives.

Nick's adrenaline surged as he drew his service weapon and gave the signal for the team to move out.

They crept through the woods, silent and alert. It was a good thing there were no neighbors in the vicinity. One less thing to contend with. One less factor to cause a complication that could affect the outcome.

Once they made it to the edge of the wood line, Nick whispered into comms, "Hold. Everyone hold."

The house was a two-bedroom ranch style. Fifteen hundred square feet. Drawn curtains covered the windows, blocking a view of the interior.

Nick watched for a minute while he slipped a tactical light on the rail of his Glock. No sign of movement inside, no shadows, no lights, no rustling of the curtains. Then he gave the hand signal for SWAT to advance.

The four-man team hustled up to the rear door, taking their positions. Using their equipment and a tactical under-door camera, two men checked the entrance for explosives. Everyone else waited, tense and watchful. A quick thumbs-up indicated it was all clear. This was it. The other two guys swung forward with a battering ram.

There was nothing for Nick to do besides prepare to enter, steadying his nerves, which were the byproduct of adrenaline. Being wired and impatient served nobody. He smoothed out emotions like ice under a Zamboni and then he was ready to rock and roll.

The ones holding the battering ram had an internal count bred from practice—fast, efficient, fluid. On the third swing they breached the door.

Boom! The force brought the door down, tearing it from its hinges.

Nick and Dash were already on the move. They swept inside the house, going in a different direction from SWAT.

The interior was dimly lit with no natural light filtering in. Nick switched on the flashlight he had attached to his weapon. Dash did the same.

The garage was on the west side of the house, where Nick and Dash were headed.

Over comms, the others reported in as they cleared rooms. No kid. No Chloe. Nothing.

At the garage door, Nick and Dash positioned themselves on either side of the frame with their backs to the wall. Any potential explosive devices were more likely to have been placed at an exterior door or window. They exchanged a glance and Nick nodded, giving the go-ahead.

Dash tried the doorknob. It would be quieter and easier if it was unlocked. The knob turned. He swung the door open and pulled back in case of any incoming gunfire.

With his gun at the ready, Nick was the first through the door. Dash followed in.

The garage was empty, and the walls were bare. There were no signs that anyone had been held hostage.

Reporting in over the radio, Nick moved back toward the center of the house.

One of the SWAT guys came up to him in the kitchen. "No basement and no attic. But we found something you'll want to see."

Nick followed him into the living room.

One half of the main wall was covered in newspaper articles. Nick swept his flashlight over the headlines and read them. Some Liam had found and discussed. Others were about the success of the Survivalist Zone video game, Theon Lasiter winning an award, Jackson selling the games and cutting the department to make billions in profit. Theon Lasiter's suicide. Jackson braving a new frontier for ETC.

Nick and Dash shared a look, then they moved down to the other side of the wall.

A picture of Jackson Rhodes with a red *X* drawn over his face was front and center at the middle of a web. Chloe had drawn lines to the connections. The nanny agency. The Duwamish site. Emma Rhodes. Maybe *web* wasn't the right word. It was a labyrinth of pain and misery that she had plotted out. All of it led to one final piece. The Survivalist Zone site—the image looked exactly like the cover of the video game.

"That's where she's holding Emma," Dash said.

"Maybe that's her endgame, where she wants to finish it. So that Jackson will know why. I mean, none of this means anything unless Jackson understands what he did wrong in her mind and why he's being punished."

"Then why hasn't she lured him out there already?" Dash asked.

Nick shrugged, thinking it through. "She hasn't had the chance. Madeline has been with him the entire time. Chloe needs him alone and unmonitored."

Dash looked at him, his eyes widening with concern. "But Madeline is on her way out there now."

Someone flicked on the light switch.

There was a popping sound. Then electricity hissed and crackled. The smell of pine and burning wires permeated the air.

"Move! It's rigged!" someone else yelled. "Go! Go!"

Nick and Dash bolted for the back door. But SWAT jumped through windows. Their exit was faster, smarter. Nick cut to the right, heading for the closest window. Raising his arm to shield his face, he dived through the pane of glass and rolled onto the grass. Dash leaped through next, landing beside him, just as the bomb went off.

Chapter Fifteen

Madeline stopped at the locked gate to the Survivalist Zone mock-up. In between the six-foot-high bars, she saw a cabin. One story with a chimney. Looked like any other cozy cabin. Part of her expected to see some kind of obstacle course, but according to Dennis Garcia the point was that intruders weren't meant to see the defenses.

She punched in the code Jackson had given her and it worked.

Pushing the gate open, she looked around at the lush evergreens, listened to the wind whispering through the soft needles. The forest was serene.

She drove through, leaving the gate open, and parked a few feet from the cabin.

At the small porch, she checked for hidden traps before stepping up on it. The doorknob twisted, and she pushed the door in, staying outside in case something had been triggered.

But there was nothing. She entered, one step at a time, looking and listening as she went.

With a quick glance around the open space, Madeline determined that no one was inside, though someone had been. The unmade cast-iron bed had been occupied recently. She put her hand to the side of a thermos on the table. It was warm.

Pushing her jacket behind the holster on her hip, she put her hand on her weapon.

The cabin had windows with no curtains, which let in plenty of natural light. The floor and walls were wood. Bare, not plastered with newspaper. Except for one.

Madeline crossed the room. On the wall, near the top, was a picture of Theon, smiling, holding a copy of his video game in one hand and in the other an award—a statuette that resembled the *Winged Victory of Samothrace* but with a head. Below the photo was a list of actions Jackson had taken that led to the obituary of Theon Lasiter. Madeline glanced over at a metal chair that was bolted to the floor and faced the wall.

Was the chair meant for Jackson?

Maybe Chloe wanted to draw Jackson here, intended to put him on trial, have him face the evidence of what she considered his crime to be.

If Chloe was out here and not at Sand Point, then where was Emma? The large open space of the cabin didn't resemble the room from the picture that Emma had been in.

Madeline's gaze fell and she noticed the twin-size bed was in a weird spot in relation to everything else in the room. As though it should have been pushed against the wall, but instead it was in the middle of the room. She stepped back and lowered to one knee.

One of the legs on the bed was positioned over a door in the floor. Madeline got up and shoved the bed to the side. She tugged on the door handle.

The hatch door lifted, revealing a hanging rope ladder that led to a lit room belowground.

Madeline climbed down, one hand on the ladder and the other planted on the grip of her gun. Halfway on her descent, she turned and came eye to eye with Emma.

A wave of relief swept over Madeline. She'd found her.

The little girl looked so much like Jackson. She was sitting on a bed that had a gray wool blanket, playing with a doll. Her glassy brown eyes flared wide as she pulled her legs up to her chest and drew back against the wall.

"You don't need to be afraid of me, Emma. My name is Madeline," she said, jumping off the ladder and looking the child over. Her face was clean, her hair brushed. Remnants of a sandwich, a bottle of water and a Hershey's bar wrapper were on a small table nearby. "I'm an agent with the FBI. It's like the police. I'm also a friend of your dad. I'm here to help you. To bring you home."

Madeline glanced around the bunker. The floor was concrete, as were the walls. Without the newspaper to hide the fact that the walls were made of bare concrete, it would've been easy to tell that Emma was being kept in a cellar. Or a bunker.

Emma leaped off the bed and ran to Madeline, dropping the doll at her feet. "Where's my daddy?" The girl's voice shook. "I want to go home."

Madeline gathered Emma into a tight hug. "Your dad is waiting for you. He misses you so much."

The girl squeezed back, and an unfamiliar warmth flooded Madeline.

She wasn't used to this struggle to balance her emotions with her job. As though the two had to remain separate in the same manner she held herself apart from everyone. Never allowed herself to get close, to become attached. Until Jackson. For so long she believed cutting herself off was the only way to protect herself when she had only been cheating herself.

Maybe she was strong enough to dedicate herself to a purpose and have a life.

Pulling back from the hug, Madeline took out her phone

and thumbed a quick message to Jackson so he'd know Emma was all right.

The message failed to send. No reception, she reminded herself.

Emma tugged on Madeline's jacket. "She'll be back soon," the girl whispered.

"How do you know?"

"She told me that someone was here. To stay quiet while she took a look and that if I didn't, she would hurt Daddy."

Not only was Chloe at the site, but she was aware that Madeline was, too.

Madeline ushered Emma to the ladder. "We're going to get out of here, sweetheart. Right now." She helped the child up, staying behind her on the ladder.

When Madeline climbed out of the bunker back into the room, Emma was staring at the wall with Theon's picture.

"That wasn't there earlier," the little girl said.

Chloe must be close to ending this if she had just hung up her version of evidence.

Madeline took Emma by the hand. "Let's go." They rushed through the door and hurried toward the SUV, but Madeline stopped short.

"What's wrong?" Emma asked. "Why aren't we leaving?"

All four tires were flat. Slashed. And the gate was closed.

They weren't driving out of there.

Chloe was close by. Probably watching them now.

Madeline looked around, scanning the woods, and hauled the little girl back inside the cabin. "Change of plans, Emma. I have—"

"Striker!" called a woman from outside.

Chloe.

"It's her," Emma said. "We took too long. She's back."

"I know you're in there," Chloe said. "I'm not letting

you leave here with Emma. Come out with your hands in the air."

If Madeline went out and exposed herself, she'd be easy pickings. "I don't think so." Better to stay put and wait for Chloe to try to get in.

"Come out now!" Chloe said. "Or I set the cabin on fire."

Emma wrapped her arms around Madeline's waist and clung to her. "I'm scared."

"Shh. It's going to be okay." Madeline stroked her hair, trying to think. "Chloe! I don't think you're going to do that. I know you care about Emma. You don't want anything bad to happen to her. So, why don't you put down any weapons you have and we can talk about this."

"You're right. I don't want to hurt Emma. But if you force me, push me to do it, then I will. Come out, hands up, or you'll regret testing me."

For a strained heartbeat, Madeline closed her eyes, thinking of a solution. A way out of this predicament. But nothing came to her.

"You've got thirty seconds to decide," Chloe said. "Once the fire starts, I won't be able to stop it."

The car was useless. Without cell reception calling for help was impossible. Madeline couldn't run, not with Emma. It would only expose the child to more danger. The best place for her, the safest place for a little longer, was unfortunately here.

Madeline lifted the hatch to the bunker. "I need you to go back down."

"No!" Emma cried. "Please don't make me. I want to stay with you."

The girl's words tugged at her heart. Kneeling, Madeline brought herself to eye level with the child and rubbed her arms up and down. "I know you do, sweetheart. But it's not safe for you out there. Lots of terrible things that could hurt you. I have to do what she says. It's the only way to keep anything bad from happening to you. Okay?"

Tears rolled down Emma's cheeks, but she nodded. "You'll come back for me, won't you?"

"Time is almost up!" Chloe said.

Madeline wanted to reassure Emma without lying to her. "Help will come. You're not spending another night in that bunker. I promise."

The little girl threw her arms around Madeline's neck and squeezed in a tight hug. "Okay."

Madeline helped her climb back down the ladder.

At the bottom, Emma picked up the doll and clutched it to her chest.

"Don't worry. I always keep my promises." Madeline lowered the door to the bunker and pushed the bed on top of the door. The idea of leaving the girl made her sick and the prospect of Emma escaping, only to get hurt in the woods, was just as horrible.

"Time's up," Chloe said.

"I'm coming out." Madeline opened the cabin door and stepped out slowly with her palms raised. She searched the tree line for Chloe.

The disturbed woman was there. Close. Hiding.

"You are not going to ruin this for me," Chloe said. "I've earned the right to see this through. With my patience. All my planning. There were lots of times in the past two years where I was close enough to Jackson to stick a knife in his throat, poison him or strangle him. I thought about lots of different ways to kill him. But I watched. I listened. Bided my time while learning about his hopes and fears, what he cared about most. Waited for the perfect opportunity to make him pay. And now everything has fallen perfectly into place and no one is going to stop me."

Madeline followed the direction of Chloe's voice and

pinpointed the general area the woman was hiding in, but she couldn't spot her. Was she flat on the ground behind a bush? Up in the trees? Her voice carried so much that Madeline couldn't be sure.

"Jackson has paid dearly," Madeline said.

"Not nearly enough. The only thing I regret is not cutting the strings on his piano to take away that bit of solace. But it would've shown my hand, tipped him off to me too fast. And he only would've ordered a new one. Well, he can't order a new CEO position, or stealth technology, or a new daughter."

"Yes, you've hurt him deeply. More than I think you realize. You can stop this now before anyone gets hurt. He has suffered every single minute that Emma has been gone. He's sick with worry and guilt."

Chloe gave a bitter laugh. "Don't lie to me. You can't fool me, Agent Striker. I have cameras hidden in the smoke detectors in his house, watching his every move. I saw the two of you last night. Together. In his bed."

Fury bubbled and spilled over into shock. Then the magnitude of it sunk in, the violation of being watched during a moment of raw intimacy. Madeline swallowed hard against the nausea rising in her throat that made her dizzy.

Sheer force of will alone kept her steady on her feet.

"He didn't look like he was suffering when he was inside you," Chloe said. The derision in her voice cut like a blade.

Clearing her throat, Madeline ignored the sweat chilling her forehead. "It's not too late to stop this."

"But it is. Even if it weren't, why would I stop?"

The bush dead ahead, forty feet away, shook. Madeline itched to draw her weapon, aim and take the shot. End this.

A rabbit darted out from the bush and hopped away.

Damn it. Where was Chloe?

"You're the first woman he's looked at, much less

touched, in years," Chloe said. "So, I think it fitting that I use you as practice. For when I bait him to come out here later tonight. You can experience what he's going to feel as I make him run the gauntlet of the Survivalist Zone. I'll make certain that he comes across your dead body and sees you bloody and broken before he draws his last breath."

The one weakness Chloe had in this was her feelings for Emma. Yes, the child was a piece on a chess board to her, but not one she wanted to sacrifice. Somewhere along the way she started to care for her. Madeline had to use that against her.

"What about Emma?" Madeline asked, redirecting the conversation. "If you take away her father, you'll make her an orphan. She'll be all alone. Like you are. You don't want that for her. I know you don't."

"She'll have me. I'll raise her," Chloe said. "Teach her. Love her. She'll barely remember Jackson after a while."

"Chloe, step out where I can see you." Where Madeline could get a solid shot off. "Face to face, we can talk this through. You don't have to do this."

A flicker of movement up in the trees near the entrance drew Madeline's gaze. She spotted Chloe, dark hair pulled back, and wearing some kind of camouflage to help her blend in with the woods.

Madeline caught the flash of an arrow cutting through the air too late.

The arrow struck her left thigh. Madeline screamed in pain, clutching her leg.

"But I do have to do this," Chloe said. "For Theon. For myself. Everything I've planned for so long is working out and I need to finish it. I won't rest until Jackson Rhodes has suffered and lost everything. Including his life. Just like my brother. I'm going to play nice with you, Agent Striker.

Give you a sixty-second head start before I hunt you down. Your time begins now."

Was Chloe serious?

Madeline only contemplated it for a second. She took off into the woods in the opposite direction.

Hobbling along with her wounded leg, she bit back a groan of pain.

Chloe had deliberately positioned herself near the entrance to force Madeline deeper into the Survivalist Zone. Not that she would've gotten far down the main road either, not with an arrow in her leg.

If only her cell phone had reception, she could call someone. Tell them. But she was all alone. No one in sight. No one around for miles to help her.

Satellites played no role in cell phone reception, so getting closer to the sky, or getting a clear shot at it, wouldn't necessarily result in a connection. Cellular reception largely depended on how close you were to a cell tower, what manmade obstructions and geographical obstructions stood in between. Like the mountains surrounding her. But a higher elevation might put her in line of sight with a cell tower and help her get that one crucial bar of coverage.

Her only chance, no matter how slim the odds, was to make her way to higher ground and hope for a cell connection.

There was a hill not too far off that might work. She looked around, scouting the best route to the top.

Spears sticking out of a bush on the right had Madeline going left. She picked up her pace, despite the agony lancing through her, knowing that Chloe was close behind.

Her ankle snagged on something. She was about to look down to see what it was when she heard an earsplitting whoosh.

Without thinking, Madeline dropped to the ground as a

heavy log swung out with tremendous force, slicing through the air where she had just been standing.

If she hadn't dropped, she could've been killed instantly, or suffered such traumatic internal injuries that she would've died slowly. But the pain that wrenched through her leg stole her breath.

With her eyes tearing up and heart throbbing, Madeline rolled onto her back and snapped the shaft of the arrow in half. She reached out, grabbing hold of a stick that was long enough to use as a cane and scrambled up from the ground.

She stumbled forward, pulling her gun from the holster in case Chloe popped up unexpectedly. It was only a matter of time before she did.

Determined to move faster, she dug in with the stick and hopped up the hill, doing what she could not to put too much weight on her bleeding leg.

Madeline funneled her anger and pain and used it to fuel her onward. To push uphill with everything that she had. She limped faster, breathing hard. Tuned out the pain from her wound and the ache from her muscles. Breath sawed in and out of her lungs. She was nearly to the top.

Dropping the stick, she pulled out her phone, keeping her gun in her other hand.

Almost there. Almost.

Madeline kept going, climbing up the hill. She just needed to reach the top, get a signal and call for help. Tell them where Emma was and make sure this area was surrounded before Liane or Chloe or whatever the hell her name was could get away.

Certain her assailant was on her tail, she darted in between trees. Stayed low.

Looking down at the phone, she checked it for bars. Nothing. Not yet. She cut between pine trees, darting behind them and crawling over fallen logs, scrambling ever higher up the hill.

Her phone chimed.

Madeline stopped and looked at her cell. Two bars.

The message she had typed earlier went through. She went to press the call icon when an arrow whizzed past her head, hitting the trunk of the pine beside her.

She looked downhill. Spotted Chloe moving like a shadow between the trees. A ghillie suit helped to conceal her.

Madeline fired twice at the woman, forcing her to duck. Then she hurried higher.

But she had to keep track of Chloe. Risking a glance back, Madeline twisted her ankle on a rock. A new type of pain ricocheted along her shin. *Oh, God.* She tried to find her footing and landed wrong, tripping on a tree limb, throwing her forward as her knees buckled.

The ground gave way beneath her feet.

Her arms flailed. She desperately sought to grab hold of something. Anything to keep from falling. The phone and gun dropped from her hands as she snatched onto thick vines at the edge of the pit, breaking her fall.

THE KIDNAPPER WAS inside Jackson's head, playing a sick, twisted game of manipulation.

Behind the wheel of his Tesla, he ran through the what-ifs. What if he did as the note instructed, yet again? Ditched the FBI and went rogue? Why would the outcome be any different this time? What if the person never had any intention of giving Emma back? What if this was another power move designed to hurt him, physically this time?

The more he thought about it and calculated the risks, there was only one thing he could do. Discuss it with Madeline. She had been right about so many other things. The smart, tough agent would help him figure out what to do.

In the meantime, he needed to make sure she got back safely.

Jackson drove down the 405, headed for the Survivalist Zone site. Madeline had no idea how dangerous the place was. From intricate booby traps to the rugged terrain that could flatten a tire. Not to mention there might be wildlife on the property.

She didn't fully understand what she was walking into, and he did.

Jackson glanced at the gun case on the passenger seat. Mountain lions and snakes posed as much of a threat as any of the man-made hazards.

His phone chimed. A new message.

Cold dread fisted in his chest. If it was another text from the kidnapper, tormenting him, taunting him, pushing up the deadline to meet, he didn't know what he'd do.

He took out his phone. It was from Madeline, not an unknown number.

Sucking in a breath, he swiped the screen and looked at the message.

Found Emma in the bunker at the SZ site. She's unharmed. Chloe Lasiter is Liane Strothe.

His mouth dried as relief tangled with disbelief.
Thank, God. Emma was alive and all right.

His thoughts circled back to Liane. Chloe Lasiter was Liane. A woman he had trusted, who he had let into his home.

All this time, she'd been watching him, spying on him, plotting how to best hurt him. *For two damn years!*

Tension bled through him, tightening every muscle in

his body. Pressure built in his chest so fast and hard, for a second he thought he was having a heart attack.

Jackson dialed Madeline, but the call didn't connect. *And Liane, what about her?* What if she was still in the area, out at the site?

A million terrible possibilities spun in his mind.

Getting into the Survivalist Zone site was one thing. Getting out could be an entirely different situation, especially if Liane—Chloe—one of the masterminds behind the design, was out there.

Rage replaced everything else and it was like acid burning in his veins. Jackson pressed harder on the accelerator, changing lanes to veer away from a slow-moving minivan. He dialed the BAU office. It rang and rang.

Come on. Someone pick up.

"Liam McDare. How can I help you?"

Weaving around traffic, he cut off a sedan and took the exit ramp off the 405 and gunned it. "This is Jackson Rhodes. I heard from Madeline. She found Emma at an old ETC site that had been used by Theon Lasiter." He relayed how to get there. "I haven't been able to reach Madeline, but I'm on my way out there now."

Chapter Sixteen

Had a vine not been handy, Madeline would've fallen into the pit. Her heart pounded in her throat as she held on for dear life. She looked down. Wooden spikes pointed up from the ground. Her phone and gun had both fallen and were three feet below her. Dropping down to get them wasn't a viable possibility. Her feet or a limb would land on a spike. There were too many to avoid.

Even if she somehow managed to drop down safely to get her phone and gun, she'd be trapped. A sitting duck for Chloe.

She tugged on the vines, and using all her upper-body strength, pulled herself up. One hand over the other. She pushed up from the ground, and forced herself to bend her injured leg, swallowed a scream.

Breathing through the hot vise of pain gripping her leg, Madeline glanced around. No sign of Chloe. But she couldn't sit there waiting for her.

Level ground was best for her leg. She had to get off the hill.

Birds flew out of a tree twenty feet away as though something had spooked them.

Every sense she had went into overdrive as the need to survive took over.

Run!

Madeline scrambled in the opposite direction. Headed back downhill.

Keep moving. Don't stop.

Run as fast as you can!

Another arrow whistled through the air, landing in bark inches from her head.

Oh, God.

Madeline ducked low, but didn't stop. She gasped for air, her mind racing like a mouse caught in a maze. There had to be a way to save herself and Emma. To make sure Chloe never had a chance to drive Jackson through this gauntlet of hell and misery.

Chloe was closing in on her. She could feel it. There wasn't much time.

In a physical struggle with Chloe while injured, she wouldn't win. Since she'd lost her gun, she had no weapon aside from what she might be able to find. A tree branch maybe.

She had to outwit Chloe. Somehow. Keep moving. Hope her text message had gotten through and Jackson had notified the BAU team. She doubled back toward the cabin instead of finding out what was in store deeper in the zone.

Heart throbbing as if it would burst, she slogged forward to God only knew where. Chloe had been over every inch of this land, knew it, had it memorized.

Despite the pain searing through her body, Madeline ran onward. Hard. Limping and bleeding.

She found herself near the area where she had started.

Her gaze snagged on the spears sticking out of the bush. Seeing the bush before had driven her away from it in the opposite direction, toward a trap. Maybe that's why it was visible. But maybe she could use this to her advantage.

She hobbled to the bush. Grabbing onto one of the

spears, she wiggled it and pried it loose. Now that she had a weapon, she needed to find someplace to hide.

Crossing a stream, she passed a tight cluster of trees and came to thick underbrush. She bent down, gritting her teeth when she wanted to scream, and crawled into a bush.

She'd have to be cautious. Listen for even the snap of a twig around her. She could do this. Had to. She was out of other options. This was the best one.

Better to try anything than let that psychopath kill her.

Fury burned through Madeline.

Bring it on, Chloe.

I won't go down without a fight!

JACKSON DROVE AS close as he dared to the entrance of the Survivalist Zone. He parked behind a stand of pine and grabbed the loaded gun from the case. Then with an eye on the locked gate, he crept through the woods in its direction.

He spotted the government SUV. His heart leaped, but there was no sign of Madeline.

Nothing moved around the cabin. No one passed in the dark windows. No smoke curled from the chimney.

With his nerves singing, he entered the code at the gate. The lock disengaged.

He slipped inside, closing it slowly, quietly behind him.

Passing the SUV, he noticed the tires had been slashed. All of them.

He made his way to the front door, careful of where he stepped, and edged inside the cabin. Glancing around, he caught sight of Theon's picture on the wall. But he didn't want to look at it. Theon was gone. As tragic as his suicide was, he was gone. Emma was alive. And here somewhere. That's all he cared about it. Finding his little girl and Madeline and getting them both out safely.

Jackson walked through the room, searching for a sign

that Emma had been in the cabin. A floorboard creaked. He stopped and walked back over it.

Staring at the floor, he remembered. Theon had constructed a bunker. Concrete walls. Concrete floor. Like the room Emma was being held hostage in.

Jackson kicked the bed aside. Found the door and opened the hatch. He climbed onto the ladder, got down two rungs and jumped down the rest of the way, sending a pang through him.

He spun around and the air caught in his lungs. *Emma!*

"Daddy!" Emma raced to him and launched herself into his arms.

Ignoring the pain slicing through his side, he wrapped his little girl in the biggest, tightest hug. "Oh, baby!" He kissed her head, her cheeks, her hair. *But where was Madeline?* "Honey, have you seen anyone else besides Liane? Did a nice woman find you?"

"Madeline?"

He set his daughter down. "Yes. Do you know what happened to her?"

Emma shook her head. "Liane made her go outside and Madeline told me it was safer to stay down here. She promised help would come. She was right." His daughter wrapped her arms around his neck.

Despite the pain, Jackson lifted her in his arms. He'd gladly endure any discomfort if it meant he could hold his child.

He climbed out of the bunker. Opening the door, he peeked outside.

"You can't hide from me!" Chloe said in the distance. "Come out and I'll make it quick. If I have to find you myself, it'll be slow and painful, Agent Striker."

Madeline is in trouble.

Jackson darted out of the cabin, making his way back

through the gate. This time he left it cracked open. Down the road, he cut into the trees to his car. He opened the back door and placed Emma inside.

"I need you to be a brave girl for me. A little longer. Stay down in the footwell." He grabbed the blanket from the seat that he always kept in the car and covered her with it. "Daddy's friend Madeline is in danger. I have to help her. Liane wants to hurt her."

"But she wants to hurt you, too."

That woman already had. "I know, baby. But I'm going to be careful. Stay here until I come back or the police arrive. Don't move for any other reason. Understand, darling?"

"YOU CAN'T HIDE from me!" Chloe said, her voice circling closer. "Come out and I'll make it quick. If I have to find you myself, it'll be slow and painful, Agent Striker."

Slow and painful it would be unless Madeline killed her first because there was no way in hell she was surrendering.

Something moved on the ground, underneath the same bush. A squirrel? Maybe a rabbit.

No, it was smaller.

Madeline didn't dare move an inch to see what it was, praying it would crawl or scamper off. But it didn't. It slithered closer.

A snake! Madeline swore in her head. She hated snakes, was terrified of them. But in terms of things to fear, Chloe was higher on the list.

Squeezing her eyes shut, she sucked in a calming breath. She hoped, prayed, it would slither past. Most of the snakes in Washington were nonvenomous. Not a concern. The only one she needed to worry about was—

A distinct rattle clacked under the bush.

Madeline gulped hard around the lump of ice in her

throat. A rattlesnake was cause for concern. It could kill her. Not on the spot. Pain and swelling would start at the wound site and travel and spread from there.

With Chloe stalking her, there was only one thing Madeline could do.

Killing the rattlesnake wasn't an option. Crawling to a new hiding spot wasn't an option.

She braced herself as the snake slithered closer. The sound of the rattle filled her ears along with the frantic drum of her heart.

The sting was vicious. Brutal. But the rattler sank its fangs into her ankle twice. The second bite caught her off guard. Though she swallowed her cry, she'd jerked back, shaking the bush.

Chloe lunged into the underbrush, snatching Madeline by the hair, and dragged her out.

Screaming, Madeline rammed the spear up into flesh with all her might. She didn't stop thrusting the sharpened pole into the woman until Chloe let her go.

Madeline's vision blurred. She tried to stand, but the leg the snake had bitten turned to jelly, and the other, wounded from the arrow, was too weak to support her, so she crashed to the ground. Her thighs and calves were aching in agony, her lungs on fire. Rolling on her back to keep Chloe in her sights, Madeline shuffled backward. But there was nowhere to go. Nowhere to hide. She couldn't even run.

Chloe's lips curled, baring her teeth in a face smudged with camouflage. The woman reached behind her, pulling something from the pack strapped on her back. A weapon. She held a rope, and on the end dangled a rock with spikes duct-taped around it.

Adrenaline sent Madeline scurrying away, scooting

across the ground until a tree stopped her retreat. She swung the spear, desperate to keep Chloe at a distance.

The woman dodged the last wild swing of the spear and kicked Madeline in the leg injured from the arrow.

Madeline screamed, but swung the spear again at her attacker.

Chloe whipped the spiked rock in the air, faster and faster, picking up speed and gaining momentum. She launched the weapon and with a powerful whack split the spear in two.

The crunch of the wood splintering resonated in Madeline's soul.

"It's over, Agent Striker!" Teeth bared and growling like a wild beast, Chloe started swinging the spiked rock again. Preparing to strike Madeline in the leg. Or chest. Or the face.

A wave of horrifying panic engulfed her. In a frantic last-ditch effort, Madeline kicked at her. With her dying breath, she'd fight. "Go to hell!"

Chloe raised the spiked rock over her head and swung. *Boom!*

The report of the 9 mm sounded like a cannon explosion, so loud it rattled Madeline's teeth. She froze, confused. Dazed.

Chloe's eyes went blank as she dropped to her knees dead before she keeled over to the ground.

Jackson rushed to Madeline, lowering to a knee. He pressed a hand to her cheek, his frantic gaze traveling over her body. "Are you okay?"

"Emma," she said, her throat tight and sore. "Did you find Emma?"

"Yes, yes. She's safe."

A helicopter flew overhead and circled back, setting down near the cabin.

She rested her head on Jackson's shoulder and looked at the body.

It was finally finished.

Chloe Lasiter was dead.

Epilogue

Three days later...

Most of the team took up every available seat in Miguel's hospital room while they enjoyed dinner together and kept him company for a little while. The only person missing was Caitlyn, who was on a date.

Madeline's thigh and ankle both throbbed, but the soreness had improved considerably after the first couple of days.

"I wish I could've brought him in alive," Miguel said, referring to the terrorist suspect he'd had to shoot.

"We all read your report," Nick said. "You didn't have a choice."

Dash nodded. "The guy had a gun to the kid's head. You had a split second to make the right call and you did. You saved a life."

"But I wanted to bring him to justice," Miguel said. "Squeeze him for information that could've ended up saving even more lives."

"We're just glad you're going to be all right," Madeline said.

"And you as well." Miguel glanced at her leg.

"I'm okay. Compared to you getting shot, this is like a

scratch," Madeline said, downplaying her injury, not liking the attention, but it was also true.

Unlike Madeline, it would be a week before Miguel would be back on his feet and another two before they'd see him in the office.

"I read your report, too," Miguel said. "You almost didn't make it out of the Survivalist Zone."

A shiver ran through her thinking how close Chloe had gotten to almost ending her life. But thanks to Jackson, that disturbed woman had failed.

For once, Madeline was glad he didn't listen to her and *had* gone rogue. If he hadn't already been on his way out to the site to help her before he'd gotten her text message, he never would have made it there in time to save her life. For a second time.

"Jackson and I ended up making a good unofficial team and saved his daughter." She smiled, though her chest ached from not having heard from Jackson.

Not that she had any expectations. No strings attached.

Yet deep in the recesses of her heart she had hoped, foolishly, that once Emma was safe, he might still be interested in her.

But there had been nothing but silence between them. Even thinking of it now, no call, no text, something inside her withered.

Shoving the thought aside and tamping down the prickle of disappointment, she turned to Liam. With his head hung and pushing his food around in his take-out container, he hadn't spoken much.

"Liam, have you and Lorelai not worked things out yet?" she asked.

He clenched his jaw and shook his head. "I messed up. A part of me was afraid to go through with it and walk down the aisle. I mean, look at my parents. Even Lorelai's folks are divorced. But now that the wedding is off…" Shrugging, he slapped his container closed. "Careful what you wish for because you just might get it."

"This isn't all your fault," Madeline said. "A relationship takes two people, and I will admit to you, because I've already done so directly to Lorelai, that she was becoming a bit of a bridezilla."

The others in the room nodded emphatically.

"It's going to be okay," Nick said.

Dash patted him on the back. "Whatever is supposed to happen, will."

"If you miss her and want to work it out," Miguel said, "then you can. One thing I know for certain is that life is too short to let an opportunity for love pass you by."

ON THE DRIVE HOME, Madeline couldn't get Miguel's words out of her head. He was right. Life was too short to let an opportunity for love and happiness pass by. But it took mutual interest, mutual attraction, mutual desire on the parts of both parties. She couldn't force something that wasn't there no matter how much she wanted Jackson.

Funny, she'd gone all these years content to be on her own, and after knowing him a few short days, he'd turned her world upside down. Had her reevaluating what she wanted, needed. Made her consider facing her fear of attachment rather than running from it.

In her condo, she kicked off her shoes and poured a glass of wine since she no longer needed her pain medication. She pulled the pins from her hair and took down the loose twist. Sipping a glass of cabernet, she figured she'd take a bath and curl up with a book tonight.

The doorbell rang.

She groaned, realizing it was that time of year again

when kids went knocking door-to-door selling candy to raise funds for their school.

"One minute." She set her glass down, grabbed her checkbook and opened the door.

Her heart flipped over.

Jackson and Emma.

The two of them stood hand in hand, smiling. No, beaming at her.

"What are you doing here?" she asked, hearing the words that left her mouth and regretting them when his smile faltered. "I mean, I'm surprised you're here. But glad." Jump-up-and-down ecstatic.

"We both wanted to see you," Jackson said. "Can we come in?"

"Of course." She opened the door wide. "Please."

"How are—?" she and Jackson said at the same time and laughed.

"I'm good," she said. "Your ribs?"

"Still healing and Emma is sleeping through the night now and back in her own bed."

Emma held out a card. "This is for you. I made it."

"Thank you." Madeline took the piece of folded construction paper and stared at the flowers and rainbow drawn on the cover. Inside was a smiley face inside a heart. Emma had scribbled, "Thank you for saving me." Emotion clogged Madeline's throat and she couldn't speak as surprising tears wet her eyes. "It's so beautiful. I'll treasure it."

The little girl gave Madeline a hug, and she bent down to tighten the embrace.

"Emma, why don't you go sit on the sofa for a minute while Madeline and I talk?" He handed her a kiddie tablet, and she went to the couch.

"How did you know where I lived?" Madeline asked.

"Caitlyn took pity on me and told me. I hope that's okay.

I wanted to talk to you in person, not over the phone or at your office."

She owed Caitlyn one. "It's fine. I don't mind."

"I wanted to come sooner, but I needed to focus on Emma. Make sure she was all right."

"She's your number-one priority. I get that."

"I can't stop thinking about you. I know big, important things about you, but I want to know more. Everything. The name of your third-grade teacher, your favorite dessert, your happiest memory. What your go-to takeout is."

"Sushi. Spicy scallop roll and tuna *tataki*."

"That's a start." He stepped closer. "Caitlyn also mentioned that you're taking a couple of days off. I was wondering if you'd like to come to dinner with me and Emma, tomorrow night. In Paris."

"Paris?" She owed Caitlyn big-time!

"Why not? You'll be on vacation and I'm not currently employed."

"You're not going back to ETC?"

"I don't know. I want to take some time. Spend it with Emma. And you." He cupped her jaw and caressed her cheek with his thumb.

She was surprised by the sudden twist of desire that stabbed through her, all the way from her scalp to the pit of her stomach. It took her breath away, and she wanted him with a force that frightened her.

"What do you say about Paris?"

"I'd love to, Jack."

* * * * *

SURVIVING
THE TRUTH

TYLER ANNE SNELL

This book is for Hannah, Ace, Madi and Kelvin. Writing this book came at a very stressful time for the Tyler household, and you all were nothing but kind to us. Roll Tide (sorry, Madi)!

Prologue

"The conclusion I've come to is an easy one, even if it is a frustrating one." Detective Lovett dropped the box on the sheriff's desk. It landed with a notable thud. "We need help—and I'm talking specific help, not just me and an unlimited supply of coffee."

Sheriff Chamblin let out a breath that sank his shoulders and protruded his belly. He was at his desk but wasn't happy about it. He was a man who liked to pound the pavement, not pour over paperwork. Plus, with the way things had ebbed and flowed from quiet to downright loud in Kelby Creek throughout the last year or so, it was hard to feel at ease anywhere, most notably behind a desk.

So Chamblin hadn't been in the best of moods before the detective had come in and now, with Lovett's conclusion, he feared it wasn't going to get any better.

Chamblin spelled out the obvious. "You want the task force."

Lovett nodded. "Normally a place so small wouldn't need one, but given Kelby Creek's history, there're a lot more cold cases that we need to look into. Ones that we thought were resolved but weren't. Ones that we thought we had the right person for but—"

"But we don't," Chamblin finished. He sighed again and motioned to the box. "We have enough of these cases for an actual task force? What does that even entail? Two people? Four? How would you have handled this in Seattle?"

The detective thumbed at his wedding band and shrugged.

"In Seattle we would have had more than enough people to switch their gears, but here?" He thought a moment. "I'm going to suggest that eventually we have two people but, considering we don't have people lining up to fill the department at the moment, I'd say try for one first. See how that goes. Worst case, it's a glorified trial period. Best case, it does what the rest of us are trying to do."

Chamblin snorted. "And what's that exactly?"

Detective Lovett smiled but didn't return the sarcasm.

"Make the town trust this department again, one good deed at a time." He tapped the box, his expression turning serious. "They're not the only ones who deserve justice."

The sheriff couldn't disagree.

"Whoever we hire, they'll need to be above reproach," he said. "Because if they're anything but trustworthy and straightforward, this town will eat them alive. It's one thing to do right by Kelby Creek when things pop up. It's another to dive into the past and muck around. Whoever does that is going to have their work more than cut out for them."

Lovett nodded. Then he pulled out a piece of paper with a name and number written on it. He passed it over to the sheriff. "That is why I think we should reach out to him."

Chamblin had to read the name twice. Just so he knew he wasn't mistaken. "You've gotta be kidding me."

Detective Lovett shrugged. "Find me a more motivated individual and I'll recommend them instead."

After a moment, Chamblin admitted defeat.

"It'll take some talking to get him back into law enforcement after what happened. And I'm not sure talking will even do anything. We talk about righting the wrongs of this department's past, but there's not a thing we can do to right the wrong of what happened to him."

Lovett's expression softened.

"He's good people and, no matter how life beats good people down, they always find a time to stand right back up." He thumped the piece of paper on the desk twice. "He'll take the job. I bet my badge on it."

There was only one way to find out.

The sheriff picked up the phone and dialed the number. It rang as he traced the name on the paper for the third time.

Kenneth Gray was either about to be intrigued or really, really angry.

Chapter One

Willa Tate wouldn't have found the box at all had she not been trying to be polite.

See, it was a curse—being polite—one she'd been saddled with from a young girl and was still burdened with at the age of thirty-one. Like a bad perm or a wine stain sitting on a white blouse for too long, being polite wasn't just something she decided to do on a daily basis. It was something she *had* to do.

It was in her DNA.

So when Missy Frye called the office in a fuss, worried over her husband and why he wasn't yet home, Willa glanced around the empty space and nodded to no one but herself.

"I can run out to the site to see if he's already gone for the day," she offered, looking for her purse.

Normally it hung on a hook next to her office door, but today she'd gone for fun lunch and, after fun lunch, her purse had a way of landing anywhere but where it was supposed to. Thanks in no small part to her friend and co-worker Ebony Keller.

Fun lunch often included a good deal of gossip, even if no one had asked for it originally. And gossip in small-town Kelby Creek? Well, that wasn't something you just left at the lunch table.

Ebony had hustled into the office, pulling on Willa's side as she'd hurriedly whispered about the newest piece of juice in town. That meant her purse had probably landed near where Ebony had dropped her two cents on what was happening over at the Dawn County Sheriff's Department.

"Oh, Willa, that would be *amazing* of you," Missy nearly yelled back, her accent a brand of Scarlet O'Hara's in *Gone With the Wind*.

Willa's ran a bit deeper and with a lot more syrup. Her family had been in the Deep South town of Kelby Creek for four generations. It was a running joke that by the time Willa had a kid and then that kid had their own, the poor soul would have an accent so thick that no one would be able to understand a word.

"I normally wouldn't even call up there," Missy added, "but Dave usually answers his phone and now it's going straight to voice mail."

"I bet he's just lost track of time is all." Willa tried to assure her. "Give me five minutes and I'll have him calling with an apology on the tip of his tongue."

Missy showered Willa with a few more thank-yous, and even threw in a "Tell your sister I said hi," then the phone was in the cradle and Willa was shaking her head.

She dug into her purse, which had wound up halfway beneath the worn love seat that had catered to many a tired worker, and pulled her personal cell phone out to make sure no one was missing her.

They weren't.

Willa sighed at the lack of notifications and locked up the office with a grumble. Up until a few months ago, she would have had one to ten messages from Landon. But, she supposed, it made sense that they would stop on account of his new—and quick-as-a-flare-up-in-an-unattended-grease-pan—engagement.

Not that Willa was holding that against him.

She *had* been the one to call it quits after all.

You also would have married him had he asked, she pointed out to herself.

Willa shook her head. "No time for feeling any type of way on that," she said aloud. "Now's the time for finding Dave."

Kelby Creek, Alabama, was caught in an awkward way lately. Mostly it had to do with the weather. There was enough humidity to keep Willa's blond hair big and unruly but enough chill to make her wish she'd worn something other than a short-sleeved blouse. Or at least had brought a rain jacket with her. She could smell the rain in the air even if the darkening sky was free of clouds. Late October in south Alabama was a mixed bag when it came to knowing what to be grumpy about when you stepped outside. Today was no exception.

The second way Kelby Creek felt a bit strange was a lot more subtle and, if you weren't a local, harder to pin down. Willa had come to town when she was a teen and had, somehow, managed to not leave it since. She had some feelings on that front but her time in the out-of-pocket place had given her a sensitivity to it. Like most locals, she'd been upset at what had happened two years ago. Hurt. Scared. Angry.

But now? Now, there was something in the air. Change. Was it good? Or was it more of the same?

She couldn't tell and most locals couldn't decide, either.

They felt the wind blowing, in a manner of speaking, and no matter which way it would eventually go, it was there all the same.

But, for Willa, she didn't think she would have to ponder on any of that anytime soon. In the grand scheme of town, she wasn't exactly top-tier important. She worked as an office manager for a construction company that catered to all of Dawn County, lived in the garage apartment of her younger sister and husband's house, and had a five-year plan that she'd already extended twice. Willa wasn't the kind of woman to be a part of the important things—the things that made ripples and waves. She was more of the person who watched the troublemakers throw the rocks into the water in the first place.

It was her lot in life and she'd accepted it. Accepted it all the way to the north side of town and right onto a makeshift lot where their workers had been parking to walk to the land they were prepping. Eventually, the lot would be bulldozed, flattened and smoothed. Then it would be turned into a small set of town houses. Right now, there were still a few trees, weeds and dirt mounds interspersed with the construction equipment.

Willa got out of her car and took in most of the area without having to do much. Dave's truck wasn't around and neither was he. Still, Willa had known the man for years and the possibility of him leaving his phone behind at a site was up there with a pretty dang good chance. So she decided to stay polite and do a quick pass over the lot, all while switching her heels for her rain boots and bringing out the light of her phone.

Dave was probably on his way home now after chatting too long with Marvin after work. He'd get an earful from Missy for sure, but maybe Willa could soften the blow by dropping off his misplaced phone.

The first half of the lot still had a few patches of mud from last night's rain. It squished against her boots and made her hurry so she could minimize how much gunk she'd have to wash off when she got home.

Her trek brought her to the back end of the lot, which still had some trees not yet bulldozed, with half attention.

When the light of her phone split between a tree, an old stump, and a half-buried rectangle, Willa moved over a few steps, passing it off as a wayward toolbox.

But then, why was it partially buried? Even with a heavy rain, it wouldn't sink underground.

So Willa went back, out of curiosity, already assuming it was some other construction-related thing.

However, it wasn't.

Willa knelt next to the wooden box. Her light showed it was worn, with cracks and matted dirt and mud. Some of the box looked a bit crushed and the metal clasp on the front was off the hinges. She propped her phone up against the tree stump and used both hands to free the box from the dirt. Not heavy enough that she couldn't move it, it definitely required two hands.

"You better not be some kind of *Jumanji* game where I get cursed by opening you," Willa muttered to the box.

It had been a joke.

A silly little thing to say in the dark to herself.

Yet, once she lifted the top, Willa's veins filled with ice.

"Oh my God!"

NOVEMBER BROUGHT IN late tropical storms to Southern Alabama and, with the second, an almost oppressive humidity followed directly by a blanket cold. That was why Kenneth Gray came into the Dawn County Sheriff's Department with his own haul in tow. It was less "make you sweat, cuss, and wish you lived someplace where the seasons stayed in their respective lanes" and more of his only chance of surviving the day.

It was Monday morning and Kenneth entered through the back of the building after swiping his card. He dropped his coffee cup on his desk and the pack of sinus meds next to it. He'd also brought something else that had nothing to do with the headache brewing in the back of his head. That was also why he'd hustled behind closed doors to his desk and not taken any time to talk about the weekend.

That "something else" knew the drill and whipped under the desk to the bed he'd already taken the time to set up his first week on the job. If he had been working anywhere else, he was sure it would be grounds for a firing.

Yet Kelby Creek had been forced to become forgiving. Along with the interim sheriff and the department that served it.

Plus, it wasn't like he brought his dog to work every day.

"Good girl, Delilah," Kenneth said to the three-year-old golden retriever. He pulled a chew toy from his bag and tossed it next to her as she settled.

In Kenneth's opinion, she was the only thing that fit nicely in the room. Everything else around them was mild chaos. The desk that butted his didn't have a chair behind it, but its top was covered in paperwork that had been shifted over from his side. There were boxes and filing cabinets in the room crowding both, and the smallest of placards on the door that still read Storage.

It wasn't supposed to be an office but it had become his.

Just as the cases stacked around him had.

A knock on the door had Delilah sit at attention though Kenneth knew she wouldn't move unless he said so. Still, he tried to block her from view of a man with red hair and crinkles at the edges of his eyes. He had a badge on his uniform and a scowl on his face.

Deputy Carlos Park shook his head in greeting.

"Smart to use the back door. Did you see the line that's out there in the lobby?"

Kenneth shook his head but hadn't missed the more than usual number of cars in the parking lot.

"Is it the same as last week?"

Park nodded. "Ever since the press conference, you, my dude, have stirred up a lot of chatter in town." He pointed at the wall, in the direction of the department's lobby. "Now that chatter has turned into a roomful of people sure as spit simmering on a sidewalk in summer they have information that can solve one of these cold cases."

Kenneth sighed. "If only it was that easy, I wouldn't have this job in the first place."

They each took a moment to glance around the room. Kenneth had known Carlos for years, but just as a passing hello, a quick conversation in the bank line or a how's-it-going while closing out tabs at the bar. But Kenneth had heard of Carlos's feats of excitement over the last two to three years and how the guy had gone from a sour-faced, angry man to a more calm and caring one. As the deputy's gaze swept over the papers and boxes, he wondered if that new side of compassion helped him see what Kenneth saw instead when he looked around.

People.

A void that couldn't be filled but could be stitched closed to make a scar instead of a wound.

However, that was a deeper conversation for another day. No sooner had Carlos's gaze moved across the space did it travel to Kenneth's desk. Or, really, the bright-eyed pup beneath it.

He cracked a grin. "I know you're having some work done on your house but I still think the sheriff will lose it if he sees Delilah here."

Kenneth wasn't that worried.

"That press conference didn't just put me in the public eye, it pushed him out there, too," he reminded the deputy. "I haven't seen the sheriff for more than a few minutes here and there, and that's usually in the break room." He paused and looked at the dog in question. Delilah must have sensed the new thoughtful attention. Her tail started to wag. "That said, give me a heads-up if you see him around."

Carlos laughed and agreed. Then he was back to annoyed. "You going to the conference room for another round of conspiracy theories?"

"I am."

Kenneth sighed, took some of his sinus meds, gave Delilah a pat, and followed the deputy out and to the room next door. Carlos didn't enter, but there was sympathy now written across his face. Someone was already seated at the end of the conference table. Carlos lowered his voice so only Kenneth could hear him. "Good luck, Detective."

Kenneth didn't say so but he didn't believe in luck when it came to Kelby Creek.

Not after what had happened.

Not after Ally had died.

Murdered, not died.

Carlos didn't seem to note the anger and resentment that had burned through Kenneth at the thought. Instead he went off down the hall, unaware the rising frustration that went along with the familiar emotions was only about to be stoked by Kelby Creek residents who liked drama a little too much.

He took a small beat, pulled on a polite smile, and settled in the chair opposite his first of, he assumed, many locals who wanted a piece of the new cold case task force and the only man heading it.

That polite smile nearly slipped off altogether as Kenneth met the gaze of a woman who was not at all what he'd expected would make his life a little more difficult that Monday morning.

Sunshine.

It was the first descriptor that came to his mind as he quickly took her in.

Shoulder-length, big blond hair, freckles across her face, dark lipstick along her polite expression, and bright green eyes that seemed to be smiling, too. She was petite yet there was no doubt by her curves and demeanor that she was late twenties to early thirties. Her outfit helped drive that conclusion home. A dark red blazer with a blouse tucked in. A gold locket around her neck. Her nails were also immaculately kept. She didn't just care about her appearance, it was most likely a requirement for a job or career.

There was also the other thing that made Kenneth place the woman older than what he might have had they met under different circumstances.

Something was weighing on her.

Something, he guessed, having to do with the wooden box placed on the table between them.

"Good morning," he greeted, keeping his gaze locked on the almost-lime green of her stare until he knew more about why she was there. "I'm Detective Gray. How can I help you?"

The woman's smile went megawatt. She extended her hand so fast he almost flinched.

"Nice to meet you!" Her voice was surprisingly chipper for someone who seemed troubled. Then again, this was the South, and Southern women had a sneaky way about them. They only let you see what they wanted you to see and, right now, the woman wanted to act like she wasn't in a sheriff's department. "I'm Willa. Willa Tate. I actually already know you, or of you. I saw that news story they did last week. The one where you wore the tie. You know, the one with the stripes."

Kenneth knew the press conference. He also knew the tie.

He'd only expected her to bring up one of the two.

"You should have seen the Bugs Bunny tie I almost wore

instead." It was a joke. And, boy, did Willa laugh. But there was a nervousness in it.

And then, like he'd flipped a switch, that laugh slid all the way down into the reason why she was there.

The heaviness became physical as she put her hand on top of the box that had seen much better days.

"A month ago I found this." Even her voice had hardened a little. No longer bright and chipper. She made no move to push the box over to him. "I unearthed it in a construction site and after seeing what was inside I... Well, I decided to take it home."

Despite himself, Kenneth leaned in a little closer.

"After everything that's happened with Kelby Creek and this department, I thought that maybe it was better to try to figure it out myself. Or, maybe get a clearer idea of what happened before I brought it in. But I've hit a dead end and I think it's time I ask for help."

"With what?" Kenneth pushed his pad of paper and pen to the side. The last round of locals he'd seen had sprouted instant conspiracy theories about dirty cops, bizarre and unlikely cold cases reaching back decades, and the ever-popular "I know what really happened to Annie McHale." None of the information had led anywhere other than to a cluster headache for Kenneth, but now he found himself intrigued.

Maybe because Willa Tate was herself intriguing.

She hesitated but answered with conviction.

"Solving a thirty-five-year-old murder."

Chapter Two

Detective Gray was a good *good*-looking man. Willa had almost forgotten her words and her thoughts when he'd sat across from her, slightly lost in her surprise.

Willa had seen the man before on the local news and in the paper more than once—it had been big news that a cold case unit was coming to the sheriff's department, even more so by a man who had returned to the job years after he'd left it behind. Then there was what had happened to his wife all those years ago that had made a news cycle or two in town. But there was just something about being close to him that changed her perspective from the man she'd never met but seen on TV.

He didn't much look like a small-town detective, lead of a task force or not. Instead he favored an actor playing the part of some big-time FBI agent in New York or Chicago. His brown hair was cut and groomed close and nice, just as his goatee beard made a controlled dusting of hair that took a good *good*-looking man and added some spice. His eyes were dark and blue and rested beneath thick eyebrows that expressed a seriousness she bet extended outside of work.

Then there was the jaw and the sun-kissed tan and the lean body and tall height, and Willa couldn't help but mentally stumble when he'd introduced himself.

But then, her reason for being there had come back

and she'd pushed any and all attraction out the metaphorical window.

Now she watched as one of his eyebrows rose with concern and not physical interest.

"A thirty-five-year-old murder?" he repeated.

Willa kept her hand firmly on the box's lid. She nodded.

"I know it sounds out there, but yes, I think I got really close to figuring it out," she said. "Because of this."

Willa didn't want to slide the box over but knew it was the right thing to do. For some reason, she'd grown protective of it. Or, at least, some of its contents. She hadn't lied to the man, she'd squashed her first instinct to go to the sheriff's department when she'd found the box because she hadn't trusted that whatever was inside could be taken care of. So, she'd done some investigating on her own… and in the past month had become attached to a story she wasn't even sure was true.

Now it almost felt like giving the box over was her abandoning that hope.

Abandoning the woman in the photograph.

But you ran out of the story, she told herself. *It's time to get someone else to help you find the rest.*

Willa upped her smile in the hope that Detective Gray couldn't see the very real cracks beneath it. She carefully pushed the box across the table.

He took it when it was within reach.

Willa let out a small breath. It shook with relief, concern, and excitement.

Detective Gray's dark eyes met hers once more before focusing on the main reason for her being there. He was just as careful as he opened the container.

Willa knew exactly what he was seeing yet still listened with rapt attention as she listed off the contents.

"A ring box. A photograph of a young woman. One bullet casing…" He paused. Willa listed the last item currently in the box for him.

"A piece of ripped fabric. With what appears to be blood on it."

No matter his intensity or looks, Willa didn't like the skepticism that stretched across his face.

"Whose blood?"

Willa shook her head.

"I have no idea," she said. "I was hoping you'd be able to help me with that part."

Detective Gray took one last sweeping look across the box's contents. Then those dark eyes were on her. The skepticism still whirling around in them.

"And you found this at a construction site? How'd you know where to look?"

She'd been ready for this question but knew the answer sounded made up.

"A coworker had gone MIA and his wife called all concerned about him," Willa answered. "I offered to go look for him at the site he was working earlier that day. He wasn't there but I thought he might have dropped his phone. I found the box instead. Dave, the coworker, was fine by the way. He said he'd gotten wrapped up in a conversation with another worker about football. I suspect he got an earful when he got home, though."

There was a small stretch of silence as the detective scanned the items again. That skepticism stayed.

"I'm not saying that what's in this box isn't interesting," he started. "I'm just not sure how you think this pertains to a thirty-five-year-old murder. One that you want me to help you solve. If I'm being honest, this box actually looks like something for geocaching."

He must've realized she didn't know what that was. He tacked on an explanation.

"That's when you have a box in a certain location and you log those coordinates on a web site and then people go and look for it. Typically, when they find the box, they either write their name down on a list or take something out of the box before putting something back into the box." He waved his hand across the worn wood. "To me, that's what this looks like. An assortment of random objects. I mean these don't even look like they all come from the same time period. The picture looks like it was taken in the eighties. But this ring? It maybe looks a few years old."

Willa wasn't naïve enough to think that she would be believed the second she tried to explain. She knew that there were a whole lot of people in Kelby Creek who had been trying to knock down the door of the sheriff's department to see the new cold case unit. Her friend Ebony had been filling her in on some of the conspiracies and gossip that had been surrounding their fellow locals trying to get their piece of the newly developed unit and the former detective who had come back to be its leader.

Yet there was a sting in his words that cut into her.

Willa wasn't used to not being trusted.

Even from a stranger.

She pushed her shoulders back, sat as tall as the chair would allow, and took great caution to keep her voice free of her swirling emotions starting up beneath the surface.

She also didn't want to betray the fact that, despite wanting the man to trust her, she was lying to him. At least, in part.

"At first, that's what I thought," she started. "That it was just random what was in there, but then I got lucky with the picture." Willa pointed to the box. The detective understood the motion. He pulled the picture out and glanced down at it before looking back to her as she continued. "That woman is Mae Linderman. I only was able to figure out who she was because, if you can see in the background of the picture, that's the old grocery store. I have a friend who works there now—you know, years after the remodel, of course. She was able to find out, through the owner and a lot of gossip, that Mae's brother worked there in the seventies. I was able to talk to him and, even though he was not a fan of discussing anything, he and the few people that I showed the picture to confirmed that that's Mae."

The detective nodded. Willa appreciated the gesture. At least it meant that he was paying attention and staying quiet long enough to let her tell the whole story.

"After I found out that it was, in fact, Mae, I learned that she passed away in '81 from a car accident."

The silence didn't last long.

"And you think it was murder? Something staged to look like an accident?"

"No," she replied a little too quickly. It was the first time Willa had said any of this to anyone. She hadn't told Ebony of her discovery or theory, and she hadn't told her sister Martha, either. It was exciting to tell someone finally. Exciting and frustrating. Especially when they were giving her a look like Detective Gray was giving her now.

"Once I learned about Mae, I learned about Josiah Linderman," she continued. "He was her husband and they married young. They had two kids and, despite the two of them working long hours, they didn't have much. They did, however, have each other and, from the few people I've talked to who actually knew them, their love was something else." Willa couldn't help but smile. She wasn't a stranger to love, falling into it with a partner or seeing it displayed by her family and friends, but a special love? True love? She didn't know if that was real. All she knew for sure was that she hadn't had it with Landon.

And if she hadn't had it with him, a man she'd been with for years, who was to say she would have it with anyone?

Across from her, the detective moved in his seat. It was subtle and... Maybe it was just a part of her imagination, but Willa thought the man had gone from scrutiny to discomfort. She kept on with the story and her theory so they wouldn't be bogged down in what was and instead find out what had happened after.

"A year after she died, Josiah said he was going to the store to get some groceries," she continued. "They lived in the house close to town limits, out near the creek. From his house to Main Street, it should've taken about ten minutes or so at a good pace to get there but Josiah'd been known to take the long way 'round to get to town. Instead of taking the paved roads, he detoured to the dirt ones that ran next to the woods, the creek, until finally he made it to Main. I mean, who doesn't prefer the long way around on a nice day? Especially us locals."

Detective Gray didn't comment, even when Willa had left him the space to do so if he wanted. She wasn't used to having a conversation so one-sided, even if she was explaining something. That might have had more to do with the fact that her sister could go a mile a minute when given the proper topic. Plus, as per her curse, Willa was trying to be polite.

She decided that this truly was the wrong place and the wrong time, so she finished the story without pausing again.

"Josiah never made it to the store and he never made it back home. According to Mae's brother, he just disappeared. A search party of friends was formed that night. They looked everywhere, but no one found a thing. He just was gone. Like snapping your fingers."

Willa motioned to the picture. "Like every town, there

were, of course, people who said such bad things about him. A father consumed with grief overwhelmed at being a single parent leaves his kids to fall into foster care since they had no other family, apart from their uncle who refused to take them, and other such nasty things, but the few people I've talked to seemed to genuinely think the man cared about his kids. Even more so after his wife passed. He knew he was their only family. I don't think, at least from what I know about him, that Josiah would willingly abandon them."

Willa let her eyes wander to the photograph in the detective's hand. It was yellowing with age and there were worn marks from where it had been folded and unfolded many times.

"Though, to be honest, if it wasn't for that picture, I think I'd be inclined to believe that that box is just filled with random mess. Some scavenger hunt that maybe never got found. But rumor has it that ever since that picture was taken, Josiah had it on his person every moment except when he was sleeping.

"Whether it was in his pants' pocket, his wallet, or in his hand because he was showing someone his lovely wife, Josiah treasured that picture. So to find it in the box with a bullet casing and a bloodied piece of fabric? I don't think Josiah Linderman just disappeared. I think someone took him. And I think someone killed him, put the evidence in that box and buried it, hoping no one would ever find it. I think Josiah was murdered and I would very much like you to help me figure out by who."

There it was. The story Willa was trying to find.

The mystery she was trying to solve.

The one box that had consumed her thoughts since finding it buried at the construction site a month before.

And now she'd finally told someone.

And now it was time to see what Detective Gray thought.

EXPECTATIONS HAD A way of being a bit wild sometimes. What you thought you were going to get and what you actually got. It was like sitting there holding an empty cup while water poured into your hands instead.

In this situation, Kenneth felt like his cup was still waiting to catch some very vague conspiracy theory about the town or a neighbor. Instead he was sitting there holding a picture, a box, and a story about a man who left his family thirty-five years ago to go to the store.

And he didn't rightly know what to do with it at first.

Mainly because the one who had poured it all in had seemed more invested in finding out what had happened than in hoping for attention that many before her had come seeking.

Willa Tate gave off the impression that she very much wanted to help.

That was why he felt just a little regretful that he was going to have to shut her down.

"It's a shame what happened to that family," he said, using the voice he reserved for civilians when it came to the job. A voice he hadn't needed to use until recently. "But I'm not sure what I'm seeing here is a direct cause to believe in murder or to even prove that a man didn't just leave his family."

Willa opened her mouth. Ready, he assumed, to jump back into what she believed was the truth.

Maybe if Kenneth had lived a different life the last seven years or so, he would've let her. And Willa Tate could've tried to change his mind.

But Kenneth's life had been changed a while ago in the most violent of ways.

Every plan, every hope and every dream he'd ever had had been destroyed, rearranged, and painfully put to rest.

Along with a future he didn't recognize had come a perspective shift.

Before he'd been looking at the world with rose-colored glasses. Now he saw the world for what it was and his eyes continued to be bloodshot for it.

He hadn't come back to the sheriff's department, to a life in law enforcement, because he'd simply wanted to do good.

He'd come back because he'd wanted answers and justice, too.

And he couldn't have either if he accepted every far-fetched story that walked through the door. No matter how much she looked like sunshine.

"The best I can do for you right now, Miss Tate, is have you give me your number and I'll give you my card. I can look into the name to see if we have anything on file here." He powered on. "Though I have to warn you, since this unit was just formed, I'm the only one working through any of the files that come along with it until we can find someone else to hire who has the qualifications we're looking for. It might take a few days for me to find what's there or to see what's not. How about that?"

Kenneth didn't have to know the woman to understand that she was not a fan of anything he'd said.

"What about the bullet casing? What about the blood? Those aren't exactly things you typically find buried unless something's wrong. Right?"

"I'll admit, it is a bit odd, but I'm still not convinced it's not anything other than maybe geocaching or coincidence. I mean why bury the evidence to a murder and have it sit underground for that long when you can just destroy it some other way? The creek stretches far and wide here in town. There's a whole lot of forest, too. You could easily hide any one of these things between when Mr. Linderman went missing and now. Plus—" Kenneth pulled the smaller box out and turned it so she could see the ring. "I'm not at all an expert in jewelry, but I do believe this box comes from Cadence Jewelers in town, and they didn't open until 2002 or 2003. Why would it be in here with the rest of these items?"

Willa's sunshine had dimmed into what he could only describe as pointed determination. And it wasn't pointed at him.

"How do you know it's from Cadence Jewelers?" she asked. "The ring box, I mean."

For some reason Kenneth hadn't expected that question. He felt the tension in his body before he heard it in his voice.

"That trim on the inside is something the owner does specifically for locals. She calls it a nice personal touch. Also, most of the more prominent jewelers have a logo of some sort on theirs."

Kenneth didn't want to answer any more questions so he stopped there, put the ring box back into the wooden one, and shut it. He was reaching for his business card as Willa pulled the box back to her.

"I'll let you know if I find anything," he said, passing it over as he stood.

Rising, Willa Tate produced her own card. Clanton Construction was typed in fine print across the top.

"Thank you." Her voice was clipped but she didn't continue.

Kenneth walked her to the door. It was only when she was through the threshold that she stopped and turned back to look at him.

"This town has had a habit of losing people, whether it be through some violent means or just by falling through the cracks." Her eyes narrowed on him. Her nostrils flared. If he had the time, Kenneth believed he could have counted every freckle across her face given how close they were. Instead he got the sharp end of good intentions and extreme determination. "Josiah Linderman may be gone but I will not let his memory and what happened to him fall through the cracks. And you shouldn't, either."

The contents of the box shifted as Willa turned on her heel and walked herself back out to the lobby.

Kenneth could have almost sworn that the hallway became a little darker in her wake.

Chapter Three

Martha could tell something was wrong. She'd been like that for as long as Willa could remember. It didn't matter if it had something to do with a bad day at school, a crush who didn't like her back, or client interaction that rubbed her the wrong way, Martha Tate-Smith had a knack for knowing when to bring the sweet tea and cookies to her sister.

"Willa Tate, I know you're in there," her sister could be heard calling at the side door at the top of the stairs next to the garage. "Not only is your car parked out here but I saw you walking like a bee was in your britches. Now open up so we can talk about it while we take in our God-given daily dose of sugar that we don't need."

Willa thought about not opening the door. Sure, technically Martha was her landlord and, sure, she was her sister. But Willa was so mad that she knew seeing Martha, cookies or not, wouldn't make that bee in her britches go away.

When Willa had gone to the sheriff's department, she'd hoped to find someone who at the very least would listen and at the very most take action. Find whatever information they could about Josiah Linderman and maybe come up with a plan for next steps. Instead she'd been given a card with a number, a vague outline of what was next, and a warning that nothing might be found or done.

It hadn't been an inspiring meeting, which was a feeling that had rolled over into uninspiring frustration an hour later.

A frustration that she was going to have a hard time hiding from her sister.

Willa took the wooden box and placed it in its hiding spot. She let out a sigh and went to the door.

"Aren't you supposed to be at work?" Willa asked in greeting when the door was open.

While Willa was big blond hair and freckles, Martha was smooth dark hair and one singular mole on her right cheek. The difference between them was all down to genetics. Willa had taken after her mother and Martha had taken after their father. But personality wise? Both sisters had somehow become more like each other than anyone else.

That was why living with each other could be disastrous on any given day.

"Don't you go sassing me," Martha shot back. She pushed inside the apartment, the smell of cookies wafting off of the plate as she passed. "I'm just here to make sure you're okay. First you say you're taking off work for a personal day and then you come back here looking all scrunched face and bothered? You better believe that I'm going to come ask what's going on."

Willa followed her sister to the kitchenette in the corner.

Despite it being above the garage, the mother-in-law suite was surprisingly spacious. The living area, including the kitchenette, was big enough for a couch, a TV, a desk and four barstools at the counter. Two of those barstools were occupied by indoor plants that, for whatever reason, Willa couldn't seem to keep alive. Martha's husband, Kimball, liked to joke those were the stools where houseplants went to die. Past them and through the doorway next to the small refrigerator was the bedroom. It was smaller but had everything Willa might need.

Though even if it had been lacking, it was still better than living with Landon right after they'd broken up. Willa liked to be an optimist, but even that situation had caused her a few stomachaches of worry before Martha had stepped in.

"I took a personal day to do a few personal things," Willa responded, taking a seat next to her currently dying plant. "That means it's none of your business unless I say so. Okay?"

Martha rolled her eyes as she took the Saran wrap off the plate. She worked part-time at a bakery downtown. Her specialty was chocolate chip and peanut butter cookies. But it was her Oreo cheesecake that was her absolute gift to mankind. That was why both Willa and Martha's husband had made a rule that she wasn't allowed to bring that specific work home with her.

"Willa, if you're using that 'it's none of my business' line on me then it has to be about a boy," Martha concluded with quickness. "Last time, it looked like you sucked the end of a lemon when we were talking about the guy you dated— what's his name? The one with the tattoos?"

Willa had to chuckle at that.

"Are you talking about Rodney? Rodney Bishop?"

Martha did a small clap. "Bingo!"

"First of all, I didn't date Rodney," Willa corrected. "I went on a date with him after Landon, and while it wasn't bad, it was better for all involved to just stay friends. Second, every time I'm frustrated doesn't mean it's about a man. I think that could be considered sexist, you know?"

Martha took a cookie and went to the fridge to pull out the jug of sweet tea. She started pouring her glass while talking around the bite of cookie in her mouth.

"Well, it's not like you're exactly out here living some kind of exciting life. No offense—"

"Hey! Much offense," Willa interrupted.

Martha kept on like she hadn't said a word. "—so excuse me for assuming it had something to do with relationships. But if it isn't about some man," she continued, "then what is it about? Did something happen at work?"

Willa might have been older by two years, but there were moments when concern for her family overtook Martha that she seemed older and—dare Willa think it?—maternal. She finished pouring her tea and leaned against the counter, nearly matching eyes on Willa.

"You can talk to me, you know?" Martha added. "I won't judge."

Willa wasn't worried about her sister judging her for what she had done the last month. She didn't think Martha would give her any grief over the fact that, for almost four weeks, she had doubled down on a mystery that may or may not exist. That her heart was starting to—or maybe, as she suspected, already had—become attached to a man and his family who had been gone for thirty-five years. Willa should have told her sister then, between the dying plant and fresh cup of sweet tea, all about the box and its collection of odd contents.

But then she thought of what wasn't in the box anymore.

The one item she had taken out and hidden in a separate place.

The one object that might have piqued Detective Gray's attention, despite his reservations about Willa's story.

She might have trusted her sister, respected and loved her, but something about what had happened to Josiah and the box kept Willa's stomach tight.

She didn't want to tell Martha because it felt like anyone else knowing would put them in danger somehow. Just like when someone can feel someone else staring at them or watching them. It was a simple feeling that Willa couldn't escape.

Though it was one she was hoping would have gone away had Detective Gray believed her.

"I know I can talk to you," Willa said, voice soft. "But I'm fine. Today's personal day was work-related and frustrating, but nothing bad. I'm just tired. I didn't sleep that well last night."

It wasn't all a lie but it wasn't all the truth. Guilt and shame pushed frustration and anger out of Willa but she stuck with what she'd said. She didn't know what was worse, though. The fact that Martha seemed to believe her or the fact it was so easy to let her believe her. Either way, the subject changed, they ate cookies together and, after a while Martha declared it was time to go back to work.

She patted the top of Willa's hand before she left.

"Don't forget family dinner will be this week," Martha said halfway out the door. "I cooked last week so you and Kimball are combining your powers to make this meal."

"Oh, I won't forget," Willa assured her sister. "Mom's already promised to send me a recipe to attempt."

Martha laughed. "God help us all!"

Willa would have taken offense to that but it was like another switch had flipped within her. Talk of a normal family dinner made her think about Josiah. Thinking about Josiah made her think of the box. And thinking about the box?

Well, that led her to the small window seat at the front of the room.

Willa looked around as if someone had somehow snuck in and was hiding in the room with her. She waited a few moments and then pulled up on the cushion.

There was no box inside. Or at least not a sturdy one.

She took the lid off of a shoebox and stared at what she should have told the detective about.

A shiver went up her spine.

Willa had never been comfortable around guns.

THE DAY DRAGGED out longer than Kenneth's sinus medication supply lasted. By the time five o'clock rolled around, his head felt like it was trapped in a vise.

"You know, Delilah, there are some people up north who don't even know what humidity is. One day you and I are going to pack our things, take a truck, and just head north. What do you think about that?"

Delilah didn't seem to mind the fantasy. She wagged her tail and then let out a yawn. Kenneth gave her a gentle pat. Despite the building pressure in his head, he smiled. There was just something about a dog that made the world a little bit better.

A rap against the door made that tail wagging go into overdrive.

He turned to see Foster Lovett filling his doorframe. Lovett was the lead detective for the sheriff's department and one of the reasons why Kenneth had agreed to return. For all the hot water the department had found itself in with the town a few years prior, Lovett had been doing his damnedest to pull them all out of the mud. He'd also, according to the sheriff, been the reason why the cold case unit had been formed. Getting each case solved and sorted wasn't just a job to Lovett; it was more important. And that had gained Kenneth's respect.

He also had seen Delilah earlier and had only smiled, polite.

That, too, made Kenneth like him more.

"Hey there, Lovett. How can I help you?"

The detective leaned in the doorway. There was a file beneath his arm and he was rubbing his wedding band with his thumb. He looked tired but Kenneth didn't know if that was from work or the newborn baby he and his wife, Millie, had at home.

"I just came in here to check on you," he responded with a smile. "I saw how crowded the lobby got today. If I hadn't been on the way to court to testify in a case, I might have given you a hand to help cut down on how many people you had to talk to."

Kenneth shrugged. "This is the job," he said simply. "Everyone thinks they have a story and it's my duty to listen to the stories... Even if it makes me want to drink more coffee than I'm sure is good for me."

Both men laughed. Most of the people in the department had a running joke about how much coffee each of them drank, especially since the county coroner, Amanda Alvarez, had come to the department to school them all on their health.

"You can't help people if you don't help yourself," she'd said. "Make some healthy choices. For starters, maybe don't drink your weight in coffee before noon every day."

No one had promised her they would cut down on their coffee yet Kenneth had been surprised to see that some had actually followed her advice, most notably Deputy Park. Though that might have less to do with his personal health and more to do with the fact that he seemed to be a big fan of Dr. Alvarez. But that wasn't Kenneth's business.

"Well, either way, I'm impressed that you made it through them all," Foster continued. "Did anyone tell you anything you think has actionable information?"

Kenneth ran his hand through his hair, using the small gesture to buy him an extra second or two to think about how he wanted to respond.

"There were a few people who gave me names and spoke about cases they believed had been filed wrong. Most of them I already knew about. Just like I knew most of the people who brought it up were directly involved with those who, because of whatever crime they'd committed, are now serving time. Still, I'll look into them, but I don't imagine we'll get anything new there. Also, there was another name I was given that I hadn't heard before."

"Oh yeah? Who?"

"Josiah Linderman?"

Lovett's eyebrows came together in contemplation. "Linderman... I can't say that rings a bell. Who is he?"

"Some man who disappeared thirty-five years ago around here. There allegedly was no proof of foul play and many thought he'd left town of his own accord. Now I have a woman who believes he was murdered instead. Thinks she found some evidence that points to her conclusion."

"Hmm. If I recognized the name, I could throw in my two cents, but even if I hadn't left town for over a decade before coming back, I'd say that's a little bit before my time. But you know Sheriff Chamblin was here then. If you think there's some credence to the story, I'd go talk to him tomorrow. He should be in-house for at least the morning before having to deal with more of the press." Lovett smiled. It was a humoring one.

Kenneth might not have worked previously under Sheriff Chamblin but he knew enough about the older man to know that talking to the press was his least favorite thing to do when it came to his duties. He also wasn't big on sitting behind the desk, yet that's what he'd been doing more and more lately. Though, after what had happened to Annie McHale, being transparent with the community and making damn sure the department was completely aboveboard might have been the most boring aspect of his job, it was now one of the most important.

Still, that didn't mean the sheriff had to like it. He might actually welcome the change of talking about a potential cold case.

"All right," Kenneth said. "I'll talk to him tomorrow to see if he knows anything."

"Sounds good to me. Are you about to head out?"

Kenneth nodded and rolled his chair back. He already had Delilah's leash in his hand. "If I don't get her home and take her for a walk, I'm sure there'll be hell to pay later on when I'm trying to fall asleep."

Lovett laughed again.

"Same goes for me and not relieving Millie from Mom duty soon," he said. "She loves our son a whole lot but you should see her pass him off like a football as soon as I make it to the property line. Not that I blame her. I don't think she's slept since he was born."

It was meant as a way to end the conversation on a casual note. Something polite to say instead of just saying "Okay, I'm headed out because it's the end of my shift." But it struck a chord that often got played when people around Kenneth spoke of their families.

No matter how many years went by, there were some moments that reminded him of his own lost family.

Of Ally's death.

Of her murder.

Of a man in a mask who had, for no reason that anyone knew of, decided to kill her while she'd been out for a jog.

Kenneth balled his fist, the leash in his grip and pen in the other hand.

He glanced down at the top of his desk and at the pad of paper he'd been writing on that day.

There were names and cases that filled the small page.

Yet there was one name that Kenneth eyed with ease among the others.

Josiah Linderman.

Chapter Four

The sheriff had been surprisingly absent the next day.

So Kenneth spent that Tuesday night sitting on his back porch, in a patio chair that had seen much better days, and watching Delilah run around.

All the while thinking about freckles and sunshine. About how something nagged at him about Willa Tate.

Kenneth had intended to talk to the sheriff today about Josiah, but when it had become clear that talk was going to have to wait, he'd dug into the files in his office, searching for any hard-copy records of cases from 1984 through 1986. Surprisingly there weren't many cases that had been challenging or unsolved from the timeframe. A robbery turned deadly. A bike theft. A complaint of harassment by an anonymous source against a man who'd owned the hardware store in town at the time.

In most small towns that would be normal—the whole "not having a lot of cases that piqued much interest"—but Kelby Creek wasn't normal. It hadn't been for years.

Delilah barked and then shot across the yard to the corner of the fence. Just as quickly as her attention had diverted to it, it switched again to the other side of the yard. She bounded playfully, just enjoying being outside. Kenneth imagined she was mostly happy to no longer be sitting in his dusty office. She was free here. At least, free from all the violence and wrongdoing that surround them both in the storage room at the department.

Kenneth reached for the beer that he had opened an hour ago. It was no longer cold but it was completely full. He rubbed his thumb along the label and snorted as a memory floated through.

I've never met a man who has such a hard time learning to relax. If bad guys can sit back and drink beer, and not worry about the law like you catching them, then I think you can enjoy a drink every now and then, too.

Kenneth hadn't heard Ally's voice in almost eight years. And that was only because, on the anniversary of her death, he'd finally mustered up the courage to listen to a voice mail he'd been diligently saving. The last one she'd left him. But sitting here now, it was like she was standing at his ear and repeating something she had often told him throughout their marriage.

"I know how to relax," he would always say, trying to defend himself.

"Whatever you say."

Ally's lips would then turn up at the corners and she would smile a brief, beautiful smile, and Kenneth would slowly start to relax. She'd always been good at that. While he was in his own head about work, about cases, she'd remind him that there was more than just what was in his head.

Kenneth put the beer bottle back down.

He looked at his cell phone and then at the card lying against the thigh of his jeans. Willa Tate's name was in bold.

After he'd gotten home last night, he had done a social media search of the woman. Mostly to see if she was the kind of person who posted all over the internet about wild, outlandish things but partially because he was curious. Kenneth had grown up in Kelby Creek but he'd spent his summers in Georgia at his grandparents' home. After he'd graduated high school, he'd moved there for a few years to go to school for criminology. Then he'd gone to the academy and right back to Kelby Creek, accepting a job as a deputy.

In his absences, he'd missed a few new faces, forgotten some old ones, and had run into several he'd wished he'd never see again. Small towns were like that. At least, he felt that way. You couldn't go to the grocery store without running into at least three people you knew, but you could go to a football game and stare into the crowd and not know at least twenty of the people staring back.

That's who Willa Tate was to him. A local in the crowd he'd just managed to never meet.

According to the internet and her public posts, she was a few years younger than him, seemed to like to laugh a lot, and was surprisingly single.

The last detail shouldn't have mattered but he found himself making a note of it anyway. A small piece of information that held no bearing whatsoever on her interest in Josiah Linderman and the box she'd brought to the department. Yet he'd wondered why a person who was like sunshine didn't have someone in her life bathing in her light. It seemed a damn shame, if he was being honest.

Apart from those small facts that he gleaned off the internet, Willa seemed like a normal woman. And by normal, he meant not the type who would try to dig up someone else's tragic past for attention or any kind of fame.

That was why he was on his back porch this Tuesday night in the first place. Watching his dog run and play, his mind coming back to Josiah Linderman, the box and the nagging feeling that he'd missed something during his conversation with Willa Tate yesterday at the department.

It took him another hour or so to realize that what he was feeling had less to do with what she'd said and more to do with what she hadn't. Also, the box itself. If it did contain the clues to an unsolved murder, why put them in a box so big? It was almost like something was missing, and that bothered him.

It bothered him as he lay awake in bed later that night. It continued to bother him on Wednesday morning as he drank his coffee and took Delilah out for one last walk. As he talked to his neighbor and thanked her for keeping an eye on his golden pooch while he was at work. And all the way to his office with the Storage placard on the door.

So he grabbed his pad of paper, pen and coffee thermos, and marched down the hall to the door that read Sheriff.

He knocked and was glad to hear a callout in response. "Come in!"

Kenneth opened the door to reveal a burly man with laugh lines, gray hair, and a cowboy hat on the desktop. He had a folder open in front of him with a stack of papers on top. He didn't look displeased to see Kenneth, but it wasn't hard to tell that, if given the choice to teleport to some faraway tropical island versus continue to do whatever paperwork he was looking at, he'd be on some sandy beach drinking mai tais.

"Hey, boss. If you didn't mind, I was wondering if we could talk for second?"

Interim Sheriff Brutus Chamblin dropped the pen like it was a snake ready to bite him.

"No offense, Gray, but talking to a wall right now would be preferable to doing this paperwork." He shook his head. "You know there were days during retirement where I'd get so antsy that I felt like I was about to run out of my skin. Now that I'm back until this town can get a new sheriff I think about fishing with an ice-cold beer in one hand and my no-good brother-in-law complaining about being too hot at my shoulder, and I'll be a daggum monkey's uncle if I don't miss it something fierce."

Kenneth laughed. "Everyone's got something to say about working, but no one really tells you what to do with retirement. Though I do think that's the point."

Chamblin chuckled then shrugged. "Well, if that ain't the truth."

His posture went from casual to a little more stiff. The humor that planted the crinkles at the edges of his eyes was gone. In its place was a man who was good at his job and wanted others to be good at theirs, too. "Now, what brings you here to me before you've even finished your first cup of coffee?"

"I met with a woman two days ago who claims that she might have information on an unsolved murder back in the eighties. The murder of a Josiah Linderman. I looked through the files, but couldn't find anything on him, not even a missing persons report, so I was wondering if you knew Josiah or knew of him?"

Chamblin took a moment to think. Then he nodded.

"It's been a while since I heard the name but, yeah, I knew Josiah. Well, I'd gone to church with him and his wife before she passed. We'd said a few words here and there but weren't close. Let's see… When he went missing, I would have been a deputy here. Not on the job too long. I can't speak to anyone filing or not filing a missing persons report, but I do remember helping our church along with others to look for him."

"And you didn't find anything," Kenneth suggested.

Chamblin shook his head.

"One Sunday he was there and the next there was an empty seat in one of the pews. After a while, the name and what happened just kind of faded. Sad to say it but true." His eyebrow rose, even more curious than Kenneth had been when Willa had first told him her theory. "This woman, did she find a body?"

It was Kenneth's turn to shake his head.

"No, sir. But she thinks she's found enough for me to look into. Before I made my decision, I wanted to see what you knew."

"I'm afraid that's all I have. It was a long time ago and, as much as I like to say my memory is a steel trap, just as it had been when I was a deputy or a detective, I'd be lying." He gave Kenneth a small but genuine smile. "I trust your judgment on this. That's the whole reason why you are the only man we had fingered for the cold case unit. You've got good instincts and a drive that a lot of people just don't have. Let me know what you decide."

Kenneth, ready to leave after he'd said a quick thank you, paused before he made it to the door.

"You know, throughout my career, at least up until this point, I've noticed that when people say someone has 'disappeared,' it's because they can't decide if that person left of their own free will or was forced. Now, if it's clear the person didn't leave of their own volition, they usually say 'taken.' And then there are people who use the word 'missing.' In my experience that typically means they've made up their mind and believe the person in question didn't just run off, that something happened to them. Something most likely that was bad."

The sheriff's brow furrowed for a moment. "I'm guessing I said 'missing,' didn't I?"

Kenneth nodded. "Yes, you did. You think Josiah Linderman was killed, don't you?"

Chamblin sighed. "I guess I do, despite there not being a lick of evidence to support the idea."

"Can I ask why?"

The sheriff didn't have to think on it this time.

"Grief or not, he loved his kids. You didn't have to know him that well to see that they meant the world to him. I don't think there's any way he would've let them willingly go into the system. He was all they had."

It wasn't a fancy answer, but it didn't have to be fancy to be a good one.

"Thanks, Sheriff. I'll let you know if anything progresses on this."

Kenneth went back to his office. He had to take care of a few things and then make a call.

IT WAS THE big boss's birthday and after lunch everyone went home. Well, everyone was told they could go home but instead the party continued on at the only bar in Kelby Creek.

The Rosewater Inn was a smattering of weird decisions.

In the first stage of its life, it had been a motel. In the second stage, it had been partially renovated to a bed-and-breakfast. When that hadn't gone anywhere, the next life stage took an even stranger turn, and the Rosewater was divided into three pieces. To the left, when standing in the parking lot facing the building, there was the portion that had been made into the bar. The middle section, transformed into storage, had been closed off to everyone but the owners for the last several years. The right portion of the building had been converted into rental office suites. At the moment, there was a salon, an accountant and a bona fide psychic—according to her sign in the window.

All in all, the Rosewater was just one of those places that was definitely unique.

It was also a place where you could find trouble if you had too many of their specialty drinks. Last time Willa had gone with Ebony after work she'd sent a text to one of her exes saying that she still wanted to kiss his face, somehow lost a shoe, and had woken up with one the worst hangovers she'd had since college. So when the party went from celebrating her boss turning seventy with cake, soda and a sandwich platter to being at the Rosewater at 2:00 p.m. on a Wednesday with a bunch of construction workers grateful for paid break, Willa made sure to enjoy herself while staying on her best behavior.

Though that plan wobbled its way out the door when her phone rang. The Caller ID read Unknown. She excused herself from Ebony's side to go out to the parking lot to take the call.

"Hello?"

Before the voice came through the line Willa had hoped it would be Detective Gray on the other end but when she actually heard his voice, her stomach still fluttered.

"Miss Tate? This is Detective Gray, with the Dawn County Sheriff's Department. We met on Monday."

"Oh, hi, Detective! What can I do you for? Did you find anything about Josiah?"

There was no hesitation on the other side of the phone.

"No, but I would like to meet with you again. Today, if possible. Would you mind if I swung by your work? I'm out of the office on some business and thought it would be easier."

Willa had a rule about not letting anyone make her feel embarrassed unless she'd earned it, but the heat of a blush was making its way up her neck and into her cheeks. Unfortunately, there was no way around where she currently was.

A bar.

On a Wednesday afternoon.

Not exactly normal operating hours.

Also not something she wanted being spread as gossip around the department if he repeated the information.

"I… I'm not at work right now. How about meeting at the coffee shop on Main? I can be there in twenty?"

Detective Gray wasn't as quick to respond, but after a moment she felt like he nodded into his answer of okay.

"I'll see you there in twenty, Miss Tate."

Chapter Five

Half an hour went by. Then another ten minutes. Before another five could pass, Kenneth gave Willa another call.

Her phone rang and rang and rang.

Then her voice mail played with her telling whoever was calling that she must have stepped away from her phone, to leave a name, number and reason for their call, and she would call them back. It was a professional message yet... There was a tone of happiness he assumed was her natural state as she said to have a good day at the end of it.

This time Kenneth left a message.

"Hey there, Miss Tate. This is Detective Gray again. I'm at the café and got a little curious as to where you might be. Give me a call back. I hope to see you soon."

Another few minutes went by and there was no Willa Tate to be seen.

Kenneth paid for his coffee, asked the barista if Willa came in to tell her to call him, and tried to walk around the feeling in his gut he was not liking at all.

He pulled her business card back out as soon as he settled behind the wheel of his SUV. This time he called Clanton Construction's main number printed beneath hers.

After a few rings, a man picked up. It was clear that, based on the noise in the background, the man was probably not at a construction site.

"This is Bobby. How can I help you this fine, fine afternoon?" There was laughter in the background along with a lot of chatter. Whoever Bobby was, he also sounded like he was having a good time.

"Hi there, Bobby. I was actually looking for Willa Tate? Is this where I can reach her?"

The sound of movement made the connection go slightly static. Wherever Bobby was, he hadn't left the commotion, though Kenneth guessed he'd stepped away from it enough to hear better.

"We actually closed early today due to an office event."

"Then Willa is with you?"

Maybe she was with her coworkers and had just lost track of time?

"Uh, can I ask who's asking for her?" Bobby's voice went from fun to focused in an instant.

Kenneth assumed he was friends with Willa, so he got to the point without giving away the reason.

"My name's Kenneth. I am an acquaintance of Willa's. We had plans to meet for coffee and she hasn't showed up, so I was wondering where she is."

The sound of movement was loud again in Kenneth's ear. Bobby called out to somebody. That person answered, but Kenneth couldn't hear what was said. It didn't matter. He realized he already knew that Willa wasn't there. But he waited for Bobby to confirm.

"Sorry, she left maybe a half hour ago. I can take a message for her if you want to leave one, though."

Kenneth didn't want to leave a message. What he did want was information. After very little questioning, he found out that most of Clanton Construction was at the Rosewater Inn. He kept his thoughts to himself as to why they were at a bar so early in the day and ended the call.

Putting his SUV in gear, he drove a little faster than he should have to the only bar in town.

It was nothing, he told himself.

Willa had just gotten sidetracked somewhere between the bar and the café.

Two days after she had brought a potential unsolved murder to him and the same afternoon that he just so happened to want to meet her and talk about it.

It was a coincidence that the woman he'd met who was so gung-ho about finding justice was now gone and not answering her phone.

Even as he thought it, Kenneth gripped the steering wheel with force.

Willa was probably fine. But he couldn't shake the growing sense of urgency.

So, a few minutes out from the bar, he decided to use his SUV's hands-free calling to try the woman's cell one more time.

He could be overreacting, the feeling in his gut there because Kelby Creek had a history of people just disappearing.

A history of phone calls being made but never answered.

Of women there one day and gone the next.

Kenneth tried to shake the thoughts that were starting to trail somewhere dark. Somewhere he never wanted to go again.

But then the phone stopped ringing and Willa answered.

Though, judging by the fact she answered in a whisper, he assumed it wasn't time to feel relief just yet.

"Detective Gray?" Her voice was low and hurried.

Kenneth slowed his speed, ready to turn off the road to give her his full attention if needed.

"Willa? What's wrong?"

The woman didn't immediately answer. Much like her

coworker Bobby, the sound of movement traveled across the line. However, unlike Bobby, Kenneth couldn't hear any type of chatter or commotion in the background. Instead there was her movement and then silence.

Kenneth eyed the console screen for second to see if the call had ended but then Willa's voice came through again.

"I'm at my apartment, above my sister's garage," she said, so low he almost couldn't hear her.

Kenneth matched her volume. Something was wrong. There was panic and fear in her voice even if it was faint.

"What's going on?"

When she answered, it was like a whisper on the wind.

Something that passed you by and left nothing in its wake.

"Someone else is here."

Adrenaline surged through him at her words. He was grateful in that moment for a memory that was mostly good. Thanks to his internet search the day before, he'd confirmed that she was in fact a local and had noted her last listed address.

He started to turn the SUV around, knowing exactly where he needed to head next.

"Who is with you?" There was no answer. "Willa?" He made sure to keep his voice as quiet as possible. "Willa? Are you there?"

She didn't answer.

The phone call ended.

EBONY HAD ONCE told Willa a story about how she was taking yoga to help spice things up in the bedroom with her husband. When Willa, who had been in the middle of filing at work at the time, had asked why, her friend had laughed.

"It's all about being flexible," Ebony had responded. "When you're flexible and bendy, you can have more *fun*."

Ebony had wiggled her eyebrows after she'd said it, which had only made Willa laugh all the more.

"And here I thought people did yoga for health benefits and strength."

They'd shared another laugh when Ebony had pointed out that being bendy was a benefit to everyone involved before Willa had admitted that she was as flexible as a straight arrow.

"Sounds like you should do some yoga then," Ebony had responded. "You never know how important it is to be flexible until you're in a situation where you want to be."

Willa had waved the woman off when she'd said it because they both knew the situation she was talking about was one in the bedroom behind closed doors and beneath the sheets.

But now?

Now Willa wished that she was a bendy, flexible person.

If she managed to get out of her hiding place, she swore to herself that she would take Ebony up on the offer of joining her at yoga.

That was if whoever was ransacking her apartment didn't find her first.

Because as much as she was okay with the size of her living space on any given day, the truth was that it was small. Thus, it would only be a matter of time before the man riffling through her things got to the window seat and, since the cushion that normally rested on top was no longer there, be able to see the seat's hinges and know that it opened.

And that an un-bendy, nonflexible woman was hiding inside trying to be as quiet as possible.

Footsteps sounded somewhere near the counter at the kitchenette. Something scraped the floor; the intruder must have moved a stool that had already fallen when he'd first entered. Willa didn't have time to replay all the ways she could've handled herself better when her uninvited guest had started trying to break through her door. It wasn't like there were many places to hide or a way to escape. She could have jumped from the second floor onto the concrete below to the driveway or tried to find a weapon. She could have done a lot of other things probably a lot smarter than smooshing herself into the window seat.

But she hadn't.

The only thing she had done that had made a lick of sense was to grab her cell phone.

Shortly after, Detective Gray had started to call. She'd been quick to put her phone on silent. Willa had wanted to answer the first two calls but instead she watched the phone light up the board beneath her. She couldn't tell exactly where her intruder was but then she heard him moving around her desk. At that point she'd been too afraid to move. Too afraid to even dial 9-1-1.

She also couldn't remember if the keys on her phone made noise as you typed in a number.

Then she couldn't remember the emergency setup on her phone. Wasn't there just one button to push? One key to alert the authorities without making a noise?

Her heart had been and was still beating a mile a minute.

When the detective called for a third time, Willa found some luck.

She heard the intruder rummaging around in her bedroom. Plenty of distance between the two of them where, if she talked quietly enough, the outsider couldn't hear her.

Then her luck, as small as it was, disappeared.

The footsteps returned to the living area and she ended the call.

Those footsteps came closer to her hiding place.

Willa held her breath.

Just go away, she silently pleaded.

She should have just gone straight to the coffee shop from the bar. She shouldn't have come home to change into something nicer. Why had it mattered what she'd been wearing?

Because you wanted to make a good second impression. Because, even though he ticked you off by not believing you, he looked darn good doing it. That's why you're wearing a sundress and not your work slacks. That's also why there's a tube of lipstick on the counter that you dropped before your bad mistake was banging through the door.

Willa berating herself was a good distraction for the moment.

Her heart didn't beat as fast and she wasn't on the brink of crying anymore.

She was just waiting.

Waiting for a man she didn't know to hopefully find her address, speed her way, and save the day from the intruder taking his dear sweet time to rob her.

Because that's surely what he was doing, right?

Those footsteps sounded like gunshots now. They were closer. There was nothing in the world that could take Willa's mind or nerves off of the fact that whoever was standing next to her hiding place was either looking out the window or looking down at the lid of the seat.

She should have just worn her slacks.

The intruder grabbed the lid of the window seat and started to pull up. The creak from the hinges that needed oiling were squeaking before the guy could even get his fingers beneath the lip.

Ice went through Willa's veins.

And sirens sounded in the distance.

Police sirens.

It was enough to change the next order of events.

As the lid rose, Willa pushed up with her back and aching, partially numbed legs, and yelled something awful.

She didn't have time to take in the details of the intruder shocked by her sudden presence. All she could catalog before she went into fight-or-flight mode was that it was a man. He was wearing a mask and an oversize jacket, and he was much, much bigger than she was.

"Help! *Help!*"

Willa's momentum and now raging adrenaline and fear toppled over the side of the wooden seat she had just sprung up from. The man, still coming to terms with her appearance, had stumbled a foot or so back. Her yelling for help seemed to shake him out of his surprise. He went for her as she hit the ground, palms first, elbows second, knees third.

His hands, large meaty things encased in gloves, planted themselves on either side of her rib cage and pulled up. It was an awkward and off-putting thing for him to do, driving his momentum down at an odd angle while she tried to roll out of his hold.

Soon both of them were on the floor.

"Help!" she yelled again, struggling with her voice.

Willa managed to flip onto her back in time to use her arms and legs to try to keep the man from grabbing at her again.

For a large man, he was deceptively fast.

He was on his feet and using one of them in a flash. His boot pushed Willa's flailing leg closest to him to the ground. She cried out in pain and then in absolute fear as he used one of his hands to grab her wrist. He pinned the right side of her body to her own living-room floor.

"Let...let me *go!*"

The man didn't relent. Willa tried to get out of his hold and move her leg at the same time. He held fast to his position. When Willa tried to use her left hand to free the other, he was unfazed. It was like hitting and clawing at a wall.

"The cops—the cops are coming," she croaked.

Willa prayed that the sirens they heard were actually heading to her location, but just as she had the thought, their volume decreased. They were heading away from them. It was a cruel twist of fate. One that the intruder must have found joy in.

He didn't speak but he did chuckle.

Every part of Willa deflated at the sound.

Tears started to prick the corners of her eyes.

She thought of her sister and her parents and her friends.

She thought of Josiah Linderman. Wondered if she, too, was about to go missing as she was convinced he had.

The intruder used his free hand and slipped it into his jacket pocket.

Willa started to fight again; a fish pulled from the creek water and struggling to get back.

He had expected that. Whatever was in his pocket, he didn't pull it out.

Instead, he did something that might've been even more terrifying.

He removed his foot from Willa's thigh and dropped to his knee next to her on the floor. Before she could do anything, his right hand went around her neck.

Willa tried to scream but he snuffed out the sound.

Blinded by fear and panic and pain, she was convinced she was about to die.

Chapter Six

Kenneth was seeing red.

Red and black and sunshine yellow.

The only thought that went through his head was not to shoot for fear of hitting Willa. Instead he did what he believed anyone else would do.

Kenneth was on the man the second he stepped through the door of Willa's apartment.

The punch caught the man wearing black off guard, but not as much as the tackle. The attacker might have been tall and wide but so was he. And if a career in law enforcement had taught Kenneth anything, it was that a person with surprise on their side often had the best advantage.

They both fell backward onto the floor though Kenneth managed to get to his feet much faster. He threw another punch with every intention of trying to knock the man out.

It didn't take.

Instead, Kenneth took an uppercut that nearly put him back on the floor.

Behind him, Willa could be heard coughing.

Then the red returned.

The anger.

The rage.

The absolute audacity of the man for attacking a woman in her home.

Of trying to strangle her.

All while wearing a mask.

The past rushed into his heart just as Kenneth's gut told him what to do in the present.

He felt that anger and rage vibrate through him, riding along with his adrenaline. This time when his fist connected with the man beneath him, he knew it was going to end their fight.

The man grunted but didn't swing out again.

Kenneth took a step back and pulled out his service weapon again. He'd placed it back in its holster when he'd realized he couldn't get a clear hit on the man without endangering Willa when he'd first come into the apartment.

Yet, the man was fast. He had his own gun in hand in a second flat.

Kenneth should fire off a shot.

But there was Willa to consider.

He didn't know exactly where she was behind him and he didn't know if he could shield her if the man got a shot off first.

"Let's keep calm," he said. "This doesn't need to escalate. I'm with the Dawn County Sheriff's Department. We can figure this out without anyone else getting hurt."

By the widening of his eyes, the only thing Kenneth could see through the ski mask was that the news carried some kind of weight. The man stood slowly, gun trained on Kenneth, but the aggression that had been pouring off the man in waves had lessened.

When his eyes darted to the door, he was forced to do the one thing Kenneth assumed he'd been trying not to.

He spoke.

"I'm a fast shot." His voice was deep, gravel-filled. It was also strained. He was hurting. "You might be able to stop me but not before I can kill her. Let me leave and I won't."

"I can't just let you leave," Kenneth said.

"Then you're about to be in a room with two dead bodies."

Willa made a noise.

Kenneth had to admit the statement was chilling.

Not to mention convincing.

The way the man was standing, his tone, despite reflecting obvious pain, was confident in his skill set and his threats.

Kenneth wished there had been a deputy cruiser closer to their location but when he'd called into the department, almost everyone had been responding to a nasty wreck out on the county road. Rerouting a couple of cars would take a few minutes. Maybe if he could get the man to talk…

"You have five seconds before you're the only one standing," the man added, certainty in his words. "Five. Four. Three."

"Fine." Kenneth shook his head. "Leave. But I'm not lowering my weapon. Willa, stand up and get behind me."

The man didn't seem to find the directive displeasing. He started slowly moving toward the door, never taking his aim away. There was movement behind Kenneth as he turned, letting him know that Willa was also following directions. By the time the man was about to escape, Kenneth felt the soft touch of her hands on his lower back.

"Leave the gun," Kenneth commanded.

The man shook his head.

Kenneth fired his own weapon.

Willa screamed as the man returned fire.

It turned out he wasn't fast. He also wasn't a great shot. At least, not after being hit in the shoulder by Kenneth's bullet.

His squeezing the trigger was as sloppy as his aim. The man's bullet embedded somewhere in the wall behind them. His gun clattered to the floor and he was out the door, running.

"Stay here," Kenneth yelled at Willa as he followed the man out, gun high. "Barricade the door behind me and don't open it for anyone else."

Willa let out a soft okay.

Kenneth was at the stairs and yelling for the man to stop.

He wasn't listening.

On solid ground, he ran off into the backyard without any indication that he was ready to slow down despite being shot.

Kenneth wasn't going to let him get away.

He jumped the last few steps leading to the concrete of the driveway and was on the man's heels.

They tore through Willa's sister's yard and right into the side yard of the neighbor behind her. A small wood fence was up ahead. If the man wanted to flee, he was going to have to jump it.

That would give Kenneth enough time to close the gap between them.

But the man made a startling choice. Instead of jumping the small fence, he barreled through it.

The crack of the wood against his legs made Kenneth inadvertently flinch.

"Stop! Or I'll shoot," Kenneth yelled out.

The man made no move to listen. His pace even picking up as he ran through the remainder of the yard and into the street.

A stitch pulled at Kenneth's side. Where he'd been hit across his face throbbed in pain. It had been a while since he'd run this hard. It had been a while since his veins had been filled with nothing but adrenaline.

That didn't mean he could keep chasing the man indefinitely. He needed to end the pursuit sooner rather than later.

As Kenneth approached the street, he tried to remember the layout of the neighborhood. Maybe there was a way to cut the man off if he—

The sound of a car's brakes locking up screeched through the air.

A heartbeat later, that same car slammed into the ski-masked man. Like the fence, he became the object that gave.

His body rolled up onto the car's hood and crunched into the windshield. The driver yelled out. When the vehicle stopped, both Kenneth and the driver watched as the man tumbled onto the asphalt.

"Sheriff's department," Kenneth yelled out to the driver. "Stay inside!"

The driver did as he was told as Kenneth converged on the masked man. This time there were no surprises. Willa's attacker was down and out for the count.

THE SIRENS CAME, along with Kelby Creek law, but Willa stayed put in her apartment. The man had broken her door so, as the detective had suggested, she'd barricaded it. First with a kitchen stool, then with an armchair that she'd pulled along the floor.

The same floor she had been pinned against.

She stood back and stared at the door, her phone clutched in one hand, her other hand trailing across her neck where a man's gloved hand had been.

Willa didn't cry.

But she didn't move, either.

Not until she heard it.

Footsteps rushing up the stairs. Heavy and belonging to one person.

"Willa?" That person called through the door. "It's Kenneth. Detective Gray."

That's all she needed to hear.

Willa pulled the armchair back enough to give the detective room to push inside.

She didn't bother moving the stool out of the way and he certainly didn't wait for her to move it.

"Are you okay?" he asked, closing the space between them, hands going up to her face but not touching it. Instead his hands hovered, concern in his eyes.

"Is he—? Did you get him?"

The detective nodded.

"The first two responding deputies are with him now on the street over." He motioned with his head in the direction he'd chased down the man. "I came back to make sure you were okay. Are you?" His gaze dropped to her neck. There must have been a mark. His brows drew together even more. He was upset. Just as he had been when he'd saved her.

"You came." She didn't answer his question but maybe because she wasn't sure how to. A part of her felt numb. Shock, maybe.

Detective Gray nodded. "You were in trouble," he said. "Of course I came."

Willa knew that, logically, rescuing people who called for it was part of the job when it came to law enforcement. That she was no different, just as her savior had reacted the same way his colleagues might.

Yet the part of Willa that was so close to shaking inside couldn't stop seeing the detective in front of her, ordering her to stay behind him, and only shooting when he knew that he was blocking her body with his.

And then he'd come back for her.

Full of concern, dark eyes running over her, trying to find out if there was something he could fix. Something he could help with.

Willa didn't realize what she was going to do until it was already happening.

She pushed up on her tiptoes and her lips pressed against the detective's with what she could only describe later as reflex. She wrapped her arms around his neck to anchor her there, anchor her against him, and let the weight of what had happened and her appreciation move through her lips to his.

The detective didn't move right away. They were still in an embrace that neither had expected.

But then he broke the kiss, using his hands to take her upper arms and gently move back.

Willa might have felt the pang of embarrassment or rejection, but the moment the cool air from her apartment, the apartment that had just been violated, hit her lips, the part of her that Willa had been holding off broke through.

Tears didn't start to prick at the corners of her eyes. They came out like waterfalls, rushing down her cheeks as her chest tightened and her breathing became hitched.

Her neck hurt, her leg hurt, her wrist hurt, her apartment was trashed, and she was afraid.

Willa hung her head.

Detected Gray didn't say a word.

But he didn't need to. Not when his hands dropped from her shoulders and, instead of pulling away, he pulled her against him.

She felt his chin rest on top of her hair as Willa lost it completely.

Her body racked against his with sobs, yet the detective didn't move.

He held her against him as though he knew that he was the only thing keeping her up.

That was good. Because he was.

THE NEIGHBORHOOD BECAME a cacophony of sound. It seemed that half of the responding deputies weren't communicating with the other half. Some went to the house and the garage apartment, some went to the street behind where the man had been hit, and others scoured each street. Looking for what, or who, he didn't know.

But he wasn't bothered. Not with what had happened or what he knew would happen next. He simply stood in his backyard, staring at a pool float shaped like a flamingo, and marveling at how some people's timing was impeccable while others' was far from it.

"Honey?"

He turned around at the sound of his wife's voice. The smile he reserved for his home life pulled the corners of his lips up.

"Yes, dear?"

She had a dishtowel in one hand and her phone in the other. She used the former to cover the receiver of the latter. That meant she was about to tell him some gossip that she'd just learned.

"Mrs. Appleton said she just saw the ambulance take a man away. The burglar Tim hit with his car."

"Is he alive?" The chain of information from two streets over wasn't always accurate. What one person would swear to be true, another would swear to be false. It made everything more challenging but wading through the verbal muck to get to the truth was a worthwhile challenge if it meant keeping you alive and free. The ability to get the facts and stay ahead of everyone else seemed to be something the man who'd been dumb enough to get hit by a car in a neighborhood that had a speed limit of twenty miles per hour hadn't possessed.

"As far as Mrs. Appleton is concerned, yes. But she said she heard he wasn't moving much when they put him on the stretcher before they got him into the ambulance."

He shook his head, his wife's eyes still trained on him.

"It's a dang shame something like this could happen in

our neighborhood," he decided to say. "It looks like I'll be double-checking the batteries on our alarm system today."

His wife nodded with fervor.

She had no idea the things he could do to her without batting an eye.

Instead, she looked at him like he was the only man in the world who could completely protect her.

That smile that he saved for his personal life grew.

"I'll be in in a second," he added. "I need to make one more call."

She nodded and was back on the phone with Mrs. Appleton in a flash.

Until he was sure she was on the other side of the house, he listened to the sirens moving off into the distance.

Then he took the piece of fabric out of his pocket.

Despite the years that had gone by, the bloodstain was as dark as it had been the day it had first been soaked.

He sighed into the afternoon air. It smelled like rain.

Rain was good.

It had a way of making everyone forget.

And what the rain wouldn't do, he would.

Chapter Seven

The sky was dark.

It matched everyone's moods.

Willa absently rubbed at her neck. She picked through the wreckage in her apartment, trying to assess the damage. She'd heard a deputy who'd seemed friendly with Detective Gray, say what had happened looked like a smash-and-grab. One that she had interrupted, despite trying her best to hide.

The detective didn't seem as convinced. Then again, Willa didn't know him well enough to understand all of his expressions. Had she been a betting woman, though, she didn't think he believed the man in the ski mask had had such a simple task in mind.

Or maybe Willa was projecting.

The most expensive items she owned were more or less intact. The man hadn't brought a bag or anything else to carry his stolen loot with. Instead, he'd turned her home over without so much as lifting her computer, her TV, or even her jewelry, which had been out in the open on the top of her chest of drawers.

Not to mention he had broken in during the daylight hours, while her car was parked in the driveway, and he'd brought a gun.

If that was a simple smash-and-grab, she'd hate to see what a more complex operation looked like.

Willa walked back to her bedroom again. She knew that Martha would be there soon and if she saw the mess and the mark around Willa's neck, she would lose it. So while the detective finished up with another Dawn County Sheriff's Department colleague, she started to straighten the room as best she could.

She didn't make it far. After coming across a jewelry dish that her mother had made her a few birthdays ago, broken in pieces on the floor, Willa sat on her bed and tried not to cry again.

If she had any more tears left, that is.

After kissing the detective, it seemed every tear she had in her had poured out onto the man.

If she cried now, it would just be her going through the movements without the mess.

A little knock pulled her attention from the broken dish to the bedroom's doorway. She felt a flush come over her as she locked eyes with the man who had saved her.

"Detective," she greeted.

He put his hand up to stop her.

"Please, call me Kenneth, Miss Tate."

Willa smiled at that. "Please, call me Willa, Kenneth."

He returned the small dose of humor with a nod. "Will do." His eyes went from her to the room around them, scanning the mess. He did that a lot. Looked around, like he was building a catalog in his mind. He was probably good at the details, which only made him that much better at his job.

He also had proved to be quick on his feet.

"You got here really fast," Willa noted. "After we talked on the phone, I was sure it would take you longer to get here. I also thought you'd wait for backup."

Kenneth was modest about it. He shrugged. "I was actually already looking for you when you answered my last call. It was lucky that I wasn't that far away."

Heat, pleasant and at the same time uncomfortable, rose into her cheeks. She smiled.

"It's a good thing you wanted to meet today." Willa felt her smile flip. She gave the man a questioning look. "I haven't had the chance to ask, but why did you want to meet?"

Kenneth didn't seem excited about his answer. Still, he gave it.

"I wanted to ask you some more questions about Josiah Linderman. And I wanted to take another look at the box—"

Willa jumped up and winced at the pain in her leg.

Her focus, however, pinpointed on the one thing she should have already thought about.

In that moment, she felt like a fool.

"The box! Of course, I'd forgotten about the dang box!"

She rushed back into the living room, purpose driving her heels into the floor. Everyone from the sheriff's department was gone, but still she lowered her voice when she got to the window seat.

"I haven't told my sister, or anyone, about me looking into Josiah Linderman or this box," she explained. "Martha is really nosy sometimes, not that that's always a bad thing, but sometimes that nosiness gets her to snooping into my stuff."

Willa lowered herself to her knees and bent over the side of the open window seat. Her hair swung down in her face but she didn't need to see to know exactly where the box was. She reached out to the farthest left corner that she could access and felt the worn wood beneath her hand.

When she pulled it out, she couldn't help but feel a little guilty about having a hiding place specifically from her sister.

"Since I found this, I've been putting it in here and covering it with blankets." She motioned to the quilt she'd hurriedly thrown out as she'd gotten inside the window seat to hide from the intruder. "Martha may like to snoop, but if it's too much trouble, she doesn't bother herself with it. So, at least as far as I know, she never found the box and no one else knows it exists."

Kenneth gave her a look she couldn't quite decipher. She led him to the counter, where she put the box on its top.

"If you're wondering about my thought process on why I hid this and didn't tell anyone about it, let me remind you that Kelby Creek doesn't have the greatest track record when it comes to mysteries. I mean during the last two years there have been some really wild ones that have overtaken the town." Willa tapped the top of the box. "I was hoping I could solve one by myself without getting caught in something slightly terrifying. In my mind that could happen if I was the only one who knew about it."

"To be honest, that is a very fair point when it comes to Kelby Creek," Kenneth conceded.

He didn't open the box right away.

Willa watched as his expression changed again to an emotion she couldn't read. She was about to ask him point-blank what he was thinking, but he pulled the lid open before she could.

Willa's gaze stayed on his expression before falling to his lips and staying there for half a second too long. She hadn't addressed the fact that she had kissed him and he hadn't addressed the fact that he'd held her for a long while before his colleagues had showed up. Maybe because they both knew it was an overflow of emotions brought on by a traumatic event, but Willa found that a great big part of her wanted to feel the man against her again. To feel his warmth and steadiness. To feel his heart beating at a steady rhythm against hers, reminding her at every beat that he was there.

But while she was daydreaming about his touch and how it had made her feel safe, Kenneth became rigid with tension.

Willa looked down at the box.

She gasped.

"Judging by your reaction, I'm assuming you're not the one who took the piece of fabric out, are you?" Kenneth's voice wasn't cold but it was clipped. Professional. He was back to being Detective Gray.

"No. I didn't," she answered. Willa's palms became sweaty. She felt sick. "No one knows about the box, just like I already said. And I was already hiding with it when that man first broke in. He had no time to take that cloth. How was it gone if he didn't take it and no one else knew about it?"

Kenneth shook his head.

"If this box contained evidence of an unsolved murder, then outside of you and me there is at least one other person who knows what was and is supposed to be in here." He gave her a long look. How she wished she could be in his arms instead of on the receiving end of words that chilled her to the bone. "The killer."

"HIS NAME IS Leonard Bartow and he's been a nuisance to this department since before The Flood."

Deputy Carlos Park had made a face when he'd said the man's name and that off-key expression only soured further as he'd said "The Flood."

Kenneth had no doubt he didn't look happy, either, at the mention of the latter, to be fair.

The Flood was a town-wide nickname for the disaster that had created a rift between the locals and those in positions of authority years before. Friends, families and neighbors had all gone from trusting those with a badge or influence to automatically assuming they were part of the conspiracy surrounding the abduction of Annie McHale, the daughter of one of the most beloved families in Kelby Creek. Or that those same people were crooked in some other way.

It was the main reason why so many closed cases needed reevaluating and why any cold case related to those who had been caught in the conspiracy were being reopened and double-checked.

Never mind the remaining cold cases that had never been solved even once.

It was why the unit Kenneth headed, and solely ran for the time being, had been created.

The Dawn County Sheriff's Department was still understaffed almost three years after The Flood.

It needed someone with singular focus and drive. Someone to help without distraction. Someone who had a unique motivation to find justice for those no longer around to seek it themselves.

"Does he make a habit of attacking women in their homes during broad daylight?" Kenneth's voice came out in a low growl.

Deputy Park sighed and crossed his arms over his chest.

"If he does, it didn't show up in any reports or complaints," he answered. "His track record in Kelby Creek over the last decade has been burglary. Unarmed at that. He went into offices, cars and residential homes when no one was around, grabbed the most valuable things he could, and then was gone. The only way we even knew it was him half of the time was through security or home cameras and eyewitnesses after he left. He might seem sloppy while he's doing his thing, but after he leaves a place, it's like he simply disappears into thin air. *Poof.*"

"But he has a record."

Deputy Park nodded. "Before he went *poof*, he was caught twice within three years. Spent some time in prison for it."

"And now he's strangling women and carrying a gun," Kenneth said with a snarl.

"It seems like it."

They took a moment of silence to think on that. A few deputies who had responded to his call for backup were behind them, chatting and enjoying their break. A few doors down, Willa and the sheriff were finishing up her official statement in the department's meeting room.

He wished he had a way to erase the last few hours from her memory, but knew trauma wasn't something one could just wish away. Instead, he focused on what he could.

"The car they found a few blocks away, which they think is his, you said it had several items in it that were stolen?"

Deputy Park nodded again. "It's looking like he broke into two other houses up and down the same street before he got to Miss Tate. Some of the items were in the car when we found it."

"Do you have a catalog of the items? Or a picture?" Kenneth wondered if the fabric from the box had been inside, even though Willa had been adamant that there was no way Leonard would have had the time to get it while she was there.

Regardless, it wouldn't hurt to look.

"Yeah, we have some pictures that Gordon took. Want to see them?"

Kenneth said he would.

It didn't take long after that to start wrapping the day up. He went to his office and finished what he could before grabbing his things and heading to the meeting room. It was good timing; the sheriff was coming out.

He wasn't in a good mood at all. No one was a fan of

what had happened that afternoon. He was quick to give
his recap of his thoughts but then patted Kenneth on the
shoulder and said he had to deal with the press.

"The whole town will know by tomorrow about what
happened. I better get prepared."

Kenneth didn't envy that side of the job and told the
sheriff good luck.

He popped his head inside the meeting room as soon as
the man was gone and locked eyes with the woman he'd
been worrying about since that morning.

Willa was standing, cell phone in her hand.

She looked lost.

"Everything all right?" Kenneth knew it wasn't, but he
had to say the words.

A strained smile righted itself across her lips.

"Just tired, I think. Maybe a little overwhelmed, too."

Kenneth didn't like the way she sounded. He didn't like
the mark around her neck. He didn't like the way she was
putting up a front of smiles and being accommodating when
she was the one who had been attacked.

It made him feel...protective.

And he hadn't felt that in a long time.

"Do you need a ride home?"

Willa nodded but held up her phone. "Kimball told me
to call when I was finished here."

Kimball Smith, Kenneth knew, was Willa's brother-in-
law. He'd been the first to arrive on scene outside of law
enforcement back at the apartment. Without announcing
who he was, he had picked Willa up in a hug and spun her
in a half circle. It was only after Willa returned the embrace with several assurances that she was okay that she
introduced the two of them. Before she'd done so, Kenneth
couldn't get around the fact that he hadn't known if Willa
Tate was seeing anyone. Sure, her online profiles might

have said "single," but that didn't mean she hadn't been dating anyone.

Now he didn't have to guess on it. She all but told him the only people who would be calling after her were her sister, her brother-in-law, her friend Ebony, and the people she worked with. Anyone else would be after gossip.

"My shift just ended," Kenneth surprised himself by saying. "If you don't mind, I'd like to give you a ride."

It might have been his imagination, but Willa's shoulders dropped a little, like the tension in them had lessened.

"That would really be nice," she said. "I think Kimball and Martha are actually out buying a new security system right now. So, yeah, if you don't mind, that would be great."

"I promise I don't. Come on. Let's get out of here."

Chapter Eight

It had already started raining in some parts of Kelby Creek.

Willa could smell it in the air.

Normally, that would have been a topic of conversation. An easy one to make with someone you barely knew, especially while in the car with them. Yet she kept quiet about it. The urge to dish out her Southern niceties was gone.

A rare occurrence for her.

Instead, she'd remained silent after the detective had finished his quick call before leaving the parking lot.

Kenneth, however, didn't seem to like the silence. He spoke the moment he started driving. "So, did the sheriff tell you about Leonard Bartow?"

Willa fought the urge to touch her neck. An EMT had told her in her driveway that she was lucky her attacker hadn't been stronger and that Kenneth had showed up when he had. A bruise was much preferable than more extensive damage that could be caused in that area. At least she could talk without it hurting. Apparently, that wasn't always the case.

The thought made Willa wholly uncomfortable just thinking about the what-ifs.

"Yes," she answered. "He said that Leonard has a history of breaking into people's houses and stealing. He also said that today's stop at my apartment was his third break-in.

Leonard must have expected me to be in the main house and not the garage apartment, which is why he attacked."

Out of her periphery, Willa saw Kenneth turn toward her.

"But you don't believe that." It was a statement. One that was true.

"I stand by what I said. There is no way Leonard got that fabric when he broke into my place. He couldn't have. I was literally pressed up against the box. *But* I don't think him being there was a coincidence. He was in my apartment for almost half an hour. Why? It's not that big a space and all of my valuables? They were just out in the open, ready to be taken. So what was he doing?"

"Do think he was waiting for you?" Kenneth's voice had gone flat.

Willa was glad to shake her head.

"If he was waiting for me, he picked a weird time to do it. My normal workday is until five and going to my house before I was supposed to meet you was a last-minute decision." Willa looked down at her sundress. It seemed so silly now that she'd gone through so much all because of wanting to wear a dress to impress the man next to her.

She shook her head again. "He had to be there about the box, right? It's too much of a coincidence not to be."

Kenneth was thoughtful when he responded.

"The timing of it all does make it more suspect. He put himself at a lot of risk to seemingly do nothing. Just breaking into a place that has a car parked outside is dangerous. Even if he might have thought the car belonged to someone in the main house. Not only did he do that, he did it during the day and then he stayed. I can't tell if he had a plan or if he's not the brightest tool in the toolshed. Either way, it's all definitely suspicious."

"It also makes it slightly terrifying." They slowed to stop at a light. She shared a glance with him before looking down at her hands. "Let's say Leonard didn't know about the box at all... Then who took the cloth?"

Kenneth didn't have an answer. Not that Willa had expected one. In fact, she hadn't expected anything from the man after their meeting on Monday.

"You called today because you wanted to talk. Does that mean you found something about Josiah?"

Kenneth's eyes were back on the road. They didn't stray her way as she studied his profile. His jaw was hard, his brow pronounced with concentration, and his lips were warm. At least they had been when she'd kissed him.

But that was part of a different conversation Willa wanted to have with the man. Not the one she needed at the moment.

"I didn't find anything on Josiah but, after talking to the sheriff and thinking on it some more, I wanted to see if you could walk me through what you've done since finding the box."

"You mean my investigation?"

Willa saw the corner of his lips twitch like he was holding in a smile.

"Yeah. I want to make sure I'm on the same page with you before I go any further."

Hope sprang eternal in Willa's chest. "So, you're officially taking on Josiah's case?"

"More like I'm going to try to figure out what's going on with that box."

Willa was pleased as punch about that. She smiled wide.

"Either way, I'm glad to hear it. I was starting to feel like one of those killers on a TV show. You know, the ones who have like a weird shrine of pictures or a bulletin board with tons of strings attached to it."

"Believe me, you're no killer."

Embarrassment took heat from Willa's stomach and pushed it up into her cheeks.

She hadn't met Kenneth before yet, as a local, she knew about the murder of his wife. There might have been the odd homicide in Kelby Creek and Dawn County but the killing of a young woman out jogging with no leads? That had been on repeat on the news.

And, if she had somehow managed to miss that, then Kenneth taking the job as the head of the cold case unit had put the story back into circulation.

Willa's heart squeezed at her poor choice of words.

"I... I'm sorry," she tried to rectify by saying. "I didn't mean to—"

Kenneth held up his hand to stop her. "It's okay. No harm done."

Willa wasn't sure it hadn't been, but she didn't say so. She quieted while the rain picked up and blurred the world around them. It helped her thoughts from sticking where they shouldn't.

That didn't last long.

Willa glanced over at the man's hand. She'd already noted his lack of wedding band on his ring finger when she'd first met him. Still, she felt the need to check again. Instead, her eyes stopped at the holster on his hip.

She must have made a noise.

Kenneth turned to her in a flash. "What?"

Willa had already blushed twice since being in the SUV with Kenneth. And for different reasons. Now she did it a third time.

Not for embarrassment or the prickling desire she suspected she was starting to have for the detective. But for the shame of overlooking the most important detail from the mystery she was trying to solve.

She gave Kenneth a long look.

"You're probably not going to like this."

THANKFULLY, THE CAR ride had been over quickly after Willa's ominous statement.

That didn't mean that Kenneth had parked the SUV in her driveway and then led the way to the garage apartment without apprehension. It was there when they walked inside of the living space that he noted that the apartment had been straightened and cleaned since earlier. When Willa turned around to face him her gaze never wavered from his as she bottom-lined why they were there.

"There used to be a gun in the box."

Kenneth ran his hand over the stubble along his jaw. He repeated her words to make sure he'd heard them right. Willa nodded.

He would have sighed in exasperation, maybe even anger, had it been anyone else who had just dropped a bombshell like that.

Instead he kept his cool. Though he had some questions.

"Why didn't you tell me when you first came to the department? That's a pretty big detail to leave out. A gun would've certainly gotten my attention a lot faster."

Willa rung her hands together. Her cheeks had turned a rosy shade again. Just as they had in his SUV. It only made part of him feel even more protective of her. Being in the room where she'd been attacked was only making that feeling stronger.

"Well, I was trying to figure out this whole situation before coming to the department in first place, since I didn't know who to trust. I mean, I know that the sheriff's department isn't like the one before The Flood, but there's just so much water that hasn't actually gone under that bridge for us locals. And… I don't know, I just didn't want to chance missing out on getting some kind of justice or answers for Josiah's family."

"So you didn't tell me about the gun because you didn't know if you could trust us. Trust me."

Willa shrugged. Those rosy cheeks became rosier.

"Well, yeah," she said. "That and the fact I didn't exactly want to bring a gun, even if it wasn't loaded, into a sheriff's department. So I decided to kind of feel you out first."

He put his hands on his hips and slid his eyebrow up question.

"You decided to feel me out first," he repeated, slightly humored.

A quick smile passed over her lips before deepening into a frown.

"Yes. But then you kind of dismissed me, so I decided not to bring up the gun. When you called me today to meet, I was going to tell you then. Or, at least, I think I would've. The day kind of got away from me, and not in the best way, as you know."

Kenneth noted the way her hand flexed. He bet she was keeping it at waist level with thoughtful intention. He'd already caught her several times lightly brushing the bruised skin of her neck.

The sight of her trying to control the reflex made his disbelief that she hadn't told him about the weapon soften. He let out a breath, purposely loosening his shoulders.

"So you found the gun and then you hid the gun," he stated. "Where is it now?"

Before they had gone into the department for Willa to give her official statement, she and Kenneth had decided to find a different place to put the box. At first, he'd suggested taking it to the department. But with Willa's adamant insistence about keeping it, despite the break-in, he'd relented. There was just something about the tear tracks down her cheeks and her bloodshot eyes that made him want to give her everything she wanted. Or, at a minimum, not add to her current stress.

They'd moved the box from the window seat to, of all places, the refrigerator. He had laughed at the suggestion but realized in hindsight that it had been a pretty good place to hide something. How many people with bad intentions broke into a home and went through the fridge?

He chuckled to himself as she went to the freezer portion of the refrigerator and opened the door. She looked inside and breathed a sigh of relief so loudly that Kenneth found another bit of tension fall away from his shoulders.

"It's in there?" He walked over and stopped at her shoulder.

Willa actually clapped. "Yes. Thank goodness!"

She moved aside as Kenneth pulled on the latex gloves he'd taken from the trunk of his vehicle. No matter what he drove, he always carried them around everywhere.

"Is…is that it?"

At the back of the freezer, next to a box of Toaster Strudel, sat a large Tupperware container. Through its clear sides, he saw something black inside.

Willa crossed her arms over her chest, defensive.

"Hey, watch that tone. I wasn't going to put a gun willynilly in my freezer. What do you take me for? An amateur?"

Kenneth was going to comment that that's exactly what she was, but glanced over in time to see her smirk. She was teasing him.

When she saw that he understood she was playing with him, she shrugged again.

"Plus, I'm a good Southern woman. One thing we have in spades are plastic containers. I've used them for leftovers, sewing needles and thread, chocolate-covered whatevers, and one time to catch a lizard and use it to put him outside. Why not add hiding a gun in the freezer to the list?"

Kenneth reached inside and gently pulled the Tupperware out.

"You know, I've heard and seen a lot of things during my time in law enforcement," he said. "But I can tell you with certainty that's the first time I've heard, and the first time I've seen, this."

Kenneth decided not to inspect the gun then and there. By her own admission, Willa had already done her own investigation, at least, as much as she could. He also decided, even if she wouldn't admit it, that Willa was exhausted. He didn't want to keep her from eating with her family and getting some rest.

He walked her downstairs to the side door that led into her sister's house, promising that he would look into the gun.

"My house is currently being worked on, so I have to take off tomorrow to meet with the contractor. But I can still look into this—" he tapped the lid of the container "—from home. I'd also like to talk to you about what you already know in more detail. If you don't mind waiting until Friday or, if you do, I can get you in with Detective Lovett or—"

"Or I can come over tomorrow morning with coffee and tell you all about it then?"

Kenneth was caught off guard by the offer, but not as much as how he felt about it.

On the one hand, he knew Willa's intentions were pure. She wanted to find out what had happened to Josiah Linderman while understanding every single thing about the box's contents. If he turned down her suggestion, he had every confidence in the world she would show up Friday morning bright and early.

But she didn't want to wait.

He could see that in her face, her movements, how she looked at the gun hidden in the container in his hand.

And Kenneth knew that feeling. The impatience that ate at you when all you wanted to do was to move forward but instead got stuck waiting.

He didn't want that for her. Just like he didn't want to be the one to put her through that simply because of something he had scheduled before meeting her. A meeting about pipes to boot.

On the other hand, he couldn't help but wonder if Willa had picked up on his shifting feelings for her.

From a stranger with an interesting story to a woman he barely knew and still felt the almost primal urge to protect.

And that was before they had kissed.

Willa put up her hands to stop him before he responded. "I don't want to overstep and I don't want to encroach on your day off," she hurriedly added. "I just want to show you that I appreciate what you're doing with a cup of coffee and a stress-free atmosphere."

She laughed. "Though, I guess cold cases, guns in freezers, and a relative stranger trying to come to your house doesn't exactly equal a stress-free atmosphere."

Kenneth knew the moment that she laughed what his answer was going to be.

"If you don't mind a construction zone, a very hyper golden retriever, and me asking you more questions than a dad asks his daughter's date before her prom, then that's fine by me."

Willa's lips stretched wide.

The rain was still falling around them just beyond the awning. Still, even without the contrast, Kenneth was sure she'd be just as bright.

"Sounds like a plan," she said. "Just text me your address and your coffee preference, and I'll be there come rain or shine."

Kenneth agreed to the plan. He was ready to head out into the rain and back to his SUV when Willa reached out and caught his elbow.

"Kenneth?"

He stopped and readjusted his gaze down to hers.

She was back to being solemn, lips downturned, and thoughts he couldn't hear weighing against her.

"Yeah?"

She didn't let go of his arm.

"Do you think Leonard Bartow broke into my apartment earlier to take the fabric only to come back later looking for the gun? Do you think it was all a coincidence? Bad luck on my part?"

Kenneth didn't say anything but he'd already gone through the same questions in his head. The last he'd heard, Leonard was in stable condition and Detective Lovett had already made plans to talk to him the moment he was conscious and able. Kenneth had also gone through the pictures found in Leonard's car. Nothing had been remotely linked to Willa, the box, or Josiah.

But someone had taken the piece of fabric.

And whether Kenneth believed in coincidence or not, he absolutely knew that bad luck could and did happen to good people.

"I don't know. But I can promise you this, I'm certainly going to find out. Starting with calling up Mae's brother and seeing if we can't find out more about the day Josiah Linderman went missing."

Chapter Nine

Willa knew that she had what some would call a bubbly personality. Again, that was another thing she could blame on her almost compulsive need to be polite. You catch more flies with honey than vinegar, and all of that. It wasn't until she was older that she'd realized she wasn't sure if that's who she was. The peppy blonde who laughed at jokes, worried if you'd eaten enough, and never had to borrow sugar from a neighbor because her cabinet was stocked with it.

Was that really her? Or had she fallen into a stereotype that she'd accidentally built because she thought it was what was expected of her?

Willa couldn't say for sure and it wasn't until she'd found the box and had done some digging that she'd even begun to wonder if she could be, or wanted to be, something else. Some*one* else.

She was parked at the curb outside Kenneth's house, once again asking herself the same questions that had been revolving through her mind the last month.

Introspection while holding a coffee caddy in a Mazda with a notable dent on the passenger-side door where a Walmart customer had unapologetically run into it with their cart. Even then, Willa had smiled, promised it was okay, and then gone on to put away stray carts from the spot next to hers.

She looked out the front window and wondered what Kenneth would have done in the same situation.

The smell of coffee warmed her.

This had been Willa's idea and now she was stalling.

She should've waited until Friday and not put the man on the spot and forced him to help her. At least, not help her from his home.

Willa tried to give herself a mental pep talk to get moving but before the gears could start turning, someone rapped against her window.

She jumped and turned to the confused face of someone familiar.

"Landon?"

Willa opened the door and Landon Mitchell stood back as she got out. A flush crossed her cheeks, if only for the fact she hadn't even thought of the possibility of running into her ex-boyfriend here of all places.

"Landon," she repeated. "What are you doing here?"

Her friend Ebony had once told her that she hadn't found love yet because of the first man Ebony had ever gotten into serious relationship with. Ebony had lamented repeatedly about how, no matter who she'd dated after, she couldn't help but compare him to her first love. From personality right on down to shoes.

"Sometimes you just meet a man who sticks," Ebony had said with a shake of her head. "And once that guy sticks, you can't help but put him up against every man you meet."

For all intents and purposes, Landon should have been that man for Willa. He'd been the longest relationship she'd ever had and the only one where marriage had been considered. Not to mention they'd lived together the last year of their relationship. He should have been whom she pictured, whether she meant to or not.

But wouldn't you know it, instead of listening for his

answer, she was retroactively comparing him against someone else.

Landon was almost the same height as Kenneth but built in a completely different way. He was thick with muscle from hours at the gym and a job that often required manual labor. Kenneth, on the other hand, was lean and toned. A lithe man who was strong *and* fast. Someone who sat behind a desk but who also could chase down a suspect in a flash. Then there was Landon's highlighted features that people first noticed when meeting him. Light green eyes, like grass after a rain, copper-blond hair that shagged this way and that, and a set of cheek dimples that flexed even if he was barely smiling. These were all details Willa had appreciated during their relationship.

Yet, there she was. Standing, with a coffee caddy in hand, in front of a man everyone thought she'd marry—herself included, if she was being honest—and thinking about... Eyes the color of deep blue water, hair cut close but just long enough to run her fingers through, and a seriousness to the way he smiled that gave off an edge with a vulnerability to it.

She might have loved Landon but, in a surprise that was making her cheeks burn, Willa realized she wasn't just at the detective's house because she wanted answers for a cold case.

She wanted Kenneth Gray.

And what a thing to come to realize while staring at her ex.

Landon's green-grass stare coupled with an eyebrow quirk. He pointed over her shoulder to Kenneth's house. "I have a meeting with Mr. Gray about his house."

"Oh my gosh! I didn't even put that together when Kenneth said he had a contractor coming over."

Of course, he would have hired a local contractor. It didn't hurt that Landon was good at his job, either.

"Kenneth, huh? Why are *you* here, Willa?"

Willa's defenses flared at his tone. She was not a fan of that one.

She squared her shoulders and held the caddy a little higher.

"I'm here to talk with my friend and drink some coffee," she said, sidestepping the truth. If she still hadn't told her sister about the box and Josiah Linderman, there was no way she was about to tell Landon.

"Aren't you supposed to be at work?" he challenged. "I know for a fact that Clanton is working two sites in town. Y'all have to be busy."

"I took the day off, thank you very much."

That eyebrow of his went higher, if possible.

If he'd heard what had happened at her apartment the night before with Leonard Bartow, she was sure he would've already commented on it. Instead, he was looking like he was getting wound up about who she was fraternizing with. Something she surely did not appreciate from anyone, let alone an engaged man.

Landon must have sensed he was straying near dangerous territory. He raised his hands in defense.

"Now don't go getting all squirrely on me, Willa. I was just curious is all. I haven't really seen you around town and here you are just sitting in the car outside of my client's house. You can't blame a guy for asking what's going on."

There was that polite prodding again. Willa decided to let his not-so-subtle poking pass.

"Well, how about instead of us standing here gabbing, we go in there so you can get to that client of yours?"

Landon conceded, but there was a hesitation to it. Like he wanted to say more but ultimately chose not to. Instead, he helped her get her bag out of the car and then walked with her up to the front porch.

She decided not to say anything as he stepped in front of her to knock on the door.

They lapsed into a somewhat awkward silence until Kenneth appeared.

It was the first time Willa had seen the man dressed down. It certainly wasn't a disappointing sight.

Landon cleared his throat before extending his hand.

"Good morning, Mr. Gray. Sorry again for the delay getting over here. I had an issue at this house in the county over because of all the rain from yesterday. Then I had to catch up a little with Willa here."

"That's no problem," Kenneth replied, shaking his hand. He shared a look with Willa but stepped aside to motion them both in without addressing her directly. "How about I show you around the house and we talk about what I think I want done?"

"That works for me." Landon's gaze switched to Willa, as did Kenneth's.

"Willa, if you don't mind, you can make yourself at home in my office." Kenneth nodded toward the door at the end of the first-floor hallway they were standing in. "Delilah will probably love the company. I shouldn't be long."

Willa's customer service smile must have been a flashing neon light. Both men seemed to hover over it as she nodded. "Sure thing!"

She handed his coffee over and then was off to the office without any more conversation between them. And that was good because she didn't really know what else to say.

While the last month had had many twists and turns she hadn't seen coming, standing in Kenneth's home between him and Landon Mitchell had never even entered her mind as a possible scenario. She was glad to escape and hang out in the detective's office.

Even more so when a ball of golden fur and excitement met her at the door.

"You must be Delilah." Willa laughed as the dog's tail whipped back and forth faster at the mention of her name. "Well, Delilah, my name is Willa, and I am very pleased to talk with you and not with the two of them."

Delilah seemed to agree, especially when her tummy became the target of a good belly rub.

Mr. MITCHELL GLANCED at the office door one too many times before he left. Kenneth thanked him for coming, after they'd gone through a standard recap of what happened next, before each half waved goodbye and went his separate way.

Before the contractor made it to his truck, he gave Willa's car one long look.

Kenneth paused by the front window to see the man drive off and then went to his office.

When he opened the door, he found himself pausing again.

His office wasn't at all like the one he used at the sheriff's department. This one was filled with books, art and knickknacks, pictures of family and friends, and a desk his father had built. The couch opposite the desk was the one his wife had insisted on buying so she could lounge and chat while he worked.

Since her passing, he'd gone through the difficult task of donating, storing and rearranging most of the things Ally had left behind. He'd needed it out of the house. He'd needed to not see constant reminders that she wasn't there anymore. His mother had told him, time and time again, it was all in the spirit of moving on and that there was no shame in how he or anyone else grieved. But Kenneth had known what it really was.

He'd needed to give himself space so he didn't drive himself over the edge.

Again.

Because, unlike most widows and widowers, Ally's death hadn't been natural. Or accidental.

She'd been murdered.

And walking into the empty house and seeing her clothes hanging in the closet, her favorite blanket thrown on the couch, and their wedding picture front and center over the fireplace had been a reminder.

Not only was she gone, but the man who'd taken her was still out there somewhere.

Every single day, every single night, every single moment he was in the house, Kenneth had felt that pain and frustration and near-suffocating rage.

That side of him hadn't gone unnoticed either. He'd been told to sell the house by old friends and family, to even leave town to start over somewhere new so the reminders weren't every place he went.

Yet, he could never do it.

Leaving the house, leaving town, didn't erase the fact that Ally was gone. It would just mean that he'd be gone too. Something about that had never sat well with him. He didn't want to leave. He wanted to catch his breath and keep going.

He wanted to heal.

He wanted to find her killer.

Things Kenneth knew he could never do if he left it all behind.

So, he hadn't, and now years later and the house was that of a single man. One with minimal tastes and a need for function over sentimentality.

Yet, the love he had for Ally had been as stubborn as the woman herself. One day he'd walked into his office and there she was. In the artwork on the walls, the books she'd loved nestled on the shelves, and the couch she'd nagged him about getting until he'd finally relented.

And now there was Willa, lying across the same couch and laughing when she saw him.

"In my defense, I didn't know if Delilah was allowed on the furniture so I made an executive decision that she was until you told me otherwise."

Delilah's tail was wagging a mile a minute as she popped up from her spot on Willa's chest and stomach. Kenneth smirked as her big brown eyes tracked him on the way to his desk chair.

"I tried the whole *discipline* thing when I first adopted her," he admitted. "While she may be well-trained out in the real world, when it comes to the inside of this house, she knows she's queen."

Willa seemed entirely amused by that. She sat up on her cushion and readjusted to Delilah's new position for being petted.

"Let me guess, you're the kind of guy who lets his dog sleep with him in his bed, but *also* the kind of guy who would never cop to that fact."

Kenneth shrugged, though she'd pegged him true.

"If I were that kind of guy then, like you said, I'd never admit it."

Willa laughed out loud again, which only made Delilah more excited. She wiggled this way and that before deciding Willa's lap was the best position to lay her head to get her favorite behind-the-ear scratches. Kenneth should have known the two would be a good match. Both were bright spots in a world that could be gray.

"All right, sorry about the delay," he said, getting to

the matter at hand. He pulled out his personal notebook, wanting to take more detailed notes than his notepad had room for.

"It's no problem. After yesterday, I decided to take today off." Willa rolled her shoulders in a wave motion. Kenneth quickly glanced at her neck. She didn't miss the attention. "I hid the bruise as best I could with some foundation Martha had for tattoo cover-up. But then I realized how small Kelby Creek is and, bruise or not, the news about the break-in and attack had already spread like wildfire before I'd even gone to sleep last night. So, I decided to give myself a day to breathe, so to speak."

Kenneth felt himself stiffen in anger at Leonard Bartow. The last he'd heard, the man was still unable to speak to anyone. Apparently, he'd hit his head a little too hard to bounce back with ease. Not that Kenneth was upset that he wasn't up and around yet. Though talking to him would get them some answers he wouldn't mind having.

"Does it hurt?" he asked when he realized he was staring.

Willa shook her head. "A little sore but not bad."

Kenneth had every intention to use that to segue to the beginning of her Josiah investigation but couldn't help himself. He averted his gaze to his notebook for a moment and tried to sound nonchalant.

"Did Mr. Mitchell know what happened?" he asked.

"I don't think so. Why? Did he say something?"

Her voice had changed. Not a lot, but the pitch had grown higher than normal. And her words came out faster.

Kenneth met her genuinely curious gaze as he picked up his pen.

"No, that's why I was wondering if he knew," he answered. "With the way you two were outside, and then the way he was looking at you in here, I thought there might be something—" Kenneth waved his pen in the air a little then put it back on the desktop "—there."

Willa outright snorted. Then her cheeks went a shade of crimson he hadn't yet seen on her.

"Sorry if I overstepped," he interjected before she could speak. "It's none of my business."

She waved off his dismissal. Delilah nudged at her hand with her nose.

"No, it's fine. I'm just not used to being around people who don't know about us."

Kenneth didn't like the *us* but knew there was no reason to feel that way. Still, he was glad for the explanation that followed.

"We dated for a few years and lived together for the last one, but it didn't work out. He's a good guy, and a great contractor by the way, but something was just *off* between us. At least for me. So I asked for a break to see if I couldn't sort out what was bothering me and realized I wasn't happier without him but I *also* wasn't sadder." She shrugged. "I thought that was worth a conversation but I guess I waited too long to have it. He started dating someone and then got engaged all before our lease was even up."

Kenneth whistled. "He doesn't waste any time, does he?"

Willa shook her head but she was smiling.

"Not with her, apparently. Though, don't get me wrong, I very much think we're better off as friends."

Even though she was being flippant, Kenneth saw the wounded look cross over her face. He liked it less than the mention of her and Landon as an *us*.

"You deserve someone who you'll miss when they leave a room and someone who will miss you if you leave a room," he said. "Anything less and you're settling for someone else's fantasy."

Willa's eyes widened slightly. Her hand stopped its

movement through Delilah's fur. Kenneth worried he had overstepped again but, slowly, the corner of her lips pulled up.

"Why, Detective Gray, that was almost poetry right there."

Kenneth chuckled. "I feel like I should be offended at how surprised you sound, but I'll take the compliment in that instead."

Willa's grin filled out into another one of those bright smiles he'd bet was second nature to her. Just looking at it, at her, and he'd almost suspect she had some kind of superpower. Willa Tate made him feel better with such little effort that his feelings of intrigue for the woman had only multiplied tenfold since their first meeting.

That made her tears as she'd sobbed against his chest yesterday something he never wanted to revisit. Her pain had become his pain.

And that meant he needed to get to the bottom of what had happened to the missing piece of fabric, the contents of the once-buried box, the mystery of the gun, and the disappearance of Josiah Linderman.

Now.

Because, if anything happened to Willa, Kenneth wouldn't forgive himself.

He couldn't.

He picked up his pen and set his jaw.

Willa picked up on the change, he noted, as her fingers stilled atop Delilah's head instead of stroking her fur.

"Now, Willa," he started, voice unintentionally low, "tell me everything. And I mean *everything*."

Chapter Ten

"I have to say, I'm impressed."

Kenneth put down his pen. The first time he'd done so in the last half hour. When he said that he wanted to be thorough in what Willa had learned, he hadn't exaggerated. He taken more notes than she probably had taken all of her college career.

"I actually have half a mind to ask you to join law enforcement," he added on. "I could use a detective like you."

Willa felt her cheeks turn hot at the compliment. Though it wasn't all deserved.

"I worked on trying to figure this out for a month and all I got was the name of a woman in a picture and an idea that a man most think left town was, in fact, killed," she countered. "I'm not sure that constitutes being a good detective."

"Don't sell yourself short. I'm not sure most people would even care to figure out what was going on."

"Probably because most people would take the box straight to the cops when they found a gun inside."

Willa watched as Kenneth conceded, his expression momentarily thoughtful.

"I can see why you didn't, though," he said. "I had worked at the department before The Flood happened and after we saw how far the corruption spread... Well, even I had some reservations about returning."

"Why did you?" Willa found herself starting to want a lot of things when it came to the detective. During her recount of all the people she'd talked to about Mae Linderman's picture and Josiah's disappearance, she'd caught herself tracing his lips in her mind—and her question was among the few she'd been truly curious about. Even before The Flood had happened the comings and goings of local law hadn't gone unnoticed. Town was too small and gossip was too fast, so news that Kenneth Gray had left the department and law enforcement a year after his wife had been killed had made its way through Kelby Creek with relative ease. But, why he'd chosen to come back to the department to work? That, Willa had no clue about.

Kenneth let out a little breath.

"I guess for that reason, and why you didn't come to the department right after finding the box. I couldn't stand the idea that the corruption could have leaked into our closed cases and may have been why some of our unsolved cases are still unsolved." He smiled, but it didn't reach his eyes. "Plus, Detective Lovett and Sheriff Chamblin sure made a good speech about why I was the perfect match for the job. I guess that also helped me along to agree to come back."

"And why are you the perfect match?"

Kenneth's smile wavered then faded. Tension crept into his shoulders.

She responded to the change, shifting the sleeping Delilah on her lap. Willa had hit a nerve.

"Because in all of my years in law enforcement, as a deputy and as a detective, I only ever gave up on one case."

He didn't explain further.

He didn't need to.

Willa chose her next words with care.

"I don't think men like you give up, Detective. Even if they themselves think they have."

Kenneth didn't look like he believed what she'd said but he didn't dispute it. He changed the subject and tapped his open notebook.

"I'm officially taking on Josiah's case tomorrow when I get to work. That really boils down to me telling the sheriff that I'm focusing on looking into what happened to him, seeing if Leonard Bartow took the cloth from the box, and why, and then going through the rest of contents in the box."

Willa tried not to get excited but she made a little squeak.

He jabbed at his notes again and kept a stern expression. "I've already started by calling Mae's brother this morning who, like you said, didn't seem that pleased to be called. But he did give me a rundown of what happened that day as he knew it, which wasn't much. He didn't seem to be close to Josiah or Mae and, since the kids were placed into foster care after he declined becoming their guardian, we can't track them down. As for other family, you were right. There doesn't seem to be anyone else. At least anyone we can find."

Willa's heart squeezed at that. Kenneth continued.

"But next I'll start with the gun to see if I can't follow the serial number and chain of sale somewhere. *But* if I can't, or if it's not connected to Josiah at all, and we don't find any actual evidence suggesting foul play, I can't guarantee I'll keep looking into him. I learned enough to follow hunches as well as leads, but I can only do that for so long. Especially since I have an office at the department filled with other cases that need looking into."

Willa rocked forward in her seat, nodding with enthusiasm. She'd worn her hair down and felt it bounce around her head with the same energy. Kenneth agreeing to talk to her was different than him agreeing to treat her theory with an official tag labeling it.

It was validating.

It was exciting.

It made her stomach do a little flip, though that might have been at the way Kenneth was searching her face to see if she understood.

"That sounds like a fair plan to me."

"Good. I can swing by your place tomorrow and grab the box." He stood and Delilah popped up like a daisy, tail already wagging.

Willa was less ready to leave the office. She liked talking with Kenneth, even if the topics hadn't been the peppiest.

"Or, I could give it to you tonight? Maybe at dinner?" The words tumbled out with such speed that Willa didn't have time to blush. "I mean treating you to a meal after you saved my life yesterday is the very least I could do."

Kenneth paused, one hand on his cell phone and the other on the back of his chair. She'd caught him off guard, which was apparent enough, but beyond that, she couldn't read his expression.

"Dinner," he repeated.

Willa stood, too, as Delilah made a break for her owner.

"Yeah, just a friendly little thing. Or we could grab a drink, if you prefer. Whatever suits your fancy. I'm not picky."

Whatever hesitation had been there shuffled off.

Kenneth nodded, though there was some stiffness to it.

"I could use a good, friendly dinner."

Willa felt her smile widen at the news.

Even if she wasn't exactly happy about the friend part.

EVERYTHING WAS LOOKING UP. Not only had she been taken seriously about Josiah, she'd also decided to finally tell Martha and Kimball about the box and everything she'd found out. Willa had decided, though, that she would tell Ebony after Kenneth did what he was going to do to make it official, and then ask that everyone keep quiet so the gossip mill didn't take over.

Martha and Kimball had been hot and cold about the information when she'd sat down with them at lunchtime. They'd been intrigued and upset that they hadn't been told sooner. They had wanted to know where the ring in the box had come from as well as the gun. They'd split in their opinion on Leonard Bartow and whether or not he was just a run-of-the-mill burglar or if it had been his second attempt to find the gun. Martha thought he'd probably taken the bloody cloth the first time.

"Whose blood do we even think that belongs to?" Kimball had asked. "Josiah?"

"That's what I think," Willa had responded. "But Kenneth still isn't sure. He thinks the ring and the bullet casing are more recent than the other items. I don't think he's convinced they're even all connected."

The three of them had pondered that for a while before Kimball and her sister had gone back to work. That left Willa feeling antsy for far too long, especially left alone in her apartment. So she did what every antsy, Southern woman did when she felt she needed to do something.

She cleaned.

She dusted first, used the Lysol second, and then vacuumed. Somehow, after that, she ended up using the disinfectant again. Then her attention went to the baseboards before pulling her to the bathroom to mop, Windex and, once more, use Lysol to clean everything. She even wiped down her newly-repaired front door thanks to Kimball's friendship with a local woodworker. He'd been quick the night before and now, although it needed paint, the door shut and locked like brand new.

By the time she was done, her small apartment smelled like lemon and she had a slight headache.

She also hadn't killed enough time.

The clock built into the microwave said it was only just after three, which meant she had a few hours before her dinner engagement with Kenneth at six.

"You could read something," she said out loud to herself, feeling like she'd drunk a whole pitcher of sweet tea. She couldn't sit still. "Or you could bake."

Willa looked at the small recipe book Martha had given her for Christmas. It was sitting on the kitchen counter. Called the "Brownie Bible," it contained over fifty types of brownies made from scratch.

Did Kenneth like brownies?

Who didn't like brownies?

Sure in herself and the fact that she believed Kenneth did like them, Willa found her favorite recipe and went to see if she had all the ingredients. She wasn't all that upset when she didn't find every one of them.

Instead, it seemed like a good excuse to eat up a little more time. She changed out of the clothes she'd put on to clean in, and danced into a pair of blue jeans that did her curves some nice favors, a frilly blouse that matched her increasingly good mood, and a pair of flats, setting the old tennis shoes she'd been wearing off to the side.

She left the apartment feeling good and with a little hop in her step.

So much so, that she didn't even mind the dark cloud hanging over downtown as she pulled into a community parking lot. She threw her purse across her shoulder, decided it wasn't too much of a run from the grocery store to the car if it started to rain, and headed into the grocery store with a song in her head and a smile on her lips.

How had she gone from being so terrified the day before to feeling like she was almost floating now?

Had Kenneth really made all the difference?

She barely knew him.

Yet, there she was buying eggs and brown sugar and wondering if he liked the center pieces or the corner pieces when it came to brownies. She was partial to corner pieces, but decided she wouldn't mind sharing. She could be diplomatic like that.

The rain still hadn't arrived by the time Willa was done shopping and her mood was still flying high, so she loaded her groceries into her car and locked the door behind her. She was on Main Street but there were shops along the parallel streets that had become a lot more interesting in the last year. The thought of one in particular pulled her along the sidewalk in the direction of the street behind her.

The rain cloud above wasn't on the same upbeat wavelength as Willa. Droplets started to dampen her hair, but she decided to not let that keep her down. She adapted by taking a left turn to cut through one of the short alleyways, one that was covered.

The rain stopped hitting her hair and Willa took that as a sign of good luck. She was ready to put that positive energy back out into the world.

Maybe she *was* that bubbly person everyone thought she was.

Maybe that wasn't such a bad thing.

Willa made it to the mouth of the alley on the far side, took a step out onto the sidewalk and looked across the street to the Pet Market, wondering what kind of toy Delilah might like.

She didn't understand at first why her forward momentum changed direction back into the alleyway or pinpoint right away why her chest now hurt.

One second, she was deciding between getting a ball or a chew toy. The next, she was being dragged backward with startling speed.

"Let. Go."

It wasn't Willa who said the words but, given how deep and harsh they were, she could feel them vibrate through her skin. Then she realized what was happening. Someone was pulling her by the strap of her purse. The same purse that someone was trying to take off her now.

Willa fell between fight-or-flight and froze as she was pulled another foot back into the alley. She tried to turn around to see a face but all she saw was a closely shaved head and a hockey mask. That was enough to tip the scales.

Willa went into fight mode.

"Help!" she yelled as loudly as she could, panting against the struggle to stay on her feet. Essentially being dragged by the strap of her purse, it rubbed against her chest like a seat belt might pull in a car accident. That's how hard the man was trying to get it off of her.

"Say anything again and I'll—"

Lightning suddenly forked in the air above the Pet Market street and the rain intensified just as a boom of thunder sounded overhead.

There wasn't a storm coming, she realized. It was already there. And that meant it was going to be even more difficult for people to see or to hear her.

She was just going to have to struggle in this alleyway until this masked man decided he was done with her.

Willa slashed back at the man's face with her nails. They weren't long but they were sturdy thanks to a lifetime of vitamins her sister always insisted she take. She managed to get her index finger beneath the man's chin. Swiping up along its path, she slid it under the edge of the mask.

At such an awkward angle, she only managed one attempt to rip it off.

Something the man did not like.

He grunted and let go of Willa to keep the hockey mask from completely coming off.

Then Willa was all flight.

Chapter Eleven

Colleen Tate had been obsessed with the *Child's Play* movies. There's just something about Chucky, the little doll possessed with a serial killer's soul, that terrified and interested Willa's mother. If you were a Tate, then you'd seen all the movies. More than once. More than twice. More than any one person should see the serial killer movie about a doll.

But, like her sister, Willa had never been a fan. It wasn't so much about the plot as it was about the victims. They had the tendency to be smart, cautious, and surrounded by weapons. And yet, as soon as that doll was seen holding a knife, it was like every victim's good brain cell disappeared in a flurry of fear.

Willa had decided that if she was ever in a similar situation, she would be the one to keep her wits about her. Leonard Bartow surprise attacking her in her apartment excluded, of course. She'd never had the opportunity to get away from him.

This time, though, was different.

This time she'd broken away from her attacker with enough room to make it out onto the sidewalk.

It was only too bad that Willa finally understood why those characters in her mom's favorite movies seldom survived. For all the smarts that she believed she possessed, instead of heading to the very same pet store across the street, Willa seemed to lose all semblance of direction. Not only did she turn and run away from the store, she was also headed in the opposite direction of where her car was parked.

It was a disappointing self-discovery. A mistake she hadn't realized she'd made until the rain soaked her through and she was a good block from the alley.

Maybe he was gone.

Maybe she'd put up too much of a fuss and he'd decided she wasn't worth robbing.

A storefront was alight another block down. It belonged to a graphic artist who designed billboards for businesses in the county. Willa had met her once though she doubted the woman would remember her.

She definitely would after Willa barged in. "Lock the doors" is what Willa would yell first, followed by "Call 9-1-1."

But just as the rest of her life this past week hadn't gone to plan, that one, too, didn't last long.

Once again Willa was abruptly yanked backward. She didn't have time to scream. The rain pounded around her, along with her heart, as she tried to replicate the same defense she had used with the attacker the first time.

But instead of him tugging and pulling her deeper into the alleyway, the movement stopped altogether.

"Willa, it's me," came a deep voice. It was unlike the last.

Willa turned and wiped at the rain collecting on her eyelashes. The man was wearing dark jeans and a gray shirt that was just as soaked as hers. More important, he wasn't wearing a mask.

He was also Kenneth.

A fact that should have put her at ease. But Willa was

starting to go numb. Fear or shock? Disbelief that within two days she been attacked by two different men?

Overwhelmed and afraid.

That's what she decided as Kenneth pulled her to him before pushing her up against the brick wall of one of the buildings. There was no overhang to this alley and it was hard to make out his face as the rain picked up. But then he bent over her and angled his chin down, and Willa understood what he was doing.

He was hiding her.

And he wasn't alone. A weight pressed against Willa's leg. Delilah was leaning against her.

Willa felt the comfort of both though it didn't last long.

The unmistakable sound of someone frustrated and running was coming upon them from the sidewalk Willa had just been pulled from. Heavy footfalls pounded the pavement, the sound much louder than it would have normally been thanks to the gathering water.

The man had followed her.

Kenneth leaned in closer, making a cage out of his body around Willa. From the sidewalk, she would be hard to see.

"Does he have a gun or a knife?" Kenneth's breath brushed against her ear. Had it been a different situation, she would've shivered at the contact.

She placed her cheek against his and whispered back to him. "I—I don't know."

Kenneth nodded, moving her head as he did so, to let her know he'd heard her.

The pounding footsteps passed their alleyway.

Then Kenneth pushed something into her hand.

"Keep each other safe."

He was off and running before Willa saw that she was holding Delilah's leash.

IT HAD BEEN a long time since Kenneth had made his rounds downtown in Kelby Creek, but he didn't need to know the exact layout or where he was on the map to do what needed to be done next. Not when he had his sights on a man running full-speed away from him, donning a white mask.

"Stop! Sheriff's department!"

Kenneth's warnings did nothing. Not that he thought they would.

It had only been by chance that, while walking Delilah from the small dog park to his car, he'd seen Willa running on the opposite side of the street.

The rain had made it difficult to decipher what, exactly, had been going on until he'd noticed the way she'd been running. It hadn't been the jog of a woman who'd forgotten her umbrella or was trying to find shelter from the weather. It had been the sprint of a frightened woman. Then he'd seen the man exit the alleyway and hesitate, looking both ways.

That's all Kenneth had needed. He'd run after Willa and cut through another alley on the next block so he could grab her. He didn't know if she was hurt, or if the man who was interested in her had a weapon, or where she was going.

But he hadn't wanted to chance that she would disappear into the rainfall. Catching her had become his main priority.

Catching her attacker became his second.

Kenneth ran through the rain in the direction Willa had been headed, noting, in the distance, the lighted storefront of a local business. His leg muscles burned as he tilted forward.

The moment he'd seen Willa, he'd wished he had his gun. Just as he now wished he had his badge. But he'd been taking Delilah out for a run at the park and hadn't thought to take either. If he ran into the man, he'd have to get creative.

And physical.

Thunder clapped overhead. The small chance of rain had turned into an active thunderstorm. The booming rattled the window of the lighted graphic artist business as he slowed to look around. A short awning gave him a small respite from the rain. Through the window, two desks could be seen at the back of the front room. The lights might have been on but there was no one at either.

Kenneth ran a hand over his face, shucking off water as he tried to figure out what to do next.

If he hadn't caught up to the man, there was a good chance he wouldn't now. The rain was only falling harder, the world around him getting darker. He was unarmed and, even though he had faith in Willa and her ability to find a safe place with Delilah to call the department, Kenneth couldn't get past the thought that if he didn't know where the man was in front of him, who was to say he hadn't doubled back and gotten behind him?

Kenneth didn't like that idea.

He made up his mind.

He would get back to Willa and wait for backup.

A man materialized out of the blanket of rain beyond the awning's cover and rammed into Kenneth like a defensive tackle going for the quarterback. A power move that gave neither man the chance to stay upright. Kenneth felt the air leave his lungs just as their combined weight propelled them right into the storefront window.

The best thing Kenneth could do in between the hit and the crash was to tuck his face into his biceps and hope the glass held.

It didn't.

Kenneth felt only the smallest resistance before momentum carried them right on through the window.

A woman screamed in the background.

Pain and adrenaline pulsed through Kenneth as he slid a few feet across tile and glass. Later, he'd marvel at how hard the hit had had to be for them to travel so far into the store, but when everything stopped moving, he knew it wasn't going to be good for him if he didn't get up quickly.

The man had the same idea.

Kenneth clocked his attacker as the man got to his feet while Kenneth tried to do the same.

The hit, the glass, the floor… It had done a number on him. Rising wasn't such an easy task.

"Dawn County Sheriff's Department," Kenneth yelled, pushing himself up and around so he was facing his attacker. He didn't mind the blood on the floor. It was most likely from both of them.

The man was wearing a hockey mask. White. It was wet and gleamed beneath the fluorescent lights of the room they were in.

Kenneth didn't like masks. Ski masks he had dealt with in his career. Protective masks for roadwork or yardwork, he could reason out.

But hockey masks? Halloween masks? Faceless things made to hide an identity in no memorable or extraordinary way?

Kenneth didn't like those.

Not since a witness had seen a man in a mask running away from Ally's body.

A nondescript mask the witness had said looked like it came from a costume, though which one, she didn't know.

It wasn't the same as the hockey mask in front of him, but to Kenneth's heart, it didn't matter.

The mask was hiding malice and violence.

Malice and violence intended for Willa and now him.

The attacker got to his feet before Kenneth could steady himself. Instead of trying to brace for another tackle or to ready his own attack, Kenneth decided if the man was going to play dirty, so was he.

He dove to the right, knee smashing into the tiled floor, and grabbed something they'd bowled over when they'd come through the window.

It was only after it was in his hand that Kenneth realized he was wielding an oversize closed umbrella.

Perfect.

The man missed hitting Kenneth after the dive and both turned back to each other at the same time. Kenneth couldn't help but smirk at his new weapon, brandishing it like a baseball bat.

Since this wasn't a gentleman's duel, he wasn't about to wait for a countdown to strike.

Kenneth stood to his full height and wound the umbrella in an arc behind him before swinging it at the man with all his might.

Now it was he who wasn't ready.

The umbrella hit the man's shoulder so hard that he stumbled. Kenneth brought it up and was about to go for another wind-up to strike again when the masked man showed his own weapon of choice.

Kenneth hated to admit it was a good one.

He flashed the gun's muzzle and Kenneth jumped to the side as a shot went off. Another scream sounded in the distance. Thunder backing it up a second later.

Kenneth slung his body into his attacker's, ready to keep the distance so close that the man couldn't get a good shot off again.

He'd miscalculated the man's true brazenness.

The next shot was so close to Kenneth's head, he howled, certain his eardrum exploded at the sound.

On reflex, one hand went to cup his ear while the other grabbed for the shooter's wrist. He connected with both.

Then Kenneth was in a game of pure strength. He'd put every ounce of it into crushing the man's arm so he'd release the gun. If he could do that, he could turn the tables on the fight.

Because he didn't want to die here.

He didn't want to die at all.

Kenneth thought of Ally, his parents, the cold cases unsolved in his office.

He thought of Willa in the rain, terrified, Delilah at her side.

Kenneth pushed his other hand against the man while the one around his wrist became an unforgiving vise.

His ears were ringing but Kenneth knew the man had to let out a yell of pain.

Because right after, the gun fell to the ground.

Kenneth wasted no time. He kicked the weapon with his heel far away from both of them. Then he closed the distance between them. Using his grip, he half slung, half pushed the man to the side.

Then Kenneth turned on his heel and ran toward the gun he'd kicked away. He managed to scoop it up before it stopped moving.

He knew it was loaded due to its weight and turned around to face the man to let him know he meant business.

The man, however, wasn't just standing around. He was at the door, about to head back out into the rain.

"Stop or I'll shoot!" Kenneth commanded. His voice sounded distorted. Maybe his eardrum had ruptured after all.

The man in the mask moved his head, as if to look at someone behind Kenneth.

It could have been a trick but Kenneth heard footsteps.

Did his attacker have a friend?

Kenneth moved with a speed he knew was only draining away and readied to defend himself against the new threat.

And it was in that moment that Kenneth knew the man in the mask would get away. That he would let him run out into the rain and disappear.

And the man in the mask knew that, too.

Because it wasn't a friend or a partner who had shuffled up to their fight.

It was a woman in tears.

A woman holding her stomach as a gunshot wound bled out into her blouse.

Kenneth got to her just as she fell to the ground, softening the blow before she hit the tile. He kept the gun in his hand and readjusted his aim toward the door again.

It was open, the sound of rain uncaring and loud.

The man was gone.

Chapter Twelve

Haven Hospital was small and the only hospital within the town limits. It was privately owned and therefore impeccably kept. It was also surprisingly modern. White, clean hallways. Private rooms that looked like they could belong in a hotel. A cafeteria with food that wasn't just convenient for the staff but actually desired.

It was all a nice picture.

Professional. Reliable. Comforting.

It didn't at all match with how Kenneth looked when Willa finally found him.

"He's okay, right?" she'd asked the nurse, a friend of her sister's named Janelle.

"Physically, yes. He had some wicked cuts but nothing some cleaning and bandaging couldn't fix. He also is going to need to take some pain pills for his shoulder I suspect, but the doctor will run that down for him when he gets back."

Willa hadn't questioned the emphasis on *physically* or the need to specify until she was standing on the other side of a hospital bed from the man.

He was in a chair next to it, elbows resting on the sheets, hands held together. His eyes took their time rising from them up to her.

Willa's heart squeezed and then squeezed even tighter.

"Oh, Kenneth."

Blood stained his shirt in an awful pattern and bandages covered spots on his arms.

But it was his red eyes and empty hands that made Willa nearly weep.

"Oh, Kenneth," she repeated, hurrying to his side. "I'm so sorry, honey."

Willa knelt beside his chair and didn't for a moment think about personal space. She slipped between his knees and the hospital bed and put her body against his until he molded around her, accepting her embrace. There wasn't enough room for her to hug him at such an awkward angle so she settled on his lap. The side of her body was flush against him. If they had been standing he would have been holding her like a husband taking his bride over the threshold. But that wasn't the case now. Willa put her arms around him and her face into the crook of his neck.

She would have never embraced someone so intimately in any other situation but, for now, it was simple.

She wanted Kenneth to know she was there.

For him.

With him.

And he didn't seem to mind. It took a moment but his arms wound around her waist as he supported her against him. Then his head went down into her hair.

The last time they'd been close—but not *this* close—Willa had been sobbing while Kenneth had remained still.

This time, neither said or did a thing.

Kenneth let her hold him and that was enough.

They stayed like that for several minutes until finally he let out a long, ragged breath.

Willa pulled back and knew their time was done. She took his chin in her hand, looked him square in the eye and knew he'd cried. Or had tried hard not to. It was all so heartbreaking, but there wasn't anything Willa could do to assuage that break. Instead, she tilted his chin so she could kiss his cheek.

Then she untangled herself from the man and stood.

Because she wasn't a fan of hospitals—who was in this town?—and Kenneth made no indication he was going to move, Willa took a small chair from the corner and positioned it on the other side of the hospital bed. It gave her a clear view of the detective and his brilliant eyes of dark, deep water staring right at her.

She wanted to give him space—because wasn't that what you were supposed to do in situations like this?—but that wasn't who she was.

And what had happened wasn't something silence could heal.

Plus, Willa hadn't seen him since their run-in in the alleyway in the rain. After that she'd gone to the Pet Market with Delilah and called in the department. She'd waited there until sirens filled downtown.

The rain hadn't let up but Willa had been readying to venture out when a firetruck and ambulance flew past. But Deputy Carlos Park had showed up for her first.

"Detective Gray sent me," he'd said. There was such a mass hesitation that Willa knew something had happened. That something was wrong. Even when the deputy had assured her that Kenneth was all right.

It had been a few hours since she'd had that conversation with Deputy Park and those hours had felt excruciating not being able to see Kenneth or to talk to him. Though she understood why.

Kenneth had resumed placing his hands on the bed between them. He gave them another long look before meeting her gaze again. For the first time since everything had happened, Willa thought he seemed to acknowledge that a significant passage of time had indeed passed. At least, it felt significant to her.

"I'm sorry I didn't call..." he started. His voice was a little hoarse. He'd been yelling. But why and at who, she could only guess for the moment. "Deputy Park said he had you and you were okay."

"I was," Willa confirmed. "Delilah, too."

That stirred him a bit more. "Is she here?"

Willa shook her head.

"She's with Martha and Kimball at the house. Don't worry, though, they're great with dogs and said they're more than happy to watch her until you're ready. I also remembered seeing the bag of dog food at your house when I was there this morning, so we went ahead and got her a bag at the store. So don't you worry, she's really okay."

If it had been earlier in the day, Willa suspected that Kenneth would shake his head, thank her, and then insist on not being a burden in some gentlemanly way that he thought was right. But he didn't do that now. He simply nodded, weary.

Willa decided not to bring up that, while the law worked to contain and sift through what had happened, Willa and her sister and Kimball had worked to settle things for Kenneth. Thanks to Deputy Park, Kenneth's keys had been taken before he'd been carried off in the ambulance to the hospital. His SUV was in the parking lot downstairs and Willa's car was back at her place.

That was one of the very great things about living in a small town with a solid support system. When something bad happened, you never went through it alone, even if you didn't realize it.

Willa didn't want to seem like she was looking for a pat on the back for their resourceful accommodation or for having given some forethought to what might happen next. Instead she waited for him to speak again.

When it didn't seem like he would, Willa was gentle. "Do you need to stay here any longer?"

On the way up to his room, Willa had run into only two deputies, one of them Deputy Park. They had been heading out. Surely that meant Kenneth could leave. "Or does the doctor need you to stay?" she asked.

That got an immediate answer.

"I can leave. I'm fine." He looked down at his shirt.

Willa's heart squeezed again.

She heard what he hadn't said.

He was fine.

LeAnne Granger was not.

A stray bullet from the masked man's gun had found her and, though Kenneth had tried his best to save her before the first responders arrived, she'd died in his arms on the floor of her business. Surrounded by blood and broken glass, according to Deputy Park when Willa had finally gotten the truth from him.

"I've never had someone die in my arms," Park had commented after he'd told her, shaking his head, a pained expression lining his face. "No one should have that happen but especially not Kenneth. Not after—" The deputy had caught himself and buttoned up the conversation. Willa found it touching that he hadn't wanted to gossip about something so sensitive to Kenneth, though it wasn't hard to put together that he'd been talking about Ally Gray.

As far as Willa knew, Kenneth hadn't found Ally, but he had been called to the scene when her body had been called in.

Holding a woman, even as she died, wouldn't have been easy for anyone. But for someone whose wife had been murdered? It had to bring back memories that were a new level of unbearable.

Willa reached out and touched Kenneth's hands. It brought his attention away from a shirt he should have already taken off.

"Here. You stay put and I'll be back in a second."

He didn't make a fuss as Willa went out into the hall and searched for Janelle.

A few minutes later, she was back in the room, a clean white T-shirt in her hands. She stopped next to Kenneth's chair and took his elbow.

"Why don't we switch your shirts out?" she said, keeping her voice soft as she tried to gently pull him up. Thankfully, Kenneth stood on his own.

He was in a daze, probably deep in his thoughts, replaying what had happened to LeAnne or to his wife or on something else that would give Willa nightmares, but he seemed to be fine with following her directive.

In one fluid movement, he pulled his shirt up and off. Willa took it before he could focus on the dried blood again and handed him the new one.

"Where'd you get this?" he asked, pulling it over his head.

Willa hurried to the trashcan in the room and, hoping he wasn't attached to the plain gray shirt, was quick to throw it away.

"I noticed a male nurse on shift who was about your size. He had a spare in his locker," she said, scooting back to his side. "He said it was no problem if you took it since he has a ton at home."

Kenneth nodded absently.

Willa hesitated before taking the lead again.

"Is…is there anyone you want me to call? That you need to talk to?" She knew about Ally but her death had been years ago. With a burning blush, Willa realized she had no idea if the detective was attached to anyone else. Sure, there was no ring on his finger, but he could have been dating someone. So far all of their interactions had been about Josiah and the box. Just because she'd been feeling a little more than what she'd let on, didn't mean that Kenneth returned those same sentiments.

So she waited, feeling incredibly selfish for hoping that he wasn't seeing anyone, for him to answer.

He did so with little fanfare, though it struck a chord with her nonetheless.

"The only person I was planning to call was you."

He reached back to the table behind him and grabbed his phone and wallet. There was also a sheet of paper. She spied a doctor's signature at the bottom. Probably a prescription for heavy-duty ibuprofen for his shoulder, like Janelle had said. He folded the paper and slipped it into his jeans.

For the first time Willa noticed that there was some blood on there, too. Along with his shoes.

"Let's go." She put her hand on the small of his back, feeling waves of protectiveness and helplessness lap over her at the same time. They stopped at a nurses' station to make sure the paperwork was taken care of, and Willa waved goodbye to Janelle. It wasn't until they were in the parking lot that Kenneth peeked out of his own thoughts for a moment when he saw they were headed for his SUV.

"I don't have my keys." He patted his jeans.

"I do. Don't worry."

Kenneth nodded. He became quiet again.

And that's how the rest of the night went.

Willa made the decisions, Kenneth went along for the ride.

She drove him straight home and let him inside his own house before sitting him down at his dining room table. She made him a turkey sandwich, got him a water, and called her sister to make sure she could keep Delilah overnight.

When he was done eating, she guided him to the shower and left him, to make another call to her sister. Once he'd changed, she shooed him into bed with little to no resistance.

He'd fallen asleep faster than she'd anticipated.

Willa paused by his bed in the middle of her current task of collecting his discarded clothes for the laundry and looked long and hard at the man.

She became misty-eyed at his face slack from sleep.

Good people watching bad things was no life to live. At least, no life to live alone.

THERE WAS A knock on the door. He could have cussed at the interruption. He'd already bandaged himself but had had to change it out twice already. The first had bled through his shirt; the second had pulled uncomfortably.

"Honey! You'll never believe what I just heard!" His wife's voice was excited, pitched high and vibrating.

He could ruin her fun, tell her he had a good idea of what she'd just heard, but that wasn't part of his plan. So he used the voice he reserved for her and called back through his closed office door.

"I'm on a call, dear. Give me a few minutes and I'll come talk, okay?"

She wasn't a fan of that but, to his surprise, had been a good wife when it came to his privacy. If he told her to not disturb him without knocking on his office door first, she didn't. If he told her he couldn't talk right then, she waited.

Just as she did now.

"Okay. I'll be in the kitchen when you're through."

He heard her pad away and continued to check on his

cuts. Then he looked at the bruise on his arm that would only get nastier.

He couldn't believe Detective Gray had hit him with an umbrella.

He also couldn't believe he'd left his gun behind.

As for the woman who had been shot by accident...

Well, nothing he could do about that now.

So he finished up and thought about his options. He became angry and then he cooled.

He was the smart one.

The patient one.

Then why did you attack the detective? You could have just let him go.

It was a question that had been bothering him since he'd escaped.

But one impulsive decision wasn't going to affect him. He wouldn't let it.

Impulsive or not, patient or not, there was somewhere else that he needed to be. Something he needed to fix.

Because that's what he did.

He fixed mistakes, especially ones that others made.

And, boy, was there one he needed to fix sooner rather than later.

For now, he checked that his shirt covered his injuries, was thankful for that bit of good luck, and left the office for his kitchen.

His wife was on him in seconds.

"That woman who got shot? The Granger lady? She died! Isn't that awful?"

She grabbed his hand and squeezed.

He squeezed it back.

"That *is* awful, isn't it?"

Chapter Thirteen

Light splayed across the foot of the bed. Kenneth blinked away sleep and took in the sight slowly.

He looked down at his hands and got lost for a moment.

His alarm went off after that. A series of chirps on his phone that annoyed him to no end, especially since he always seemed to wake a minute or two before it. He rolled over and slapped at his phone on the nightstand, dismissing it.

Then he saw the charging chord attached to it.

Kenneth tried to think back to the night before. Plugging in his phone was always the last thing he did before sleep, but he knew for a fact he hadn't done it last night. In fact, he'd lost track of his phone entirely somewhere between food and his shower.

Kenneth sat up, ramrod-straight.

Willa.

He looked around his room, expanding his attention to detail.

A pair of jeans sat folded on top of his dresser. He got out of bed, walked through the pain in his shoulder that made him wince, and held up the jeans.

They were clean.

So were his shoes, sitting stain-free on the floor next to him.

His gray shirt, however, was nowhere to be found.

That didn't surprise him. Not after—

The sound of dishes clattering together pulled Kenneth's attention again. When he opened his bedroom door and walked out into the hallway, he could smell something that made his mouth instantly water. He followed it out and down the stairs to the kitchen, minding the pain as he took each step.

Kenneth turned the corner and saw sunshine in his kitchen.

Sunshine trying to reach a plate on a shelf too high for her.

"Let me."

Willa whirled around, hand going to her chest.

"Kenneth!"

The day before felt like a lifetime ago but Kenneth knew Willa had changed from the outfit he'd seen soaked through in the alley and then again in their quiet conversation at the hospital. She was casually dressed, with her hair down, framing her face, and jeans and a light blue blouse that clung more than it flowed. There were no shoes on her feet but there was a pair of socks. They were pink and had hearts all over them. Cute was the word that came to mind for them.

Beautiful was the word that came to mind for her.

"I didn't hear you moving around," she added after his quick look up and down her body. Her cheeks took on a rosier hue. Then her eyes widened, her brows knitting together. "I didn't wake you, did I?"

Kenneth shook his head and went for the items she'd been trying to reach. With effort, he hid how it hurt to grab plates and bring them down.

"I always wake up around now," he assured her. "I think it's part of my DNA at this point."

Willa took the plates from him and waved him to the doorway that led into the dining room.

"Well, now that you're up, let's go ahead and eat. I hope you like bacon and cinnamon rolls because that's all we have."

Kenneth told her that he did and soon they were seated at the small table, each with food that smelled delicious, and a pot of coffee.

Everything had all happened so fast that Kenneth hadn't thought to question any of it until he was one cinnamon roll deep. He supposed he must have been hungrier than he'd thought.

"I didn't know I had cinnamon rolls. Or bacon, for that matter."

Willa looked up from her food and smiled.

"You didn't. Actually, you didn't really have anything, but Martha is a ridiculously early riser and offered to bring some of each over. She baked the rolls and the bacon. She's big into breakfast." Willa averted her eyes and grinned. "I guess I should have opened with that instead of hoping you'd thought I was the one who went through the trouble of making them."

Kenneth shook his head.

"Hey, if it had been just me, I would have had the coffee and saved a buck fifty for the vending machine at work. This—" he motioned to his plate "—is much appreciated, whether you physically made it or not."

Willa seemed cheered by that. Her smile widened. "Well, for what it's worth, I do make a mean everything-in-it omelet."

He believed her. "I'll have to try it sometime."

They lapsed into a silence while they finished their food. It wasn't like the night before when Kenneth had locked himself in his own head. This time he was trying to backtrack, to see outside his thoughts about LeAnne and the hockey-masked man.

Kenneth had made it home, in a new shirt, been fed, directed to the shower, and told to go to sleep. He'd had his clothes washed, his phone charged, and had been served breakfast.

And all because of Willa.

"I wanted—"

"Willa—"

Both spoke at the same time and both stopped.

Willa's face tinted pink.

Kenneth chuckled. "You go first," he said.

Willa obliged.

"I just wanted to say I hope I didn't overstep by staying here last night. Or by invading your privacy and making some decisions without your input." She got up and walked over to where her purse was sitting on a chair that seemed to collect junk mail.

Willa fished inside it until she pulled out a keyring. It and the keys belonged to him. She set them down next to him on the table and took her seat again.

"For instance, driving your car around without your consent and for also letting Martha and Kimball keep Delilah overnight when you don't even know them. And, well again, staying here after you'd gone to sleep." She shifted in her seat, outwardly uncomfortable. "I just didn't want you to be alone is all, and thought I could help. I hope you're not too mad or think I'm a loon."

Kenneth didn't have to think about what to say. It came out with a smile he hoped she realized was genuine.

"I was going to thank you, Willa." She gave him an apprehensive look. "I mean it." He tried to drive his appreciation home. "Last night was hard. You didn't have to help but you did. You made everything a little less…" Kenneth couldn't find the right word. He let it lie and reiterated his first point. "What I'm saying is thank you. I mean it."

Willa tucked her chin a little. She was back to smiling. It was small but sincere. But then it faded.

He knew what came next.

"I'm the one who should be thanking *you*." Her hand fisted around the handle of her coffee mug. "And apologize again. If you hadn't grabbed me when you had, that man would have caught me, I'm sure of it." A shadow passed over her face. "But if I had run the right way or if I had been more aware of my surroundings, LeAnne…you… None of this would have—"

"No." Kenneth's voice was pure force. It made Willa's gaze snap up to his in a flash. "This isn't your fault. Not one ounce of any of it. Not LeAnne's death. Not me getting hurt. Not even him trying to take your bag. The only person to blame is the person who actually did every single one of those things. You got it? Willa?"

She sniffled, surprising him that she'd been so close to tears, but nodded. There she had been, helping him while also riddled with self-imposed guilt.

A feeling Kenneth knew all too well.

He softened again. "It's a hard lesson," he admitted. "Easier said than done, too."

"Then let me remind *you* that LeAnne's death isn't your fault, either. It was that man's. You did everything you could to save her."

Kenneth couldn't help but look at his hands. After he'd called for help, he'd tried to use them to stop the bleeding. But the lone bullet had done too much damage. He'd lost a heartbeat before the EMTs had arrived. Still, he'd gone with her to the hospital, tied to her in death since he'd been the one to face it with her.

The way she'd looked up at him before she'd gone…

Kenneth could feel it pulling him back into himself again. Just as it had last night.

"You can talk about it, if you want." Willa's voice was small but strong.

Kenneth didn't want to talk about it. Yet he did.

"I've seen death before on the job. Some things I've tried very hard to forget and other memories sneak up on me sometimes. But last night was the first time I'd seen anything like that since Ally passed." His felt his jaw harden. "I knew LeAnne wasn't going to make it and, when you can't save someone, the best you can do is be there with them—really be there—at their end. To see them out of this world with compassion and attention."

Kenneth shook his head slowly. His eyes found the sunshine across the table from him. He felt shame. Deep and cutting.

"But I couldn't even give LeAnne that," he said. "I knew she was going, but when I looked down at her, all I could think about was Ally."

He hadn't wanted to tell anyone that truth. In fact, he'd planned to bury it so deep within himself that it would only haunt his nightmares.

There was something about Willa, though. Something that made him feel comfortable and able to give in enough to show her that he valued her presence.

He valued *her*.

Kenneth thumbed the spot where his wedding band had once sat on his ring finger.

"I don't know how much you've heard about what happened to my late wife, but she was killed and left out in a field. Shot. Like LeAnne. But alone. No one with her as she bled out. Just her and the grass and the sun overhead."

He took a breath. The ache that never went away sent a pulse of fresh pain through him. "Holding LeAnne, seeing her like that… All I could think about was if that was how it had happened with Ally. If she'd tried to stop the bleeding, hoped someone would save her. Or if she'd known there was no hope and given up out there. Closed her eyes and then never opened them again. All alone. And I hate that. I hate that I couldn't give LeAnne the focus she deserved. I couldn't save her and I couldn't get out of my own head to say goodbye to her."

That was it, he realized. That was why he'd gone into his head after he'd seen LeAnne was shot. That was why he'd operated on reflex and muscle memory.

It was why he'd let Willa take over.

That, and because he trusted her.

No small feat, he reckoned, but didn't have the head-space to think more on just yet.

He watched Willa push back her chair and come to his side. She took his chin in her hand as she had the night before in the hospital. Instead of kissing his cheek, she bent her head. Her lips were soft and warm and quick against his.

When she broke the brief kiss, her cheeks had gone rosy again.

"If I'm keeping count, that's the third time you've kissed me," Kenneth found himself saying. The world didn't totally feel real at the moment, caught between a nightmare and a dream.

Willa let his face go but held his attention like she was a bright, stunning flame and he was a moth with a mighty need for light.

"I should apologize for that, too, but I won't." She held up three fingers and ticked off each point as she made one. "The first kiss was because I needed comfort. The second one was because you needed comfort. This one, the third, was only for the fact that you're a good, good man, Kenneth Gray, and I don't want you to ever think otherwise. You got that?"

Her lips had been soft. Her tone now was not.

She meant what she said.

And she wanted an answer from him. No smart-alecky remarks and no backtalk.

So he didn't give her either.

"Yes, ma'am."

Willa nodded, straightening. She smoothed her shirt down and tossed some of the hair that had fallen over her shoulder at her earlier movement across her back again.

"Good," she said simply. "If you need more reminding that none of this is your fault, just let me know and I'll kiss you quiet again."

Kenneth could tell she hadn't meant to say that by the way she paused and her cheeks turned a darker shade of crimson, but he laughed all the same.

"I'll keep that in mind."

She nodded again and was off with their dishes into the kitchen.

Kenneth went back to his bathroom to get ready and change.

After giving the office a quick call, he made his way to the living room. A folded blanket sat on the couch's end, a pillow on top. She'd slept on the couch.

Because she hadn't wanted him to be alone.

Kenneth cleared his throat as Willa joined him in the living room.

She looked expectantly at him. "It's not a coincidence, is it?" she asked. "Leonard Bartow happens to break into my apartment, the bloody cloth goes missing, and then a man tries to take my purse or me two days later."

Kenneth didn't think so. Not at all.

He said as much.

"I think it's all connected." He sighed. "We just don't know how yet."

Willa pushed her shoulders back, determination hardening her usually soft features. "Then what can we do now?"

Kenneth could already feel his anger rising.

She shouldn't be a part of this, but there Willa was, right in the center it seemed.

How he wished she wasn't.

Kenneth locked his eyes with hers and hoped she felt every vestige of intent behind his next words.

"Now, we fight back until this entire thing is over."

Chapter Fourteen

They should have known that, at some point, living in a small town would have unforeseen complications. What they hadn't expected, though, was that they get two steps into the sheriff's department's lobby on a Friday morning and find one.

The man had a Guns N' Roses tattoo on his forearm and anger in his eyes. He lunged at Kenneth before anyone could stop him. Willa, tucked at the detective's side, didn't see what was happening until Kenneth moved to become a wall in front of her. His protection cost him a right hook to the jaw.

A deputy and two civilians in the lobby jumped up to step in. They separated the men enough to get the story behind the attack.

The man who had delivered the hit was Jason Whitmore, LeAnne Granger's fiancé.

And he was grieving.

"I've been there before," Kenneth told Willa after assuring her for the umpteenth time within the span of a few minutes that he was okay.

He'd smiled; it was strained to the max. "We picked up my pain meds for my arm. They'll help my face, too." He'd looked over at the still-riled-up Jason. "I need to talk to him. Why don't you go get started on filling in Detective Lovett while I do that?"

Willa had agreed and was escorted to the lead detective's office by Deputy Kathryn Juliet. They'd gone to school together but hadn't been more than acquaintances. Still, Juliet, as she'd told everyone to call her growing up, said she was glad that Willa was okay.

It had been a nice sentiment and Willa thanked her for it.

Then she was looking at Foster Lovett, another local. Though, he had left the fold with his high school sweetheart only to come back years later, divorced but accomplished. He'd been the first new hire to really make a difference, according to Martha and Ebony's opinions, in the department since its name and reputation had been tainted. The job suited him, as had his experience. Because of them, he was well-liked, had gotten married and, most recently, had become a father.

"Willa Tate." His smile was weary. Everyone's seemed to be lately. But maybe that was Willa's own mood projection. It didn't stop her from being polite.

"Foster Lovett, the man who returned."

He came around the desk and bypassed a congenial handshake. His hug of greeting was quick but proper. When he stepped away, he chuckled. "Hey, I heard you'd left, too."

He motioned to the chair across from his desk. Willa noted a framed picture next to the nameplate on the desktop. It was his wedding picture. It was nice.

"I went to college," she said when he'd settled back into his chair. "I'm not sure that's the same thing as going across country for a decade."

He ran a hand through his long hair. "You say it like that and I just feel old all the way to my bones."

"Don't feel too old. I'm only a few years behind you in

age. Making *me* feel anything other than young and relevant would be impolite."

He snorted and held up a hand in defense. "Well, I don't want to be impolite. Not when your sister is still in town. She'd never let me hear the end of it."

The only reason Willa was friendly, or at least had been before Foster had run off, was that he'd been actual friends with Martha. Along with his ex-wife. Though Willa decided not to bring any of that up.

She wasn't there for a social call, after all.

Foster seemed to remind himself of the same thing.

He leaned forward in his chair. Something all detectives apparently did when things became serious.

"I talked to Kenneth this morning, briefly, on the phone. He said that he believes the break-in with Leonard Bartow and the attack on you downtown yesterday are connected. But we've designed the cold case unit to act independently from active cases, so I'm afraid I'm out of the loop. Bring me up to speed, if you don't mind?"

Willa didn't.

Like she had done with Kenneth, she told the detective everything. Even about the gun, which Kenneth had brought in, along with the box.

Foster didn't take notes but his eyebrows stayed furrowed as he listened. When Willa tied up the story, his look of concentration was still there. Though his gaze had shifted to the doorway.

Kenneth stood within it, the side of his face red. "What do you think?" he asked Foster.

Willa noted his hand was fisted at his side. Whatever conversation he'd had with Jason hadn't been a fun one.

"I think that, if it was anywhere other than Kelby Creek, we'd need more to go on to call this a web instead of several different non-connecting threads." He shrugged. "But this *is* Kelby Creek and, from experience, I can tell you that it may be small but it has a knack for finding a way to be a massive pain in the backside."

He gave Kenneth a questioning look. "That is why I'm going to make an executive decision for our sheriff, who's out dealing with press and the mayor, to keep you in charge of this. So what do *you* want to do? What do you need from me?"

Willa could tell Kenneth hadn't expected that. He did, however, have an answer ready.

"I want to address anyone who isn't actively patrolling or on a case. Now."

Foster nodded, not at all offended by the command. He stood. "Then let's get to it."

Willa thought she would stay in Foster's office or be taken to Kenneth's, but instead she was led to a large room filed with tables, chairs and a whiteboard.

"I hope you don't mind, but I'm going to ask you to tell your story one last time," Kenneth said to her as staff who were available started to file in a few minutes later.

Willa's stomach fluttered with nerves but she told him she didn't mind.

That lie turned into more nervous twitches as the door closed behind the last person to attend the impromptu briefing. There were almost twenty people inside the room.

Kenneth started the meeting off.

With an absolute bang.

"My name is Kenneth Gray, but a lot of you know me as the man who left this department several years ago after my wife, Ally, was shot dead in a field."

The room fell into an absolute hush. Kenneth knew without looking at her next to him that Willa's eyes had widened in shock.

He wanted to tell her he was shocked too at how bluntly he'd said it.

After speaking with Jason Whitmore, something in Kenneth had snapped. Or maybe exploded. Whatever the action, its force was still propelling him now.

At first, Kenneth hadn't known exactly what he was going to say. But he had known it wouldn't be the pep talk about catching bad guys that everyone might have expected. Nor would it be a meeting with a summary of what had happened so far. It certainly wouldn't be the cry for help that he himself had expected.

He'd known that from the moment Detective Lovett had asked him what he'd needed.

Because what he needed wasn't just something he could do on his own.

"For those who don't know that about me, know that I left the department because I couldn't find one lead, not one, in her murder," he continued. "Other men, or women, might have stayed to put more good out into the world, but I wasn't one of them. *But* then, as we know, The Flood happened and the damage from it was enough to get me back."

Kenneth paused, but not for dramatic effect. Instead he searched the faces of the men and women looking at him. He decided that he knew what needed to happen next.

"Raise your hand if you were hired or transferred in after The Flood took place."

To his surprise, six people raised their hands.

"Raise your hand if you were hired or transferred in a year or two before The Flood took place."

More hands went into the air than before.

"And raise your hand if you were heavily investigated by the FBI task forces that came in after The Flood to root out corruption because you had been here for a good chunk of time before it happened."

No one raised a hand.

Not even Detective Lovett. He had been a new hire after The Flood, despite being a local.

Kenneth raised his own hand.

He could see the surprise on some of his audience's faces. He'd never told anyone that and, as far as he knew, the interim sheriff was the only one in the department who knew. Even Lovett couldn't hide his sudden curiosity.

He lowered his hand, knowing he now had everyone's full attention.

And that was good because he had a point to make.

"Everyone knows the story. You've heard it from the gossip mill, the news, and maybe some who were directly affected. But let me make it clear exactly what happened."

Kenneth started to pace. All eyes were on him as he did so.

"Annie McHale, daughter to the beloved and quite rich McHales, went missing one day," he began. "If it had been anyone else, the reaction wouldn't have been as swift, but the McHales were a special family. Humble, compassionate, and powerful. Everyone loved and respected them, and that love and respect trickled down to Annie...

"So when a ransom call came in, it wasn't just a family worried about her. It was a whole town ready to fight. But that's not exactly how a ransom demand works. You can't have an entire town in on it without putting the very person you're trying to rescue in more danger. So the McHales turned to their best friend, and godfather to Annie. The sheriff at the time. He decided to handle the swap—five-hundred thousand dollars for Annie."

He paused again, the memory of seeing what had happened next on TV popping into his mind. As well as the memory of hearing it from his neighbor, who'd yelled at the news when her friend had called after witnessing it in person.

"We all know what happened next. There was an ambush by the kidnappers. It became a bloodbath in the park and five people were killed, several were wounded, and Annie McHale was never seen. The kidnappers managed to get away and Kelby Creek made national news because they'd hacked into the town's web site and played a live video of Annie, beaten and bloodied, begging to be saved while a kidnapper asked for a million dollars in three days or she would die."

Several people in the room seemed to physically readjust how they were sitting at that, as if trying to move away from the ugliness of the past. While the video had been taken down, it had been online long enough for recordings to be made and saved. Kenneth wouldn't doubt that everyone in Kelby Creek had seen the video at this point.

"The first FBI agents came in then to help sort everything out. One of them, Jacqueline Ortega, was the first of the two to have a hunch and follow it. She left a message on her partner's phone and disappeared. *Then* the thunderstorm came, bringing with it a nasty flash flood. That flash flood is what sent the mayor off the road and why Ortega's partner stopped to help him. That's how he found Annie's necklace in the mayor's car, and that's when he followed his new hunch that Annie's kidnappers might not be strangers at all." Kenneth looked to Willa. She was paying rapt attention. He hated to put her on the spot, but he wanted to prove that what had happened was public knowledge. "Can you tell us what happened next as you've heard it from the news and locals, Miss Tate?"

Willa's cheeks darkened but her voice was loud and clear when she spoke.

"He was able to connect the sheriff and the mayor to the

kidnappers and figure out that they had been behind it all
along. The FBI sent in another team to investigate. They
learned that the corruption went far back and had spread
like a cancer throughout the sheriff's department and other
positions of authority across town. During their investigation, several people were fired and arrested. Some disappeared." She quieted a little. "Annie McHale and Jacqueline
Ortega were never found."

Kenneth nodded. She gave him a small smile then was
back to watching him like the rest of the room.

"Now let me tell you what they didn't advertise in the
news or through the back channels of town gossip." Kenneth rolled his shoulders. He was tense. He was antsy. He
was tired of not having answers.

"When the FBI first started looking into how the corruption had infiltrated this department, they were utterly
overwhelmed with what they found. I only know this because, when they came to my door, they questioned every
single detail of every single case I had assisted on or helped
close. Every detail. Then, when that was done, they focused
on everything else. Traffic stops as a rookie. Speeding tick-
ets. What I was doing when a shooting had taken place or
when a drug bust had gone down. Where I was when my
wife was killed."

Rage at that, no matter how earned the question had
been, would never, ever, go away for Kenneth. To be questioned in the home he'd shared with Ally, after tirelessly
looking for her killer, only to fall into an obsession and
then a depression, had been a pain that he'd never thought
he'd feel. Yet, he'd had to power through it to keep his
name clear.

"It was only after I passed muster that one of the agents
admitted they hadn't expected so many others to be suspicious. Never mind guilty. He also told me he wasn't sure

the town could ever recover. Or that the department would even survive the gut job it was going to get.

"To be honest, I think at that point I was tired and angry and I said some things I probably shouldn't have. Things like there were still good people in the department. In the town. That trust might have been broken but that's the great thing about trust. You can only ever break it or earn it back. Since it was broken, that just meant it was time to earn it back."

Kenneth had gotten to his point, even if he'd taken, as Willa called it, the long way around.

He kept his gaze sweeping his audience.

"But I was wrong."

Kenneth flipped the whiteboard over. He'd written a number on it before everyone had come in. The number wasn't exact, but it was well over one hundred. "That's how many cases and incidents were directly affected by the corruption the FBI and the rest of us managed to find after The Flood. That's what this department did. The corrupted made fools out of any of us who fought the good fight and did it all for personal and selfish gain. That FBI agent was right, we shouldn't even be standing with that kind of cloud above our heads." He shook his head. Angry all over again. "And that's why the criminals in this town have become more brazen. If we can't police or catch the criminals among ourselves, what hope do we have of doing anything to them."

A few nods waved through the group. Lovett's was one of them.

"That's why I'm here, right now, in front of you." Kenneth looked at Willa. "Miss Tate, here, is going to explain how she launched her own investigation into one of our cold cases and I'll tell you how we're going to help her."

This time Willa's blush was gone. She'd seemingly lost any nerves she'd been carrying.

She was curt and quick to tell them about Josiah Linderman and the box.

Then Kenneth brought it home.

"Everyone in here is now on this case and the break-in by Leonard Bartow, as well as the attempted mugging and subsequent attack by the man in the hockey mask. But I'm going to tell you two things that you probably won't hear again in this building."

Kenneth knew he could be commanding, just by his body type alone. He could make himself seem taller and wider, and turn his face into stone, while his voice flattened and swung low. He did all of those things standing there in front of the people who would hopefully help solve several mysteries all at once. He wanted them to not only hear him, he wanted them to listen.

When he was confident they were, his voice seemed to reverberate off the walls.

"You are not to trust anyone, but most specifically anyone currently in the department or who has formerly worked for the department. The town doesn't trust us for good reason. We're going to remember that reason while we work. No stone left unturned. No one is above suspicion."

He held up two fingers to show he was at his last point. "You will tell no one outside this room what we are doing. Not spouses, not friends, not coworkers. If you question someone, you find a way to tell the truth without giving it away. Someone is out there making moves that we didn't anticipate and we couldn't stop. So, even though it's a big ask to not trust and to not talk, remember that it might be the best way to find justice for people who deserved better from this department. From us."

He didn't say their names but three immediately swam behind his eyes.

LeAnne.

Josiah.

Ally.

Kenneth turned to Willa.

He refused to add her name to the list.

"Now, come to me one by one for assignments," he barked out to the room. "We've got a job to do."

Chapter Fifteen

The gun went with one person, the ring and the box with another, someone was given Leonard Bartow, and Willa thought she heard another being assigned to shuffle through files relating to anything that had happened the year that Josiah Linderman had gone missing.

Kenneth was the head of the hunt and held the authority with sangfroid. In turn he was given the reverence that Willa believed he'd earned by his speech. Though, to say she was surprised that the speech was meant to make each person in the room not trust a soul, was an understatement.

It was also the first thing Kenneth addressed when they were alone in his office.

"Telling someone they can't trust anyone, especially during an investigation, usually makes them uncomfortable and cautious. It makes them choose their actions carefully and double-check their work. Not a long-term solution but, for now, I need everyone sharp, fast but thorough, and knowing that I'm not talking just to talk. I want this handled."

The way he spoke, with such conviction, gave Willa goose bumps.

She asked how she could help.

Kenneth checked his watch. "I need to do a few things here, but do you think you could reach out to your boss, or whoever was in charge of making the agreement to develop the land you found the box buried on? I need as much information on it and the developer as possible. Maybe if you ask about it, you'll get less scrutiny than if I send a deputy or even go myself."

Willa felt a little shame that she hadn't thought of that herself, but nodded. "I can do that."

"Good. We might not know yet who buried the box but maybe if we found out why it was buried *there*, we can follow it back to some answers."

Willa agreed. She was already thinking about the paperwork she could find herself as office manager when Kenneth announced she wasn't going alone.

"You're the common denominator in the attacks, so you're not leaving my sight until this is over." Willa might have normally scoffed at the somewhat sexist and demanding statement but there was no denying she felt relief. For more reasons than one.

She didn't want to be alone.

She didn't want Kenneth to be alone.

"I thought you didn't want anyone to know what we were doing?" She couldn't imagine Bobby Thornton, her boss and connection to the developer, wouldn't stare at Kenneth's presence when she spoke to him.

"I'll stay in the car." He held up his cell. "I can still make headway from my phone."

It took them a few minutes as Kenneth finished up, but it wasn't long before they were headed to her office.

Willa had already spoken to Bobby that morning, just as she had the day before about taking some personal days off. When she stepped through the front door solo, he came out into the small lobby with arms wide.

"Willa." His tired eyes drank her in before he was all hug. Bobby was pushing seventy but had made it a point to tell anyone who would listen that retirement was for the birds. And he wasn't a fan of flying.

He gave her a quick squeeze and then stepped back to look at her, full of concern. Along with wanting to die behind a desk instead of anywhere else, Bobby was known for his absolute love for his wife. Willa was surprised to not see her there. The very few times Willa had called off, she had come in to help out. Unlike her husband, she fully believed in relaxing after decades of working.

"How are you?" he asked, seeming to accept that, at least physically, Willa appeared to be all right. "I thought we agreed that you should take a few days. I mean, after what happened, I can barely focus on the work and I wasn't even there."

Kenneth might have been spouting the rule to not tell anyone about the investigation into Josiah and the two current attacks, but that didn't mean news of the latter hadn't already spread. Kelby Creek had been known to have the occasional uptick of excitement since The Flood but, as far as she could remember, no one had been outright killed. At least, no one innocent.

LeAnne Granger's death had changed things.

It wasn't gossip that had put the mugging turned deadly out into the town, it was facts.

A man had attacked one woman and killed another.

Neither piece of news was to be taken lightly.

Willa patted Bobby's hand, still on her shoulder.

"I'm not here for the day but, you know me, always working up here." She tapped her temple with her finger and smiled. That smile was tight and a mask for the discomfort of stepping around the truth to the boss she respected. "I was thinking about a new filing system to take when we need to be on-the-go and was wondering if I could ask you a few questions about some of our current jobs. About some details I realized I didn't have. You know, to keep my focus at home instead of worrying about everything else outside of it."

Willa swore when this was all over, she'd buy Bobby a big ol' steak and apologize for her dishonesty. Until then, she was glad—and filled with guilt—when Bobby nodded and said it was a good idea.

He led her past her own office and into his, then Willa got down to business.

Twenty minutes later she was saying goodbye, telling Bobby that his wife didn't need to worry herself with bringing Willa any homemade pie, and promising to see him Monday, bright and early.

When she got into Kenneth's SUV, he was finishing up a phone call. He waited until he was done to start driving.

"Did you find anything?" he asked her in greeting.

Willa sighed.

"The name of the company who bought Lot 427, Red Tree Development, but that was all the information we had on file. I'll have to call them and see if I can get more specific. Maybe we'll find something useful."

Willa wasn't sure of that but she had hope.

"Who was that?" she asked, turning her attention fully to him.

Kenneth was tense.

"Remember I told you that Leonard Bartow woke up but only talked long enough to get himself a lawyer?"

Willa nodded. Part of her had been glad he'd been silent. Her hope was that he'd take that silence and let it, and the evidence against him, earn him a jail cell.

"Apparently he wants to talk. To me."

That made her eyebrow pop up. "Did he say why you?"

Kenneth shook his head. "No. Just that he'll only cooperate with the man in charge of the cold case unit."

"Does he realize that man is the same one he attacked and threatened?"

"No," he said again. "I don't think so, at least. I'll find out soon."

Instead of angling the SUV in the direction of the department, she noted he'd turned in the direction of the hospital. Not her favorite place. But, after all, Leonard had been hit by a car, so it stood to reason that he was still in Haven Hospital. The thought that he'd been in the same building when Willa was with Kenneth the day before made her skin crawl.

Kenneth placed his hand on top of Willa's. His was warm. He was also sensing her unease.

"You don't have to see him. You can stay out in the hall with the guard on duty," he assured her. "Or, if it makes you feel better, I can take you back to the department."

Willa shook her head. "I might not like the man but I want to know what he has to say."

Kenneth nodded and put his eyes back on the road.

Yet, he kept his hand right where it was until they parked at the hospital.

LEONARD BARTOW'S ATTORNEY was shaking his head as he left. Kenneth didn't blame him. He'd just been dismissed by his client in words so loud they'd reverberated through the third-floor hallway.

Willa watched him go, Kenneth watched Willa. She hadn't said a word since she'd agreed to come with him to see Bartow and now he wished she had. Kenneth couldn't tell what she was thinking. Not at the moment, at least. Other than obvious concern, there was something beneath the surface.

Something he wished they could talk about.

But now wasn't the time.

Not with Leonard ready to talk.

The hospital's security guard—the man's nametag read Billings—moved from his spot next to Leonard's hospital room door.

"He's handcuffed to the bed," he said in greeting. "But everyone's said he's been a good patient. Hasn't kicked up a fuss since I've been here, either."

"I suppose he saves that for the women he attacks," muttered Willa.

It sobered the guard.

"Yeah, that's not right." He turned to address Kenneth directly. "Between hospital security and the deputies sent our way, Mr. Bartow hasn't been alone since he was brought in. We've been on him 24/7."

"Good." Kenneth didn't think Leonard would try to pull much considering he had a broken leg and arm. But, after the week he'd had, Kenneth wasn't about to assume anything. "Willa, are you good to stay out here or—"

He watched Willa flinch and cover her ears at the same time he felt the urge to do the same. An alarm screeched throughout the hallway with awful intention.

"Is that the fire alarm?" he asked Billings.

"Yeah, it is," he shouted over the piercing noise. "But we don't have any drills scheduled for right now, especially since there's surgery going on downstairs."

Billings took a step back and began to talk into the radio he'd pulled from his hip.

Kenneth reached out for Willa and took her hand.

Her eyes were wide.

He gave her hand what he hoped was a reassuring squeeze.

Billings stepped closer. "There's someone attacking staff downstairs outside room 203!"

Kenneth's heartbeat galloped to attention.

Room 203 was where Leonard Bartow was supposed to be. It was only on the recommendation of Detective Lovett that Leonard had been moved to another room after the second attack on Willa. "It might not do us any good to be the only ones who know where he really is, but it might do whoever is helping him or involved some bad to not know where he really is," he'd reasoned.

Maybe Foster had been right.

"I have to go," Billings yelled over the alarm. He started to turn but Kenneth grabbed his uniformed arm in an invasive move and kept him steady. He pointed at the door and at Willa.

"You guard them. I'll go downstairs!"

Kenneth didn't wait for an audible confirmation. He did wait for Willa's.

"Go," she insisted.

So, he did.

Gun out and ready for anything.

WILLA DIDN'T LIKE it but she was ushered into the room Billings had been guarding and right into the sights of Leonard Bartow. True to the guard's words, the big man was attached to the hospital bed by a set of handcuffs.

When their eyes met, it was instant recognition.

Willa made sure not to reach up and touch the skin of her neck that was still slightly bruised from the brute's hands. The foundation her sister had given her was the only reason no one had so far commented on it.

"What's that damn noise for?" Leonard yelled at Billings.

He didn't answer him.

"I'm going to be right outside the door," he said to Willa instead. "No one will be coming in but me or your detective."

Willa cast Leonard an uncertain look.

Billings caught it. "He's cuffed and I'm the only one with a key. You'll be fine."

Billings's concern for her was nothing compared to Kenneth's. He was out the door, letting it shut behind him, in a second flat.

Then again, guarding Leonard and her had been his most recent directive.

"What's going on?" Her former attacker's voice was filled with a mixture of anxiety and anger. The same thing she was feeling just looking at him.

"That's the fire alarm," she responded, pointing up. The noise wasn't as deafening in the room but they still had to raise their voices.

"If there's a fire then why are we still in here?" His anxiety notched up to an easily discernible panic as he pulled on the handcuffs. They stayed right where they were on the bed rail.

"It's an alarm, I don't know if there's an actual fire," she snapped. Her own rising panic wasn't as easy to control.

Was it a coincidence that the moment they were about to talk to Leonard, the fire alarm went off? That some man was fighting people downstairs outside the room the sheriff's department had moved him from?

No.

There was absolutely no way in hell.

Willa worried for Kenneth with such acuteness that she physically grabbed at her chest as she looked back at the closed door.

"You were with Detective Gray, weren't you?"

The question caught Willa wholly off guard. So much so, she told the truth and nodded. "Yes, he was about to walk in when the alarm went off. He had to go downstairs to check it out."

The man might have looked like an ogre but it almost

seemed like he was doing some figures in his head, working something out.

To her shock, he had.

"He wouldn't have left you here to go downstairs if there was a fire. He would have taken you with him." Leonard's frown deepened.

The fire alarm cut off.

The silence behind his words was eerie as he continued. "He's coming for me because I'm a loose end."

Willa wasn't about to dismiss the thought. She took a tentative step toward him.

"Who is he? Who are you—?"

A sound that was becoming all too familiar to Willa made her scream.

It was a gunshot and it had been out in the hallway.

Willa didn't have time to react further before two more shots sounded.

She was clutching at her shirt, terror thronging through her body, when Leonard's voice managed to penetrate her fear.

"Get in the bathroom, Miss Tate."

It was a simple, straightforward statement said in a calm, even tone.

Willa looked Leonard's way because, for that moment, he was the only sturdy thing in the room.

"Don't make a sound," he added.

Someone yelled out in the hallway. Another gunshot sounded.

It was enough to make her move.

Willa hurried into the attached bathroom. She shut the door and turned out the light. Not even a second later, the door to the other room banged open.

She placed her hands over her mouth, hoping to hear Billings or, even better, Kenneth.

Instead the only voice she heard belonged to a stranger. He was loud and quick.

"Sorry."

It took everything Willa had not to scream as one last gunshot went off.

Chapter Sixteen

The bathroom was dark but the light from the room poured inside and surrounded the woman.

Kenneth could have cried in relief.

"Willa?" He dropped his gun to his side and flipped on the light. Her wide, worried eyes took him in as his did the same to her.

She didn't appear to be hurt.

"There was a man…" she started. "I heard him say sorry and—" She placed a hand over her mouth. "Oh God, he shot Billings and Leonard, didn't he? They're dead, aren't they?"

One day he wished the only news he would give Willa was good. He couldn't control that now.

"Yes. They are."

Willa's eyes welled with tears. Kenneth could hear security and responding deputies running through the halls. It had been over ten minutes since the fire in the stairwell had been set, the man downstairs had attacked a nurse and a patient, and the barrage of bullets could be heard exploding overhead. When Kenneth realized his error, his grave mistake of leaving Willa's side despite promising not to, it had felt like his feet hadn't even had time to touch the ground with how fast he ran up the stairs that weren't blocked.

His stomach had fallen to his feet when he'd seen Billings on the ground outside the open door.

Then Leonard, motionless in his bed.

Kenneth didn't know what he would have done had he opened the bathroom door and Willa not been there.

"Are you hurt?" he asked, reaching out to take her hand.

Willa shook her head. Those tears began to spill over her cheeks.

"No but I... I'd very much like to leave here," she stammered out. "If...if we can."

Kenneth hated to keep the bad news coming.

"We can, but not yet. The hospital is on lockdown until the man who did this is found. So I'm going to need you to stay in here for a little bit longer. Okay?"

Willa shook her head but repeated his last word.

"Oh...okay."

Kenneth dropped her hand and positioned himself in the open doorway of the bathroom. Out of his periphery he saw Willa move against the wall behind the door, blocking any and all sight into Leonard's room. Thankfully, from their angle, the blood from both Leonard and Billings couldn't be seen.

The hospital was in lockdown but it started to fill up with law enforcement. Even reserve deputies came out and each floor was swept from top to bottom for the mystery man. Detective Lovett had been one of the first to show and had called Kenneth after reviewing the security footage.

"He knew where to walk to avoid being seen head-on by the cameras," Lovett had said, his words heated. "I can't see his face for anything, just like I can't see how he got in or if he got out."

After that call, Kenneth had made several others. All while keeping his spot in the doorway and his hand on his gun.

He didn't move an inch when the sheriff or his other colleagues arrived to work the scene. By the time the county coroner and friend to the department, Dr. Amanda Alvarez, appeared, the search within the hospital was done.

"It would be better to take her out now and have her close her eyes than wait," she told Kenneth in a low voice. "Things will get messier before they get cleaner."

"Thank you," he replied, taking the thoughtfulness for Willa to heart.

He also took the advice.

"We're going to leave, but I need you to close your eyes, Willa."

The woman had no objections. In fact, she didn't say a word as Kenneth decided picking her up and carrying her past Leonard and over Billings's body would be the best way to keep her from having to deal with haunting images.

"We're in the elevator now, so I'm going to put you down, okay?"

Willa nodded but didn't open her eyes until her feet were against the floor. Kenneth pushed the button for the lobby. Willa stayed against him, silent.

"Are we going home?" Her voice was so small, so soft.

Kenneth found himself nodding.

"Yes. I've already cleared it with the sheriff. We can go."

The car ride was, he suspected, much like the one the night before. This time, however, their situations were reversed. Willa kept quiet while Kenneth worried mindlessly for her until he was able to take her into his house and set her down on the couch.

There her silence broke into a flood of tears.

"He...he told me to hide in the bathroom after the first shot."

Kenneth pulled her against him, cradling her much like she had him after LeAnne's death.

"Who? Leonard?"

She nodded, her hair brushing up against the bottom of his chin.

"He...he told me not to make a sound. I don't understand. Why did...why did he do that?"

Kenneth stroked the back of her hair and held her tight. He admitted he didn't know.

She continued to cry until her sobs slowed into deep breaths. Then into a quiet that managed to fill up the room.

Every tear, every gasp, and every breath, Kenneth felt in his bones.

"I want you to stay here tonight," he said with nothing but honesty.

It wasn't a question but Willa still gave him an answer. "Okay."

After that their world sped up a little. Willa excused herself to the bathroom and then called her sister while Kenneth made several calls of his own. The witnesses who had seen the fight told their descriptions of the gunman but it didn't sound like anyone they recognized. It was only luck that Kenneth saw two bandages on the man's right arm in the security footage from where his sleeve had slipped down. That was enough to make them suspect that he was, in fact, the man in the hockey mask who had killed LeAnne, his bandages hiding cuts he'd gotten from his and Kenneth's tussle. There was an all-points-bulletin out on him and a sketch artist from the next county was coming over to work with them to see if they couldn't put his face out there since he'd avoided the hospital's security cameras.

Everything else on the technical side of what had happened was being handled by the sheriff. He'd been the one to suggest taking Willa somewhere else and keeping an eye on her.

Regardless, even if he hadn't, that's exactly what Kenneth would have done.

Because, as much as he hated to admit it, it felt like two things were happening at once and neither of them was good.

Someone was cleaning up loose ends and someone considered Willa part of that mess.

THAT NIGHT CAME to find Willa in better spirits.

Though *better* was starting to become a relative term.

She wasn't better compared to her life before she'd found the box, but she was a lot better than she had been before two people near her had been shot dead while she'd hid in the bathroom.

The worst part about finding the box was the constant death it seemed to bring with it.

The best part about finding the box was the man who woke her from her nap to offer her a peanut butter and jelly sandwich for dinner.

"I almost let you keep sleeping but realized I couldn't remember if you'd eaten anything for lunch," he said. "Also, not trying to push, but your sister has already called me twice. I think she wants to talk to you and not hear from me that you're okay."

Willa smiled, not an ounce embarrassed.

"Good of you to wake me. Though I barely convinced her to go stay at Kimball's parents' place. I'm not sure she'll believe I'm okay."

Kenneth slid her the phone and excused himself to give her some privacy. She ate her sandwich and spoke to Martha until it was gone.

"You should be with me," Martha insisted one last time before the call ended.

Not if I'm a target, Willa thought, and not for the first time. She skirted repeating that and took a more judicious route.

"This is only temporary, Martha. I'm good here, and you know that."

Martha didn't respond with anything cheerful but did let Willa off of the phone without any more pushback. Then it was time to finally return the several texts from Ebony, though Willa did so with a call. Guilt at keeping what was happening from her faded away as she gave the Cliff's Notes version of everything that had gone on since she'd found the box.

Ebony had, understandably, freaked out.

Then she'd reverted to nothing but concern. She'd asked Willa what she'd needed and accepted her answer of time alone to process.

Or, at least, time alone with the only person who she felt safe being with.

Willa ended the call with promises of checking in later and took her plate to the kitchen. Kenneth was finishing off his sandwich over the sink. He grinned and took the dish from her.

"I hope you don't mind my lack of chef's excellence," he said. "As you probably saw this morning, I need to go grocery shopping something fierce."

Willa situated herself leaning against the counter so she was facing him. He made quick work of cleaning the plate, despite the dishwasher being close by.

"You won't find me complaining," she assured him, weirdly warmed by his show of domestic gumption. "I *was* hungry and that *was* a great sandwich."

Kenneth chuckled. He dried off his hands.

The conversation hit a small lull.

Delilah, dropped off by Kimball along with a bag of Willa's things packed by Martha right after lunch, decided to break it with some pointed licks to her hand. It made Willa laugh.

"You know, for a moment, I think Kimball was thinking about asking if Delilah could stay with them a bit longer." Willa scratched behind Delilah's ear. Something she seemed to be very fond of. "I wouldn't be surprised if, when this is all over, he talks Martha into getting their own puppy."

"Can you blame him? Look at this stunner."

Kenneth surprised her by heading to the living room and dropping down into a crouch. Delilah became hyper at the movement and followed, as did Willa. Delilah lapped at his face while he rubbed down her sides, exciting her even more. She gave a few barks and then was pure speed as she ran out of the room in a wild gallop. It made the humans in the house laugh.

"And that's what you call the zoomies," Kenneth explained. "She's about to treat this place like an Indy 500 track, slow down long enough to need to go outside, and then she'll pass out shortly after."

"Ah, such a simple life sounds fantastic right about now."

True to his word, Delilah zoomed around the house. She managed to get both of them to chase her, extending the fun until, sure enough, she ran to the back door and barked.

"Coming through," Kenneth called, running from his spot behind the couch where he'd been playing hide-and-seek with her. Willa laughed from her spot behind a chair opposite. She went to the back door and watched as the fully grown man resembled a carefree kid, running around in the backyard. It was only after Delilah did her business that he slowed.

And it was only when he led the dog inside the house that the carefree kid turned back into an adult.

The one with bills and fears and pain.

But maybe Willa was projecting her mood again.

Because, for all of the smiles and laughter she'd taken part in, there was a growing weight that couldn't be ignored.

It must have showed on her face.

When Delilah went to lap up some water from the kitchen, Willa admitted that she was still tired. And that there was a good chance some of that was from a collection of bad days and not just what had happened at the hospital.

"It just feels like we've been trying to walk up a hill while it storms," she said. "Every step we take up, we slide back two."

Kenneth sighed. It was an impressive sight from how close she was standing next to him. He was in an undershirt since being home and it was tight enough that the movement showed a hint of lean, muscled chest. Though she'd already seen his upper body when she'd made him change at the hospital the day before, there was something different about seeing even a tease of it now.

Or maybe she was just getting caught up in more and more details about the man.

His shirt, his cleaning habits, how his eyes crinkled at the sides when he laughed while playing with his dog. How he'd handed her a napkin with her plated sandwich.

How he'd let her into his home to protect her.

How he was looking at her now, making her feel like she was the only person in the world.

Those eyes of his, filled with depth and a storm-clouded sky, empathized with her.

"Believe it or not, I know how that feels."

He motioned her to follow him and was soon giving her a rundown on his bathroom and the shower, if she wanted to take a spin, as he called it.

"All my bath soap and shampoo smells like cologne, but it'll at least get the job done cleaning-wise if Martha didn't pack yours," he said, showing her the various bottles lining the shelf in the shower. "There're also clean towels in that closet and, if you're feeling fancy, a robe I may or may not have accidentally stolen from a hotel in Kipsy, Alabama, when I went to visit a friend last year. Don't worry, it's clean, too."

"I have to say, Mr. Gray, you're very accommodating," she said.

The man smirked, more playful than usual. "Something all men love to hear from a beautiful woman."

That made Willa's cheeks burn up in an instant. Luckily, Kenneth had excused himself to give her some privacy. But that didn't stop her from thinking about the comment as she showered and readied for bed.

When she was finished and dressed in her flannel pajama set that looked like it belonged in a family Christmas movie, Willa hoped the blush that was lying low beneath the surface would stay there.

No such luck when she saw that Kenneth had changed, too.

Instead of jeans, he was wearing a pair of nearly matching flannel sleep pants.

"Well, great minds, I guess?" she said, pointing to the obvious.

Kenneth chuckled. "I have to say I think you wear them better."

That blush lifted itself to her face again. She had no choice but to fight through it, especially when she saw a bandage peeking out of his shirtsleeve.

It was like cold water to her face.

Another two steps back on the hill.

Kenneth didn't notice at first. He was moving around the bed, adding a new blanket.

"I'm going to give you the bed, and don't try to talk me out of it because that's a fight you'll lose. I'll take the couch downstairs," he said, unaware that the mere mention of him being somewhere else made Willa's anxiety rise. "As for Delilah, you're going to have to keep the door shut to keep her out. She's gotten used to sleeping on the bed because *someone* has let her do it almost every night of her life."

He cracked a grin and finally faced her with full attention.

"What's wrong?" He was all serious in a second flat.

Willa averted her gaze. Then thought, *Who cares?*

They'd already been through a lot together as it was. She looked him in the eye.

What would this hurt?

"Could you stay with me? At least until I fall asleep?"

It sounded like a simple request—and maybe it really was simple—but Willa felt her heartbeat speed up as the questions came out.

Never mind when Kenneth didn't even blink before he answered.

"I won't say no to that."

Chapter Seventeen

Willa slipped beneath the cool sheets, taking extreme care not to touch Kenneth as she did so. It wasn't for lack of want—hadn't she struggled with the fact that she *knew* she wanted the detective for the last week?—but out of respect.

And…well, fear.

Not the sickening kind that had gone through her several times recently.

No.

This fear had everything to do with her feelings. Her desires.

The fact that she didn't know if they were reciprocated by the detective.

Or, to be truthful, deserved.

That thought rattled her more than she'd meant it to and, no sooner had the man been laid out on his side of the bed, than Willa finally give voice to a thought that had been growing unchecked within her.

"It's my fault," she said. "It's all my fault."

Kenneth was on his back but readjusted to look at her, his hands behind his head and elbows against the pillow. If she had thought he was a big man when standing, he somehow seemed to command a bigger presence in the bed. Willa felt tiny in comparison.

"Because you found the box and didn't let it go."

Willa nodded because he was exactly right.

"Three people have died and, why? Because I wanted to solve a mystery? And what if there's nothing really there to begin with? What if it was just a box of random things like you first said?" Willa rolled onto her back and stared up at the ceiling. The only light in the room was on the nightstand next to Kenneth. It was small and cast shadows against the popcorn ceiling. "What if everything that's happened could have been avoided had I just kept my mouth shut and my curiosity at bay?"

Willa thought of LeAnne, Billings, and even Leonard.

They would all be alive had she done things differently.

The sound of fabric moving against skin preceded Kenneth's hand sliding beneath the covers to find hers.

The contact startled her but she didn't move away.

Instead, she listened to the warm rumble of his voice.

"I've never told you about the day Ally died, have I?"

That question was more unexpected than the impromptu hand-hold. Willa shook her head. He must have heard the movement because he continued without a verbal answer.

"Most know the gist of how she was found, in Becker's field with two bullets in her, but no one knows why she was there in the first place." He shifted a little but kept Willa's hand. His voice stayed even and warm despite the topic. "See, Ally was one of those crazy people who loved to run. I'd say it's all just exercise and she'd fuss at me and say running wasn't just a way to try to stay in shape, it was a lifestyle. A way to get and keep control of your life while also giving you freedom."

He laughed. It sounded old and worn.

A laugh recalled from a memory he'd no doubt had with his wife.

"But for me? Well, it was just a fast way to make you sweaty and hungry." Willa felt through the mattress's rising and falling that he'd taken a deep breath. When he'd let the breath out, the warmth in his voice had gone with it. "The last time I saw her alive, she wanted to break in her new running shoes and go on a trail at the park to shake things up. She asked me to go with her. I didn't."

There was unmistakable pain in his voice.

Willa wished she could make it better. She knew she couldn't. At least, not entirely.

"No one knows where she was actually killed, just knew that she wasn't shot there in Becker's," he continued. "And to this day, I have no idea what would have happened had I gone with her instead of staying home. So, I blamed myself then for her death just as I still blame myself now sometimes for it, too."

"But you didn't do anything wrong," Willa piped in. "You couldn't have known what would happen."

As she said the words, Willa realized why Kenneth was telling her about Ally now instead of all the times they'd been together in the last week.

He gave her hand a squeeze of pressure.

"Unless you came up with the plan, carried it out, and pulled the trigger, it isn't your fault." He sighed again. It sounded lighter somehow. "But I know it's a hard truth to accept. What-if scenarios put bumps in the road to acceptance."

Willa started at that.

"Well, if that isn't a poetic way to put it, Mr. Gray. I'm impressed."

The mattress moved as his laugh rumbled through it.

"You have my mom to thank for that," he said when he was done. "She more or less said that same thing about a hundred times after I left the department the first time. I guess it stuck."

"You're just taking the long way 'round to healing if you

keep tormenting yourself with what could have been and how things would have turned out had you chosen differently. It's a good sentiment."

Kenneth laughed again and this time he rolled over onto his side, sliding one arm beneath the pillow and letting her hand go with the other. Willa mimicked the move. She was on her side, facing him, hands in a prayer stance between her cheek on the pillowcase. Suddenly it felt like two friends at a sleepover, shooting the breeze about life, love, and also trivial things.

Never mind that they were in their thirties, had both survived attacks meant to kill in the last few days, and were a single man and a single woman.

"You know, I was born in Kelby Creek and grew up here, and I've heard a lot of Southernisms, but 'long way 'round' is new even to me. When we met, it was the first time I'd heard it."

Willa snorted.

"I have a theory on that," she said. "See, there are tiers of being Southern and only us top-tier families use phrases like that. 'Like a hair in a biscuit,' 'madder than a wet hen,' 'full as a tick,' 'worn slap out,' and so on. 'Long way 'round' is just something I grew up hearing from my family. Though it can be a pain in the backside to use when you're trying to give someone directions on where not to go, especially since the long way 'round isn't just a measurement of distance."

"It isn't?"

She shook her head. Willa had washed her hair but had quickly braided it to her scalp. It would be a mess in the morning when she unleashed it, but she was trying to save the man's pillow from being soaked through. She'd gone through his bathroom cabinets and there wasn't a hair dryer to be found. There was nothing, in fact, aimed for use by a woman. It had split her emotions down the middle.

On the one hand, she imagined Kenneth cleaning out Ally's things after her death, maybe slowly or maybe through the years. On the other hand, she was pleased to see that no other woman seemed to have been entertained by the man in recent years. Or, if they had been, they'd brought their toiletries in and then taken them out.

Willa's braids smelled like spice and something woodsy as she shifted her head to look up at him a little more easily. It wasn't an unpleasant thing.

"Sometimes it just means you took the challenging way. The road less traveled."

"I suppose that makes sense. Though my favorite Southernism hands down will always be 'bless your heart.'" He grinned. "I've never heard nastier fighting words than those."

"Ugh. I *hate* that phrase," Willa said, honest as a nun in church. "Your contractor's—Landon Mitchell—mother used to say it to me all the time. She disapproved of my job, my hair, and my disinterest in learning to knit. I mean... don't get me wrong, I don't judge those who do knit, but after she told me I needed to do it to be a good mom, I made a promise to myself to never touch a knitting needle out of pure pettiness." She shook her head. "That woman blessed my heart so many times it'll probably get to heaven before the rest of me ever follows."

That really got Kenneth going. He was laughing so much that it turned her growing grumpiness at the memories into following his contagious laughter with her own. It was nice to hear the man happy. It was nice to be the reason why he was smiling, too.

"I never would have guessed someone could dislike you

at all," Kenneth said after he'd composed himself. "You re-mind me of sunshine, and who dislikes sunshine?"

Willa didn't know how he'd meant the compliment to land but it was a powerful hit. She was glad he couldn't see her cheeks that were, no doubt, flaming to life.

"People have called me bubbly and bouncy, but I'm not sure anyone has ever said I was like sunshine."

He hesitated. The first time he'd done so all night.

"Not even Landon?"

Willa shook her head again. She wondered if he could read the change in emotion moving through her chest.

"No."

It was a simple response. A true one.

And Kenneth responded with only three simple words before the house around them became quiet.

"Bless his heart."

ON SATURDAY MORNING answers started to come in.

Much like the rain.

Willa emerged from his room around eight, dressed and with her hair still in braids. She held up her phone to show a social media post from their local news station.

"The weatherman promised no more rain for a week after today."

Kenneth didn't rightly believe him.

By the time noon rolled around, he was sure it had been raining for years.

An annoyance that normally wouldn't have affected him, not being able to go outside felt limiting. Plus, the man who'd entered the hospital hadn't been found. Neither by the all-points-bulletin nor from their working sketch thanks to witnesses at the hospital. Whoever he was, he wasn't in the department's system and he hadn't made a scene out-side the hospital. That only made the rain more frustrating.

It limited their search and it improved his chances of staying hidden.

Willa brought Delilah in from a quick bathroom break in the yard, shucking rain off the umbrella, and in an increasingly foul mood. Earlier that morning she had been doing her own investigation into the developer who had bought the lot where the box had been buried and was still waiting for a call-back from someone.

"I know I didn't tell them about the urgency of the matter but, still, it's only polite that when you say you're going to call back in a few minutes you actually call back within a few minutes. Not make the person you promised wait."

She grabbed for the towel Kenneth had put next to the side door to the yard and absently began to pat dry Delilah, who sat still, used to the process.

"I swear, Dee, you've got better manners than most humans," Willa muttered.

Kenneth had overtaken his dining room table despite having an office to utilize. He blamed the paperwork that was starting to pile up across its surface but, the truth was, the night before had changed something between him and Willa.

At least, in his mind.

Kenneth had already believed Willa to be a beautiful woman, but the sight of her sleeping in his bed, wet braids dampening his pillow, hands folded against her cheek, face slack and at peace, had utterly bewitched him.

She was a light in the darkness.

Not just sunshine. She was the moon in the night sky, too.

It was another poetic statement—though, this one he kept inside his head—that he hadn't known he believed.

But he did.

That's why he decided to work at the dining room table.

It gave them both room to work together. Even if it was in silence, it was a companionable one.

The kind he enjoyed just as much as watching her do the simplest of things like wiping the rain off Delilah or asking him if he wanted anything while she was up.

Kenneth knew that part of that might be the fact that he had been lonely over the last few years, shying away from true connection, but the other part?

That was all Willa.

The woman let Delilah run wild while she tucked back into the kitchen. She offered him a fresh cup of coffee, which he said he'd gladly accept.

It was still brewing when his phone starting ringing.

The Caller ID read Foster Lovett.

Kenneth answered on the second ring. "Gray here."

There was a rustling on Lovett's side of the phone. He asked Kenneth to give him a second.

Willa came in with an empty coffee mug, curious. She watched him as Lovett found a better position to talk.

"Sorry, this rain is a kink in the kitchen sink, I tell you." He didn't wait for a response. "Gray, we found a few things that we don't have context for yet but…well, it's a heck of a few things."

Kenneth got that feeling in his gut. That *everything is about to change* feeling.

But, like life, there was no other way through it than to go through it, so he said, "Okay, hit me."

Lovett took a breath. The noise behind him had quieted considerably. He must be inside now.

"We ran down who the ring belonged to, or did years ago."

"Who?" Kenneth grabbed his pen.

"A Joshua Kepler from out of town bought it eight years ago, and the only reason why the owner of the jeweler's remembered his name and the ring is that Joshua used to have a different last name when he lived in Kelby Creek. Linderman."

"Linderman?"

Willa's eyes widened as Kenneth wrote down the name.

"Josiah Linderman's son."

Kenneth couldn't believe it. He said as much but then that feeling came back when Lovett said that wasn't all. Not by a mile.

"You're at home now, right?" Lovett asked before explaining. "Willa is still there with you, too?"

"I am," Kenneth said slowly. "She is."

Willa mouthed "what," but Kenneth's attention had been pooling around the phone call until there was nothing but Lovett's voice.

He sounded reluctant and sorry all at the same time.

"The bullet casing inside the box... Well, after looking into old unsolved cases, we actually found the bullet it matched."

Kenneth knew then. He wrote down the name but waited for the detective to finish before dropping his pen.

"Gray, the casing matched one of the bullets that killed your wife."

Chapter Eighteen

Willa was in the kitchen while the sheriff and a deputy she didn't recognize spoke with Kenneth in his home office. It wasn't at his behest that they get more privacy, but Willa could tell that the news had knocked Kenneth off whatever balance they'd become comfortable with since they'd met.

Willa wasn't surprised.

Though she wished she knew the full extent of what was going on, and not just what Kenneth, as if in a daze, had repeated to her after the phone call had ended.

It was while she was feeling sad for Kenneth and trying to foresee what the news of the potentially connected cases would do to their investigation that the phone call she'd been waiting for came in.

A man named Ronaldo said hello and all the nice things you said to a stranger on the phone before asking what he could do for her.

"I'm the office manager with Clanton Construction here in Kelby Creek. I was updating some files and realized the file on the town houses on lot 427 in town had been misplaced. I was hoping to fix that, if I could, by next week so my boss doesn't think I'm lousy with a computer."

Willa hurried to grab the notebook that Kenneth had let her borrow and searched out a pen. "I've managed to find most of the information, like your company, Red Tree Development, is the one that purchased the lot and hired us to do the work. But there's a spot here for the person who was in charge of accepting our bid. Mrs. Reynolds from your office said that that information was with you, which is why I left the message with her to pass on."

Willa had learned at an early age that if you talked long enough, made the words sweet enough, and gave the person you were talking to the chance to be a hero, most people were mighty inclined to help.

Ronaldo was definitely one of those people.

"Ah, I certainly can get that information for you, Miss Tate," he exclaimed. "You're in luck because I often work from home and all of my information is here. Give me a second to get my computer booted up."

They talked non-talk for a little bit—professional chit-chat, as she liked to call it—until he'd brought up the Clanton Construction account.

"Ah, Lot 427. The town houses…" he said. "Let's see… Well, won't you know it. There are three people listed here with Red Tree who helped facilitate the bid and buy. I'm afraid I don't have more details other than their names, but their contact information would be on the company web site."

"Oh, that's okay. I just need to put down the names. If we need more, I can reach out later."

Ronaldo gave her all three names and wished her luck with her computer skills, something that made Willa blush considering she'd lied.

And then she was left staring at three names she didn't recognize.

Maria Clements, Nadja Loren, and Terry Page.

Willa was about to Google them when the men came out of Kenneth's office.

Not a one of them looked happy.

Willa put her notebook back on the dining table and smiled at the group. The sheriff took his tried-and-true cowboy hat off, gave her a nod, and said he had to get going. The deputy followed.

Kenneth shut the door behind them.

He locked it.

Willa took a tentative step forward. She didn't know what to say, let alone ask.

Thankfully, Kenneth had become more forthright with her. Instead of leading her to the table or the office, he took a heavy seat on the couch. Willa was much more delicate as she perched on the cushion next to him, angling her body to face him.

"They were looking through cold cases with the same kind of caliber bullet that matched the casing found in the box," he started, no segue. "They found only two unsolved in the last thirty years with the same kind—Ally's and an older man who'd been killed in a robbery gone wrong. Ally's was the only case where a bullet and one casing were missing. The one in the box was a perfect match with the one that was…was in her."

Willa took his hand. At this point, it was something they'd both done several times. It didn't faze either of them.

"So what does that mean?" she asked, hoping some of her warmth would seep through her skin and right into his heart. She hated how tense he'd become since the call.

Kenneth let out a long breath.

"It means that, somehow, Josiah Linderman and Ally are connected. Whether it's by a killer or something else, I don't know."

Willa again couldn't believe that one box could cause such confusion and devastation.

She also couldn't believe what he repeated from Detective Lovett to her next. Not only had Joshua Linderman come back to town, the engagement ring he'd bought had been found in the box too.

It was a lot to process.

"What about Joshua Linderman? Or is it Joshua Kepler? Maybe he can tell us something?"

"That's what Detective Lovett is deep-diving on now. Our best guess for his name change is that, after he went into the foster care system, he was adopted by a family and changed his last name to theirs. Foster is trying to find Joshua through his new name but so far he can't locate him."

"What about their uncle? I could reach out to him again. Maybe he knows more about the children than he let on about the first time around. Why else would Joshua be back in town?"

Kenneth nodded. It was like he'd aged ten years within half an hour. "That would be nice."

Had this been at their first meeting, Willa would have gone about her task without another word. But now she could tell there was something that Kenneth was holding back.

She moved her hand from his and brought it up to his cheek. "What else?"

A smile passed over his lips. It was brief.

"Josiah's most prized picture, Joshua's engagement ring, and the bullet that helped kill my wife... I'm now almost afraid to know how the bloody cloth that used to be in there connects. And why it was the only item stolen from the box."

"Do you still think the man in the hockey mask is the one who stole it from my apartment before Leonard showed up?"

It was a theory they'd kicked around earlier that morning. Why else would the man at the hospital walk in and kill Leonard the way that he had?

Kenneth nodded.

"I think Leonard was about to tell me who his partner was, or his employer, if he was a hired hand, and I think that's why he was taken out. He's the only one who could have given us real answers. Not just conjecture and theories—which, by the way, I'm not a fan of."

Willa let her hand slide down to his chin. "We'll get to the bottom of all this."

She didn't need to do it, but she did.

Willa used her hand to tilt his chin down enough so she could place a chaste kiss on his lips.

When she pulled back, it took him a bit longer than usual to look up from her lips to her eyes.

"That's the fourth kiss," he noted. His voice unreadable. "What was it for?"

Willa smiled.

"Faith."

Kenneth tried to return the smile but it didn't last. The three names she'd found slipped right out of her mind as the need to talk to Josiah's brother-in-law took over. Surely, he had answers.

At some point someone had to.

JOSIAH LINDERMAN'S FORMER brother-in-law was less talkative about Josiah and Mae's children than he had been about his sister. Mostly because he'd felt guilty, as he said in his own words, that he wasn't able to take the children and that's how they'd wound up in foster care.

"I already told you I didn't take them in. I was having my own problems and...well, I couldn't raise no kids. The last time I even saw 'em young was right after Josiah went missin'. Didn't seem to be anything I could say to be helpful and I knew if they saw me again, it would make it hard for everyone."

Willa had been delicate about how she handled the rest of the conversation—she wasn't blaming him or anyone for the choices made in the wake of tragedy.

"You said the last time you saw them was when they were young. So does that mean you haven't seen them as adults?"

Turns out, he had. Something he'd kept from both her and Kenneth the times they'd called before.

"I'd heard Joshua had come back in to pay some respects to his mama's grave on the anniversary of her death. I went out to find him there." Willa could hear the pride in his next statement. "He looked good. Tall and healthy, you know. Smart, too. Said he'd found a family who liked him to read a lot, and so he'd learned a thing or two. He even said he'd gotten him a woman who liked books and all of that, too. Said he was thinking about marrying her but had to do some things first."

He didn't know what those things were and, when Willa asked if Joshua spoke of his sister, Mariam, he was openly upset by his own answer.

"Joshua said him and Mariam got split up in care when they both were still real young. She got adopted a year before him and they'd kept up with letters for a while but then lost each other." He cussed. "We can only hope she got as lucky as he did."

There wasn't anything else to ask once he admitted that was the last time he'd seen Joshua, and the last of what he knew about him.

Willa bid the man a thank-you and a goodbye, feeling a heaviness in her heart as she did so.

A family that had started out steeped in what people

called true love between Josiah and Mae had turned into mystery and loss.

Willa wished she could snap her fingers and make it all go away. Bring back Mae, keep Josiah from walking to the store that day, and watch Joshua and Mariam be raised by two caring parents.

But she couldn't and she went to the bathroom to become weepy about it for a few minutes.

By the time she was done, Kenneth was off the phone and ready to listen to what she'd learned. He conferenced Foster in on the call and both men were quiet as she recalled the conversation.

"Finding kids in care, who aged out of care, and who were adopted, is a hard get in Alabama, so finding Mariam might be a lot harder than we hope," Foster commented when she was done. "Especially since Joshua is our only lead and he apparently lost touch with her."

"What about Joshua?" Kenneth asked. "Any luck with Cadence Jewelers' owner and tracking down any information on him?"

"The owner's still looking through his boxes of records but thinks we can get an address off of the receipt when he finds it. I'll keep you updated. On everything. Thanks for the help, Willa. And, Gray? Can you switch off speakerphone?"

Willa used the need for privacy to take Delilah out into the backyard. The rain had downgraded to a drizzle but was in a way refreshing. She tried to forget for a moment how quickly life could change for the good or the bad and turned her face up to the sky.

After a minute or so, she felt better.

She took Delilah back inside, patted the pup off, and found Kenneth in the kitchen.

He was staring out the window.

"I know this question is becoming moot, but is everything okay?" she asked.

"I've had better days, I suppose." Kenneth snorted. "That is one reason the sheriff has decided that I need to take the rest of the afternoon off. 'Take it easy while you can.'"

"You don't strike me as a man who appreciates that suggestion."

Willa moved to lean against the counter, facing him again. The casual stance was becoming a habit the longer she was in the house.

"I'm not good at sitting still. Usually when I'm alone with my thoughts, I end up being as far from relaxed as possible."

Willa shrugged, silently conceding that a lot of people rarely got peace of mind when alone with their thoughts.

"*But* you're not alone now," she said, smiling wide and true. "I'm here."

She was about to list off reasons why the sheriff's advice wasn't bad—being run ragged never helped anyone, half the department including the lead detective was working on every angle of their investigation, and they themselves were really just waiting for call-backs—but then Kenneth did something peculiar.

He just stopped and stared down at her.

Willa felt her cheeks heating up. Her eyebrow rose in question.

She didn't get a chance to ask a thing.

Kenneth went from standing tall to swooping low. His lips pressed against Willa's moments before his arms encircled her.

In that moment, the world went out the window as far as she was concerned.

It was made up of just two people, kissing in the kitchen.

Kenneth did not seem to want to keep that status for long, however.

One fluid motion was all it took for the detective to take her from standing to up in his arms and then on top of the counter itself. A glass clinked against the top as her backside must have pushed it aside. It was loud enough to make Kenneth pause.

He broke their kiss to inspect the clatter.

"Are you okay?" he asked, voice filled with gravel that felt like it was rubbing against all the right places on her. "Willa?"

That pulled her attention from her hammering heartbeat but didn't give him the answer he wanted.

"What was that kiss for?" she found herself asking.

He might have thought it a play on their already-established small kiss inside joke. But, for Willa, it was exactly the question she wanted answered.

The absolute lack of smile but very present loosening of control was a good sign.

"That was because I want you." Slower than the last time, tentative almost, Kenneth pressed his lips back to hers. It was tender but deep. Willa had to force her eyes open when he pulled back. "That was to show you the first wasn't a fluke. And—" He came back for another kiss.

It was torture. Willa loved it, though not so much when he stepped back again.

"—that was to hopefully give you a taste of the rest of my intentions."

Willa sounded more breathless than she felt.

She did manage a smile, though.

"How about now we just assume that anything that happens between us is because we both, really, really want it? No need to stop and talk about it."

Kenneth's eyes became hooded. Then his gaze went to her lips.

"Sounds like a plan to me."

Chapter Nineteen

The rain had stopped sometime in the middle of the night.

Kenneth only noted the lack of sound because in its place was something better. At least, to him.

Willa Tate didn't snore, but she made this small murmur on occasion as she slept. It wasn't something he'd witnessed the night before when he'd stayed until she'd fallen asleep but, after remaining in the bed with her, a long while after she'd fallen asleep, he'd been able to listen to the soft murmur until he'd also drifted off. Before that, he'd watched her sleep, stroked her hair when her cheek was against his collarbone, and then marveled at how warm she was when he pulled her flush against him, arm over her hip protectively.

That's how he'd woken up the first time early Sunday morning.

Willa under his arm and back to his chest.

He'd felt her breathing in and out and was happier for it.

Happier than he'd been in a long, long while.

So much so, he dozed off until an hour or so later.

Willa wasn't in his arms any longer, but she was still in his bed. He blinked a few times before realizing she was awake and staring at the ceiling. Her brows were knitted together in a way that made him instantly alert.

"What is it?"

Willa jumped a little. He reached out and found her hand

beneath the covers. He realized then that they were both still naked but didn't comment on it just yet. Not when she looked so concerned about something.

"Sorry," he added. "I didn't mean to startle you."

Willa's cheeks flushed but she gave him a small, dismissive wave with her free hand.

"Oh, don't worry. I probably am the one who woke you with my moving around. Sorry."

Now she really had his attention. her voice sounded off.

Kenneth rolled onto his side and propped himself up to look at her. "Willa, what is it?"

She released a long, heavy sigh. It made the sheet ruffle a little at the movement.

"A thought was bothering me and I couldn't figure out what it was but now I know. But saying it feels like a not-so-cool thing to do given where I am and the fact that I'm very naked." It was one long, hurried statement.

Kenneth went from his side to sitting upright. "Whatever it is, you can tell me."

Willa also straightened. She brought the sheet along with her and covered herself.

She was self-conscious now.

Did she regret what they'd done?

Because he definitely didn't.

"I was thinking about you being tickled that I say the 'long way 'round,'" she started, not exactly meeting his eye. "Then I thought about you and everything we've been through, and then I thought about Ally." She let out a sigh of frustration this time. Then she was staring at him full-on. "I know this isn't the right time but... I mean I suppose there really isn't a *right time* to talk about it, but you said the day she was killed that she went out to the park to break in her new shoes, right?"

The entire conversation had caught him off guard but

Kenneth nodded. "Yeah. She liked going to the park downtown. Before it was sectioned off into a dog park."

"The one off Main that backs up to the woods," she offered.

He nodded again.

"And she was found almost near the town limits, nowhere near the park, right? But that wasn't where you thought she was killed?"

That look passed over her again. The one she'd worn when she'd been staring at the ceiling.

Deep thought. Not all of it good.

And she sounded like she'd been working on the idea for a while. How long had she been awake?

"Yeah. We never found the second bullet that went through and there wasn't…a lot of blood where she was. We expanded the search to include the park, though, and found nothing. Why? What are you thinking, Willa?"

She chose her words carefully.

"I had this friend in school who got these new running shoes and needed to break them in ASAP for a 5k she was doing with her boyfriend the following weekend. She wore them everywhere and, even though they hurt her feet, she'd insist we walk back to the dorms through the wooded path because it was hard terrain. She thought it would make the process easier or faster or something."

Willa angled her body so there was no mistaking where her attention was. "Maybe Ally did something similar and instead of staying at the park—"

Kenneth tensed.

Adrenaline shot through him.

An idea.

A thought.

A potential lead.

"Maybe she went the long way 'round because it isn't always about distance, it's about the challenge," he finished.

Willa nodded. "And if I was going to take the more challenging path from that park, and I'm also a local who enjoys going the distance with running, then I'd leave downtown and follow the woods up to the creek before coming right on back."

Kenneth threw the covers off him. He was out of bed in a flash and at his dresser looking for a new pair of boxers.

"That, if you kept in a relatively straight line, would put you really close to someone else's idea of a long way 'round," he said, words clipped and quick to maintain his excitement at possibly finding an answer. "Josiah Linderman's."

Willa was out of bed, too. She took the blanket with her. There was no denying she was feeling the same energy he was.

"Exactly," she said, picking up on his thoughts. "And that can't be a coincidence, can it?"

"I don't know but let's go find out."

KENNETH DROVE TO the park while Willa laced up her shoes. Delilah was with them and she was picking up on their excess energy. The moment they left the park's old running path and went into the trees, she was all tail-wagging and sniffing.

Kenneth would have normally been more playful but he couldn't be now. Not when he was trying his best to think like Ally. He took every bit of knowledge he'd ever known about his late wife in the years they'd dated and the years they'd been married and moved through the woods at a slow but thoughtful pace.

Willa trailed behind him, quiet.

She was giving him space and, one day, he was going

to let her know just how much he appreciated her thoughtfulness. And her patience.

Kenneth had a feeling that not all women would be keen on sleeping with a man only to go out the next day to look for the place his late wife had been killed.

Then again, Willa wasn't at all like most women.

Sure, she was sunshine and moonlight, but she was also so much more.

Someone he wanted to know more about.

But someone whom he let stay behind him while he became lost in another woman he'd cared deeply for.

That's how they stayed for half an hour or so. Kenneth moving across parts of worn paths and parts of the woods that he imagined Ally would prefer. He started to doubt that their lead was anything more than wishful thinking and, even if it wasn't, it had been years since her death. If they did find the spot where she'd been killed, there was a good chance they'd never know it.

They made it to the creek soon after he started to lose faith.

"She wouldn't have gone across it," he disclosed. "This is when she would have turned back."

Willa nodded and said she agreed, but didn't follow him right away. Instead, she went to a nearby tree. It wasn't dead, but there was a hollowed-out space at the bottom of its trunk. It looked as though an animal had made it into a den. Dirt, leaves and other debris had collected inside.

He paid it no mind.

But Willa did what Willa did best.

She surprised him.

He paused, watching her bend down.

When she straightened again, she looked caught between excitement and disbelief. She pointed down.

"I don't know why this keeps happening to me, but I've found another box."

It wasn't actually a box but a cigarette case. One of the fancy, vintage ones. Metal, with an intricate design on its top, it was ultimately worn and covered in grime. It had seen much better days.

Willa took Delilah's leash as Kenneth donned a set of gloves he'd brought with him, as always.

He paused to take a breath before opening the case.

He didn't know what he'd expected to see but a folded piece of paper and a small, whittled-down pencil wasn't it. He shared a silent look with Willa before setting the case aside and unfolding the paper.

It was a list of names. Ten in total. All but two had a cross through them.

Kenneth wasn't sure if the cigarette case was a clue to what they were searching for or just something someone had misplaced. Still, he read the names out, as if hearing them could give him some clarity.

"Grant Milligan. Terry Page."

He sighed. He shouldn't have let his excitement get the better of him. What were the chances that they'd actually find something after all these years?

Kenneth looked back at Willa to voice his opinion.

He stopped the second he saw how wide her eyes were. She didn't wait for him to ask her what had changed.

"If you think me finding that was a coincidence, wait until I tell you where I've heard one of those names before."

Two days later and Kenneth was wearing a suit, a skinny tie, some boots, his badge and gun, and something akin to excitement across his lips. Willa watched him from the window of his SUV. She would have joined him but her own best-dressed self was trying to keep her heels dirt-free. Plus, in some way, it felt like Kenneth walking along Lot 427 was an intimate thing.

He was seeing where it had all started.

Just like she had when she'd first found the box.

It was night, timed that way only because they'd lost track of the clocks on their phones while going over their plan again.

A plan Foster Lovett wasn't happy about.

"Getting a warrant to search his house and workplace would be safer," he'd told them both that morning.

Kenneth had already thought about that.

"There's no judge in the world who would okay it," he'd said. "No matter what any of us think, the truth is we have no hard evidence. It's all circumstantial."

That was the understatement of the century.

Not only did they have no evidence that said Joseph Page—the same Terry Page who had been part of securing and championing for Lot 427 to be built upon—was responsible for murder, they had no idea which murder that was.

He wasn't old enough to have killed Josiah Linderman... but his son, Joshua? Maybe. Since Foster had done his digging into Joshua, he'd found the number of the woman he had been dating seven years ago. Her name was Lottie and she'd told Kenneth a troubling story when he'd called her.

A few days before Joshua had talked to his uncle at his mother's grave, Lottie had all but broken up with Joshua.

"He loved me but couldn't seem to love the idea of committing to me," she'd told him. "I wanted to get married and have kids and he, well, he told me he didn't know if he could do that. So I told him he needed to figure that out and, if his answer swung our way, that he knew where to find me. He agreed to that and took his things and left. I guess he made up his mind. I never heard from him again."

From there Kenneth had said he'd been delicate when

presenting the possibility that Joshua hadn't come back because something had happened to him. Then, when he'd asked after Joshua's adoptive parents and any friends or coworkers and why no one had reported the man missing, she'd rounded out the story with a deep sense of pity.

"His adoptive parents died two years apart from one another. After that he became very closed off to people. As for where he was working, he was between jobs. He wanted to be a journalist but was having a hard time getting hired."

Kenneth didn't say so on the phone but Willa had summed up his feeling after he'd recounted the conversation.

"Joshua really did just fall through the cracks, didn't he?"

The fact that his father had done the same thing weighed heavy on both of them.

Two Lindermans who had disappeared into nothingness.

Lottie had emailed Foster a copy of an old letter Joshua had given her after that and, at the very least, they'd been able to match the handwriting to the note in the cigarette case.

Had Joshua been investigating his father's murder as an adult? And, more important, had he found a lead that had brought him to Terry Page?

If so, then how did Ally Gray fit into it all?

There were too many questions still, and hunches that they couldn't back up.

So it felt like the only reasonable play left was to be a bit unreasonable.

And that's why Willa was wearing a party dress, why Kenneth was in a suit, and why Martha was waiting for them to drop Delilah off at her house.

They had a party to crash.

A party that Terry Page would be attending.

"What will that accomplish?" Foster had asked when they'd told him of their plan. "Are you just going to ask him if he's been killing people over the years?"

Kenneth had tensed. Willa knew the anger coming from him hadn't been meant for Foster but it eked out of his words.

"When I look him in the eye, I'll know if he's guilty."

Willa had known he was amped up…and emotional. It wasn't just about Josiah and his son. Ally was involved.

The one case he'd been forced to give up on.

So she'd pulled Foster aside when there had been a break in the conversation.

"If Terry Page is behind even one of these disappearances or, what we believe are in fact murders, then that means he's either the man from the hospital or he knows him," she'd said. "You know me and you know Kenneth. I can get Terry talking and Kenneth can guide that talk to something we can use. We have to at least try. If we show our hand to him first and he is guilty and we don't have a way to prove it? What's to keep him from running, or worse?" Willa had lowered her voice then. She'd looked toward Kenneth. Her heart had constricted and fluttered all at once. "He deserves answers. Just like Ally and the Lindermans, and *this* is the only way we can think of to maybe get some."

Foster had sighed but had agreed to the plan after that.

Though he'd been sure to point out it wasn't much of a plan all the way up until they'd left Kenneth's house.

"I'll be close," he'd called after them. "You say the word and that party will have more guests than they ever bargained for."

Willa found that image wildly comforting.

Though now she was starting to get nervous as she watched Kenneth and Delilah walk around Lot 427 like a man paying his last respects to a place before leaving it forever wasn't helping. They'd stopped on their way to Martha's at Kenneth's request.

If Terry Page *was* guilty, what would happen next?

What would she do? What would Kenneth do?

She watched as the man and his dog started to walk back to the car. His blazer was unbuttoned. Willa saw the glint of his gun beneath it.

For just a moment, Willa wished she'd never found the box.

And hoped that its discovery wouldn't take any more lives than it already had.

Chapter Nine

Chapter Twenty

The associates of Red Tree Development were celebrating two things.

One reason to have a party was that they'd just completed a long-standing project in a nearby city. Something, according to Ronaldo—the man who hadn't held back when talking to Willa on the phone after very little maneuvering on her part—that was a long time coming. It was a strip mall and, apparently, had been a pain in the entire company's collective backside over the last year. Closing the book on the property had been reason enough for celebration, yet they'd decided to be less obvious with their disdain for their work to share the party with an employee's birthday.

Her name was Wendy and her husband had a good bit of money when they'd married.

"Ronaldo said that's why, when Red Tree does decide to party, they usually do it at Wendy's place," Willa explained. They'd parked her car in a line of vehicles along a long drive. It wasn't McHale money but it wasn't some house out in the middle of town, either. "Not only is this place big, it apparently has dock access to the creek at the back of the property and a gazebo somewhere else."

Kenneth had cut the car's engine and quirked his eyebrow at that.

Willa seemed to pick up on his thoughts.

"Ronaldo seemed to like Wendy, but he had a lot of thoughts on people who own gazebos, and not all of them good," she said with a shrug. "Then again, he said if he had gazebo money then maybe he wouldn't dislike them so much."

Kenneth took the keys out and tucked his badge into his pocket. He wanted it on him if he needed it, but he didn't want to spook anyone until then.

"It's amazing to me how powerful your small talk is," he'd noted, not for the first time. "You call Ronaldo back to thank him for helping you and scoring points with your boss, and somehow you manage to get yourself an invite to a company slash birthday party with no one you know. *And* with a plus one." He shook his head and laughed. "It's a Southern superpower."

Willa wiggled her eyebrows at him.

"A superpower I'll use for good but don't think for a second I won't also use for it evil if it suits me."

Kenneth put his hands up in mock surrender and laughed.

Then the reason why they were there was staring at them through the windshield.

The house was large and set within the woods for privacy. Kenneth had only been by the home once when he was a teen and that was to turn his car around when he'd missed the dirt road to another dock access a few minutes before. He suspected since then the house had been renovated and given an addition or two. He also understood why Red Tree asked to party there and not at the office or a bar. It looked like something out of a movie. The two-story was lit up like a Christmas tree. Outdoor lights hanging from rustic-looking wooden poles every few yards led the way before the house lights inside and out took over.

Music could be heard thumping, even before they got out of the car.

Two more pulled up behind them.

"I can't tell if it's a good thing or a bad thing that so many people are here," Willa commented. She'd lost her earlier humor. "Surely if Terry Page is our bad guy, he won't try anything with a crowd like this around?"

Kenneth grit his teeth for a moment. "He better not."

A sigh escaped Willa's chest. "Then let's get this thing going."

Kenneth caught her hand before she could reach for her door handle. Willa searched his face, confused.

But he wasn't.

Not at all.

"Willa, you already know that I don't like you being here—and *yes* I know you don't care because you're a strong, independent woman and the perfect 'wing woman' for this adventure," he said, loosely quoting her from earlier when she'd said her not going with him wasn't a negotiation. "*But* I have to say, I am glad you're with me."

They'd already shared a lot in the last week or so, including many intimate conversations between his sheets, but Kenneth felt the need and acute desire to share more.

He just didn't know how to say it exactly. Not when they were on the trail of a murderer. Not when they were fighting to hopefully find justice for Ally.

Not when there were so many unknowns that could still spell disaster for them.

So the short statement would have to do.

Though Willa didn't seem to take it lightly.

She took his chin, gave him a quick kiss on the lips, and broke it with a smile.

"For luck."

Kenneth returned the smile.

"Better than a rabbit's foot for sure."

They left the car without any further comment and headed to the house.

Willa took his hand before they went inside.

THE RED TREE employees and their significant others were a nice enough bunch. Willa vaguely recognized a few of them. She and Kenneth, dressed to impress, blended nicely, drinks in their hands and good company at their ears.

Ronaldo was there, all smiles. He pulled Willa and Kenneth into a friendly conversation that lasted several minutes with him and his husband. For half of those minutes, it all felt so normal.

But Willa caught a look across Kenneth's face that she probably hadn't been meant to catch. He might have been smiling but his eyes were like daggers as they surveyed the people around them.

It was a reminder for the rest of the conversation that they weren't on some fun double date. They were looking for a man with a thin-but-there connection to a box containing items related to two disappearances and one murder. Not to mention a cigarette case that held his name.

Terry Page.

Since learning his name, the sheriff's department had undertaken an in-depth investigation for information on the man. Unfortunately, he hadn't been listed in any criminal database and his social media profile had been scarce if not practically inexistent. The company's web site bio page had one single picture of him, but it was old and somehow managed to be absolutely unmemorable. If Terry Page wasn't guilty of something nefarious, he was guilty of online evasion.

Ronaldo and his husband suddenly excused themselves to take a call from their babysitter. Willa eased into Kenneth's chest and stayed close as she spoke so only he could hear.

"Ronaldo said everyone from his office is here, and that includes Terry Page. We need to mingle faster."

Kenneth nodded and then they were off. Sipping drinks, utilizing small talk and polite hellos, and passing compliments when sucked into someone else's orbit. It happened more than once and Willa could tell the routine was starting to wear on her partner.

It made her want to do something drastic to help his heart, which had to be hurting right now. He could, after all, be in the same room with the man who'd shot the woman he'd vowed to spend the rest of his life with.

Willa couldn't help the pain in her own chest at that truth. If Ally had never died, she never would have come to know Kenneth the way she had. Never felt the warmth of him, the rumble of his laughter, or the delight of seeing him joyful. She wouldn't be wondering about their future or if it would exist beyond the hurdles they were currently being thrown. She wouldn't have an affinity for Delilah and how much he loved her. And she wouldn't be standing in a crowded room of people fervently wishing to hold only one person's hand.

Willa knew in her heart that she would give it all up in an instant if she could somehow turn back time to save Ally.

Because that's how much she cared about Kenneth.

She wanted any and all of his pain to be replaced by unending happiness.

Willa sighed. She knew that was a pipe dream for every soul who walked the earth. That there would always be hard times. That happiness wasn't every second of forever. Still, she scanned the new room they entered with hope that they would at least find some helpful answers.

But there was no Terry Page.

There was, however, a familiar face that bobbed into view just ahead.

"Missy!"

Missy Frye and her husband were also dressed in their Sunday best and holding obligatory cocktails.

As they approached, Willa couldn't help but note that Missy's mass of curls put her own big hair to shame while Dave looked like he wished he was anywhere else than in stiff clothes at some fancy-schmancy house party.

Missy dived in, bypassing any type of hello. "What are you doing here, Willa?"

Outside of Missy's calling the office to hunt down her husband, Willa only saw and socialized with her by bumping into her at places like the grocery store, hair salon, or any Clanton Construction functions. Missy was younger and had been more of Martha's crowd growing up.

Dave, though, wasn't a true local. A nice guy who had been down on his luck, he'd been passing through Kelby Creek when he'd taken a job as part of a construction crew. Instead of leaving, he'd married Missy quick and, as Martha had not-so-politely said, been her prisoner ever since.

To be fair, at the moment, he really did look the part of husband there against his own will.

"We were invited by a friend from Red Tree." Willa sidestepped a direct answer. She'd say Rolando if she had to, but wasn't sure why Missy and Dave were there at all. Missy worked in the county over at a nail salon and spa. So, Willa just asked, "What are y'all doing here?"

Missy was beaming. She'd been a social creature since she was in diapers, according to Martha.

"The same! And we just couldn't pass up the invite. Look at how stunning this place is!" She seemed to realize that Willa had someone with her and waited, pointedly, for an introduction.

"Missy, this is my friend Kenneth Gray. Kenneth, this is Missy and Dave Frye. I work with Dave at Clanton."

Kenneth was poised and professionally polite. He shook their hands, smiled like he was supposed to, and jumped right into a conversation about the almost-gaudy house around them.

Missy wondered aloud why the woman of the house would still be working if they clearly had money and Dave said that sometimes people did things that didn't make sense because outsiders didn't know the whole story.

They all agreed with him and Missy looked like she was ready to go another round of pure chatter when Kenneth pulled his phone from his pocket. Someone was calling him but Willa couldn't see the Caller ID.

Whoever it was, he gave her an apologetic look. "I need to take this."

Willa nodded and motioned to the next room. She hadn't seen anyone go in or out of it in a minute or so.

"Go ahead. It's fine," she assured him.

He excused himself from the group, saying it was work, with a quick squeeze to Willa's hand as he went. She watched him transform into downright focused as he hurried out of the room, answering.

Willa hoped it was good news.

She wasn't sure if they could take any more of the bad.

"Speaking of work, I guess this is as good time as any since your date isn't here, but do you think I could talk to you about one of our current jobs?" Dave looked downtrodden just bringing it up. "I was going to talk to you about it last week but you were out."

"For good reason," Missy added.

He nodded, immediately apologetic.

"Oh yeah, I'm not blaming you," he interjected. "I just mean that's why I didn't see you there."

Bless his heart, Dave had always been a somewhat simple man. He talked straight, was respectful, and became flustered fast.

Willa was more than happy to help ease his embarrassment, even if that meant talking about work at a party.

Being polite was in her DNA, after all.

"Don't worry about it. What do you want to talk about?"

A new song from the DJ in the main room kicked up. It wasn't as loud here as on the rest of the first floor, but it was annoying. Dave glanced at the door along the wall she presumed led out to the back.

"We can go outside, if that'll be easier for you?"

Dave nodded.

Missy huffed.

"I'm off the clock, so I'm staying inside," she announced. "Y'all just come back in when you're done. I'll tell Kenneth where you are if he comes back before you."

Willa thanked her and followed Dave outside into the night air. The lights hung out around the front of the house were sparse in the back. Though a path that led down a ways to what must have been the dock was faintly visible with lights in the distance.

If Ebony had been there she would have said, "You can't hide money."

But her friend wasn't there.

No one was really outside where she and Dave were.

It was good and private.

"So, what's up, Dave?" she asked, readying to try to help with whatever might be bothering him.

Dave set his drink down on the ground and looked back at the closed door. When his gaze went to hers, it had doubled down on apologetic.

So much so, she started forward, hand out as if she could help him with whatever it was that was weighing him down.

But then he spoke and Willa stayed right where she was.

"Missy shouldn't have called you that night. You shouldn't have gone out to the lot to look for me." He took a step forward. Willa had never noticed how big of a man he was until then. "And you should've never taken the box."

Before she could utter a word, move an inch or even scream, something hit her hard from behind.

Just as the world around her went dark, Willa had one last thought.

One day I've got to learn how to be a bitch.

Chapter Twenty-One

"One of our witnesses called in and said they lied about the man they saw at the hospital." Detective Lovett's voice was clipped and undoubtedly angry.

Kenneth made sure no one was in the room with him. It looked like a small office but without all the trappings of work. Just a desk, some nice chairs and a few wayward books. When he was certain no one would overhear him, he spoke.

"They *what*?"

Lovett talked fast. He was clearly on the move.

"The witness was one of the two people attacked on the second floor of the hospital to, as we assume, draw you and security away from Leonard Bartow's room. But before anyone could help, the attacker was able to say enough to scare both of them into giving a false description. Since they were the only people who got the best look at the guy, it was enough to tank our entire image of him."

"Did the witness decide to help us with a more accurate one?"

They'd been looking for the wrong man for days. Kenneth swore beneath his breath in the space between his question and Lovett's answer.

"I did us one better. I sent him a photo lineup of sorts using several different people. He picked one picture out immediately as the man who was at the hospital. I just met with the second witness. I did some fast talking, and he agreed to cooperate. It was instant recognition with him, too. They both went for one man."

"Terry Page?" Kenneth felt like he was vibrating out of his skin in anticipation.

Lovett didn't make him wait a second longer.

"Terry Page," he confirmed. "That means we have enough to get him now and we're on the way. I'm ten minutes out. Deputy Park should be there before me. Play it safe and smart until we arrive."

Kenneth snorted. "Safe and smart can kiss my ass. I'm going to go find Terry Page and arrest him."

He ended the call, whirled around on his heel with all of the righteous vengeance in his chest, but came up short.

He hadn't heard the man enter the office, but he couldn't ignore the timing.

Or the strappy shoe that was in his hand.

It belonged to Willa.

Dave Frye looked sincerely regretful to be exactly where he was, but that didn't stop him from using a voice that was nothing but commanding.

"Throw your phone on the desk—and your gun, too," he said. He shook the shoe. "Or else this will be all that's left of Willa."

Kenneth's blood was boiling. "If you've hurt her—"

"Just put the gun and phone down, and we can talk."

Kenneth weighed his options. It was smart to keep his gun when Dave didn't appear to have any weapons on him. Yet, Willa's shoe brought him up short. He should have never left her. Even when he'd thought she was with friends.

He put the phone on the desk but hesitated with his gun in his hand. Instead of dropping it, too, he took the clip out and slid it into his jacket pocket. Dave watched with a raised eyebrow.

"So neither one of us can use it," Kenneth said.

It surprisingly didn't offend the bigger man.

Instead, his brow scrunched. When he started to speak again, it sounded like he was saying something he'd been forced to rehearse.

And Kenneth imagined he had been.

"You have two choices now. You can either die here alone or you can die outside with Willa."

Kenneth couldn't describe the anger that rushed through him. But he decided to bury it to keep the situation calm.

"Why are you doing this?" he asked, genuinely curious. If Terry had been the man who'd killed LeAnne and Billings, and Leonard had been the man who he'd fought at Willa's apartment, then how did Dave fit into any of this? "I thought Willa was your friend?"

The big man nodded.

"She is but friendship doesn't get you out of gambling debt."

"But murder does?"

Dave didn't seem to like that question. He made a disgusted face.

"I don't murder anyone. I only find things and then return them."

Kenneth wanted to point out that he'd just given one hell of an ultimatum for someone who didn't plan on killing anyone but realized then just how Dave fit into everything.

"You're the one who stole the piece of fabric from her apartment."

Dave didn't deny the accusation.

"It wasn't Willa's. It didn't belong to her."

It didn't make sense why Dave hadn't grabbed the box

when he'd taken the bloody fabric yet, his ultimatum was still ringing clearly in Kenneth's head.

There wasn't time for any more questions.

The feeling must have been mutual. Dave's face hardened.

Apparently, Kenneth had been too swift to discount Dave. The bigger man reached into the back of his slacks and pulled a gun from its waistband.

"You die either alone or together," he reiterated. "Those are your only options."

WILLA WAS SICK right into the water. It was a miracle she'd even made it to the side in the first place—or maybe just instinct. Once she'd become conscious again, she'd heard the water, blinked against the dim lights strewed along wooden pillars, and had known if she got sick right where she was then her night would only head that much more downhill.

When she was done, the pounding pain in her head had only lessened slightly.

And the man who had dealt the blow seemed more annoyed than he would have been otherwise by the act.

"I didn't hit you that hard," he sneered. "You don't have to be that dramatic about it."

Willa wiped her mouth with the back of her hand. There was blood on it but she realized she must have grabbed at the spot on top of her head before passing out.

"You hit me hard enough to lose consciousness," she said with some added spice she hadn't realized would be there. "I'd say that counts as just painful enough."

Willa stood slowly and took a few steps back, trying to orient herself. She saw the path that led to the dock from the house again but, this time, from the other side. Somehow the house seemed farther than the dock had. She could hear the faint thump of music. She could also feel the wooden planks beneath her bare feet.

Her shoes were gone.

She took a shaky breath and finally met the eye of the man who had done this to her.

Terry Page looked as average as his name sounded. Apparently, his Red Tree bio picture had in fact done him justice. Short brown hair, brown eyes, clean-shaved. A man who looked as though he said things like "accounts receivable" and "return on investment" several times during his workweek.

Not a man who had become the center of a web of death and loss.

"We don't have much time," he said, smiling like it was a business transaction.

"Before what?"

He shook his head. "I'm not going to tell you that. Though, if you scream, I will kill you, hand to God." He moved his blazer and pulled out a gun, true to his word.

Willa wondered where Kenneth was and then hoped to high heaven that Dave, nowhere to be seen, wasn't with him. She didn't want to ask about the former in case there was any chance that Terry didn't know Kenneth was there with her. Instead, she did what they'd come here to do in the first place, even if it was under much different circumstances.

"What do you want with me?"

Terry sighed. Again, so average-looking of him.

"Well, to be honest, I really want to say I'm impressed with how you handled my initial mistake. When I first buried that damn box, I knew it was a bad idea. But I was in a hurry and Lot 427 wasn't even for sale, so I let that decision ride for too long. Then, when it finally went up, and I decided to try to retrieve the box, I realized I'd forgotten where I'd buried it." He snorted. "To be fair, it was a while ago and things were a bit hectic."

"So you convinced Red Tree to buy the lot for development. Why?"

He rolled his eyes. "It seemed like a good idea at the time. I'd rather keep my eye on the place than have someone else find it and take it."

Willa shook her head. It hurt.

She thought of Dave. Her heart squeezed a little. He'd always been so nice to her. Yet, he'd taken her outside so Terry could attack her.

So Terry could kill her.

The only connection that she could come up with through her pounding head and fear was Clanton Construction.

"Is that why Dave is here?" she asked. "He was trying to find the box for you?"

Terry's nostrils flared. She could see it clear as day from the distance between them.

"Trying is the operative word," he growled out. "I had him looking for weeks and then you just stumble across it because his wife has control issues and needed to know where he was every second of every day. Ridiculous. Then again, I'm betting the rain helped you with that. There's just something about this town and flooding that uncovers things it shouldn't."

He took the smallest of steps forward. Willa wanted him to keep talking.

She also wanted answers.

"Is that why you sent Leonard to my apartment instead? Because Dave failed to find the box the first time?"

A look she couldn't gauge crossed over his face.

"Dave failed his first job, not his most important one." That confused Willa but he kept on before she could ask anything else. "But I did have the hope that hiring Leonard to get the box would work out but I guess strike two and three for outsourcing. I hired him to find the box, which he didn't, and then he went and got caught. So, I decided it was time to do things myself. Though, I admit things got a little sloppy."

He smiled like the cat who ate the canary.

"Like you killing LeAnne? Leonard and Billings too?"

Willa knew that Terry had been the one to kill them. Still, she needed to hear it.

He actually shrugged again.

"Like I said, things got a little sloppy."

Willa hated him. Right then and there she hated everything about him and everything he'd done. From the top of her hair to the tips of her toes.

"But why?" she asked, voice pitching higher. "Why go through any of the trouble? You didn't have a target on your back until you created all of this madness trying to get the box. You made yourself all the more suspicious. Nothing *in* the box even linked to you. If you hadn't tried to find it at all, we might not even have—"

All at once, Average Terry became enraged. He took two giant strides forward, which only made Willa shrink back that same distance until she was closer to the edge of the dock.

"Because I earned everything in that box. It's mine, no one else's."

Willa's heartbeat was all-out racing.

She hadn't expected that.

But she decided to use it.

She kept her voice as low and nonthreatening as possible.

There was something else that she knew in her heart but, again, she wanted him to say it. First, though, she made sure her words were clear to lead him there.

"Because you killed Joshua Linderman and Ally Gray."

Terry's nostrils flared. When he laughed, Willa knew that she was beyond "in trouble." The man in front of her wasn't stable.

And had no intention of letting her go.

"I didn't kill them. I fixed his problems," he said. "Even after he died."

Willa didn't want to look toward the house but, at the same time, she was hoping to see Kenneth. Coming for her. Though she also didn't want him here. Not with the man who clearly had no problem killing.

"He?" she asked, hoping to keep him talking. The longer he did that, the longer she had hope of getting out of this.

Terry snarled, leaving any trace of his laughter behind.

"My father made a mistake over thirty years ago and here I am still correcting it," he snarled. "That's why the box isn't for anyone but me. *I* deserve it."

Willa took the smallest of steps back. A splinter bit into her foot. She didn't care.

"Josiah Linderman," she whispered.

That seemed to trigger the man more.

"My father thought he was untouchable. Getting drunk at home wasn't enough for him. He had to take it on the road. But then, there was Josiah, out walking." He clapped his hands together, the gun between them briefly pointed at her. Willa held in a flinch. "My father couldn't even handle burying the body. So, there I was at fourteen burying my first. I barely could lift him."

So, Josiah Linderman hadn't abandoned his family. He'd been killed by a drunk driver and then buried to hide the evidence.

"Joshua didn't believe his dad had left town," she guessed.

Terry snorted.

"I thought he did until he showed up at my house, asking questions about a piece of a car he'd found. Because, of course, my father couldn't be bothered to clean up his own mess."

"So you did."

He nodded.

"All I had to do was wait for him to go walking and follow."

Willa didn't say it but she believed Joshua had suspected the attack from Terry was coming. He must have thrown his theory, the cigarette case and the list, in the only place he'd time to—the tree in the small clearing in the woods next to the creek and not too far away from the back road his father had been walking.

Terry made another snarling sound.

"I shot him, but wanted to talk. So I made sure the shot wouldn't kill him fast, but we were interrupted."

Ally Gray.

"Stupid runner. Shot her after she hit me good. It's the only reason they got away."

That was news to Willa. Ally's body had been found, Joshua's hadn't. Had Joshua gotten away?

Her hope didn't last long.

And that had everything to do with Terry sensing he needed to crush it.

"Don't worry. They didn't make it far. Though Joshua sure was a pain to track. I'll give it to him, he made it a lot farther than I thought he would, but he made it easier, too. Buried him in the exact spot he asked me for mercy."

"But you didn't get to Ally in time?"

"No. She'd made it out to Becker's field and was spotted before I could deal with her."

He sighed, as if now bored.

"You shouldn't have taken the box, Miss Tate. It wasn't

yours." His body language started to change. He was becoming angry again.

And it was all directed at her.

"The sheriff's department has it now and knows everything I do. Killing me, doesn't do anything."

He shook his head.

Willa's veins turned to ice. This was it.

Whatever he was planning to do, he was about to do it.

"Not true." His voice was like a knife dipped in venom. "It would make me feel better."

Everything happened in the space between heartbeats.

Willa turned around and dove into the water with enough force to go as deep as possible. Had it not been raining as much as it had, she would have gotten to the creek bed a lot sooner. Thankfully, it wasn't until she was completely submerged that a gunshot pierced the water behind her.

Willa kept her eyes shut tight and changed course as best she could. She was a good swimmer but when it came to holding her breath under water, she would never win any medals.

She struggled as another muffled shot sounded. She was going to have to surface soon.

Was she far enough away?

Had Terry been able to track her?

Would she be able to get back under to avoid being hit? Or could she escape through the other side of the creek?

Willa's chest started to burn. She started to swim up, terrified.

Even more so when something big splashed into the water somewhere behind her.

Willa kicked upward and broke the surface. She hoped the deep breath she'd taken in wouldn't be her last.

"Willa!"

She was seconds from submerging when she realized the

man who yelled for her was Foster Lovett. He had his gun drawn down at a body on the dock. She could just make out the color of Terry's suit.

But who had jumped in after her?

"He's in the water, looking for you!"

Willa felt another flare of fear before the meaning sunk in.

"Kenneth!" she yelled, treading water.

It was like her voice was tied to the man.

One second it was just dark water. Then it was the face of the man she'd fallen in love with.

Kenneth was a few feet away but the moment he saw her, Willa could feel his relief.

"Willa," he breathed. "Are you hurt?"

She shook her head. In a fluid motion that didn't seem real, he swam to her and then pulled her with him to the other side of the creek. The minute his feet could touch the ground, his arms were around her.

"I thought he hit you before I got him," he said, still out of breath.

Willa noted his face had a few extra cuts and marks than when they'd arrived at the party, but she didn't focus on that.

Instead he needed to know that she was okay.

So she told him that she was.

Kenneth kissed her on the tail end of her words.

When he pulled back, he let out another sigh of relief.

"What's that one for?" she asked with a shaky laugh. Adrenaline was still surging through her.

"That kiss was for deciding to wear shoes that I could use as a weapon," he said, joining in with his own burst of tired laughter. "Dave never stood a chance."

Chapter Twenty-Two

Terry Page died on the docks. Kenneth had every reason to pull the trigger—to avenge his wife and to stop a cold-blooded murderer once and for all—but the truth was that he'd made the kill-shot for one reason and one reason only in the moment.

To save Willa Tate.

Once he'd realized that she was okay, he'd taken a minute to revel in that. Something made easier by the fact that Deputy Park had found and detained the unconscious Dave in the house and that, true to Foster's word, almost the entire department had shown up to help.

Which worked out nicely considering everyone at the party was confused and that confusion turned to anger. Specifically, Missy Frye. After seeing her husband carted off in handcuffs, she'd attacked a deputy.

It would only be later that she admitted to him across from an interrogation table that she'd had no idea about her husband helping Terry do anything other than work on his golf swing.

"They were friends," she'd tell Kenneth, still shell-shocked. "They're both good men."

Dave's own words echoed that sentiment when he was questioned later. Right before he told them everything he knew and had done.

"We met at the bar and, after some talking, Terry offered me a way out of debt. I couldn't say no to it. Plus, it wasn't much to ask. He wanted me to look for a box and then he wanted me to just focus on a piece of fabric."

When Dave had said that, Kenneth and Foster had shared a look. Foster had asked what Kenneth had been thinking.

"Why not take the entire box when you stole the piece of fabric from Willa's apartment? Why did he send Leonard in after you?"

"And why not tell Leonard exactly where the box was so he could find it when he did break in?" Kenneth had added.

Dave had seemed to think the answers were obvious and easy.

"When I went the box wasn't hidden. Well, I mean it was under her bed but easy to find. She must've hidden it later. And about the fabric, Terry said it was important to get it first so he might could have more time to deal with it before anyone realized it was missing. That wouldn't work if I took the whole box the first time."

"Why?" Kenneth had asked, genuinely confused.

Dave's answer had been simple.

Though wholly troubling.

"Because it wasn't his."

Kenneth and Foster had shared another look.

"Then whose was it?" Foster had asked.

Dave had shrugged.

"I don't know but he said he gave it back to the man it originally belonged to. I didn't ask past that and I don't think he would have told me had I done so. It's the only time I've seen him look nervous."

That was all Dave gave them but it was enough to send them back to the Page home to do another sweep, this time looking specifically for the piece of fabric.

They never found it.

"I think we just found our next possible new cold case to look into," Foster had said when they were done.

Kenneth didn't disagree but needed to put to rest everything—Terry Page first.

Natalie, Terry's wife, along with his coworkers had bucked and yelled about Terry being a good, decent man. No one had any idea that Terry was, in Kenneth's opinion, a sociopath. A killer. A man who was always one step away from deciding to end someone's life.

Those feelings, however, changed when Josiah Linderman's body was found in the backyard of the Page family home. He'd been wrapped in a tarp and buried deep. Terry's father, Kevin Page, had long since passed away but the medical examiner had found enough evidence to corroborate the story Terry had told Willa on the dock.

Josiah had been struck by a car and had most likely died instantly.

A week after his body was found, his son Joshua's was, too.

Though that had had nothing to do with what Willa had learned out on the dock and everything to do with Lottie, Joshua's girlfriend at the time of his disappearance.

After Terry had confessed to killing Joshua, Kenneth had reached out to her because he felt that she deserved as much. They'd talked awhile about it all. At least, as much as he could, until Lottie told him a story about the first time Joshua had said that he loved her.

She wasn't from Kelby Creek and Joshua hadn't grown up in town, but he'd taken her out to his mother's grave a year before his death. He'd told her about how she'd liked this one spot where the honeysuckle grew so thick that it smelled like heaven on earth. Joshua had taken Lottie there and professed his love.

"He said he'd never been happier," Lottie had said, tears in her voice.

Kenneth had then asked where that spot was and, to his surprise, she'd remembered. Her directions from Mae Linderman's gravestone to her favorite spot in town had been spot-on.

Not far from where Ally had been found in the field.

Kenneth didn't take Willa with him when he went to check because he already knew that's where Joshua would be buried.

And that's where they found him, surrounded by honeysuckle waiting to bloom in spring.

The burial had been a hasty one, though, and among his things was a note that Terry had overlooked.

It was that note now that Kenneth held in one hand, the cigarette case that Willa had found near the creek in the other. Willa was at the window of his office, staring out at the parking lot. She was wearing church clothes and had even fixed her hair up into a complicated-looking bun. She wanted to look respectful but not too sad, she'd told him that morning standing in front of her closet wearing nothing but his T-shirt.

Kenneth didn't want to point out that once she read what was in the note, she wouldn't care what any of them was wearing, but he also realized Willa was trying to step away from her own emotions on the matter. There was no getting around that Joshua had left one hell of an impression with his last words.

She hadn't asked outright, but Kenneth knew that Willa had guessed his reaction at reading the note for the first time had been rough. In fact, he'd cried like a baby in Mae Linderman's favorite spot.

He'd tell her later but, right now, he wanted to be as professional as he could.

When Willa excitedly said Lottie had pulled up, he made quick work of seeing her into the meeting room. There, Willa gave Lottie a long hug before excusing herself.

She paused next to Kenneth in the doorway, surprising him.

"This is for you two," she said so only he could hear. "I'll come back when you're done."

And there she went, polite and true.

Then Kenneth began with the part of the story that Lottie didn't know and what the letter had helped fill them in on since the two of them had last talked.

"My wife, Ally, heard the shot and tried to help Joshua. From what we can guess, she hit Terry hard enough that it almost knocked him out. But not before he was able to shoot Ally twice."

Kenneth had a hard time with his words but managed to get through them. "After that, Joshua took them as far as he could before Ally couldn't go on. When he knew that he was getting close to dying himself, he left her body near a spot he thought would be found. He then went in the opposite direction, hoping that, if she wasn't found, he might be, so Terry wouldn't get away with it."

Kenneth slid the note over, along with the cigarette case.

Lottie laughed through tears in her eyes at the case.

"Joshua wanted to be an investigative journalist, you know? But instead of carrying around some kind of notepad, he put paper in that thing and golf pencils." She took the case and ran her finger over its top. "But this thing couldn't hold a lot, so the man was always stuffing paper and little pencils everywhere. It made doing the wash a nightmare. I can't count how many times we fought about it."

She laughed again then took a shaky, long breath.

At least now Kenneth knew how Joshua had gotten the paper and writing utensil.

"So this is the last thing he wrote?" she asked, looking at the note.

Kenneth nodded. "It's small, but he had enough time to say a lot. And it's addressed to you."

She touched it. Took another deep breath and shook her head.

"I thought he gave up on us. That he didn't want me anymore. I… I thought so many things about him since then. And now all of this? Can you— Can you read it to me? I… I can't."

Willa had warned him that, if she had been in Lottie's place, she might ask the same, so Kenneth was ready. As ready as he could be.

He straightened, smiled, and said sure.

Then he read aloud Joshua *and* Ally's last words.

"'Lottie,

'Terry Page shot me out by the creek. A lady named Ally, too. She tried to help me, but he was fast. We got away for a while, but Ally didn't make it long. I told her she shouldn't have tried to help, but she said she had no regrets in life and she refused to have any in death. Then she passed. I left her near the road. Hopefully someone will see her. But I'm worried he will, and will hide us all away, so I left. I decided that was a nice thought to die to…no regrets. But I have one—I should've proposed to you *already* but I was scared. I wish I hadn't been.'"

The handwriting had worsened as the note went on. Joshua had been dying and knew his killer might find him, so he'd finished the note with a simple thought.

"'I hope you live a long, good life, Lottie. Love,'"

Kenneth thought he probably meant to sign the note but had heard Terry coming and had hid it the best he could.

But not signing his name didn't take anything away from what he'd said.

"We also guess that this was on him when he passed. A jeweler in town sold it to him the day before. He said he was going home to propose to the love of his life."

He produced the engagement ring that had been in the box Willa had found. It had been Terry's trophy from Joshua just as Mae's picture had been from Josiah and the bullet casing had been from Ally.

Lottie took the ring. She started crying so hard that Willa appeared at her side with a tissue box and hand on her back.

Kenneth watched her try her best to soothe the stranger.

It would be a few weeks later that Kenneth would open up to Willa about the note and admit through tears that, without Willa, he would have never found out that Ally hadn't been alone when she'd died.

And that, to him, was the most peace he could ask for.

After Lottie left, Kenneth simply took Willa back to his house and put on a movie. He couldn't for the life of him remember what it was, but with Willa next to him and Delilah across his lap, he didn't much care.

She'd been staying at his place more and more and he was happy for it. Even though her apartment had been fully repaired and now sported a new security system, Kenneth felt a whole heap better with her at his side. Though, that had more to do with the woman herself than security concerns. Now Kenneth gave her a kiss on her cheek as she laughed at something that was said on the TV. She turned to him, cheeks rosy, and gave him a smile that put the rest of the world to shame.

"What was that kiss for?" she asked, hand absently stroking Delilah's fur.

Kenneth decided not to tell her that he'd just realized he wanted to spend the rest of his days like this, with her. So he told a little fib.

"For being warm," he said.

Willa laughed, caught his chin in her hand and pulled him in for another kiss.

Kenneth couldn't help the one word that came to mind at the touch.

Sunshine.

* * * * *

COMING SOON!

We really hope you enjoyed reading this book. If you're looking for more romance, be sure to head to the shops when new books are available on

Thursday 2nd September

To see which titles are coming soon, please visit
millsandboon.co.uk/nextmonth

MILLS & BOON

THE HEART OF ROMANCE

A ROMANCE FOR EVERY READER

ODERN

Prepare to be swept off your feet by sophisticated, sexy and seductive heroes, in some of the world's most glamourous and romantic locations, where power and passion collide.

STORICAL

Escape with historical heroes from time gone by. Whether your passion is for wicked Regency Rakes, muscled Vikings or rugged Highlanders, awaken the romance of the past.

EDICAL

Set your pulse racing with dedicated, delectable doctors in the high-pressure world of medicine, where emotions run high and passion, comfort and love are the best medicine.

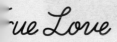ue Love

Celebrate true love with tender stories of heartfelt romance, from the rush of falling in love to the joy a new baby can bring, and a focus on the emotional heart of a relationship.

Desire

Indulge in secrets and scandal, intense drama and plenty of sizzling hot action with powerful and passionate heroes who have it all: wealth, status, good looks…everything but the right woman.

EROES

Experience all the excitement of a gripping thriller, with an intense romance at its heart. Resourceful, true-to-life women and strong, fearless men face danger and desire - a killer combination!

To see which titles are coming soon, please visit
millsandboon.co.uk/nextmonth

LET'S TALK
Romance

For exclusive extracts, competitions
and special offers, find us online:

- �f facebook.com/millsandboon
- 🐦 @MillsandBoon
- 📷 @MillsandBoonUK

Get in touch on 01413 063232

For all the latest titles coming soon, visit
millsandboon.co.uk/nextmonth

MILLS & BOON
Desire

Indulge in secrets and scandal, intense drama and plenty of sizzling hot action with powerful and passionate heroes who have it all: wealth, status, good looks…everything but the right woman.

MILLS & BOON
True Love

Romance from the Heart

Celebrate true love with tender stories of heartfelt romance, from the rush of falling in love to the joy a new baby can bring, and a focus on the emotional heart of a relationship.